THE LAST IMMORTAL

ALSO BY NATALIE GIBSON

THE WITCHBOUND SERIES

For the Love of Magic

The Dying Art of Magic

The Magic Number

The Nature of Magic

The Veiled Threat of Magic

The Magic Moment

THE LAST IMMORTAL

NATALIE GIBSON

bhc press™

Livonia, Michigan

THE LAST IMMORTAL

Published by BHC Press

Library of Congress Control Number: 2020940781

ISBN: 978-1-64397-254-1 (Hardcover)
ISBN: 978-1-64397-255-8 (Softcover)
ISBN: 978-1-64397-256-5 (Ebook)

For information, write:
BHC Press
885 Penniman #5505
Plymouth, MI 48170

Visit the publisher:
www.bhcpress.com

My villains are easy to write.
I just imagine the horrifying depths I would go,
and the absolutely terrifying things I'd be willing to do,
to spend forever with you.

To my Eric,
I love you

Dear Reader,

The Last Immortal is one of the most unique and original horror novels that we have ever read. In this chilling gaslight-era Gothic tale, a young woman with hidden talents must break free of a secret bloodthirsty race that breeds and collects paranormal powers.

Natalie Gibson writes novels filled with otherworldly violence, sexuality, and the supernatural, and she enjoys mixing horror, magic, fantasy, and romance into her writing. Her stories always have powerful females who change the world, magical creatures that battle their baser natures, and seriously evil bad guys who don't.

Recommended for those who enjoy Gothic horror, extreme horror, Anne Rice, *Mexican Gothic*, *The Death of Jane Lawrence*, or the television shows *Penny Dreadful* or *The Frankenstein Chronicles*.

We feel we must issue a warning, however, before you begin reading this book. In the words of Lady Ramillia Winmoore: *I must warn you: this tale is not for the faint of heart. Highborn Victorian Lady that I was, my life was one of violence and cruelty.*

The novel contains the following content: graphic violence and gore, language, scenes of a sexual nature including rape, BDSM, SA, self-harm, and child SA. It's impossible to list all potential content that may be disturbing to some readers, however, we did want to include this letter to help guide you in your reading endeavors.

Sincerely,
The Team at BHC Press

THE LAST IMMORTAL

PART ONE

HATEFUL BURDEN

They say I killed my parents at age twelve. Savagely butchered was the wording I believe my doctor used. I couldn't speak to the truth or dishonesty of the statement. I had no memory of the event, nor those that led to such an act by an innocent. That night, like many of my childhood, was a black spot in my memory. I cannot help thinking that was a blessing.

1

I realized too late why my father had married my mother. She had money, but that wasn't the reason he selected her. Her dowry and his standing in the community made them a good match. They were invited to all the best balls, received all the noblest callers. They lived in the right neighborhood and had the proper number of servants. Except that wasn't the horrifying reason he secretly desired her.

Mama was a striking woman though not in a conventional way. She had an angelic face, with a small proper English mouth and large doe eyes, framed by golden curls. She rarely wore stays, except when society and etiquette demanded it, allowing her unique figure to show at home.

My father chose her because she had the body of a child and would until her death.

It was the same body I had and we often wore the same cut of dress. Papa demanded it. Infants and children of both sexes were dressed alike in "skirts" at that time. In our home, Mama and I always matched, Thaddeus too, when he was a child. A stranger would not be able to tell which of us were adults. Our skirts never got closer to the floor than mid-calf and, while it was proper for Thaddeus and I, it was obscene that Mama's stocking covered ankles were always exposed. She wore her hair down in ringlets, not up in the sophisticated fashion her age and status should have dictated.

At twelve, it was apparent that my body would not stop maturing. I would not be the living portrait of prepubescence that she was. Already my breasts were budding and there was a hint of roundness to my hips. These were things I knew my mother did not have because my father told me. They have a name for her disorder, however, no one spoke of it then. He only spoke of it that night to lament the fact that I was not lovely like her. I was quickly becoming grotesque to him. I was in Papa's study when he informed me of those disappointments.

I blinked, trying to banish the warm tears that were growing, and my eyes opened many months later. I was strapped to a bed in an asylum for the criminally insane. In my day, those institutions were not what they are today.

There were no group sessions nor recreational rooms, no spa treatments nor gourmet meals. They were places of nightmares, run by people with a love of torture and the obscene.

A doctor was there when I opened my eyes. He was older, with gray hair that reached nearly to his rounded, hunched shoulders. His eyes had a yellow tint, similar to the color of his teeth. His features were sharp and cruel. He smelled sour, like spoiled dairy. With clothing tailored yet thin, he wore more layers than was fashionable to make up for the deficiency. He listened to my heart, shone a light in my eyes, looked down my throat, and felt around my belly. He didn't answer my questions about my whereabouts or condition. He gave pause when I demanded to see my family.

"You know your parents are dead," he stated plainly. "You recounted their grisly murders to me on several occasions." Despite my young age, I had somehow managed to rip my father to pieces and choke the life from my mother with such force that her head was almost severed. The servants had found me naked, covered in their blood. It took four fully grown men to subdue me. That was at least ten months prior. I was sent here by the magistrate and would remain until the good doctor proclaimed I was no longer a danger.

"There must be some mistake," I speculated. "I am not dangerous. You have me confused with someone else." I was scarcely grown, had not enjoyed a single season in London, nor been presented to my sovereign.

He laughed. Going to the door, made of solid wood with a square opening at eye level, he spoke to someone on the outside. The door had no pull nor knob on the inside. It slowly opened inward. "Tell that to him."

A man, a full head taller than the doctor, slouched down to come through the door. He was bald and bruises covered his face. His right arm was bandaged in a sling. He looked at me in a way that made my skin crawl. That man had plans for me and none of them would be pleasant.

The doctor let the man's stare settle in before speaking again. "This is your handiwork from a fortnight ago. His arm was broken so severely the bone protruded through the skin. Your tiny fists punched him unconscious and then you bit his ear off and ate it. *You*, my dear, are the most dangerous person I have ever housed."

∽

The days spent in the West Freeman Asylum for Lunatics ran together in a blur of what the educated men of the era considered appropriate treatments for my malady. This was just as much a result of the prescribed laudanum as the two physical treatments I alternated between. The doctor informed me they were successful with other patients and the giant man, whom I had come to name "Turnkey" because he was my jailer, was present for each one. Forced ice water baths and electroshock therapy might possibly relieve me of my rage.

There was no rage that I could remember. I cried a lot and wanted to go home. The contrast between the relative luxury of my fine home and this place was remarkable. The smell was pungent and no amount of scrubbing would rid the stones of its stench. Fear and hopelessness were almost palpable and if it were possible that those two emotions could be made solid somehow, it would be here. Exhaustion overwhelmed me as there was no rest in a place like this. It was never silent and even a dulling of the sounds was often broken by the screams of someone in pain or the mad laughter of the truly insane.

I was rarely taken from my room and, when I was, it was only for treatment, and I often wished to be back there in that cold, bare place. There was no furniture, save the table that doubled as my bed. It caused sores because I was always forced to lay in one position. I could not huddle in a corner to keep warm or even turn on my side and tuck my feet in. There was mold on the walls and one section was constantly slick with a mixture of oozing water and mildew. The dark-green growth was rimmed with orange. I can still see it if I try, so frequently did I stare at it. I was the sole inhabitant of my room and for that I was glad. The worst part about West Freeman was the other lunatics. They and the vermin, I mean.

Doctor Federick was as cruel as he was ugly. He knew my fears and used them against me. He frequently had my food laid just out of reach when I was the hungriest. I could only watch as it was contaminated by insects. I felt their tiny legs on me and cried with frustration that I was secured and could not even brush them away. The doctor often spoke of other patients gnawed upon by rats. In the dark, I could hear their squeaks as they ate the remainder of my meals. I barely slept for fear of them feasting upon whatever body part tempted them.

My greatest fear was of this place as a whole, that I would never know freedom again. He used this against me also. "You would be strung by the neck if it weren't for me. I took you in when even the crown herself wanted to see you swing. The gallows are overly good for the likes of you, I say. You are at my mercy and with no family left living, none that care about your existence anyway, you will never leave here."

The doctor said I had dementia praecox, which is no real disease recognized by the educated of the modern era, although it was widely diagnosed during that time for every madness they could not explain. Many years later it was renamed schizophrenia, however, that word did not exist at the time of my incarceration, nor did it have anything to do with my condition. The doctor declared me incurable, my episodes worsening, and my condition and mind deteriorating over time.

If these treatments did not work they would be forced to take more extreme measures. I tried to be compliant. When it became unbearable, the darkness came. Blessed darkness that always ended much too soon. When the spell was over, I would come to with the doctor shaking his head in disappointment and Turnkey staring at me with his yellowing, bruised face.

Whatever happened during the blackness was wrong. The doctor said I was not responding to the treatments and was headed toward the operating table. Lobotomy was a fail-safe way to cure the incurably violent patient in those days. Although this wasn't something I wanted, at least it would leave me in a condition where the horrific treatments were no longer necessary. Even if they continued, they would not bother me.

But surgery was not to ease my suffering.

Instead a letter came. I wasn't allowed to read it. The doctor announced that he finally had his benefactor and that his facility was to become modernized. People would beg to be in his care. He kissed my hand and stated my stewardship was a blessing. With no further explanation, I was wheeled from my cell into a proper room. Turnkey grudgingly freed me from my bed and left with the horrible, strapped thing. It was the last time I would see either.

Sally, my better half, says I am telling this story all wrong. I am throwing in what I know now where it shouldn't be. I didn't know that day that I would live to see my two hundred thirty-second birthday and be able to read medical journals on mental health. Or that I would never see Turnkey again; in fact, I lived in fear that he would spirit into my room at night when no one could save me from his revenge. Sally has never led me astray so I shall defer to her judgment. I will do my best to tell the story as she suggests, just as it happened, without my hindsight.

2

I, weak from so long in restraints, explored my new accommodations as best I could. They were large—larger even than my parents' back at home. The first thing I noticed was the relative quiet. I could still hear the asylum around me but it was less prominent. The smell and fear were lessened within my room also. It was relatively clean, and neither bugs nor mold climbed the walls.

I was drawn to the fireplace. Someone had started the fire and the space was already warming up. I stood with my back to it and looked out into the room. By the fire was a settle with a tall back that trapped the heat and kept away the drafts within the room. Just on the other side of that specialized warming bench was a sitting area with furniture that was worn but nicely made. There was even a desk with a stool, stationery, a choice of quills, and an ink pot. A square table and wooden bench completed the reception area. Although they were not new, the furnishings had not been there long, and I envisioned some family's parlor stripped bare of all their worldly possessions. I wondered what visitors I would be receiving to warrant the set up. At the far end there was a real bed with a plush mattress that smelled fresh and a bed curtain to close it off from prying eyes and sickening drafts.

The only other piece in the room was an armoire. Since I was freezing in my shift, even with my back against the burning fire, I was hopeful when I noticed it. I risked leaving the hearth to check it for extra layers. It was empty and I quickly made my way back to the heat source. I pulled the settle close—it was much lighter than it appeared—and stretched my legs out, putting my bare feet as close to the coals as I dared.

I must have fallen asleep. A loud clang woke me. I was relieved at the level of noise it made. No one would be able to sneak up on me, even while I slept. The clang was followed by a low but loud scrape as the crossbar slid open. The door itself swung open soundlessly. Although the room was nicer than the cell, the door was still locked from the outside. I was still a prisoner.

Kneeling, I peered over the back of the settle, terrified of my visitor's identity. Making a mental note of the fireplace poker's location, I knew I could get to it should Turnkey enter.

A pile of garments with legs entered first, followed by a proper, young woman in a respectable dress. The doctor came in after, looking at me suspiciously. A short discussion and possible disagreement arose between them. In the end, the woman must have won because the doctor left, closing the door behind him.

"I think Judith and I can handle one half-starved, half-frozen girl without protection," the young woman muttered after seeing me peeking. She swiftly joined me by the fire and held out her hand. I took it. It was warm and soft and instantly I knew that I liked this woman.

Judith, who I assumed was behind the moving wall of cloth, made her way blindly to the bed and was spreading out the various pieces. She came over to the fireplace, stirred it with the poker and then added a log. Although it had died down, the coal bed was hot and the lumber had no trouble catching.

The woman who wasn't Judith pulled me from my seat and examined my face and hands. "There's nothing to do about your hair except wait. They are terrified of lice and each new resident is shorn within minutes of arrival. If you lived in the commons, they'd do it every week. Now that they know you're a woman of means, they will allow it to grow back. Don't fret. I shan't let them cut it again."

She slipped a white sleeping cap on my head before shaking her head and removing it. "Not near warm enough without hair underneath." She reached into her pocket and pulled something out. "I didn't want anyone to see my first attempt but you will freeze to death with nothing on that head of yours." The knitted cap was form fitted and soft. Next she added an indoor cap. "Put a bonnet over that and no one will even notice that you're bald. Goodness, how I go on with you standing there in only a shift. Come. Let's see if any of my dresses will fit. They aren't as fancy as what you're accustomed to, and a few years old in cut and style, but they'll have to do until yours get here. Are you used to ladies' corsets or still wearing children's shapers?"

I stared at her. It was the most conversation I had heard from anyone since my nightmare had begun. I shook my head no.

"No stays at all? Well, you'll have to start with lady's since my childhood shapers are long gone." She had me step into some drawers and slipped a new chemise over my head, letting me put it in place before pulling off the old, dirty shift. No less than five petticoats were added. Then the corset came. Once it was tightened and straightened, I couldn't breathe but I was getting warmer. One underskirt, overskirt, blouse, bodice, and jacket later, and I was dressed. I sat on the edge of the bed as Judith pulled on my woolen stockings and buttoned up the ill-fitting boots. I was surprised to see my breasts peeking from over the bodice top, hidden from view by the lacy chemise to anyone but myself. They were surprisingly rotund compared to the last time I had seen them.

The young women helped me stand again and they seemed pleased with their work. I wondered what I looked like. These were so much more grown-up than Papa had let me wear. I couldn't breathe although I found the tightness and many layers mildly comforting. It made me feel strong. Secure.

"I am Hester Federick, the doctor's wife." I was a little taken aback since the doctor was so old and ugly and Hester was anything but. She was barely eighteen, shapely and fair. Her hair was plain brown—not dull—and was styled nicely on the top of her head. Her face was round and its features were wide to match. Taken separately, her large eyes, wide nose, and broad mouth might have been ugly, though together they seemed right.

"Judith, serve Lady Winmoore her tea."

"Ramillia." I tried to find my voice. I had been silent for so long, not wanting to incur the attentions of the doctor during our sessions. I cleared my throat and said a little louder, "You may call me Ramillia." I wanted so much to hear my Christian name, not surname, from her lips.

Hester smiled. It was generous and kind. She took my hand between hers and patted it. "You and I are going to be the greatest of friends, Ramillia. I will come to see you every day for afternoon tea. If you need anything, just let me know. Your treatment prior to this…well, let us never speak of what must have been quite an ordeal." She shooed the subject away with her hand as if it no longer mattered. "This is your room. No one comes in here without your permission. Absolutely no men are allowed as it would be inappropriate for a young woman of your standing to receive male visitors in her bedroom."

Hester pushed me back. I sat in the settle again; she smoothed my dress and rubbed her knuckles down my cheek. I think she was trying to be motherly, except mine had not acted that way, so it was odd. As she stared at me, I felt a flush growing up my cheeks to meet her touch. I felt…warm and tingly. I felt a desire that would become commonplace, that Hester would touch me again. She pulled her hand away reluctantly.

Judith brought in a tray and poured hot water through the strainer with its crushed tea leaves. Giving it time to steep, she put a scone on the dainty plate beside my cup. My mouth watered. It looked like a princely feast compared to the flavorless gruel I'd been force-fed. When I'd been allowed to eat, that is. My stomach growled in a most unladylike manner.

Hester chuckled. When I tore my gaze from the scone, her eyebrows were raised. She had asked a question but so caught up was I in my food fantasy, I hadn't heard. She repeated herself, "Do you have any hobbies? Needlework, crocheting, silhouettes?"

I shook my head.

"You need something, dear. What did you fill your days with before?"

"Books," I whispered, knowing it wasn't proper for a young girl to fill her head with such things. I harbored a secret desire to go to university but I wouldn't admit it to Hester.

"You like to read? We will have to check with your betrothed for his approval before any books can be brought for your consumption. I have some ladies' magazines barely six months old I can send up that no one could take issue with. Anything else?"

Thinking I should say something to improve Hester's opinion of me, I admitted, "I was learning to play the pianoforte before…" I let the word hang, not knowing how to end it.

Hester nodded as if that hobby was more suitable, graciously passing over the pause. "A pianoforte is a large order. I will see what I can do." She pressed an envelope into my lap and whispered, "Sir Julian Lawrence sent an impressive stipend for you and has promised to spare no expense if he thought it might ease your time here. You are lucky to have such a fine and wealthy man as your fiancé."

Hester admitted that she hadn't been able to keep the doctor from reading my letter. She apologized and left me staring at the package of parchment, my scone completely forgotten.

∽

Sir Julian Lawrence, my distant cousin, was a knighted gentleman and had attained the highest rank a man without peerage and in trade could gain. He was a doctor on the wealthy side of town and he specialized in the treatment of women. There was a rumor that he also treated poor women and prostitutes, regardless of whether they could pay or not. His criteria for patients was his own and had not to do with money. The education he had and his refusal to accept payment marked it as a hobby and, as such, was respectable. No true gentleman had to work. He could not claim to have any profession and still be thought of as refined.

I remembered him as he had dined with us a few times. He had bought my hand when I was little except no one mentioned it and it had fallen to the back of my mind. I thought about him with his letter in my hands and had a hard time recalling his face. He was an Englishman of Italian descent with money but no peerage. His dark curly hair was all I could pull from the depths of my memory. I wondered if it was still dark or if the gray had crept in. Would I, like Hester, be married off to an already old man? Sir Lawrence must have been forty, maybe even fifty, by now.

Though I had little of him in my memory, he seemed to remember me distinctly. His words were kind and gentle and read as if we were familiar. Making apologies for taking so long to find me after the tragedy and for being away on business that dreadful night, he assured me that I had done nothing wrong. Sir Lawrence wrote that I was innocent, while at the same time, addressed the death of my parents as unavoidable. I read that part several times. Using their names confirmed my parents were dead, just as the doctor had stated. He lamented not being present to witness their deserved deaths—even expressed pride in my strength and will.

My father had not mistreated me, not that I recalled. He had scarcely been a part of our lives. It was only because we dined together every evening that I knew Papa at all. He did not deserve to die. My mother had been cold, but not cruel. I had not killed them, could not believe it of myself and did not like reading that he thought they deserved what happened. The desire to throw my sole earthly possession into the fire was overwhelming, yet I resisted destroying it and put it in the writing desk.

Whatever my true feelings were concerning Sir Lawrence did not matter. He was my betrothed. He had promised to save me from this place and make me his wife, no matter what my mental health or legal status was determined to be. Until he managed to do that he swore that I would want for nothing.

Thaddeus lived with him now, as I would when Sir Lawrence and I were wed. Neither would be allowed to see me until I was freed. They would both write and Sir Lawrence begged me to answer their letters. He was sending trunks filled with all new clothes. He wanted me to dress as a lady, not a child. I did like that idea. It had been immodest the way Papa had Mama dress.

The next letter insisted on a few peculiar daily routines, asserting that exerting myself daily to the point of perspiring was healthy. A book was sent detailing the exercises he suggested. I was to bathe every day at a minimum. He was paying to have running hot and cold water piped into my own private bathroom, not the terrible running water of the city houses. Admitting he was likely paying for the doctor to have the same privilege, Sir Lawrence was to put in a water station building on the hospital grounds that had its own water well and heating mechanics. He found it well worth the money to have me clean, healthy, and well looked after.

True to his word, "my" trunks arrived—overflowing with gowns and dresses, skirts and bodices, bedclothes, and undergarments. I had never seen any of the items and they certainly weren't mine from my home. They came with a seamstress, who trembled with fright at being locked in the room with me. She took my measurements, her fear of displeasing Sir Lawrence overriding her fear of me and left with the items that needed altering.

Hester came in for teatime and would not rest until she had me dressed in the finest items. She fingered the details of each piece not chosen and put them away in the armoire and trunks. Hester assured me they were the latest fashions and very expensive. Her longing was so obvious that I offered to let her have one. I was tall for my age and they would probably fit. She declined, saying it wouldn't be right. When I suggested Hester wear one for tea, her eyes lit up. It would be our secret—playing dress-up. Plus, I had no mirror. How was I to know how fine they were and how nice they looked without her to model them for me?

I sold her on the idea.

We had a grand time at tea, though it was cold by the time we got around to drinking it. Neither of us minded.

3

Hester was right from the beginning. She and I were to become the greatest of friends. It didn't take long. Much less time than it took for the pianoforte to arrive or the bath to be installed. Both of which we enjoyed together.

One of the pieces of music that came for me to learn—as Sir Lawrence was happy about my willingness to learn the instrument and had opinions on everything I did—had a flute part in it. Hester had once been to a concert that featured a flute soloist, a wedding present from the doctor. She admitted she had always wanted to learn to play the flute except it was seen as frivolous by her family and now by her husband. I wrote to Sir Lawrence that night and had the newest Boehm model, a shiny metal flute, within a fortnight.

Hester was forbidden by her husband from accepting gifts from Sir Lawrence, though the good doctor certainly had no qualms about spending my betrothed's money himself. So, the flute was mine, not Hester's. She learned to play it but insisted that I should learn it as well just in case the doctor—whom she called John when we were alone and Mr. Federick if Judith was in the room—should ask. I agreed only if she would learn the pianoforte as well.

Bathing was much the same. We shared my baths as I would not bathe unless she joined. We, as most girls of that century, were taught that water was dangerous. It carried disease and washed away our body's natural defenses against the hysteria women were prone to. She insisted that I bathe first each time, using my same water after. I took mine as hot as I could stand, explaining it was my preference, although in reality it was so her bath would be the correct temperature.

We bathed nude, discarding the bathing gowns we were supposed to wear. It was quite scandalous and we took every precaution so we were never caught.

I looked with envy at her womanly body. She assured me that I was maturing and would be a beautiful woman, not an adult in a "childlike" body as my mother. She recognized the stages my body was going through as the very same she had experienced. We spoke of things, intimate things, that no ladies should speak of.

I knew about the differences and workings of the male and female body. This was when it was desirable to have a bride as ignorant of happenings in the bedroom as possible. The consequence was women, proper women at least, came to their wedding chambers unprepared. Most developed apathy for marital relations, if not disdain. They were not allowed to discover what they enjoyed; indeed they were not allowed to enjoy it at all. It was thought that too much sex led a woman to madness. Hester did not want me to be traumatized by my wedding night as she and every woman she knew had been. She surmised that Sir Lawrence wanted me to be versed in all manner of subjects as his broad sweeping permission for reading suggested.

Hester also read the books Sir Lawrence sent. He started out with a library he thought every young person should have, filling my rooms with works from every culture. The words of Coleridge and Wordsworth; Tolstoy and Chekhov; Dickens and Keats; Wilde, Poe, and Twain; and Verne and

Baudelaire were ours to enjoy. He even sent female writers like Jane Austen, the Bronte sisters, Elizabeth Barrett Browning, Mary Shelley, and Emily Dickinson. Anything I was interested in, he provided literature for.

Once Sir Lawrence wrote:

> *I cannot say how very much it pleases me that you have a love of learning. I share that with you. If you would allow me, I would suggest that what books are not read for pure pleasure and that which help you pass the time should be read for a better understanding of the inventions and scientific discoveries that are being made every day. I would have my bride be well-versed in germ theory, chemistry, and, above all, biology.*

With that letter came a paper called "Experiments on Plant Hybridization" by Gregor Mendel, which Sir Lawrence himself had translated for me. He insisted that I not only read Darwin's *On the Origin of a Species* and *The Descent of Man* but be intimately familiar with them.

> *I would encourage you not to give credence to moral, philosophical, and religious writings of the day. The men of this age have it wrong and I would like to save you the heartache believing them will bring you. There is nothing except life and that which is not life. There is no sin, except mistreating yourself. Anything done to keep oneself alive is good. So-called experts in these cursed fields will say that is not so. I say, are we less than the lion who kills daily? The lion would stay alive and at the top of the food chain. It is no sin if he must devour the gazelle and even, if it threatened his position in the pack, his own offspring.*

My time there was not all music and reading and teatime with Hester. Every few months, the doctor would give me an evaluation that consisted of two parts. The first was traumatic but bearable; the second was not. The verbal half was filled with questions about my parents and their murder, which I always answered the same. It was true that I had no memory of that event. The physical examination was by far the worst.

The doctor now claimed I was possessed by a demon. It was not very scientific of him, I know, but then the line between superstition and science were blurred. She—he claimed the demon was female when everyone knows demons and angels have no gender—was responsible for the blessed darkness that saved me from the experience and memory of pain. In my mind, that hardly made her evil, even if she had killed my parents. In the reasoning of Sir Lawrence, she was my lioness and she killed to stay alive. She kept me alive. She was, therefore, good. The doctor did not share my belief. He designed the examinations to anger her and bring her to the surface. A priest was at the ready to exorcise her when the doctor succeeded.

Unfortunately for me, pain is what brought out my demon.

The first of these physical examinations startled me. Not seeing Hester on those mornings signaled I was not allowed to dress. Given a shift and nothing else to wear, they took me back to my old cell where a table and stool had been added. I was instructed to sit with my back close to the door and given a metal pipe.

"Bend the pipe." The doctor gave the order from outside the door.

I thought he must be mad and furrowed my brow.

"Bend the pipe," he commanded again.

"I cannot."

"Yes, you can. I have seen you do it. You have one last opportunity to do as you're told." Only he did not give me an opportunity. A sharp, hot pain on my back jolted me and made me clench my teeth so hard I thought they would break. Then blackness.

When I woke, I knew the demon had been there. The pipe was bent, folded in half.

After that I performed whatever task he asked of me without hesitation. I did not believe in demons as Sir Lawrence had informed me they did not exist. I deduced that the darkness was just me, blinded by rage or pain. Either way, I did not want to lose control. I amazed myself by accomplishing feats that no strong horse would have been able. I had freakish strength and speed, could lift and carry ten times my meager weight of scarcely nine stone. I broke rock, bent metals, moved furniture, and indeed did everything he instructed.

No matter what happened, his report was the same. According to his expert analysis, I still suffered from my illness. He stated I would never recover, though it might be diminished under his skillful hand. He wrote to Sir Lawrence and told him as much, requesting longer stays for me with each letter. I was never allowed to write of my treatments, although Sir Lawrence often asked. I knew that if I did, not only would those letters never be sent, but that I would receive more attention.

The priest was frightened by my abilities and, as his attempts to free me from my demon failed to elicit any change, his pursuit was abandoned.

While the priest's desire to rid me of my ailment was driven by an honest desire to help me, it was easily discarded when it challenged his beliefs. The doctor did not want to see me better. He only wanted me dangerous enough to never be released. Sir Lawrence's money was the doctor's only motivation for my treatments.

∽

Each time I mastered a physical activity, Sir Lawrence would suggest another. He would send books about the subject, equipment, special attire, and sometimes even instructors. I learned to ride a horse as well as a bicycle and unicycle. I played tennis, badminton, and became skilled at fencing. I learned to shuffle and deal cards but not to play games. I became quite good at shooting both a gun and a bow. I cross-stitched, wove, crocheted. Sir Lawrence wished for me to learn every physical thing I could because the body and muscles remembered even when the mind could not, and these skills would be useful in our future together.

Everything I did, Hester did also. I had freedom to walk the grounds with her. Items that could be used as weapons were not housed in my rooms, however, Hester kept them with her. I couldn't be allowed to escape, after all. I was a milch cow for the doctor. Once Sir Lawrence had me relocated, he sent all new furniture for me, although these furnishings had found their way into the doctor's house. It was Hester's furniture I found sitting in my rooms the day my life changed. She was embarrassed by this but I was pleased because it meant my rooms were now like her home and she felt comfortable there, more so with me than in her real home with the doctor.

Hester was my first and only friend. I loved her, but then again she was all I had. I wasn't sure if she was a truly exceptional person or if she just seemed that way because I had led a life without any acquaintances except my family. She was almost as isolated from the world as I. The asylum, as I found out after gaining a small degree of freedom, was located in the country. How far outside London, I wasn't certain. Hester did have Judith, her maid-of-all-work, however, since she was the lady of the house, etiquette required that she treat her with a certain disdain as well as maintain a personal distance. There were washerwomen and cooks and such employed at the institution though they were hardly companion material for a social climber.

Sir Lawrence's money allowed Hester to hire more maids, which in turn, forced her to distance herself from them further. Servants were status. The more one had the less one was allowed to interact with them. My rank as daughter of an Earl made me Lady Winmoore, but not the sort of lady that should be called Dame as I would be once Sir Lawrence and I were wed. I was a true lady and quite above Mrs. Federick; nevertheless, we were the best social match for one another by a day's journey, at least.

My station dictated a need for at least a lady's maid. Hester served that purpose since I was allowed none. She dressed me, bathed me, did up my hair—though she allowed the seamstresses to mend my clothing. For those services, she was given my old clothes and since Sir Lawrence saw that I was dressed in the newest fashions, it wasn't long before we were both dressed so finely we would not have been shy at a meeting with the sovereign herself.

We were dressed so one afternoon on our walk in the courtyard after my seventeenth winter had passed. Spring had not yet started and Sir Lawrence had sent my new wardrobe a few weeks earlier. We were enjoying the fresh, moist air and cool breeze without so much as a shawl.

"John has said that Sir Lawrence will not be put off much longer. Your betrothed is determined that you will see your first season in London this year." Hester smiled at me.

She offered her arm and I took it, wrapping mine around hers so that my fingertips, stripped of their gloves, might just touch that strip of her skin between her gloves and sleeve's end.

It was invigorating—that small touch. We both felt it. We stared into each other's eyes as we walked. The words between us all spoken, except the ones that were never permitted aloud.

"You must know that I could never go without you, Hester. I couldn't bear it. I shall find a way to bring you along. This will be your season as well," I vowed to her.

Her eyes glistened with unshed tears. "I am a woman married to a man of no standing. I am no governess. I cannot even come as your lady's maid. Servants aren't allowed to marry as the possibility of children could take them away from their duties."

Her tears began to fall and I pulled her behind a shrubbery. "Then you will be my companion, husbands be damned." We stood face-to-face. I placed my hands on her bare shoulders. They were creamy and soft, though darker than was fashionable and with freckles. My thumbs rubbed over her clavicles. I was unable to stop them. I leaned in to kiss away her tears and was stunned when Hester turned her head so that my lips landed on hers.

I froze, as did all time and space. Even now, I can recall every detail of that kiss. The way her hands wrapped around my waist, pulling me closer. The rustling sound our dresses made when their skirts and bodices rubbed together at their fullest parts. The extreme close-up view of her large eyes, closed, and the way her long lashes rested on her cheeks. The obscene softness of her lips. The way they, so much larger than my small, well-bred ones, fell on the outside of my mouth on all sides. I was shocked by the wet warmth of her tongue when it darted out to trace the line between my lips. I parted slightly, allowing mine to graze hers.

She tasted sweet. I laid another kiss on the corner of her mouth, then her cheek, catching the tear that had been my original goal. My mouth trailed along her jaw before I worked up the courage to move on to the soft spot below her ear, which beckoned to me. Moving my hand to her hair, I gently pulled her head to the side to better access her neck, kissing my way down until reaching her shoulder. Upon arriving at my destination, I laid my head down and she mirrored me. We stood that way until footfalls warned us of someone's approach, pulling apart just as the doctor rounded the corner. The look in his eyes was furious and he ripped Hester away, leaving me standing alone in the garden. I stood there trying to decide what it was I wanted from Hester. I wanted to be naked with her, but that wasn't it completely. We had been naked together many times. I wanted to touch her—have her touch me. Although I wasn't sure what to do after, it made me think of dark nights, skin lit by moonlight, and sneaking around. It made my stomach flutter and I looked forward to this evening after dinner when Hester would come to my room to help me undress and get into bed.

4

Hester didn't come that night. No dinner was served. There was no fire. I unsuccessfully tried to start one. I lit as many candles as I could find a place for. They were beeswax candles, of course, and it made me happy to think of wasting the doctor's money from Sir Lawrence. My fiancé wouldn't hear of me using rushlights or even candles made of tallow.

I wasn't worried about Hester. Back then I didn't fully understand the control a husband had over his wife. The law recognized them literally as one person, and no one could stop a man from hurting himself. I honestly had forgotten that the doctor and Hester had any real connection, so disjointed were they in my mind. I only thought that he had kept her from coming to see and tend to me.

I decided no letters would be written to Sir Lawrence until I acquired what I wanted. My silence might force him to action. I wasn't sure what that was except Hester was an intricate part of that unknown. I read to pass the time. Although there was no clock, by the time I finished reading, the last five-hour candle had burned out and I determined it to be at least midnight. I thought about going to bed except there was no one to help me undress. With a wardrobe as expensive as mine, at least one servant was required to assist.

In addition to my dress situation, I had no way to secure the door that would put me at ease to sleep. The door locked easily from the outside with a series of bolts and a sliding wooden bar. Hester was the only one with the key that locked the door from the inside. She used it to protect our privacy and my honor while we bathed or dressed.

I jolted awake. I must have fallen asleep as I sat. A woman's scream had woken me. Was it real or imagined? I waited; the sound did not repeat. I decided to look for Hester.

If I wasn't to be locked in, then nothing was keeping me from my search. It was just as well I had burned every last candle. The other patients had no light and mine would have served as a beacon. I allowed my eyes to adjust to the lack of light and found that it was quite easy to see in the dark.

I pulled the heavy wooden door open. The sound that had always comforted me now filled me with dread. It had served as a warning of invaders and now it warned anyone around that I was coming. I waited for several minutes in the doorway, uncertain if all was as quiet as it seemed or if my thudding heartbeat just drowned out everything else. Satisfied that Turnkey wasn't waiting for me in the hall, I stepped out.

It was empty. The right led to the examination rooms, the treatment center, and down into the commons. The population that lived there was dangerous and mostly left to their own devices, although they would be locked away at nighttime. Unless, of course, their keepers had forgotten about them as mine had about me. I shuddered and turned left.

The corridor was long. I seemed to be the only resident and started to turn back when I saw a door. It had a waist high slat cut into it that was approximately a hands-width tall. Two fingers poked out, wiggled to get my attention, and then beckoned me.

I approached slowly, my eyes shifting between the fingers and the doors just past this one. There were ten or so in all but there was no movement or sound, save the snoring from a few. The simple smell of substandard human hygiene gave way to an overpowering stink, and I decided I could go no further. I could see that the inmate on the end had the habit of pouring his excrement through the food slot of his door and out into the hall. When the stench hit me full force, I stopped.

"I can smell you, Carrier." The voice from behind the door was raspy and male.

I wondered at his statement, for how could any smell break through this stench? My curiosity outweighed my fear that this could be an ambush and I squatted down. I peered through the opening and found myself looking at a very dirty face, well…the nose and mouth part anyway. His teeth were rotten and black. Sores surrounded the ridges of his lips and openings of his nostrils, almost sealing them off.

"How?" was all I managed when I wanted to ask how anyone in his condition could smell at all.

His mouth fell open. "A woman!" he whispered excitedly. He smiled, a few of the pustules on his mouth splitting. They oozed as he spoke. "I can, because we are the same. I be a Carrier, too, my lady. If you don't mask your scent, as I do, they will find you." He licked at a drip of pus.

"Who?" I whispered. The man was obviously insane. He was in an asylum for a reason. Then again, so was I.

He didn't answer but just shook his head. "Getting put in here was clever, especially if you have money. You can live well here and they won't bother you as long as you are locked up. What fun is that for them? I had no money. When he came for me, I did the only thing I could to deter him from taking me. They put me in here for it, because only the insane would do this to themselves." His head moved a little, bringing his eyes into view.

Or rather, the place where his eyes should have been.

His empty sockets were dark and the lids sunken. The bottom didn't quite meet the lid, leaving a horrifying gap. The stillness of the area was most disturbing, muscles atrophied by disuse. Blinking wasn't needed when there was no eyeball.

I gasped and then choked. The air I had taken in was stiflingly thick. I fought the need to cough and it only made things worse. The monstrous man chuckled and apologized. "I know how I must look and I am sorry to shock my lady. It is important that you know the lengths I went to to keep myself safe from them."

"You did that?" I asked through a layer of my dress I had brought up to cover my mouth and nose.

"Aye. And you'll do the same, if you love your life when they come for you. For none of them would want a body that couldn't see, even if it is a fine female."

I stood quickly. I'd had quite enough from this man. He reached out and grasped my skirts. I had decided to do him harm just as he released me. "I made that. It will help you resist him when he comes to claim you. Blue is true. Yellow, don't trust the fellow."

I rushed away, not waiting for him to explain his statement. After a cursory glance into my rooms, assuring myself that Hester had not appeared in my absence, I headed toward the examination rooms. I had to do something productive with my rare freedom and since they were the only real unpleasant part of my life within those walls, I determined that I would destroy them.

The first was the "ice bath" room. Just being there made me blind with rage. After snapping every restraint on the cursed chair that could be lowered into the vat, I realized how little that actually did to hurt this room's effectiveness. Straps could be replaced, though at high cost. The chair itself was metal as was the mechanism that put the seat into the frigid liquid. I tore the chair from its post and twisted it into a corkscrew and tossed it aside. I destroyed the mechanism for good measure, crumpling each gear so that they couldn't be repaired. I hiked my skirts up and kicked the porcelain tub repeatedly until it was no more than a pile of wet rubble.

No longer concerned with noise and confident in my ability to handle anyone who it might bring running, I tore the door from its hinges and used it to ram the next one open. I stood staring for a moment. This was a storage room and the shelves were filled with torture devices. Some I recognized and others I did not. I destroyed them all, breaking each component down so they could not be rebuilt.

I made my way along the corridor getting closer and closer to my ultimate goal—the doctor's office. It was at the very end and had no ordinary door. It was a wonderful piece of tinkering designed for exactly the opposite purpose as the other doors, to keep me and my fellow lunatics locked *out*. It was the only one made of metal, and I had heard the clicking key pattern, the hiss of steam, and the grinding of gears that signaled its lock release. I wondered what my strength would make of that technology.

I kicked down the remaining cedar doors and they shattered into satisfying splinters. I hummed to myself as I destroyed the apparatus in each room, finding new ways to enjoy my uncommon strength. No one would be tortured using these rooms again. In the last room, one which I had never been inside, I found a dead body.

The room was for surgery and the instruments were alien to me. I wrecked them all. This room wasn't for treatment or curing. It was for killing or maiming until one wished for killing. The room's last patient was pale and gaunt, strapped to a table. There was dried blood coming from her nose and tears had washed the dirt away in streaks down her cheeks. Her lips and feet were blue and there was a horrible reddish-brown stain between her legs. I forced myself to look at her and accept responsibility for her situation. I should have used my power to end this long ago. I could have saved her. When I had the full weight of her death upon me, I turned to go.

Then I heard it. Soft yet steady; she was breathing.

Carefully I ripped the ties that bound her. She opened her eyes. They were the palest of blue and they begged me. I picked her up gently. I couldn't—*wouldn't*—leave her there. She moaned and pointed back into the room. She wanted something on the table and I took her back to the one bit of furniture still standing. On it was a glass jar filled with amber liquid. I bent down and she picked it up. She smiled at me, cradling it against her. That's when I saw there was something floating inside.

The savages had saved the unborn baby they had torn from her womb. Had they done that procedure before or after the lobotomy?

∽

I took her back to my rooms. She was asleep before I put her in bed. She clutched that jar so tightly I couldn't even check that the lid was secure. She didn't know I wouldn't take it from her. I just accepted the possibility that my mattress might get that liquid in it. I didn't plan to be in that room much longer anyway. As soon as I got Hester back, we were leaving.

I punched a hole in the stones of my exterior wall, letting in the moonlight so that I could look the girl over. She was malnourished and the bruises spoke of anemia. Other than that and the part of her brain that was altered, she wasn't injured. There didn't seem to be any broken bones and the bleeding seemed to be slowing down but I was no midwife. I was unsure what level of bleeding was normal. I satisfied myself with knowing that she would live through the night and then turned my attention to the entrance.

I needed a way to lock ourselves in. I looked at my door closely and made a plan. I carefully removed the pins and dismantled the hinges, leaving them hanging on the door. Then I lifted and spun it around so that it fit in the opening, only backwards with the bolts and sliding bar on the inside. I went back into the hallway and pulled the metal off the wall that the bolts went through. I brought them inside and punctured the stone walls with them so that the bolts had a place to fit with the door facing this way. I hammered the hinge ends into the wall on the other side of the doorway with my hand and then slid the wooden crossbeam into place.

I stood back admiring my work. This should keep the doctor and his henchmen out while we slept. I suddenly felt tired. My rampage left me feeling drained in a way I had never felt before. I stumbled back to the bed. I got a second wind when I realized I still had my dress on and no lady's maid to help.

It was my favorite from the new spring group Sir Lawrence had sent but tonight's activity hadn't done it any favors. No doubt the rotting man's touch had ruined it early on. I tore it off and wrapped it so the dirty skirt was inside and no danger to my other clothes, shoved it in the bottom of the trunk filled with my winter dresses. I struggled with the hooks of my corset and then just expanded my chest and rib cage until they bent straight and came unhooked. It fell to the floor and I climbed into bed next to the girl whose name I didn't know.

I was asleep before my head hit the goose down pillow.

5

I could have kicked myself for not thinking it through before punching a hole in the wall. Morning sunlight, normally banished at this time of day, shone in a beam straight onto my face. Groaning and stretching, I sat up and realized the girl was no longer beside me. Looking around, I threw the covers off and stepped into a pile of dresses.

The trunk I knew they resided in was the largest I had. When I tentatively called out, "Good morning," it jumped. I selected a dressing gown, the only thing I could put on myself, not wishing to be indecent. I had no idea where the poor girl's sensibilities might lay.

I looked at the trunk trying to decide what to do to lure her out. An impossibly light blue eye appeared in the large keyhole. I smiled at her and she backed away. I had no food but knew the girl was famished. I had almost starved before Sir Lawrence sent my stipend. West Freeman obviously cared little for keeping its patients healthy. Having not been served any dinner, I didn't even have scraps to offer her, although I did have a tin of biscuits. Once I had retrieved them, I knelt down beside the trunk.

"Would you like a biscuit?" The sky-blue eye appeared again and locked on the cookie I held up. "They are good. Lemon flavored with a hint of sweetness." I took a bite to show her they were safe and then opened the box so she could see them. "They were a gift from my betrothed for my birthday. They aren't a true meal, however, they are all I have and you are welcome to them."

The lid raised slightly. She was sitting up, using her head to lift it. I was cautious with my movements, not wanting to startle her. She peeked out from the space between the lid and rim, her eyes gazing at the tin and its golden treasures. I held them toward the opening and her hand shot out and snatched the whole thing. The lid fell and I could hear her eating. I wished I had kept a couple out for myself but I quickly pushed those thoughts away. She needed to eat more than I did.

I hummed as I put the dresses on the bed, trying to convince her I wasn't a threat. Goodness, what she thought of me…what she must have seen the previous night. Picking out the most adjustable gown available, I laid it out for her. It was probably too long, however, it was the best I had to offer. Leaving her alone, I went to wash up.

When I returned, she was still in the trunk but the lid was open. She was shivering. Holding up the gown, I explained that it was for her warmth. She blankly stared at me. Her mouth hung open at an odd angle and a tiny bit of drool pooled to one side. Her eyes were gorgeous. They hadn't been able to take that away even if they were probably more vacant. Her brown hair was filthy and hung in clumps, and I wondered why they hadn't cut it off yet, as they had mine.

She signed to me for more biscuits. I shook my head apologetically as there were no more. Then she pointed to the lid, still lying on the floor, and I picked it up and gave it to her. She fiddled with the lid in concentration, turning it every possible way, and succeeded in placing it atop the tin. She clapped for herself and laughed a little. She set it on the floor of the trunk next to her jar and smiled happily at her two possessions.

I needed to search for Hester but couldn't leave the girl here alone. The doctor might come and take her away while I was out.

∽

That very evening the doctor did come for her. I could hear him in the hallway yelling about the girl. Her husband was coming to pick her up. He had dropped her off for those procedures and now wanted his new and improved wife. I knew he realized she was most likely with me since I had destroyed every other room in that wing. I heard him stop outside my door.

"Where is Hester?" I asked. I had to know where she was.

I could almost feel his ire rise. He did not care for me using her Christian name. "*Mrs. Federick* is learning to accept her place. I have been teaching her what her duties are to me as my wife," he said pointedly before pausing a moment. "Her lessons could be over. Perhaps if you give me Moira, I will let Mrs. Federick back into your life."

I learned her name was Moira. It sounded Irish to me. I had no intention of handing her over to the doctor. "And perhaps if you bring *Hester* back, I will not tear your asylum down room by room until I find her."

He stormed off.

It was another week before Moira came out of the box on a regular basis. Even when she started to live out in the open, she slept in the trunk. She often retreated to it when she was anxious. I began to think of it as hers. Though I put bedding inside, trying to make it more comfortable, she always threw it out. She liked it the way it was. There was only room for her, her tin, and her baby jar.

She let me bathe her and wash her hair. Only then did I learn she had red Irish hair to match her Irish name. It was beautiful. I knew nothing about fixing hair so I just combed through it and left it hanging to her shoulders. It was quite long when wet but the curls took half its length by drying.

It had to be the husband who stayed the doctor's hand when protocol would normally demand it be cut. I could think of two reasons he might have done this. One was that he loved her, admired the way she looked, wanted to help her with some ailment but not steal who she was from her. That one didn't seem probable. The second was that he had found a way to use her looks against her. For what purpose I couldn't surmise. I was an innocent, completely unaware of the workings of the world.

Every once in a while, I caught a glimpse of the woman Moira once was. I could see that at one time she had been quite stunning. She was no girl either. She was a tiny woman, like my mother had been, only she didn't have that baby look. Moira was petite and pleasantly curvy once I began to give her my daily rations.

Moira's husband came for her. The doctor tried to claim an earthquake had destroyed her wing and that she was killed by falling debris. He even showed him the area I had wrecked, however, the man did not accept his explanation and demanded to see her body. That was when I threw open my door and invited him in.

Moira was sitting at my table with Hester's magazines. She liked to go through them and tear out words and drawings she thought were pretty and then put the little scraps into the biscuit tin I'd given her. She jumped when he showed his face. I put my gloved hand on her shoulder and promised I wouldn't let anyone hurt her again.

The man, who I now felt certain was *not* her husband, stood in the doorway. "Me and the boys really missed you, Moira." I knew he was a pimp. Grinning at us, he rubbed his manhood through his pants. I knew exactly what he was thinking before the words left his mouth. "No bitch is going to keep me from my biggest moneymaker. Men pay big money to fuck a pretty, little Irish pussy."

I smiled as he made his way into my rooms. Someone in the hallway tried to warn him, but he was so confident in his ability to best a couple of women that he didn't heed them. Instead, he raised his hand to backhand me. Before he started his downswing, I caught his meaty paw, twisting it behind his back, forcing him forward. I bent him over the table, pressing his face down. He snarled and grabbed at Moira with his free hand, refusing to accept that I'd won.

I tempered my strength and punched down, crushing his hand between my fist and the table. I felt the bones break and then wrenched his other arm until it popped. He was saying the most horrible words, promising to do terrible things to Moira and me. I brought my knee up between his legs and there was a soft, squishing pop. I backed away, stunned by my violence. I had never hurt a person, not that I could remember. Things I had broken, but not people.

I half expected Moira to recoil to her trunk. Instead, she laughed and skipped to me.

Smiling at me, she slipped her hand into mine. Her pimp slithered out the door and I realized something important. Violence is only horrifying when it is done to those who don't deserve it. This man had hurt Moira: sold her body, had her baby killed, and her personality sliced away. It would be a long time before he would be able to hurt anyone again—with his manhood or his fists.

The man was dense and might need clarification for why he was being punished. "Send another woman here and I will find you. You will die, choking on your own entrails. If you ever come after Moira, you will *wish* I had let you die that way." Not waiting for him to reply, I slammed the door closed and slid the bar home.

Although I wasn't sure I could follow through with my promise, the effect it had on Moira was worth it. She wasn't afraid anymore. I was fairly certain I had a friend for life.

∽

When I woke, Moira was standing by the bed looking proud. She had spent all night practicing the fasteners and buttons on the gown she held up. Moira helped me dress and, though my corset wasn't as tight as I preferred, I felt more ready to fight and face the world than I had in a week.

With Moira by my side, I decided to search for Hester. She lived nearby, although I had never been there. I wasn't positive if she lived on the grounds, with quarters like mine, or in a house close by. I felt confident we would find her. No walls could keep me now.

A wondrous smell came from the hall and my stomach gurgled in response. I opened the door to find the cook with his cart filled with pudding so firm and dense with fruit that I exclaimed, "Easter pudding, Moira. It's Easter pudding," like a small child. If I hadn't been so excited about the change in menu, I might have noticed he didn't offer us servings from top of his cart but rather from underneath. I ignored the way his hand quivered as he offered me two bowls. I took them, thanked him, and pushed the door closed with my foot, not bothering with the locks.

Moira joined me at the table and we both dug into the hearty, sweet breakfast. It had a bitter aftertaste, however, I blamed it on the cook's ineptitude. He probably just forgot to properly burn off the alcohol after dowsing the pudding. I continued to eat in a most unladylike manner, ignorant of Moira's head slowly dipping down toward the table. I finished my bowl before I felt the effects.

I heard the door creak behind me just as my eyelids got too heavy to keep open. I knew something was happening except I couldn't focus. I was moving, being jostled, manhandled, undressed. I couldn't care; my mind floated in a cloud even as my body was strapped down. I laughed. There were no straps that could hold me. I tried to break free but the drugs were having an effect. I felt something being held against my face and knew they were giving me more. The wire frame and absorbent netting covered my nose and mouth. My breath became heavy and wet. The sweet, cool smell of ether was pungent.

I tried to open my eyes, stop them, anything. I could only hear and accept. The doctor spoke and it sounded as if it were coming through a pipe. He asked, "Why didn't you kill that pimp when I gave you the chance? I had two problems that you could have remedied with one action. Now that man will be trouble for my business. If I couldn't deliver his bitch, I needed him dead. You could have easily killed him and then my problem with you would also be solved. I could have easily gotten a court-ordered lobotomy if you had killed again with witnesses this time. None of this would have been necessary if you had done what you wanted to, what you threatened to. Instead you force me again, except this time either way you choose will end with the same result."

That was when I heard it. A woman cried. It was somewhere near, not far away like the doctor. She said my name over and over. "Ramillia. Ramillia, wake up! *Ramillia*."

Ice water, thrown over my naked form, did what Hester's voice bade me to do. I woke with a gasp. The doctor's voice was coming through a copper pipe that ended in a large horn near my ear. "Kill my wife or I will bring enough pain that your demon will come and do it for you."

I saw her huddled in a corner. Face beaten and bruised, her beautiful body broken and starved. My beloved Hester. I had time to scream, "*No!*" before the pain hit. I was sitting on a chair made of lightning. Every muscle in my body clenched. It was excruciating and then there was blackness.

I knew in that escape from pain, Hester was dead. Whether or not it was me or a demon, terrible things happened when I plunged into the darkness.

6

I woke up covered in blood, naked, standing in the middle of my room. Moira was peeking out from her trunk. I didn't blame her for being frightened. I was a monster…capable of killing my own family…best friend… *anybody*. Flinging myself upon the bed I screamed in rage and sobbed uncontrollably, my sorrow and self-hatred too much to bear.

A familiar voice shushed me, soothing my back with her soft hands. She lay on the bed next to me, stopping me when I attempted to look at her. "Don't. Please, I can't bear for you to see me like this. Not after what you just went through for me."

I couldn't help myself. "My Hester. Oh, Hester, is that really you? I thought I had kil…"

"Shh…Shh. Everything is going to be all right. I am fine. We are both alive. No one will ever keep us apart again." She reported everything that had happened after my blackout.

The stool I had been on was a special design of the doctor's. It was metal and connected to a control box by wires that delivered a high voltage shock to the seat. The doctor had found that electricity to the genitals was by far the most productive application of pain. Water was thrown on me to increase the effect. He had only delivered one shock to me. When I succumbed to the darkness, I had not passed out. Hester explained that my body seemed to operate quite normally—well, normally for me. She had never seen anyone as strong or as fast as me, which we talked about much later.

That night she only said that I stood and used the stool to destroy the room and equipment. She was frightened. When she saw my red eyes she thought it was the demon, but it was the result of the electric current that had passed through my body, breaking the blood vessels in my eyes.

I never looked at her. I tore the door from its hinges and left. She followed me to the doctor. He was still speaking into his tube, completely oblivious to what was happening outside his mechanical door. The gears and workings were sealed inside the door itself and my hands slid off the metal casing. Before I had time to test my ability against that invention, Hester stepped forward and keyed the code into the enameled number pad. The familiar grinding and hiss warned the doctor that someone was coming through. His gun was pointed at me the moment I stepped in. Although he tried to shoot, I moved much too fast and was beside him before he finished pulling the trigger. Hester said it looked like I only meant to pull the gun from his hand, but I pulled the hand from his arm. He screamed, blood squirting from his severed wrist.

When he saw her in the doorway, he called out, asking her to help him, asking her to call off her lover. Hester said nothing and quietly closed the door. She went directly to Judith, who helped her get dressed. Hester found Sir Lawrence's address in her husband's records and wrote to him at once. She gave the letter to her brother, who cared for the horses, and he rode out that very minute on the horse Sir Lawrence had bought for me. He would not arrive in London until the morning and then it would take most of the day for Sir Lawrence to come. But come he would. She knew it.

She paused in her retelling, and I noticed her expression change. Hester's husband was dead. As soon as the thought entered, I expressed my sympathy for her loss. Smiling, Hester assured me there was no need for my compassion, she was only sad because now she would have to wear mourning colors. I laughed and told her she looked good in black.

She rubbed my back, kneading the muscles as a baker might his dough. When I was relaxed, she went to the foot of the bed and started on my legs. I gasped when she reached my buttocks. She used a cool unguent on the ring-shaped burn there. It should not have felt as good as it did. The pain made the pleasure so much sweeter.

∽

I was anxious the next day. I was leaving to meet my betrothed. What if he didn't care for me after so many years apart? What if I hadn't turned out as fine as he'd expected? What if he turned me away? I would have nothing, no one, nowhere to go. Hester was a widow and Moira was a ward. If I suddenly had no status, they too were doomed.

Hester assured me that was not going to happen. She bathed me, petted me, caressed me, and described every inch that she found beautiful. I had grown into a woman during my time at the asylum and was considered quite tall for the era, with high, round breasts and well-shaped legs and buttocks. My skin was flawless, save the newest injury, which Hester said would heal with her constant application of salves. I was quite excited by the thought. She washed my hair, which was the perfect golden shade, and put it up in an elaborate style. She did all this while hidden beneath a black veil. Her face was a bruised mess and I pretended not to notice.

We packed my clothes into the trunks we had, minus the one Moira had claimed. I insisted that Hester was to come with me as my lady's maid. I knew now Sir Lawrence would have no objection since she was now a perfect, somber widow. She had no belongings, none needed in her new position, save her sole black ensemble. Hester was ready to go.

We decided that Moira was a bit of a problem. There was no question in my mind that she would come with us, although I did not know how Sir Lawrence would feel about freeing a mental patient. I decided that she would stow away in her trunk, to be loaded with the other luggage, and I would just explain her at a later date. We left a few bed clothes out to put on top of her in case anyone opened her trunk to check its contents.

Satisfied with our plan, we sat down to lunch. I was too nervous to be truly hungry so I nibbled. Hester's brother, excited and exhausted, came in with a letter from Sir Lawrence. He handed it to me and I stared at it while Hester insisted he get some rest. It was my first correspondence that had not been previously opened and perused. I took it to my settle and read it privately while the two other women finished eating.

It read:

> *Lady Winmoore,*
>
> *I received the letter from your friend, Mrs. Federick, and have taken action to free you from that place. She, of course, is welcome to accompany you, and any of her maids. Have your trunks packed and I will be there with carriages no later than 1 p.m. Leave your books. You will find that my library has all that you need or could ever dream of.*
>
> *I have applied for a special license to marry you, however, you must be presented at court and out to society before that will be authorized. I intend to marry you as soon as is decent, as soon as you are ready. I would like to give you a London season, show your beauty to everyone of rank, boast that you are to be mine, before making you so. I have servants at your family's London home cleaning and preparing for your return. You cannot reside in my home until we are wed, but you will be shown the utmost in luxury and comfort that your status and breeding demand from this day on.*

I dream of the day you will allow me to call you by your given name. Until then, I will adhere to any etiquette you deem necessary.

Forever yours,
Julian

I gave the letter to Hester to read since a portion of it concerned her. She sent for Judith at once, the reply being that Judith would not be going with us to live in London. She had a beau in the small town and wanted to stay on at the asylum, for the next doctor would surely need a maid-of-all-work. It was decided that Moira would wear a dress of Judith's and pose as our maid. I wondered what arguments Hester had used in her letter to Sir Lawrence and she assured me that she wrote nothing of the night's events. She only stated that because of her husband's passing she was now free to speak about the abuses he and his staff had inflicted on the patients. She said I had one chance to leave. It was the short time between her husband's death and the arrival of a new doctor and administrator. She informed him we had become great friends and that I dreamed of nothing but the three L's: London, liberty, and Sir Lawrence.

Hester was excited about the special license for marriage while I knew nothing about what made it so extraordinary. I asked her what it meant and she lamented my coming of age inside the asylum. We would have to work hard for me to learn to act according to my station.

She, a tradesman's wife and laborer's daughter, Hester explained, had been married by the banns. This meant it had been announced three Sundays in a row and anyone could object to the marriage, forbidding it for any reason. It put her honor and history up on the stand. The doctor had done that instead of buying a license because he wanted the opportunity for any of her past questionable behaviors to be brought to light.

A special license was very expensive and only obtained by the noblest, as they were only issued by the Archbishop of Canterbury. They enabled a couple to be married at any place and any time. It meant that Sir Lawrence would have me and no one would—*or could*—deter him. It also meant he was wealthier than the doctor had guessed and better connected than his ranking of knight might suggest.

∽

Sir Lawrence arrived right on time with a wagon for luggage and not one but two carriages, both the finest any of us had ever seen. We met them at the gate after observing their approach from inside. There was nowhere to have him in or let him rest. My trunks sat lined up, waiting for loading, as I had placed them before anyone could see me lifting a weight I had no business being able to lift.

As they pulled to a halt, I was scared by the number of men hanging off every available space on both the carriages and the wagon. There were more horses than were usually necessary, likely added to pull the extra weight of the men. More startling was how heavily each man was armed.

Two jumped from the wagon before it was fully stopped and started loading my trunks. One man climbed down from the front carriage and went back to the second to open the door and lower the step. From that smaller yet much finer carriage, Sir Lawrence emerged.

He was overdressed, and I assumed like me, he wanted to make the best first impression possible. He was very handsome and fit though quite a bit shorter than me. When he removed his top hat and bowed to me, the dark curly hair I remembered showed no sign of lightening. He straightened and I curtsied, bringing my bosom down to his eye level. His gaze hungrily took in the view. I blushed and stood holding my breath as he evaluated my appearance. I studied his face as he studied mine. He was unmistakably handsome with Roman features any woman would be happy to live with.

The inspection of my betrothed had come to a happy conclusion when I locked eyes with him. They were amber with gold and copper flecks. Like a wild animal, they were beautiful and filled me with terror. Seeing my reaction, he stepped forward and grabbed my unoffered hand. Deaf to Hester's gasp and objections, he stripped off its glove and clasped it between his own. Touching his skin had the most comforting effect. All my worries melted away and I knew I could trust this man with my life. He bent and put his lips on my exposed wrist.

He smiled and looked up at me through lush, dark lashes and then led me to the finest carriage. I barely heard him say, "Mr. Oliver will help you two into the first carriage where you can be at ease with no men to observe you, for it is a long ride." His voice was smooth and low, making me think of nudity and sliding hands.

Hester asked, "Shouldn't I act as chaperon, as you are not yet wed?" She sounded uncertain of the proper way to broach the subject with no time for consideration.

Sir Lawrence never looked away from me. I knew what he wanted me to say and I did. My voice sounded drunk or on the verge of sleep. "Do not fret, Mrs. Federick. I will be quite safe with Julian." He smiled at my use of his Christian name and helped me into the carriage. I knew she wasn't worried about me but rather about my honor, although I didn't acknowledge her concern. Julian followed me and closed the door, shutting out any further dissent.

7

To be honest the four-hour ride was a blur. I remember what we talked about though the exact words are lost in thick feelings. Being in such close quarters with him, all other senses cut off from the world by the black of the carriage, was intoxicating. The thoughts I had were unheard of and best not spoken. Julian Lawrence was titillating and made me feel lustful, but easy and comfortable with what should have been shocking.

He sat on the same side as I and hadn't released my hand. The feeling of extreme comfort and ease continued. Our hips pressed against each other's. When he spoke, he did so by putting his mouth so close to my ear that his breath kissed and caressed my neck. Every time his lips grazed my lobe, I melted, relaxing a little more. He, on the other hand, seemed to become more and more excited.

We talked about my stay at the asylum in hushed tones. Julian was not shocked by any of my abilities or my application of them. Exceedingly strong and fast, he too dealt out violence when circumstances demanded it. My fiancé knew I had killed. Happy to have my parents out of the picture, Julian swore that, had he known what was happening, he would have killed them himself. The only thing that gave him pause was how I could not remember it. He brushed it off as a young mind's attempt to protect itself from trauma. I should not have been forced to act at such an early age. The more we talked about it, while touching, the better I felt about it. About everything.

"I am excited beyond anything in recent memory. It is…frustrating." He removed his jacket, laying it on the seat opposite us. He rolled up his sleeve and had to let my hand go to do so. I came back to my senses momentarily, although not far enough to resist when he put his arm around my bare shoulders. He put his other hand on my lap.

"I will not look, my dear. Only let me touch you."

It seemed a reasonable request at the time. I don't know why. Touching was much more intimate than looking. I leaned my head back to rest in the crook of his elbow in acquiescence. The hand of that same arm lightly fingered my throat, my clavicles, my chest, before slipping down inside my bodice and corset to palm my breast. My legs fell open only a fraction but he noticed.

He fisted my skirts, pulling up the bunches of fabric, until its hem lay above the knee. He pulled my leg that lay closest to him over his, opening me more. Sliding his hand further and further inside my leg, he stopped to groan when his fingers touched the bare leg above my stockings.

"So soft. So perfect." He tarried there, whispering compliments for how long I do not know—so caught up was I in the comforting blanket of his touch. I jumped when he moved north, to the junction of my legs. His sliding fingers were agony. I knew what would happen if he touched me right.

I whimpered and squirmed until he did just that. I moaned loudly and may have heard laughter from the outside of the carriage. "I love this body. I long for the day I will be inside of it." Such wanton words I had never heard and I thought I might combust with need. "Oh, how I wish…" he muttered almost to himself, "such thoughts are folly."

My head rolled back and he retrieved a leather bundle from his jacket pocket. Untying the thong, he unrolled the pouch onto his lap, revealing an assortment of tools that were unfamiliar to me. Touching each one, he mentally weighed each option, before settling on a small, shiny scalpel. A series of short, quick movements were made before the implement was replaced. Julian laid his head back next to me and his expression matched my own. He was satisfied and made it known with a long drawn-out sigh.

I looked down at a sudden burst of color. "Julian, your arm is bleeding," I mentioned in a calm, almost drowsy voice. It was an observation, not a concern as it should have been. The red welled up from the five tiny parallel cuts in his forearm and slowly dripped onto his pant leg.

He had me roll up his handkerchief and then tie it around his arm like a common bandage, even though it was made of the finest cambric and must have been expensive. The red immediately soaked through and made the most beautiful blotchy designs. I nestled myself into the hollow of Julian's arms and he drew on my skin with his fingertips. I was awash with sensations and cried out his name.

"Yes?"

I opened my eyes to find I was alone on my side of the carriage. Sir Lawrence sat on the other side looking as if he'd been there the whole time, his clothes straight, his book open in hand. His eyebrows were up in question. "You drifted off. I saw no harm in letting you sleep since the ride was very long. I was lost in my book when you called my name. You must have been dreaming." He smiled and it looked devious to me.

The carriage came to a stop and there was a tap on the top, signaling our arrival. He moved to exit, his handkerchief slipping from under the cuff of his shirt. He tucked it in quickly, saying, "I find it pleases me to hear it from your lips whether you are conscious of saying it or not," as the door opened.

It had looked a bit bloody to me.

∽

Julian dropped us, my trunks, and the bulk of our security escort at the postern of my family home in the West End residential area of Mayfair. His house was on Park Lane overlooking the great Hyde Park. Both were in the respectable area of London but his was on *the* ritziest residential street in the city. He left and promised to be back in the morning to help ready me for presentation at court. Tomorrow I was to be presented to the queen herself and I hadn't even been to a proper dinner yet. I wasn't ready.

The house was nothing like I remembered. It seemed smaller, but that could have been because I lived there when I was smaller and therefore it had seemed bigger. The furniture, fixtures, and fillings were new. From Julian, I had no doubt. The servants, who had lined up according to position to greet us, were unfamiliar. They were also all male. I asked the butler, who introduced himself as Darville, why this was when male servants were so much more expensive both in salary and in tax.

He apologized profusely and explained that all the women who had interviewed had been too frightened to work for this house. With the pause between the words "for" and "this house," I felt he was implying they were afraid to work for me. He was glad I had brought my own lady's maid as he hadn't been able to think of a solution to the house's lack thereof.

I introduced my entourage as Mrs. Federick, my lady's maid, and Miss Moira, my personal chambermaid. They were to be treated with respect at all times and were the only personnel permitted in my private chambers for any reason. The men accepted this and I instructed Darville that, though he could divide up the household chores as he saw fit, my maids took orders only from me. He nodded in agreement and added that dinner would be served at nine.

I went to refamiliarize myself with my home. Hester and Moira followed closely behind. They looked on in amazed silence, stunned that I had grown up in such a grand house. After seeing the parlor, dining room, and all the public rooms, we took a walk in the gallery. Here, nothing had changed.

The same dreary faces stared down at us from the walls of the corridor used for housing the ancestral portraits. My father and mother were at the far end along with my brother and I. Thankfully, no one mentioned my mother's odd attire or appearance.

Hester admitted, "Your brother is quite handsome. You look nothing alike." She blanched. "I didn't mean…That is to say… You are quite fine also. It's only that my brother and I are so similar."

"Don't fret. I took no offense. People often note our differences." Where I was light, Thaddeus was dark. Dark hair, dark skin, dark eyes—he looked more like an Arab than an Englishman. Darville was standing far enough away to give us privacy but adequately close to be of use should we need. I called for him and asked how my brother was.

He looked embarrassed and I didn't understand since my question was commonplace. "You will need to ask Sir Lawrence, my lady, as Viscount Dathmoore has not resided here since I took my post."

My father had been Henry Winmoore III, Earl of Brooksberry, making his first son, my brother, Viscount Dathmoore. Brooksberry was a large estate held by entail, meaning that this house, the Brooksberry country estate, family fortune, and title of Earl belonged to Thaddeus now. I only wondered why Darville hadn't referred to him as such. Thaddeus was of age, older than I, and should have taken his rightful place here.

I took my maids up the grand staircase to the drawing rooms, library, and study.

I was uneasy in the study. This was where my parents had died. The floorboards were bleached white when I know they had been dark before. I blanched as I realized that must have been to remove the stains their blood had left. Wordlessly, Hester pulled us from that room and up still more stairs to the family's private rooms.

The furniture here was the same. Julian must not have seen any reason to update these furnishings. My trunks were resting in my parents' dressing room. It was to be mine. There, the walls were covered with photographs of Thaddeus and I. When Hester inquired about them I informed her, "It was a hobby of my father's. He was obsessed with taking our portraits."

I studied one in particular of my brother and I, remembering the day it was taken. We were not allowed to touch—mine was not a home filled with affection—but on this day, Papa had positioned us so that Thaddeus' hand lay on my bare arm. As I stood in front of him, my back against his front, a hardness in his pants grew and pressed against me. At that time, I had not known what it was. I did now and was grateful it was not visible in the photograph. The look on his face shouted almost as loudly, though.

Hester called from across the room, "I didn't know you were a twin."

I went to her. "I'm not."

"Then, who is this?" She pointed at a picture of me.

I furrowed my brow. "That's me."

"And this one?"

"Me."

"Are you quite sure?"

"Of course."

"Sorry. It's just that in this one you look like you, but this one, you are shorter and stouter," she said, pointing out the differences. "You are wearing the same dress so the time between them could not have been much."

I looked closely at the two photographs in question. The girl Hester thought was someone else looked like me but there were differences. She looked angrily at the photographer as I would never have dared. Her clothes and hair were slightly disheveled, as if she'd been running. Her eyes were much darker than mine, though photography of the time did not allow me to tell the color. It was a portrait of a girl capable of the violence I had administered. Was this a picture of my demon? I stifled a shiver, took the picture down and hid it in the dressing room, a closet that held the wardrobe for my first London season. It was stocked with new and expensive ball gowns of every color in the rainbow. Once there, all thoughts turned from the odd frightening picture of me and toward gowns.

∽

After dinner, which turned out to be mostly an etiquette lesson from Darville for me at Sir Lawrence's request, I asked Hester to stay with me in my room for the night. It had been a stressful day and I needed to rest before tomorrow, which promised to be even worse. I needed something familiar and comforting and Hester was that to me. Truth be told I would have rather had Julian with me, even from that very first night, but I would never have said that aloud. Moira took her trunk into my closet and seemed quite comfortable there.

Hester agreed to stay. She wanted to talk to me about what happened between us that last night in the asylum, wanted me to know that she wasn't one of the "third sex" women who sought out erotic relationships with women. With no desire to be the male of any family, she was, adamantly, not a lesbian.

She loved me, though. Something came over her when touching me. It inflamed her unlike the touch of any other person. The most carnal thoughts were born from even the most innocent of skin on skin. Admittedly, she had felt it the first day we'd met when brushing my cheek in what she thought was a motherly way. Confused and ashamed—no one should think of a child that way—she had initiated aggressive sex with her husband.

I assured her it was all right. I was a woman now and quite capable of handling the advances. I patted her hand in an attempt to soothe her and before I knew it we were naked. I kissed her bruises and she said they felt better. We touched each other softly, as if firm contact would shatter the delicate equilibrium we had.

After, while she slept, I explored my parents' room. Their things were all removed; this was my room now. Only the family jewelry remained in Mama's standing jewelry cabinet. The burglar-resistant safe was in the same place behind a wooden panel in the wall. Though I knew where the box was, I had no idea where its key was kept. I also did not know what Papa had kept inside. The money and valuables, other than the jewels my mother kept in her cabinet, were downstairs in the study safe. I decided that if I could not locate the key tomorrow, I would simply tear it open. I had always wanted to know what secrets he kept there. With Julian's words about my father, I wondered if it held a story of my childhood different than the one I had in my head.

8

I had no time to search for the key the next day. I was woken at daybreak. Julian was there for breakfast. We had lessons in etiquette for a few hours. Not the kind Darville had done, but rather a review of the rigid rules for being presented to the queen. The few times I got anxious and flustered, just a simple touch from Julian and I was right as rain again.

The dressmaker and her assistant arrived at lunch with my gown for that day. It was more formal than anything in my closet, if that was possible. It had a train exactly three meters long as was dictated for court. It attached under my bustle and could be removed so that the same dress could be worn for dinner or a ball. It was revealing, with the neck and shoulders completely bare, as was required for all ladies at court no matter the weather of the day or health of the lady.

Hester fixed my hair, hiding once again behind her black veil. She helped me pick the perfect sapphire and pearl jewelry for my dress that was then sewn in place. It was a beautiful pale blue with creamy accents, dark blue ribbons, and a bow worked into the elaborate skirts. I did not recognize the beautiful woman who stared back from my mother's mirror. I had not seen my image for six years and I was quite changed.

The final touch was my headpiece of blue, green, and yellow feathers, with three from a peacock's tail. The rule required feathers that could be easily seen by the queen upon a girl's entrance into the throne room. Mine was nearly two-feet-high, shorter than most required because I was so tall.

Julian was waiting for me in the great hall, his clothing old fashioned with knee breeches, buckle shoes, and a sword that completed his attire. The look on his face bolstered my courage as I clearly was pleasing to him. He fussed at Hester for her choice of jewelry. A lady's maid should know it wasn't proper to put jewels the same color of the dress on her mistress. He had her remove the necklace and earrings. I was about to defend her choices and locked eyes with him. I was filled with the same awe and fear as I had been that first time. He appeared relaxed and quickly grazed his knuckles across my cheek, banishing my worry.

He handed me a large box, calling it my "welcome home" and "coming out" present. Inside was the most expensive jewelry I had ever seen: a necklace, earrings, a bracelet, and a comb, all emerald and yellow diamonds set in gold. He insisted on putting them on me himself, his small touches melting away any remaining fear.

"It is bad manners to show at court wearing jewels that rival the crown jewels, however, I would have every Londoner of rank, including Her Majesty, see how beautiful my beloved is," he whispered intimately as we made our way through the house.

The carriage waited outside. Just as before, it was weighted down with serious men all intemperately armed. Their eyes were focused outward, watching for any danger.

"Are this many men really necessary for a simple trip?" Hester asked as Oliver helped her up the steps.

Julian helped me inside before answering. "They are. I would have more if more the carriage could hold. You greatly underestimate the value of the contents of this ride." He settled in on the seat across from us and opened his newspaper.

Hester looked at my neck and earlobes in awe. She thought he was speaking about the jewels I wore. The lust in Julian's look said it was me he sought to protect and that he would value me more had I nothing on at all.

∽

The ride to St. James Palace was short and I was glad my skirts would not be rumpled when we arrived. Julian exited first and turned to help me. We walked forward together, leaving Oliver to help Hester. She was not a person of rank and could not be presented or even allowed inside. It was still a great day for her, as the servants and chaperons gathered in a side room.

My train folded over my left arm, I was ushered into a gallery ten times longer than mine at home. When I arrived at the door pointed out to me, the lord-in-waiting took my train, let it down, and straightened it behind me. I panicked when he asked for my card. Julian gave it to him before stepping away.

His touch removed, fear crept up. I had to do this without him. The lord-in-waiting announced me as, "Lady Ramillia Winmoore, daughter of the late Henry Winmoore III, Earl of Brooksberry," and I walked forward toward the throne. Everyone's eyes were on me. The room was filled with fine ladies and gentlemen, nobles of all the highest ranks. There were whispers behind hands and I knew it was because of the "late" in my title. Few of the nobility met an end such as my father.

When I reached the dais, I curtsied as low as I could manage, my knees almost resting on the ground. I barely remembered what the queen looked like, so focused was I on not making a mistake. She studied me and when satisfied, reached out to touch my head, holding it steady to place her kiss upon my forehead. I was, after all, a peeress.

I knew something was wrong when her lips tarried a bit longer than expected. Her fingers dragged across my cheek and chin before she reluctantly released me. She spoke to me although I cannot remember what was said. I stammered, "Thank you, Your Majesty," and exited, placing one foot behind the other. It is against the rules to turn your back on your sovereign.

Once I was in the gallery again, Julian was there to take my arm. "Prince Albert will have a time tonight." He chuckled at a joke I failed to understand. "You should have locked eyes with Her Majesty." When I looked at him quizzically, he said, "You really have no idea of the power this body contains, do you?" I knew it was rhetorical because he didn't wait for my answer and led me out to where Hester stood waiting with my wrap.

∽

Julian assured me I behaved appropriately and had most certainly made quite an impression on both the queen and her nobility. He had spoken to several important people while I was being presented and had been offered no less than four ball invitations on my behalf. Many calling cards were expected in the morning.

He had lunch with me, saying that servants, no matter how fond I was of them, could not dine with us if there was a guest in the house, even if that guest was just him. There were rules to this society, like every society, and if we were to excel we must follow them. "In Caesar's Rome it was the same. The number of folds in a free man's toga were strictly enforced and any man caught wearing more than his station allowed was sternly treated," he said, sounding as if he spoke from experience.

He went to his club for an afternoon of port, smoke, and billiards. He left all of his guards with me. "Now that everyone has seen you, it isn't safe to be unprotected." My house was filled with servants as it was; I could hardly reason why this security was needed though it was oddly flattering. He thought I was valuable, on that count there was no doubt.

I wondered what women of rank did with their afternoons but didn't have to wait long for the answer to come. It was not a half hour after Julian left that the parade of footmen began. Cards detailing the names and ranks of people I did not know filled two different salvers in the great hall. I watched from my drawing room window and noted that no carriages were as nice nor horses as fine as those belonging to Julian.

Around three in the afternoon, I was startled when a large woman got out of a carriage and approached the door beside her footman. A caller! I was uncertain as to my own ranking and didn't know who it was proper to receive or not. Darville came up and asked if I was "at home." He gave me the card that announced the caller's name as "Dowager Lady Ernestine Wharlow, Countess of Edgington." Two names were written below and I assumed they were her daughters. Darville told me that a countess was surely a high enough rank that I should not cut her by turning away her visit. I nodded and he left to fetch her.

Hester made sure I looked presentable and then hurried Moira out. It would not do for servants to sit with a countess.

The countess came in and I stood, as I had been instructed. She was followed by two plump, pleasant girls similar in age to me, who she introduced as Lady Wharlow and Lady Charlotte. We all curtsied and I offered them a seat. A few awkward moments passed as we sat. I really had no idea what to say.

Once Countess Ernestine started talking, however, there really was no stopping her. They had seen me at court. Lady Charlotte had also been presented, Lady Wharlow having come out last season. Lady Wharlow seemed mortified at that bit of information but the countess assured her that she would find a suitor this season and have her married that year. A girl wasn't considered a failure unless she went through three seasons with no marriage proposal.

I expressed my relief at having that decision already made for me in Sir Julian Lawrence. A great weight seemed to be lifted from both Wharlow daughters at that. I would not be vying for the affections of any men they had their eyes on. They both warmed up to me and I found the call was over before I was ready. We had barely spoken but no call was ever to last more than a quarter of an hour.

They left after my assurances that I would return the call as soon as I was able. My name would be left with their steward. I would never be left standing on the curb waiting to see if they were "at home." I blushed and started to make apologies but they wouldn't hear it. Today had been my first as the Lady of a great house and they had boldly stepped up without an invitation. They had not expected immediate entrance. The countess was pleased that having her stand on the curb and wait would boost my standing in Victorian high society.

When they had gone Darville brought up an envelope. The Wharlows were having a ball and I, after they found me so charming, was cordially invited. I suppose it had more to do with the fact that I was already spoken for than my charm.

∽

Julian was at my door before it seemed decent the next morning. We went riding in Hyde Park. He was very happy with my training and claimed I rode like I was born to it, with grace and ease. The young Wharlows were there and I stopped to speak with them. I accepted their invitation to the ball. Though they did not say so directly, I understood that they were happy to have a young woman there with which the gentlemen could dance and who was otherwise unavailable for consideration. They had to have an even amount of males and females since it wasn't proper to dance with the same gentleman more than three times in a night. Lady Charlotte gushed about the gown she was having made until Lady Wharlow chastised her for public vanity. They invited me to breakfast. I declined because Julian was having a private breakfast with me. They seemed scandalized by the idea and moved on.

After breakfast, Julian went through the cards and gave me a list of those I had to return with cards, those I should ignore, and those I should make calls on. I dreaded making calls. I had nothing to talk about. He practiced with me.

I should only say that I was making calls to announce that I was in London, as I had been gone for some years. That vague reference to the asylum without actually mentioning it would instill a feeling of sympathy. I had, of course, been wrongly imprisoned. I should also say that the first order of business was to be properly presented to my sovereign, and wasn't she a regal woman? I would then say how proud I was that such a woman was the face of this great country. Now I was out into society and intended to enjoy it for it would be my only season. I should tell everyone about him and how happy I was that Papa had come to an understanding concerning our marriage before he passed. He promised that by the time I had said all of that and they had responded in kind, it would be time to go.

He could not make calls with me. It wasn't considered proper, but, since I knew no one, I didn't have to go until afternoon. Normally, I would always be free to go shopping with him in attendance, however, today he had a special treat. As if on cue, Darville brought in two young men to my drawing room, not announcing them. They stood waiting. Julian offered me his arm, which I accepted and he led me out.

I spent the morning learning to dance. One young man played the piano. The other was my instructor who had informed me that at a true ball there would be a string quartet. He taught me the quadrille, which was long and tedious. It was also the dance that every ball was opened with and talked through. He wasn't concerned that I know every step as long as I knew the figures so that I might walk through the dance satisfactorily. I would most likely not be asked as the quadrille was most often danced by the hostess, her daughters, and their family. It was a boring formality that needed to be completed before the real fun began.

The waltzes, gallops, and polkas were the main attractions of the ball. These put couples in close proximity, and more focus was on the dancing and not the conversation. The constant swirling of the waltz was my favorite and I know a few times I laughed aloud at the sheer joy of it. After a while, my instructor was so bold as to lean close and whisper in my ear that it would please him if I would drop the mister and call him James. He planted a kiss on my cheek and I stopped dancing. Julian stepped in immediately, shook the instructor's hand, and asked to cut in. Smoothly taking the impolite man's place, he clasped my hand and waist, and we resumed dancing. The instructor appeared dazed for a moment and then began calling out instructions from the side. "That, my dear, is why you should wear gloves when you dance. No one should touch your skin save me," Julian whispered into my ear.

I had no time to question him as he swirled and lifted me. I loved it and the longer we danced the more comfortable I became. When the music stopped, I noticed Julian was breathing hard and looking at me with hunger in his eyes. The two young men were shown out. Julian grabbed my hand and walked me to the gallery, the place farthest from Hester and Darville. He pressed me against the wall and kissed me passionately, my fingers threading through his hair. He spoke with our faces close, "Just what have you released on the streets of London tonight, my love?"

He left just as Hester and Darville reached us. Hester, chastising the whole way, took me to my drawing room. That was not the way to behave and I should have slapped Sir Lawrence for his impropriety. He ought to know better. First the carriage ride alone—she whispered *alone* like it was a salty word—and now this. She would have to remain closer if he was going to take every opportunity to act scandalously.

I accepted her tongue lashing. Everything was all right. There was nothing wrong with his behavior that I could see. I skipped lunch. I was much too tired and relaxed. I took a nap. Hester sat by my bed. That was all right also.

9

My calls went as Julian expected, and I actually enjoyed them once the conversation topic was decided. I was forced to take no less than six guards, plus the driver and footman, Oliver. More than one person I visited made mention of this oddity but, when they heard I was engaged to Sir Julian Lawrence, they nodded to themselves as if that made perfect sense. He always traveled with an entourage.

Though I was exhausted by dinnertime, Darville forced me to eat, saying that Sir Lawrence demanded it. I could not let my body waste away. In bed, Hester petted and rubbed until I fell asleep. She wanted more. I pretended not to notice while she pleasured herself next to me.

For weeks my days were spent that way. Riding on Ladies' Mile, breakfast, receiving calls and cards, shopping, lunch, more calls and cards, tea, and then dinner. The only changes were the addition of dinner parties, visits to the opera—where Julian had a balcony box—and the balls. It was a whirlwind of conversations about nothing and social posturing.

I was flooded with invitations. Most came with apologies for arriving so late, giving me no time to prepare. I had just come out and no one knew that I was in London until then. Starting with the Wharlows, I went to twenty-seven balls, almost one every other day those first months. I loved each and every one.

Though my dance card was always full, Julian insisted on the first waltz, the dance right before supper break so that he might escort me, and the last dance of the night. It was scandalous that he often wrote his name more than the acceptable three times per night. A few times he even had me remove my gloves for our last dance. With mine tucked into his pocket along with his, we danced skin to skin. While there were whispers all around us, I was comfortable with it.

It was on one of those nights, after dancing hand in hand, he had the driver stop before we reached home. Julian helped me down and we walked toward home, the carriage never too far away. He pulled me into an alley and pressed me against the bricks, as he had in my gallery that day. He rubbed his stubble-covered cheeks and chin on my neck and shoulders and whispered about the things he wished he could do to me. I was so relaxed I didn't notice the group of men approach until one of them spoke.

"Gimme your money and them jewels." Julian stopped kissing me and smiled. The man must have seen me clearly then because he said, "Well, what have we here boys? No respectable lady would be out without a chaperon at this time of night. If you're not a respectable lady, what might you be?"

That was met with a laugh and the speaker used a knife to back Julian into the arms of two waiting men. One of them mocked, "Looks like she needs better company than this prissy boy is providing."

Another taunted, "I'm sure she'll find the man she needs with one of us."

I should have been terrified but wasn't. All was well. Something wet splattered the wall next to my head. "What the…" The man with the knife never finished. Julian threw him back and he hit the opposite building with a crunch.

Julian gave me my gloves and put his on too. There was blood on one of them. "I am sorry about that. You excite me so I find I have little control." He looked satiated. When he got us back to the street and signaled the carriage to catch up, I looked back into the alley. There was no movement. There were several man-sized heaps on the ground.

"Don't fret. All is well."

And it did seem that way.

∽

Our wedding was shortly after that. It was a beautiful morning. Julian was as handsome as ever and my gown was more expensive and extravagant than any I had ever seen. It was a deep purple trimmed in real gold and there was even some lace at the neckline made entirely from the precious metal thread. I had new jewels, even though it was considered wrong to wear jewels so early in the morning.

We each had a matching cameo pinned to the place right above the heart. Men did not wear cameos, no matter how lovely their design or subject. It seemed terribly romantic to me that he would insist on breaking with tradition, so enamored was he with me. They were our images, mine on his and his on mine, carved into ivory and affixed to giant pieces of amber.

I had no gloves as Julian insisted our hands touch at all times. It also better displayed my betrothal ring, one that belonged to Julian's mother. Though its design was indeed old-fashioned, it appeared more like a piece from antiquity than a mere generation ago. It had no gems of any kind. It was thick gold with a flat circle hammered into the top displaying two figures. The two nude figures were not separate, instead they looked to be becoming one. It marked me as his and I was to wear it at all times.

The wedding was, as all were at that time, a private event. I wondered where my brother was, for surely he would show to this even when nothing else could bring him out. I asked Julian about it after.

"Thaddeus was executed after he confessed to the murders of Lord and Lady Brooksberry." Julian looked at me oddly, as if I should have known this already.

"When was that?" I asked. I was told that his death served as my release papers and had occurred the day of my release.

Julian said, "How else did you think we bought your freedom? Her Majesty's government does not often release convicted murderers and lunatics back into her kingdom. I had hoped another key to your freedom would present itself. Alas, when none did, I used what was available."

Thaddeus had felt no pain and had skipped happily to the gallows. It was many years before the fog of Julian's presence lifted and I understood what had happened to my dear brother. Many years passed before I was allowed to mourn him. On this day, nothing felt wrong. Everything was as it should be, with Julian's hand in mine as we became one.

The ceremony was in St. Paul's Cathedral—no less would do for a bride of Sir Julian Lawrence—and officiated by the Archbishop of Canterbury, having come in for just this occasion. It did not seem odd to me that there would be so much religion surrounding our special day when my groom had issued only statements of disdain for the church. Marriage was a religious right at the time; Jews and others had no right to marry at all.

The marriage was not announced. Julian said the danger was too high. No one waited outside the cathedral save his guardsmen. There were people at the breakfast wedding feast, though they had not known it was a wedding celebration until Julian announced it in a toast. The Wharlows were there alongside most of the other high-ranking people I had grown accustomed to seeing at balls and soirées.

The women all complimented me on my dress and jewels and on my husband's, now my own, lavish home. The countess wondered why I had not chosen white, as so many brides did to honor and imitate their sovereign, for the event's attire. I explained I had not chosen it. Julian jumped in from across the room. His attention, as ever, was on me even when he appeared to be engrossed elsewhere. He said the queen could have any color and had chosen white, for all the world knew who she was. He decreed my nobility by dressing me in the royal colors.

The girls envied me, having such a doting groom, and the bachelors envied Julian, having such a rich bride. They were remiss to have let such an orphan slip through their fingers, for such a dress had obviously cost a small fortune. The banquet was long, much longer than the ceremony had been. Several times during its courses Julian had whispered that he lamented the need for such celebrations, as they kept guests in our home when all he wanted was to be alone with me again. Tonight, unlike in the carriage on our first day, he would look as well as touch. He would be inside my young, supple body as soon as he was able.

Thankfully our guests, who no doubt would be shocked and offended at his coarse comments, did not hear him.

∽

When our wedding breakfast guests were gone, the procession of callers began. It would not do, to not attend the bride. Everyone was admitted. No one was to be offended by being cut on such a day as this, Julian said.

A letter was brought to me, a congratulations, from the queen herself. It had her privy seal and was addressed to "the Right Honorable Countess, Lady Brooksberry, new bride to the Earl of Brooksberry, Viscount Dathmoore, Sir Julian Lawrence." It seemed I was more closely related to Julian than I had known. Upon the death of my father and brother, the knight had taken both their titles. I was the wife of the Earl, Lord Brooksberry. Our first son would be Viscount Dathmoore, that is if Julian gained no further titles throughout our marriage. His ambition told me that would not be the case.

Then there was lunch, which Julian and I took alone in the breakfast room. Hester, still dressed in her mourning black, a bombazine so dark that she seemed made of shadow, arrived later with my trunks. I was not to move back home but live here with Julian. I was frightened and excited by the idea. It seemed silly that it had not occurred to me earlier that this would be the case.

Hester helped me out of my wedding gown and into a tea gown, which was much more comfortable and lighter. She noted that there were no more female servants here than there were at my family home. The male servants here were all so fine, so handsome, but also stoic, with half of them only staring at her when she asked a question, a blank look in their eyes. She was glad to have reprieve from them when I explained that, with no appropriate female family members, she would accompany me on my honeymoon.

"I never had a proper honeymoon. I wonder where Sir Lawrence will take you. Will we go by train, I wonder? Perhaps across the Orient. Or will you sail…maybe to his ancestral homeland? Italy is so romantic."

"Neither, and I am Lord Brooksberry now, Mrs. Federick." Julian's deep, smooth voice startled us. He came into my dressing room without shame. Even a husband wouldn't normally have such access. I realized why when he opened the door to another closet on the opposite side of the room containing men's clothing. We were to share and I wondered why in a house of this size. "It is far too dangerous to take my bride abroad."

His valet came in and began to remove Julian's clothes. Hester rushed out, flustered by the indecency. Julian caught my hand as I tried to follow her and once I felt his touch I knew it was right that we were this open. I sat on an ottoman and waited. He smiled and brushed my face.

"I will take you out into the world after we are properly bonded together and it is no longer possible for another like myself to steal you away."

He dressed and we went down for still more visitors. We had tea and then a simple dinner without changing clothes again. While the footman served my soup course, his smell assaulted me and I was filled with the desire to hurt him. My violent daydreams were vivid and imaginative. The man withdrew without ever realizing his offense. It wasn't that the man stank; it was something deeper, something primal. I was an Indian mongoose and he a venomous snake.

Julian's boisterous laugh broke me from my fierce thoughts. Smiling at me from his end of the table, he smartly shooed the footman away before I could act on my impulse.

After dinner we went into his study. After the steward poured our ports, we were alone for the first time since we wed. He let me empty my glass and then poured me another. This one was indecently full. Lighting a cigar—it was unheard of to smoke in front of a lady, even with her permission—he saw me staring and got something from his desk.

He handed me a small cigar about the size of my pinkie finger. "Puff it, don't inhale." He held a match to the end and I did as he instructed. The smoke tasted sweet and rich. "We will do many things alone that are deemed quite unacceptable to society. Any desire you might have will be indulged as I expect mine to be indulged by you. I plan to spoil you, Ramillia, and I have the means to do it well."

He sat. "You and I are not normal, nor should we quest to be so. I have brought you into my home, into my life, so that you are safe knowing the truth. You read the books I gave you on genetics?"

I nodded.

"Good. What I have to tell you will be better understood." He took a big drink from his snifter. "You are a Carrier. Your parents' genetic traits, as mine, combined in such a way that the recessive trait was brought to the front and the dominant, or common trait, was tossed away. A majority of humanity has this recessive trait but it is very rare that the right man and the right woman come together. Often, even when the right man and woman do join, the circumstances are such that a Carrier child is not conceived and a normal human is born. This age of fidelity has quite limited our reproduction efforts. Thank the gods for the superfluous women. Of the times when everything is perfect and a Carrier is issued, seldom is one female. What I am saying to you, dear, is that while I am rare, maybe one in several hundred thousand, you are one in several million. I have only ever heard rumors of female Carriers, so guarded are they."

Julian let this sink in while he refilled his glass. He downed that one and filled it again. He should have been sloppy drunk, with the five or so glasses of claret at dinner and now the brandy and port, but he did not seem affected. "You must have questions. Come. Let's have them now. There is nothing you can say that will garner my scorn."

"What does this mean for me?"

Julian smiled. "What advantage is it?" I nodded and he laughed. "That is my lioness," he said proudly. "You already know of your exceptional speed and strength. You are immortal. I, myself, am aged some twenty-three hundred plus years."

"Why are you so concerned with my safety if I am invincible?" I interrupted.

"Ah…I didn't say you were invincible. You can be killed. You are an immortal. You will not die of old age. Next question." He urged me as he smoked.

"Tell me how I may be killed."

"I do so love the way your mind works. Yes, of course that is the next subject. Now that you know the value of your life, you must look to protect and prolong it." He leaned back, throwing his leg over the arm of his chair, and thought for a minute. "It is not as easy a question to answer as you might think. It is too broad. There is much that can ruin our immortality. The short answer is this: your brain is where you reside; protect your mind and you protect your life. Be more specific."

"Can we be put to death by sword?" I asked quickly without thinking.

He frowned at me. "That is not specific enough, my dear. Try again."

I thought about it carefully. I did not like to displease him. "A blow to the head that severed the brain would kill me though I could sustain many blows to the body that would, inflicted on normal humans, be fatal." His smile returned and he nodded approvingly. I continued. "A brain needs ample blood to survive. Could I then bleed to death?"

"Though good reasoning, I cannot answer that. Not definitively. We heal so quickly that it is difficult for us to suffer fatal blood loss, most wounds sealing before more than a few drops are shed. I have never heard of it happening, but it is possible to die if blood could not get to our brain. Yes. Keep going."

His answer for that really answered most questions I could come up with. I reasoned aloud, "It is then our bodies that are special, not our brains. Our flesh can take damage and recover; our minds cannot."

"I did not say that exactly. Your mind, for example, sustained psychological damage in your youth. For that I am truly sorry. It is only physical damage that our brains cannot heal from."

"What of air and food; can we die of starvation or suffocation?"

Julian clapped twice. "Yes, and we have appetites in addition to human ones."

"You speak of violence."

"You do not beat about the bush, do you, my dear? I do speak of violence, such as the kind I dealt out in that alley a few nights ago, the kind you perpetrated against your parents and that doctor. While those outbursts are not necessary to our survival, they are pleasurable and you should feel free to act on those impulses whenever they come upon you."

I did not mention that I could not remember any of those events. He knew that already. I thought it best to change the subject. "Papa and Mama were Carriers then."

"Goodness, no. The woman you lived with was not your mother. Her deformity did not allow for conception or childbearing. You and your brother were placed with them because they were poised for a social climb. I found a place for you that would allow for a good marriage. I have been arranging pregnancies for centuries in search of you. When you were born, I was overjoyed. I almost took you home then and there, alas, I knew this way would be better for the long term. You grew up with a good family name and now it is beneficial for us both to join."

"And our children?"

"You have struck on your true value now. Every child you birth, whose father carries even the slightest hint of the genetic trait, will have it also. You could birth an entire nation of them."

It made me think of the letter he wrote years before about how a lion would devour his young if it served to secure his position in the pride. I changed the subject again. "Tell me, who are my enemies?"

"That list is much too long. I will say that any Inco…Carrier you have contact with is a danger to you. They will stop at nothing to possess you."

"Because I am so unique?"

"And because of the possibility of the army you could birth. A powerful man with you and your offspring on his side would be unstoppable."

I did not ask him if that was why he wanted me as his wife so badly. Maybe I did not ask because I already knew the answer and could not bear to hear it. Mainly I did not ask because he chose that moment to undress me. I should have protested, asked to retire to our bedchamber, but I could not. It felt proper to be completely nude in his study even though any servant could pop in and see me.

Julian studied my naked body from every angle. He expressed how pleased he was with how I had grown and taken care of myself. He touched me and I felt contented and relaxed.

10

I had no idea what time it was the next day when we woke, or even if it was the next day. Weeks or even months could have passed as I slept. I was so comfortable in my marriage bed, Julian ever at my side. He was so sweet and attentive those first few days. I wanted to do anything he needed and everything he wanted. His flesh was covered in scars, both large and small, and I got the distinct feeling they were self-inflicted, as I had seen him do in my carriage ride to freedom. His small leather pouch with the tiny implements of torture was never far from him, and I often saw him use them.

We needed exercise so we went out into the courtyard to spar. He had me remain in my day clothes. I must learn to fight in every level of dress. If I was attacked they wouldn't wait until I was appropriately dressed.

He gave me a sword; the one he held was its twin. I parried, he thrust. I lunged, he jabbed. We danced round and round and I knew he was holding back. Several times he slapped me with the side of his blade hard enough to make a sound and let me know he could have hurt me. It was exhilarating.

At first it was just us in the grass and gravel; soon many servants followed. I grappled with each and every one. Julian said that I should not touch them but try to stay my distance. The sword was an advantage to me in particular because it meant I could fight from further away, keeping my opponent at more than an arm's length. When Hester and Moira came out to see what was going on, Julian made them go inside.

I took a rest and the servants stood around waiting. Julian rubbed my shoulders. They were already getting tired. I had learned to fence in the asylum, never using such a heavy weapon. The footman who had incited my violent visions came from the house. He stood close to where we stood, Julian petting me. He did not seem to see us at all. His eyes were empty. He seemed sluggish and I did not want to fight him.

The primal feeling of needing to rid the world of this one came back once he was within smelling range. I didn't hate him; it was nothing so emotional. Simply wanting him dead and gone, I saw in my head what would happen to him once I was finished. I saw his eyes open in the shallow grave, not blinking away the flies that landed there to lay their eggs, saw his flesh rotting, moved by the maggots that would strip his bones.

"Some strains of the Carrier traits clash with others. You sense in this one something that is a threat to you," Julian whispered in my ear, his lips caressing my lobe, filling me with a sense of rightness. "He is my wedding gift to you. He is yours to..." He left his statement hanging as if to say there was no limit to what I could do with the servant.

"He has done nothing to me, this man. He doesn't deserve my ire." I remembered the epiphany I'd had after hurting Moira's "husband." Violence was only horrifying when it was done to those who don't deserve it. I could not make sense of hurting this servant, however, instinct told me to do it anyway and worry about the morality later.

"Oh, he does, if that's what you need to believe to do what is in your nature. He hurts children...and takes babies from their mothers." He rubbed me more and I knew he spoke the truth. I needed to kill this man. There was nothing wrong with any desire I might have. Julian left quickly.

I felt the darkness coming and for the first time I pushed it away. I believed Julian when he said this was who I was. I wanted to do this. I wanted to feel. I wanted to remember. If only I had let it overtake me that footman might have lived. The darkness might have saved him from my unholy lusts. It definitely would have salvaged the little bit of me that was still good.

I pushed the darkness away. I am tempted to omit the following depiction. I would like you to see me in a certain light, but you deserve the truth and so here it is. You must understand the reality of the world you live in. You must know to fear those like me.

I shredded the man's livery until he stood nude. I beat him mercilessly with my fists, until his body and face were lumpy and discolored. My blows had an unexpected effect. His manhood grew and stood erect. This enraged me. The dead eyes came alive. He laughed as I beat him. His eyes sparkled golden at my rising violence. He accepted every blow without retaliation. When we took up our swords, it was at his request. He said I must not hold back.

We fought. He instructed, critiquing my technique. He did not turn his edge away when he made contact as Julian had done. I bled. He was the better fighter. I had to try something different if I were to best him. Then I remembered what Julian and I had talked about that first night of our marriage. My body could heal from almost any wound. As long as I protected my brain, I would live.

I surprised him. I took a thrust that I could have avoided. It stabbed through my shoulder. I chose that spot to trap the blade while allowing the least damage to my vital organs. Julian's insistence that I learn something from every subject suddenly was of use to me. He released his sword and came toward me with panic and concern in his face. Again, the blackness attempted to overtake me and I shoved it away. At the same time I pushed my own blade into the footman's forehead. I could have been smart and attacked his weakest spots; there was no need. My strength knew no bounds and I breached his skull with ease.

His death was not enough for me and I wrenched my sword from him. As he fell, I relieved him of his head. As it flew from his shoulders, I turned away from the gruesome sight, my senses coming back as the instinctual need to kill dissipated. Julian came out of the house, clapping. I heard the body drop and the sword clattered from my hand onto the gravel.

Julian rushed to me. He petted and patted me and all was well. I was not horrified by my actions as I should have been. I barely took notice when he pulled the sword from my shoulder. Then he said something that confused me. "You almost got me that time. I underestimated you. I will not do that again."

I had no idea what he meant. He hadn't been anywhere near me until after I had dropped my weapon. It did not matter. Julian cradled me against him, making sure to allow as much of his skin to touch mine as was possible. He carried me inside to bed, where we remained for the rest of the day. I suppose the servants had to clean up.

∽

Though we spent the majority of our honeymoon nude, Julian never rutted. It seemed he was unable. No matter how long or intensely we touched, no matter how excited Julian became, his manhood remained shriveled and flaccid. Because of Hester's frankness, I knew how this should go and worried that I was doing something wrong. Julian became frustrated but assured me that this was not my fault.

We did not speak of it further, and he stopped exposing me to his member. He wore undergarments at all times and often I would see blood seeping through. It seemed to me that the area there was swollen. It was getting bulky, lumpy, and I could tell by the way he moved that it hurt. He appeared oddly pleased with the pain. After he finished with me at night, he would leave. When he came back with beads of sweat atop his forehead, I knew he went away to hurt himself.

He felt it was more important to keep my body happy than to worry about the failings of his. He was very skilled with the manual manipulation and release of my female humors. That was his specialty as a doctor. He took me down through the house one night and into his treatment rooms in a building behind the main one.

He had such machines housed there. All of them specialized to massage a woman's body, ridding her of the "hysterics" that plagued all females. He used every one on me and was pleased with my responses.

I know Sally says I shouldn't, however, I need to explain about the era in which we lived. No one considered any of these actions as sex. Penetration was sex. Homosexuality in males was punishable by death, mainly because there was penetration. What females did together amounted to nothing and while that was discouraged, not much was done to stop it. The word "lesbian" wasn't widely used. Women spent much time alone together, and many shared beds on the nights their husbands were either away or were disinclined to share their beds.

The pleasure from these machines was not sex. It was medicine. Doctors made house calls. Men allowed doctors to service their wives because it wasn't sex. Moreover, it saved them from the labor of having to spend the time it took to bring a woman to orgasm. Female orgasm wasn't sex because it wasn't necessary for reproduction. What occurred on the exterior of a woman's body, including what women did together, was acceptable to men because it didn't make a cuckold.

Over a short period of time, I realized that Julian wasn't concerned with that either.

∽

One evening we had unusual guests come calling at a very late hour. A fancy lad and the gay female companion of his employ were admitted through the back entrance. Julian sent them up to one of our great bathrooms to wash up. When I questioned his actions he answered only with another question.

"You want to be a mother, do you not?"

Julian took me to bed then. We lay together, I naked and he nearly so, rubbing and kissing, as we usually did. I was becoming quite comfortable with our brand of sex, for I was convinced that was the name for what we did together, penetration or not. I was so relaxed by the time our guests had finished with their baths and had entered the room that I made no move to cover my nakedness.

Now clean, I could see they were quite fine, common though they were. Thinness from a lack of access to enough food only accentuated their muscular stature. Though this woman's shoulders, face, and hands were tan from offering her services during the day, the rest of her was quite pale. Likewise the man's face and hands were seasoned. I was drawn to the man's hands. They were meaty, ruddy, and callused. I wanted to feel them on my tender skin. I blushed at my thoughts. After all, my smooth, manicured husband lay next to me.

I looked to him and he laughed. He got out of bed and went to them. He was larger than the woman and much smaller than the man. He ran his hands along their arms. "No need to be embarrassed, my love. I procured them for you. I would not take offense at what I myself had arranged." He gestured that I should approach. "Come. Touch. I mean for them to be our pleasure tonight. If you find him desirable, he will take your maidenhood."

Shivering at the thought, I rose. I did want to know what it felt like to have a man inside. I slid my hands along the planes of his chest and stomach. As with the footman, my touch had an effect on his manhood. It grew and stood erect. This time, unlike with the footman, it did not enrage me. Was it because he was only an ordinary man and not a Carrier? I looked to Julian.

He was seated with the woman in his lap. He stroked her hair, now kinking and lightning as it dried. "His body is yours."

I took him into my hand, amazed by the dichotomy of the soft, smooth skin covering the hard column seemingly made of stone. Further than that I did not know what to do. At Julian's encouragement, the woman joined me. She pulled me down to my knees and, kneeling next to me, showed me how to please a man by hand and mouth. It was shocking and stimulating at the same time.

Julian wrapped his arms around me, lifting. He brought me back to the bed and I lay on top of him, my back pressed against his front. He spread my thighs, showing the man how ready I was. "Be gentle with her, ruffian, or your night will end very badly."

I expected the pain Hester had described when she told me of her first rutting. It did not come. When he was finished, after his boneless limb jumped inside me and his seed filled my womb, he made a bawdy joke about how many women he'd deflowered and how I, while a lady, was no "lady." I was so comfortable and relaxed that I made no attempt to defend my virtue.

Julian climbed from beneath me, elevating my knees on several pillows, and covering me with the softest of bedclothes. I was floating in a cloud filled sky as I watched Julian through heavy lidded eyes. He backhanded the man, who went sprawling across the room. The woman looked like she would scream when Julian approached her, but he clamped his hand over her mouth. She instantly—visibly—relaxed. Julian soothed her and cooed her and propped her up on pillows next to me so she could watch as he beat her owner.

"You were paid ten times your normal fee for a night of pleasure. Surely you did not think the pleasure would all belong to you. You insulted my bride."

"I'm sorry, me lord. I meant no offense. I spoke the truth. Look, no blood." He pointed to his prick, still shiny from our time together, now as limp and useless as Julian's. When he saw the anger in Julian's eyes, he tried to explain. "Touching her…y-your wife made me bold."

Julian turned and smiled at me. He inclined his head slightly and a dark black curl fell onto his forehead. "She does indeed have that effect on all of us."

I fell asleep to the cadence of fist hitting flesh.

11

When I woke, the prostitute and her manager were gone. Julian was there, washing his hands in the basin. The water was pink and had dark clumps in it. I stretched. "Good morning."

Julian dried off with the hand towel. "Good morning to you." He brought me my gown and robe, helping me into them himself. "Are you sore?"

I shook my head and smiled slyly. He took my hand and we went downstairs. We passed Hester in the great hall. She curtsied. We went out through the courtyard and into Julian's doctor's office building. He asked if it would be all right if he examined me. Everything was all right as long as Julian was there. He put me on my back on a table. My feet were fitted into stirrups and he made me relax my knees.

He used what is now called a speculum to open me for examination. It was uncomfortable, not painful. He would not have done this before the activities of last night or if I had been sore. He was gentle with me, as always. When the examination was over, he helped me up and we went into his study. The one in the house was wonderfully warm and filled with entertaining books; this one was for his trade.

It was cold. Clean and bright, there were no decorations, only metal tables and stools. He had me sit while he made notes in a book and checked his reference books. He closed the books and laced his fingers, resting them on the metal desk before speaking to me.

"Contrary to popular belief, lack of blood is not a guarantee of sexual amorality. Blood is caused by the tearing of the hymen, a thin membrane inside a woman. It usually occurs during first intercourse. Usually, not always. Sometimes it is broken by natural means, such as physical activity, and often the girl is completely unaware. I understand this and so reserved my judgment until I could properly examine you."

He could see I was increasingly uncomfortable and so he came to sit beside me. He put his hand on mine. "The modern value of innocence is not shared by me. An experienced bride, one who has proven herself to be able to issue children, was desirable when I came of age. I do not care who he was, the one who deflowered you. I do not mind in the slightest that mine is not the first body to lay next to yours. I only wish to know where the babe is now."

I do not remember what my reply was. It was little more than stammering and half phrases. I did not truly understand what he was asking.

"Ramillia, I am ecstatic that you are an able breeder. My only desire is to find your baby and bring it here. I am anxious to start our family."

My mouth hung open in a most undignified way as I shook my head. "I have no baby."

He looked at me. He was not angry, but I could not read his expression. "I am a doctor, my love. Over my life, I have examined more women than live in the whole of England. I can clearly see that you have indeed birthed a child."

"I would not—*could not*—lie to you, husband. I can only say that I have no memory of being with child, nor birthing one."

He was nonplussed. "Never mind, my love. I will find this child you have no memory of and bring it here to live. Think nothing more of it. Come. I am hungry and the morning shadows shorten." With that, we went back to the house and devoured enough breakfast for twice our number.

∽

We went back out into society as a married couple. Julian was a very wealthy man. We did anything I desired. He purchased anything I wanted. I ate anything that tempted me. He indulged my every whim. He denied me nothing. He watched as I enjoyed.

We went to dinner parties and I flirted with whatever gentleman was seated on my right. We went to balls where I secreted off with my third dance partner for stolen kisses in a dark recess. Julian was always hidden somewhere nearby, his touch assuring me all was well.

The night that changed my life started out just like any other. We went to the opera and, unlike most in attendance, Julian watched the story. It was sung in Italian and he could understand every word. He loved the opera and theater, though he would have preferred a sporting event where men of extraordinary strength would compete, as they had in his time.

I enjoyed it but that night, bored, I looked down into the audience from our private box. Everyone was dressed in their finest and I judged the dresses more interesting than the stage. I found several faces staring back up at me, their rapt attention startling. I tried to pull my attention away and back to the stage but I found it difficult to pay proper attention with those eyes so focused on me. I could feel them on my face.

I opened my fan in an attempt to obscure my mouth as I whispered to Julian. It took him a moment to tear his gaze from the large soprano and her companion baritone belting out the first act's finale. When he did, his demeanor changed from relaxed enrapture to worry. He wanted to leave right away but it was not safe to leave until the crowd was out at intermission.

He called our box attendant and instructed him to have Oliver pull the carriage around. We would not be waiting for the second act. He paid the man extra to carry out his orders quietly, without attracting attention to our early departure. His panic was beginning to get to me until he placed his hand on my neck and assured me that I would not fall into the hands of the likes of such commoners.

At intermission we meandered our way around, greeting and visiting with those of a high enough station. We made our excuses and headed to the exit, saying we were simply using the facilities and getting refreshments. Once outside, the carriage clattered up to the sidewalk. Julian didn't let it stop fully before wrenching the door open. He tossed me in, rather than helping me up, and tumbled in after, stepping on my dress. He closed the door on my skirts and the carriage took off at a mad speed.

I fell back on the seat with Julian on top of me. I laughed, so unaware of the danger was I. He murmured how he never should have brought me from home before the bond was complete. I had been to the opera before and couldn't see how now was any different, except that we were married. The

Royal Opera House in Covent Garden wasn't that far from Park Lane and our residence.

The streets were busy and though the gas streetlights meant that events could happen any night, not just those around the full moon, they were dark and hard to navigate. We took corners sharply, lifting onto two wheels more than once. I expected to see Buckingham Palace before Julian lowered the blinds. I saw the shops of Pall Mall instead. Julian said that when in a hurry, they always avoided the royals. A fast-moving carriage weighed down with armed men could be seen as a threat by the palace guard and it was best to steer clear.

It meant the route was busier. We wove in and out of the traffic on the street filled with vendors at what I thought was breakneck speed. It was invigorating. I squealed with delight when I was tossed from one side to the other, Julian close behind. My dress was torn from the first dash to the left.

When we turned onto an alley that went behind our home, the seriousness of the situation hit me. One shot rang out from somewhere behind us and then several from our own guard answered it. Julian threw me to the floor of the carriage. Laying atop, he shielded me with his own body. We entered the courtyard and the rear gate crashed closed behind us. We stopped quickly, the horses rearing with the force of the pulling on their bits, ending our race right outside the postern. Julian gave the riding guards time to climb down before he handed me to the waiting men.

He climbed down after me, covering me with his cloak. Wrapping his arm around me, Julian guided me to the rear entrance. It was only a dozen steps or so. The guards surrounded us tightly. I got a glimpse of more men at the gate, in the yard, and even on the rooftop.

Once inside, Julian left me to Hester to undress. He went to see to the house's security. Hester looked horrified as I regaled her with my story of carriage chases and gunfire fights. She got more excited the more my flesh was exposed. I could smell her arousal as she slipped my sleeping gown on. Julian entered before she could act on her desires.

He ushered me out and down into his study. I could see that every window had its shutters closed and a bit of iron had been fitted on this side of the glass. The doors, I knew, were secured in a similar fashion. Julian opened a drawer of his desk and reached back inside. Something clicked and a small part of the wall opened a crack.

I clapped. A secret room! How exciting. He pulled open the panel and we went in. It was pitch black once he closed the hidden door behind us, but I was not afraid. How could I be, with Julian clasping my hand? I heard the strike of a match and then the hiss of a gas lamp.

One by one the lamps lit, showing me a beautifully decorated bedchamber. Julian urged me toward the luxuriously dressed bed in the center of the room. I realized then that I had not had a sip of any liquid in many hours. I was overcome by a tremendous thirst and was happy to see a decanter of red wine and a goblet laid out on an end table at the foot of the bed.

I poured a full glass and drank greedily from it. Despite gulping the odd copper-tasting wine, it did nothing to quench my thirst. I poured and drank two more glasses before collapsing back onto the bed. The bed sank as Julian climbed in beside me. My eyes closed and I submitted to darkness.

I jumped awake with that sinking feeling that jolts you when you fall asleep unknowingly. I sat up expecting to see the new, secret room and was surprised to find myself in my childhood bedchamber. I threw my covers back and my legs over the edge of the bed. My bare feet hit the floor and I heard running.

Soft but swift steps thudded out on the landing. I turned toward the door just as the footsteps stopped outside my door. I watched as *I* came through that door. It wasn't me now; it was me as a child. She turned and braced her back against the door, catching her breath. She seemed as surprised to see me as I was to see her. We studied each other.

I recognized the dress she wore. It was one I had only worn a few times before it had disappeared. Mama had scolded me mercilessly for its loss. I looked at it now, hanging on the childhood me, and wondered what had happened to it all those years ago. It was unbuttoned in the back and hung off one shoulder where the sleeve had come unstitched. Her hair was tussled and I had a moment of worry that Papa would be displeased.

"How did you get here?" she asked me in my own childish voice then continued without waiting for my answer, which was just as well since I had no idea. "You shouldn't be here. This is when I live."

At first I thought I had misheard her. Then she yelled at me, "You cannot be here! This is mine!" She thundered toward me. She put her hand on me and I knew real fear, solid like a wall. She pulled me to the window and I knew something terrible was about to happen to us. She opened the window and shoved me out into the nothingness that surrounded that memory. I heard cloth rip and rhythmic grunting before the darkness tightened, blocking out everything.

I fell for a long time, much longer than it would take to reach ground from a four-story drop. As I dropped, I struggled against the black blanket that trapped me. I wrenched it from my head and the rhythmic grunting came back.

I fell from that nightmare and into a reality much worse. I was back in my own time and I wished for the comfort of home. I was lying on my back on Julian's desk with the steward hunched over me. The grunting was coming from him as he rutted. My legs were spread wide, my hands above my head, my gown torn. I was as exposed as I could be and there were many to witness my humiliation. Five of the highest-ranking male servants stood around in various states of undress.

I pushed at the steward and struggled to get away. He smiled and moved his hand to my throat. It wasn't so tight that I couldn't breathe; it meant I was not supposed to move. The other men moved in to help him and if they all focused on holding me I was not positive I could break free.

I took hold of the steward's jaw and he sucked my fingers into his mouth. I gripped the jaw with my fingers around his bottom front teeth and my thumb pressed under his chin. I brought my foot up and, placing it on his chest, kicked him away from me. He flew across the room screaming. His tongue and a large amount of indeterminate torn muscles hung down in front of his throat. I still held his jawbone.

I quickly stood on the desk and leaped over to him. As I dropped, I brought his jawbone down with all the force I could muster. The pointed ends slid through his skull and into his brain as easy as they would have through butter. His head split and blood poured down his face. He crumpled under my weight and I came to stand on his rumpled heap of a body.

There was a pounding on the secret hidden panel door and I heard yelling behind it, "Get away from her. I will rip you to shreds if you damage her!" The other men in the room still had not moved. They looked from the sound to me as if they had no more of a clue what was going on than I did.

"Julian! Is that you? Help me, Julian!" I grabbed the poker from the hearth and held it between me and the slack-jawed men as I crossed back to the desk. I tried the drawer where I knew the release latch was and found it was locked. I looked frantically for the key on the desk, while trying to keep an eye open for any possible attacks. One of the footmen pointed to me and then to his neck.

I looked down. The key hung on a chain around my neck. I tore it off, opened the drawer, and slipped my hand in almost to the elbow before finding the latch. It was slick with the steward's blood and I slipped twice before I pulled it. Nothing happened. "Julian, it seems to be stuck. I cannot get it open."

"Leave us!" he shouted. The servants realized he was talking to them before I did. They fled the room. "Have they all gone?"

I looked over to the meat pile that was the steward and decided that "all" didn't include him. "Yes."

"Be sure. I wouldn't want any of them to overhear. The latch is a puzzle that only I know how to open." He spoke more quietly now.

I went to the door and looked out. The house was as still as the grave. I wondered about Hester and Moira and if they were suffering at the hands of the male servants. I couldn't hear anything and I knew that Hester would not take abuse silently. I went back to Julian and assured him we were alone.

He still spoke softly. "Grasp the lever with your first and last fingers of your right hand only. Turn your wrist clockwise forty-five degrees and then counterclockwise until it stops. Then pull."

The panel popped open and I ran to Julian's arms. They were stiff and unforgiving. He was angry with me and my only thought was that somehow he considered me a ruined woman. It would not have been uncharacteristic for a man of that time to have trouble forgiving a woman for being raped.

I couldn't have him put me away. I couldn't bear the shame of divorce. I couldn't bear to be without Julian. I dropped to my knees in front of him and begged his forgiveness. I was confused when he only uttered, "He was my favorite. So tall, so refined, almost aristocratic."

I thought I was his favorite though now was not the time for my insecurities. I was relieved actually. He already knew I was capable of murder. He had himself cultivated that part of me. "I thought you were angry that I had…that those men had…"

He looked puzzled. "You didn't do it on purpose." He said it as a statement but I could tell he was questioning.

"Certainly not. I just woke up and they were…I was scared and he wouldn't stop and I reacted with force. I did not intend to kill him."

He helped me to my feet and rubbed my bare back until I was calmed down. He would never put me away. Everything was all right. He picked me up and cradled me against his bare chest. He carried me up to bed, once again leaving a victim of mine to be cleaned up by his own.

He was talking to himself as I slept in his arms. "She shouldn't… I was too impatient. Next time I must take my time. I must take root."

12

We received no visitors the next week. Julian had the new steward, previously the butler, whose position had, in turn, gone to one of the footmen, tell everyone that we had decided to go on a foreign holiday after all. We had decided suddenly and left apologies for not giving goodbyes. The house stayed shut tight, with no one going in or out. Groceries were delivered as far as the gate and it did not arouse suspicion because even if we were gone, there was a whole house of servants and guards to feed. It wouldn't matter if groceries stopped coming. He had enough food stockpiled to keep us all alive for three months at least.

The men who had watched, ready to join in as I was attacked, remained in our employ. I did not question this, indeed never spoke of it. All was well with me and my household as long as Julian's touch was not withdrawn. Hester, who was my whole life before I came here, was a virtual stranger to me now. I only saw her when it was dressing time or undressing time. She did my hair and saw to my person.

"Your behavior is quite changed. Lord Brooksberry has an almost intoxicating effect on you. Is it true that you killed two of the household servants?" she asked me one day.

I smiled at her and described my actions. Julian often wanted me to retell the stories and I found Hester's reaction startling. She was repulsed by the acts and said that was exactly what she meant. No woman should be that flippant about killing. "Can't you see how wrong everything has become since we came here?" The question hung there with no answer—because I could not see and because Julian had entered. Though I loved Hester, my need for Julian was greater. I knew she always wanted to speak with me alone, but I only wanted Julian and his peaceful touch.

That touch, I was to find, came at a price. It was a price Julian paid with his own body. I brushed across his crotch one day when we were alone and expressed my shock at its feel. Instead of the flaccid member I recalled, it felt as if he had a pocket of snakes. He agreed to show me only after he had petted me into a near catatonic state. Only then did he undo his trousers and present me with a bouquet of penises. It would have been funny if it weren't so horrific. Every time we were together, my touch making him crave a release he could not find, he mutilated himself. He repeatedly split his member down the middle and used bits of wood and cloth to keep them from healing back together. He said the pain was enough and then something that confused me. "I will not need this body for much longer and it gives me pleasure to mangle it before I destroy it."

When a half dozen days had passed, Julian again took me into the secret room. He again unobtrusively kept me from drink for a number of hours before. I did not even realize he was doing it. He just nonchalantly distracted me whenever I started to drink. Upon entering the room, I felt the same thirst as the first time. The same decanter and goblet were there. The wine was darker, thicker, more coppery with a hint of iron this time. It was difficult to get down and I choked on it more than once. Julian's touch even soothed my gag reflex. I knew that I needed to drink until it was gone.

My body felt heavy and I found I could no longer hold myself up. I lay back paralyzed, like a lead blanket covered me. Julian was there. He joined me on the bed and took my hand. I wasn't worried by my paralysis. Everything was going to be all right.

I found myself back in my childhood bedchamber. That same falling sensation woke me from a sleep I wasn't aware I'd taken. I heard muffled noises coming from my armoire. I sat up, threw the covers off, swung my legs over the edge, and went to investigate. I opened the wooden door fearlessly.

The same version of ten-year-old me that I had seen before was there, huddled on the floor of the armoire, hugging her knees. She was crying. She had bruises on her arm and an angry handprint on one side of her face. I reached out. I wanted to comfort her. She scooted away from me. She was mumbling, "Do not touch. Bad things happen. Thaddeus says. My skin is poison. A brother ought not feel that way about his sister. My fault. Thaddeus says. Do not touch. Bad things happen. Thaddeus says."

I squatted down so I was near her without getting into her space. "Who hit you?"

"My skin is poison. A brother ought not feel that way about his sister. My fault. Thaddeus says." She looked at me with blind eyes. "I did not break the rules. I did not touch. Papa made Thaddeus touch. Touch made Thaddeus mad. Mad made Thaddeus…man."

I suddenly knew what day this was. Papa had only made Thaddeus touch me on one occasion. The photograph. I had felt what my touch was doing to him except we couldn't move. The photograph would be ruined if we moved. It had to be that day. I tried to remember what happened after the negative was set and Papa had closed the lens.

I couldn't. There was nothing after that. I tried to piece it together. I had felt a hardness pressed against my back. It grew. Papa warned us to stay still. Thaddeus' fingers dug into my arm. It hurt. Then… There was nothing. No memory of that day after that second.

I tried so hard, willing myself to remember. I shook with the effort. No. That wasn't me shaking. The ground vibrated and the armoire wobbled back and forth, threatening to topple. My porcelain dolls fell from their shelves, crashing into the hardwood floors, their beautiful ivory faces shattering.

The girl in that armoire looked at me from the darkness and acknowledged my presence for the first time. In a flash I saw that she was not me. She looked like me but she was herself. Her eyes were blue, bright vivid turbulent blue, not the warm golden honey of mine and Julian's.

I stumbled back. She lunged at me. I scuttled out of the way. There were no broken doll pieces on the ground. I looked up and they were all in their places on the shelves. They had never fallen. She stood over me.

"You cannot be here. This is mine." She grabbed my arm and she was stronger than me. When we touched again, I was certain that something terrible was going to happen to me/her. In unison we turned to the door. "You must go. You cannot be here. He is coming."

She pulled me to the window again. "Who is coming?"

"Pain," was her only reply.

"I am strong. I can help you. We can fight…him." I begged her. I did not want to go back and leave her here for whatever horrors were coming through that door. She pushed me out and I fell. There was not just blackness as before. She peered out the window at me and I saw her face.

I saw, rather than heard, her say, "You are. You can. We do."

I was so tired of falling. Why couldn't I fly instead? As soon as I had determined that there was no reason I couldn't, I was back. I stood in front of the full-length mirror of my dressing room, the one I shared with Julian. I was nude. A noise startled me and I spun to locate its source.

Hester lay on the bed lightly snoring. She was naked also and the smell of sex permeated the air. I looked at her. I did not understand what was happening to me. Had the darkness taken me to lie with Hester? That did not seem likely. Before, whenever the darkness came, I had woken to find that terrible things had happened. Making love to Hester did not fit.

I bent over to pick up my robe from the floor and a flash caught my eye. The key dangled on its chain around my neck. Just as before. I fingered it, thinking. Did this mean that Julian was locked in the hidden room behind the secret panel? How was he getting in that predicament repeatedly? I put on my robe and went out into the hallway. I had to get to him. I was afraid to be in this house without him.

I passed servant after servant who went down to one knee. Each one without fail knelt. Why? Why now? They looked at me differently. They looked at me the way they looked at Julian, in fear and awe. I was the lioness, the predator, and the prey knew their place. I liked it and could feel my confidence bolstered, my shoulders straightening, my spine stiffening. The new steward met me at the door to Julian's study.

"She is still secure, my Lord." I did not know who he meant. He put his hand on my arm and I glared at it. I knew there was rage in my eyes when I lifted them to his.

He removed it quickly and stammered out an apology. I snapped, "Leave us!" as I had heard Julian do before. I was going to operate the secret latch and he wouldn't want anyone else around to witness it. The steward practically ran from me.

I went into Julian's study and strode to the desk. I could hear Julian muttering behind the wall. I unlocked the drawer and released the latch in the same way I had before. The panel popped open and I waited for Julian to come out. Nothing happened. I waited a bit more, my confidence draining with every second.

Unable to wait any longer, I opened the door myself. Julian lay on the bed. He seemed old and weak for the first time. His skin was moist and glistening in the candlelight, his hair plastered to his forehead. He was a man in the throes of a fever. I went into the room. I quickly poured water into the basin and took it and the hand towel over to the bed.

I was tired suddenly. All I wanted to do was lay down but as I got closer, Julian began thrashing. I stayed awake. Julian needed me. I dunked the towel into the water and squeezed it. I used the damp cloth to dab the sweat away from his face. I cooled his head and neck with it.

It was working. The longer I was near him, the stronger he got. I was oblivious to the fact that I seemed to be getting weaker at the same rate. At long last his eyes shot open. Mine drooped and closed. It felt so good to rest, but it was not to be. Julian grabbed me and towed me out of the room, throwing me onto the ottoman of his study.

"Are you trying to kill me?" he railed.

He paced and I felt stronger. Stronger, not strong. He pulled me up to a seated position, gripping my arms tightly. He shook me. "How did you do it? You must tell me. To whom have you been speaking, Ramillia?"

I didn't answer, not because I didn't want to but because I couldn't. I did not know. He slapped me hard across the face. I barely had a chance to register the pain before the familiar soothing darkness took me. I heard a woman's soft laughter.

∽

I woke locked in my bedchamber. The one in my husband's house. The servants would not let me out. They would not even acknowledge my pounding and begging. I was weak, too weak to tear the door from its hinges and it was a normal door, not a heavy, solid wood one as I had in the asylum.

I examined myself in the mirror. I was bruised though they were already fading, my accelerated healing almost finished repairing my body. Julian had given me a beating. It wasn't uncommon. It was his right. I was his wife, his property, his to do with what he liked. If I displeased him, no one would judge him for doling out punishment. I didn't remember it happening but I knew it was true. I did not begrudge him.

Hester came to the door and whispered hurriedly. She didn't have much time. Lord Brooksberry would put her out if he found her talking to me. She couldn't let that happen. She wouldn't leave me alone in this house with him and his men. She informed me that the Earl was very angry. He questioned her all night long. He wanted to know the name of every visitor I had at the asylum and didn't believe her when she confessed that no one was allowed to see me. He wanted to know of any woman who had shown any particular interest in me, no matter how innocent it seemed.

He pressed on when she told him again that there was none. He wanted to know about any callers I had when he wasn't present. Any correspondence? He wanted to know who Sally was. He declared Sally dangerous and that if any whiff of that name ever tickled her nose, she was to come tell him right away.

She must help him protect me against this Sally. I would not get to come out until the accursed blood was out of my system.

Hester rushed off and I was left wondering. I looked around my room. There was something here that I needed to find. I did not know how I knew but I was certain there was something. My eyes fell to Moira's trunk. Hester acknowledged that Julian questioned her all night. She hadn't shared anything about Moira. Bright blue flashed in the keyhole and answered my silent query.

The lid lifted slightly. I went to her, moving slowly. Moira was likely to shy like an unbroken colt. I knelt beside her trunk. "Do you have something for me, Moira?" The lid lifted a bit more and the corner of a piece of paper poked out. The small, folded slip fluttered to the floor and the lid slammed down.

I picked it up and examined it, sure that every detail was important. It was crumpled, probably due to Moira's worried hands. The paper was thick and expensive, and my name alone decorated the front. My Christian name, no titles, no husband, just "Ramillia" written in a dark maroon ink. The handwriting was unfamiliar to me.

I opened it slowly, as if it could hold an attack, coiled and waiting for me. Inside there were only four lines.

He will not be your Incola.
Fear not for I am with you.
Trust in your friend Sally.
You must consume this letter.

I could not bring myself to do what it instructed. I did not know who Sally was or why I should trust her. She had not helped me get free of the asylum. Julian had. She had not given me a home and fine clothes and a place in society. Julian had.

When Julian came to the door I confessed to him about the letter I had found. I slid it to him under the door. As he read it I declared that I did not know what I had done to offend him but if he would tell me, I would never repeat it. I would strive to be the wife he wanted, the wife he deserved.

He opened the door and came inside. He gathered me up and soothed my hair and whispered that he forgave me. "You were right to show me this. Sally is the one not to be trusted. She is out there somewhere trying to take advantage of your special abilities. You are almost rid of her. If you had eaten this letter as she instructs, you might have gotten tangled in her web again."

Julian rolled open his kit and lay out his tools on the bed next to where he put me. He cut into my arms, through the veins, inserting tubes to keep me from healing. I bled through those tubes into small basins. He petted me and loved me as he drained me. My body melted under his touch. I had no worries, even though I knew that blood loss could kill me. When a bowl filled, he took it and replaced it. Bowl after bowl he filled until I was so weak I could not keep my eyes open.

He took the stints from my arms and left with all his equipment. He would now find out how that letter had made its way into his home, how that blood had made its way into his precious wife.

∽

I do not know how long I was in that room. I did not care. Julian came to see me and that was all that mattered. He bled me many more times. I did not mind. He touched me and all was well. He was tender with me. He fed me with his own hand. He even left food for Moira. No other letter appeared and Julian was pleased. He had found the crack in his defenses and sealed the leak.

Hester was gone. Julian sent her away with a competency large enough that she could live handsomely. He had ensured she was happy and well cared for, but he could not have her in his house. I believed him and let the subject go. He knew I needed a lady's maid but would not suffer a possible spy for Sally. The woman was obviously well-connected and smart.

He would leave me Moira. He found her acceptable. With her dimmed intelligence and near zero exposure to the outside world, she posed no threat. She would have to do. I was glad. I felt vaguely responsible for her and wanted to see to it that she was cared for and protected. Deep down, I must have known that Julian could not be trusted to ensure that and so I did not tell him that the letter had actually come through her, not Hester.

He said I was clear of Sally's control and he threw open the doors. I was greeted by a great cheering from the household staff. It was to the sounds of their applause that I made my way down the grand staircase and into the dining room. Julian had all my favorites prepared and he sat with me while I feasted. When I could eat no more, they brought in the port and cigars.

I smoked and drank like a common whore and in proportions only a sailor could manage.

13

Several evenings after that, Julian asked if I would care for a new game. I was eager to please him and so I agreed. He explained that because his condition kept him from participating fully in our bedroom, he could derive pleasure from watching others. He insinuated that I might decide that I enjoyed being watched. I could never be sure where he was—his home was designed so that he might access any room—and he could be watching at any time.

He refrained from touching me. Speaking softly and close so that his words and breath caressed just the same, he said he had been watching while I dressed in the morning, while I bathed, while the waste flowed from my cunny, while Mrs. Federick fingered me, while I sipped absinthe and rubbed my breasts. The list went on, enumerating any time I thought I had been alone. I felt anxious though the fluttering feeling in my stomach was pleasing. The thought of his eyes on me during such private times aroused me.

When I was wet from the unusual anxious sensations, Julian rang for the servants. He instructed me to choose from those who answered the call. I should pick the one who I liked the looks of the most. I should choose carefully because I would spend the night with that one. I would do lewd acts with my choice, while Julian secretly watched.

By the time the six or so men filed into the room I was in a froth. I was certain my life was bolder than any other's had been. I would experience things none other would. They stood, not looking at me, waiting for my decision. I wondered if they knew they were being evaluated.

I walked around discreetly so that I might smell them without their notice. Thankfully none aroused the need for violence that the footman on my first night in this house had. I did not want to kill tonight. Without preamble, I went to the first one and kissed him on the lips. His lips were gloriously full. The next one's most attractive feature was his eyes. I looked deep into the vibrant green that reminded me of life and I ran my fingertips along his face.

I went down the line, touching and testing each one according to their strengths. The last man had an impressively wide chest. I slowly unbuttoned his livery—starting with jacket, then waistcoat, and finally the stiff shirt before slipping my hands inside his undershirt to run across the planes of his chest. Once I had touched each one, the effect I had stood out plain as day in their trousers.

Very aware of Julian's eyes on me, I bent over and looked down the line, comparing the bulges. I chose the one that delighted me the most, the tall one with the green eyes. Julian dismissed them all and the one with the lips protested, "Sir Lawrence, it is my turn. I need this!"

Julian chastised, "Would you displease the Lady of this house by denying her choice? No, that will not do, Charles. Adjustments must be made to fit her into our lives." He shooed the man away with the others. He spoke again, "Also, I am an Earl now. You would do well to remember my title, no matter how long you have been with me."

"Apologies, my Lord." Charles inclined his head to me as well. "My lady." He closed the door behind him.

∽

My selection came to my chamber that night and we were intimate. I was constantly aware that Julian was watching and my imagination had me seeing him peering from every cracked door, closet, painting, and vent. I was so preoccupied with trying to ferret him out that I did not notice him looking at me from the most obvious place.

The session was good, and the techniques he employed with his mouth and hands were not unlike Julian's. His rutting was satisfactory in both stamina and speed. I lay with my legs up, allowing gravity to aid in keeping his seed in my womb, with my most private parts pointed in the direction I thought Julian could best see.

The man dressed himself and seemed a little rusty with the operation. He bowed to me before leaving and I noticed two things. His eyes seemed lighter and the key hung around his neck. The first I dismissed as a change in lighting. The second had me intrigued.

When he left, I followed him with what I hoped was stealth. I knew Julian probably watched me and it made my escapades all the more exciting. The rest of the house was asleep so, as long as I avoided being seen by the man himself, I could wander undiscovered. The man, my evening partner, left the house after retrieving some money from Julian's desk.

Since Julian was most likely watching I did not doubt that he knew and I was not responsible for reporting the theft. I stood at the desk, pondering. Did his possession of the key mean that Julian was in the hidden room? I pressed my ear to the hollow panel yet heard nothing. Perhaps the secret room held its own secrets—passages to other parts of the house, maybe.

I glanced at the open book on Julian's desk. It appeared to be a register. I would have passed it over had I not seen my name. It was written in my own script. I stared a moment and turned the page. Finding it blank, I returned to the original page and then back one more. My name was on this page as well among a list of others.

I looked at the pages more carefully, aware that if Julian did not want me to see this, he would come out of his hiding place. It was a catalog with several columns following each name. There was a date, a number of hours, another number of hours, and then a set of letters. A few of them had another date at the end. Most often the two numbers of hours were close if not exactly the same. Mine were not at all similar. On one page the numbers beside my name were twelve and one. The other had twelve and three.

I flipped through the book looking for a table of contents or key. At the front the columns were headed:

Used Date Intended Actual Activities Death

It was Julian's handwriting. I would recognize it anywhere. It was the only view of the outside world I'd had all the years I lived in the asylum. I flipped back through to see which entries had a "death" date. Then I noticed Thaddeus had many entries. For a time, he had more entries than any other. The last entry with his name had a death date.

I put it back as I found it. On that open page there was my name at the top, then three others, then the last one. The man I had spent the evening in the arms of, the one who had written here most recently, was named Albert. He had written his name, today's date, seven intended number of hours and, in the activities column, the letters "SLR."

I curled up in the most comfortable chair in Julian's office. It had a high back and sides. I leaned my head on one of the wings. I wanted to talk to him the instant he decided to come out. I must have fallen asleep because I awoke to Albert standing over me. I jumped, not because he startled me but because he looked so wretched. His hands, the hands that had caressed me hours before, were battered and bloody from fighting.

He smiled at me and there was blood around his teeth. His eyebrow was matted and swollen, his nose crooked. "Waiting up for me. Flattering." He looked at his pocket watch. "I have enough time, if you want me again." He reached for me with his grotesque hands and I pulled back.

"I just want Julian… Lord Brooksberry."

This made him smile more broadly. He went to the desk, unlocked the drawer, and reached in. When the door panel popped open, I became confused. How did he know how to operate the latch? Julian had said only he knew. Now I did also, but Albert? He hardly seemed like a confidant for the Earl, unless my choice had somehow elevated his status in the house.

Several minutes later Julian and Albert came stumbling out. They both seemed weak; the latter was barely upright. "Pull the bell, my love." I did and as we waited for the servants, Julian smiled at me.

The footman came to help Albert to his room. Julian declined his valet's offer of help. He put his arm around my shoulders and together we went to bed, all questions and worries erased from my mind with a few touches from Julian. As always.

14

I found my gaze often drawn to the secret panel. Rationally I knew I should stay away but something drew me. I scarcely heard what Julian spoke of, so preoccupied was I concerning the hidden room. The strangest things occurred after I entered the first few times.

Julian noticed my inattention. "Quite right. The time has come for us to be properly bonded. I want to complete the ritual while I am certain no other has introduced their control back into your system." He operated the latch and the door opened. "Tonight I will sink my root in you so deep that no other will ever find their way in."

I entered. The thirst was there, as was the carafe filled with the cure. Julian kept me from drinking and we lay on the bed together.

He talked while working. "You should not be able to push me out. The only remedy I can think of is that I must give you a place to go. I offer you mine. When it is time, and not a minute sooner, we will return." Julian opened my vein and put in the stint, one in each arm. He attached a tube to one, and when it was filled with my blood, he shoved the dripping end into his own arm. When his face was ruddy and puffed from the pressure, he put a stint in his other arm. Attaching another tube where his blood gushed out, he quickly connected it to the open stint in mine.

He spoke in Latin. My blood flowed into him and his into me. The heavy blanket covered me, threatening to bring the darkness, but Julian forced me to stay awake as long as possible. My body felt less and less like my own. I could feel myself—my life—inside Julian and I did not want to go. His foreign words told me to follow the blood, to ride along the path of immortality.

I jolted awake. I turned over in my childhood bed and came face-to-face with the girl who looked like me except had stormy blue eyes where they should have been amber. She had been crying and I felt sad for her. As always she said, "You should not be here. This is mine."

"I know and I am sorry. Julian says—"

"How dare you say that name to me! He is trying to take my place. He has no idea what he is dealing with. He could not handle the pain we have dealt with daily. No, do not say his name to me." She threw back the covers and dragged me to the window.

"I cannot go out the window this time. You do not know what happens. Please let me stay. He said I could return only when the time is right and not a minute before. If I do he will bleed me and lock me in my room. He may even take Moira from me."

She glared at me and then shoved me under the bed. "I will figure this out. You may stay here this time although…it will not be pleasant. I have tried to keep this from you." She turned her head to the door. A beam of light could be seen under it. "Cover your ears. Do your best not to hear. Whatever happens, do not come out from under there. I am not sure what will happen if you see."

She straightened when the door opened. I heard my mother's voice. "Who are you talking to and why are you out of bed? You know we are to play the game tonight."

I could see Mama's tiny childlike feet cross the floor. In all my childhood, I could not remember my mother ever playing a game with me. I wondered why the blue-eyed me was so worried that I might see my mother playing a game.

They both climbed into the bed above me. It was only a second before the door opened again and I heard the hard footsteps of my father. His boots came to a stop at the bed and I pulled back, afraid he knew I was there. He spoke quietly. "Well, look what we have here. Two little girls overdue for punishment."

There was a rustle of cloth and then my mother said, "Yes, Papa. Ramillia and I were very naughty today." I heard the young me crying.

There was more rustling and Papa's britches dropped. "Stop crying or I will give you something to cry about."

"John, no. I am over here. That is Ra…"

I heard him slap my mother. "Shut your mouth or I will take the whip to you. I have chosen. You will remain quiet."

I covered my ears quickly when the bed dipped under Father's weight. I tried to think of anything else. I could remember the day Mama had come to breakfast with a bruised cheek. She was pleasant through the meal but when Father left, she'd turned to me with rancor in her eyes. "I hope you enjoyed yourself last night, you disgusting, ugly orphan. You will never please him as I do. You are too tall, your shoulders too broad. Your hair is yellow like straw, not golden like mine. You will never be beautiful. Soon you will be old and I will always be young. He will choose me and we will marry you off to an old man."

I had never known why she had said such things to me. I had forgotten them, in fact, until now when they made sense. I could not remember the horrible event occurring above me. I did not try. I squeezed my eyes shut and covered my ears completely. As I lay on the cold wooden floor, the bed above me began to rock.

∽

I woke slowly. Julian was there petting…always petting. He was as weak as a kitten and surprised to find I was not. He shrugged it off, saying only that there were no female Carriers who could say what was normal for us. He was happy and so I was happy. I pulled away and stood on shaky legs.

I relieved myself in the bedpan. It stung and I winced, cutting off the flow several times before emptying my bladder. Something was very wrong. I slid it back under the bed.

"Did you enjoy your night?"

I shrugged.

He laughed as if I had shared a joke. He held out his hand. "I will take the key back now."

I gave it to him and then went into the dressing room long enough for Moira to help me into my riding dress. I needed to go home. I needed to know if what I had seen was real. I sent Moira out to have them put the sidesaddle on my mare. She never spoke so I don't know how she communicated with the other servants though she seemed to be managing nicely in her new position.

"I am going out."

He mumbled. "Yes, yes. Of course. You are quite safe now that the bonding is done. No Incola will make a move at you. You reek of me." He turned away from me. "Now I need my rest. We will have lunch together when I wake."

I went straight to my home. I needed answers to questions that hadn't even fully formed yet. There was as good a place as any to start. The ride was quick and the fresh air did me good. The stablemen helped me down and held my horse. They looked at me oddly and I assured them I wouldn't be long.

I went up the grand staircase to my parents' bedchamber. The few footmen and servants who had served me for the short time I had run this house lay around the room. They were nude, sleeping. I was astonished at their bold behavior. To move themselves into the family quarters was unacceptable.

I wrenched the door off the hidden private safe. The sound was loud enough but none of the men did more than stir. Inside my father's most secret place was only a stack of folders, each with a date scrawled on the front. Though I don't know what I expected, it wasn't that. I took them and went up to my childhood room.

There was nothing there out of the ordinary. No little girl trapped in pain and fear, no ghosts of my past. Only my furniture haunted this room. As I was leaving, I noticed the dolls perched on their shelves. I grabbed the one in red velvet that had kept me company under the bed where the truth about my childhood had come out. I took it with me, terrified that, without it, I might lose the memory again.

∽

Once home on Park Lane, after Moira had helped me change into a day dress, I sat in my sitting room. The parlor was much too public for what I was about to uncover. I opened the first folder. Stunned, I flipped through the dozen pages and closed the folder. I opened it and went through them again. There was no change.

They were still photographs of me as a child, nude and in compromising positions.

There was a folder filled with images of my naked mother with her child-like body. In some of those she employed the use of phallic objects. Another folder held photographs of my brother, Thaddeus. Even he, as a male, was not spared the humiliation of appearing without clothes in the photos that held such fascination for my father. That was all the variation there was. The remaining folders were of me between the ages of around six and eleven years.

I vomited, however, I hadn't had anything to eat or drink that day so I produced nothing. I almost wished I had something to vacate from my stomach, for without it, I continued to dry heave with no reprieve.

I had absolutely no memory of these photographs being taken. The taking of photographs was no quick matter. I had stood for long periods of time while the negative was exposed. Nude. That should have made an impression on my young mind. No matter how I tried, I could not recall a single sitting such as these. I risked another look and confirmed my thoughts.

The girl in these was the same as the one I had hidden in my closet. This was not me. This was the girl who looked like me but was shorter and stockier. Her face was angry and her eyes dark and stormy. These were portraits of her, the girl who lived in the pain.

"Your father's handiwork, I presume." I had not heard Julian come in, so lost was I in my confusing discovery. He set a plate of fruit on the small table beside my chair. "You missed lunch." I glanced at the clock on the mantle. It was quarter to three. How many hours had I sat there? I wondered. "You really should eat something. Riding often leaves us without an appetite though the body needs nourishment."

He waited until I had put a bit of apple into my mouth before he moved to sit. He took the folders with him. He looked at a few and then turned his face away. "Your father was a very sick man. Though I believe with the value this culture and era places on innocence, more will follow in his footsteps."

"Did you know?"

"That your father's tastes ran toward little children? Certainly not. He was already married when I found him to be a Carrier with the dominant trait easily passed on to his children. I assumed he'd married her for her money and connections. She was a very eligible woman. I did not suspect that he had chosen her because of physical attraction. If I had I would have taken you away, birthright be damned. Look at me, Ramillia." He waited to go on until I complied. He reclined on the ottoman. "You are alive. You will outlive the pedophile by thousands of years. You gave him the death he deserved, though if I had a say it would have been more prolonged."

"You told me Thaddeus had killed them."

"No. I said that Thaddeus had *confessed* to their killings—that he was executed. He was quite innocent, as innocent as any Carrier can be. He could not have killed them as he was already my valet and was with me half a world away." Julian sat up to look at me. "You really cannot remember, even now?"

I shook my head. A tear ran down my cheek. My brother had gone to the gallows for me, for my freedom, and I could not even recall the crime for which he had been executed. "Oh, Thaddeus."

Julian pulled me up into a hug, my confusion and anger of the day erased. "Your tears are misplaced and a sign of your feminine weakness. I gave your brother a gilded life for all the years of your incarceration. I never made him fight. I walked him up those steps happily because he had lived more than most men three times his years."

He walked toward the door and I sat back down. He held the folders up. "And these? Should I put them away for you or destroy them? I often wish that such a thing had been invented when I was a boy. Memories fade much faster than these images." When I did not reply, he nodded as if I had. "Right. Now is not the time for such decisions. I will lock them away. If you want them you need only ask. Now go and get dressed. We have a very special party tonight thrown in your honor. There is a new gown waiting for you in our dressing room."

With that he had glossed over and dismissed my whole horrific childhood, the murder of my parents, and the execution of my brother. I felt content with it. There was a party to attend and a new gown to wear. I felt that all was well.

15

My gown was exceptional, even more exquisite than the one I had worn to meet the Queen, as that was a day dress and this one was for the night. Fabrics were allowed to be richer, details more elaborate, jewels more expensive. I was the definition of opulence. Julian declared it fitting as tonight we would be among royalty—just of a different sort than England's sovereign.

This was my first Carrier party and it was in my honor. I did not know what to expect though Julian said there was nothing I could do that would be wrong. There were very few taboos at a Carrier party, and even those were broken regularly. The men would treat me as he did, as a treasured child to be indulged and spoiled. There would be few, if any, women in attendance.

The party was not held in a home as I was accustomed, but in Julian's club on Pall Mall. It was a beautiful, old building and women were not normally allowed. The rules had been changed because of me, and I was admitted not only as a guest but as a new member. Our host had been my sponsor and this party was to celebrate the grand achievement of my having been accepted. It was as much a sign of his power as it was my great value.

At first I thought the club was ablaze, so many lights shown from the front windows. Julian helped me from the carriage, explaining that a Carrier party was an exhibition of sorts and many lights were needed so that all could see. There was a large lounge room with tables, comfortable chairs, and couches at the front of the house. Next was an oversized square sandpit like the one I had seen at the circus when I was a child. All around the pit was a wide boardwalk, alternated with steps. Landing, steps, landing—turn corner; landing, steps, landing—turn corner. It went round and round the edge of the pit, making a square, spiral staircase.

There was actual fanfare when we entered. A purple carpet was rolled out over the sand so that I would not have to sully my shoes or the hem of my gown. I stood center while hundreds, possibly thousands of men, stared at me from all levels. There was polite applause and everyone was well-mannered. After a few minutes, Julian took me by my gloved hand and we started our ascension. Our seats were at the very top, where the view was best.

It was quite a walk and we had to pass in close proximity to everyone in attendance. I could tell that every man wanted to touch me and, though Julian had me wear long gloves and a wrap, not one attempted it. Under each staircase there were hidden alcoves where even more men sat. On every level connected to the landing was another lounge.

The highest was usually also the hottest and I was glad to find they had refrigerated air cooling the upper level. It was simply fans that blew over large blocks of ice, not the sophisticated air conditioning units we all have now. It was the best thing I had ever seen at the time and I was glad of it, or I would have been perspiring by the time we reached the final landing.

A man who looked very much like Julian embraced him in a familiar fashion. This was our host, I discerned, and Julian's oldest friend. He turned to me remarking, "So, you are the miracle Julian cannot stop talking about." He took my gloved hand in his own and placed a kiss on the knuckles. "I will dispense with the titles and, though you are certainly deserving of them, I do not believe those worthy of you have been invented yet." I am certain that I blushed. He continued, "We use first names, you would know them as Christian names. Though why that religion has taken hold, I will never understand. May I call you Ramillia?"

I looked to Julian and he inclined his head. I nodded to the man. "Certainly, you are obviously a great man. You honor me with familiarity." He clapped with pleasure just as Julian often did. He showed me to my seat. It was next to his on the dais. A smaller chair sat on the other side of mine for Julian. He seemed unperturbed at being in the lower place. "I must apologize. I am at a disadvantage. I do not have even a Chris…first name for you. Before tonight, Julian never mentioned you."

"No, he wouldn't have. Afraid of the competition for your affections, I imagine. It is I who must apologize. I dispensed with titles and inadvertently tossed out my manners as well. I am anxious to meet and please you in a way I am unaccustomed to. Allow me to introduce myself. I am Paetus."

"It is a pleasure to meet you, Paetus." My chair was more of a throne and was plush and comfortable. I was served the beverage of my choice and a young woman brought in a tray of food. She was young, but not very beautiful. Her features were foreign, although not in the exotic way, just the strange way. I was happy to see her just the same. "A woman Carrier? Julian said I was the only one on this continent."

"By the gods, no. This is one of my human companions. She is allowed to feed me by her own hand because she has provided me a beautiful, olive-eyed Carrier. I brought her tonight because I thought it might put you at ease to have another of the gentler sex."

"I am pleased to meet you…" I started.

"I am sorry. She is from quite far away and does not speak the Queen's English. She is not for conversation, just comfort."

We ate from the tray for a few minutes and when Paetus had enough and had ensured I was satisfied, he dismissed the woman. I was quite comfortable with Julian on my elbow and Paetus at my ear. The exhibition began below. There were many acts. Dancing, juggling, feats of strength and speed were enjoyed by all, but I could tell this was not the main event. When I asked Paetus, he seemed surprised. He spoke quietly to a man who walked away with an odd gait. When the man returned, I asked what was wrong with his legs and if there was nothing that could be done for him. We did live in the greatest age of medical advances of all time.

Paetus and Julian laughed. This time I knew it was at me, not with me. Paetus believed that this was by no means the greatest time of anything—I would understand when I was his age. He knew there was nothing wrong with the man's legs. "He has a new Incola eager to exercise his control."

Something passed between the two old friends but the final act before the main event was too engrossing for me to remember to ask what an Incola was. Across the way, a man in a ridiculous costume stood on the rail. He took a step off the rail and walked out onto what looked like thin air. Paetus pointed out the wire pulled taut from the rail where the man started to the banister right before us. I clapped and shrieked as he balanced, making his way over toward us.

He made it all the way across and jumped down from the rail, flipping several times, before landing on the dais in front of me. A bouquet of flowers appeared out of thin air and he presented it to me. I loved magic and I reached to take them from him. There was a note tied to them but I didn't have time to examine it.

The primal feeling that I needed to rid the world of this one came on me suddenly. I could not think. I was made of desire—the desire to hurt the tightrope walker. It was his smell. It was a signal that I needed him dead and gone, just as it had been with the footman. Before I realized I had moved, I flipped the fake flowers over so the metal stems pointed up. I shoved them up through his chin, through his mouth, and into his brain. I jerked the flowers left and right, effectively scrambling his brain as a kitchen maid might a batch of eggs.

I stood, bringing him with me, and tossed him over the edge. He was dead before he went over and long before landing. The performer laid on the sand, his limbs twisted at grotesque angles, blood seeping from his eyes, ears, nose, and mouth. I came back to myself to the roar of approval. Paetus led me back to my chair and I started to shake. Why had I done that? I killed a man for no reason other than his nondescript aroma.

Julian realized I had been too long without his calming touch. He stripped off his gloves and mine. He soothed me using every available patch of my skin.

He kissed my face and rubbed his cheek along my collarbone. He whispered that the man had deserved it. "Everything is all right." I believed him.

Paetus gave the signal and the main event began. He joined me on the dais, all smiles and twinkling eyes. "My dear Ramillia, I cannot think of a better way to start the fights. You are truly the crown jewel of our community." Below us four men battled in the sand.

An angry man attempted to approach me, however, Paetus stepped between us. "Leonus, she is the guest of honor. Do not disgrace yourself or my club by seeking revenge."

"She destroyed something of mine. He was not for the fights. He was a feature. I demand the blood price. That was my most valuable Carrier. I will have satisfaction." The man was not just angry; I had embarrassed him by killing his man.

Paetus took him by the throat. "By satisfaction, do you mean a child of hers? Can I guess that is what the note he bore proposed?" Leonus managed to look embarrassed as Paetus choked him. "I gave explicit instructions that there would be no talk of Carrier trade, nor offspring, and yet you sought to disobey me. Then you did not have the decency to let it go and challenged our guest! It will not be tolerated!" Paetus released his hold.

Julian spoke up. "I will pay for the loss of your feature. And, because I am feeling generous, I will pay the blood price, not to you but to the house by way of fights."

"You would risk her in the fights?" Leonus blurted out. He turned to Paetus for justice. "That proves he does not deserve her if he would sacrifice his favorite."

"I do not offer you my favorite. I offer you her favorite." Julian seemed to salivate with excitement. I was quite sedated, watching the whole exchange through a rosy fog. "If you can best him, you may have your choice of my Carriers. Present company excluded, of course."

Though Leonus seemed unhappy with the deal, he did not argue. He looked at me with what I thought was longing. He asked me, "Who would you have pay your blood debt?"

I just stared at him. I had no experience with this situation. Julian put his hand on my face and turned my head toward his. He kissed me and asked, "Who among our Carriers is your favorite, my love?"

I did not need to think long. "Albert pleases me most."

Julian seemed angry for a moment. He stood abruptly and excused himself. He left his coat on his chair, departing with Leonus, and explaining that I should stay with Paetus. No harm could come to me in his club while he was at my side. My focus came slowly back to me.

"It is a shame. Leonus has as many centuries as Julian and I, and yet he has accomplished next to nothing. What an embarrassment he is." And with that bit of club business finished we got back to the games. Several rounds had concluded and the body count was piling up. Paetus watched me with his peripheral vision. His hands hovered over mine. He looked at me to ask permission. "May I?"

I smiled and nodded. What harm could it do? I thought.

Little did I know at the time.

He started with a small touch. His eyes got big and he ran his hands up my arms. He pulled me to stand and I came without a fight. He wrapped me in his embrace. I slid my hands up his side, under his clothing, and placed my palms on his back. He laid kisses along my shoulders and neck, rubbing his face against mine.

He pushed me forward so that I was trapped between him and the banister. He rested his chin on my shoulder and we watched the scene below. The pit was cleared and two men came onto the freshly raked sand. Albert was there and another man twice his size, both stripped to the waist. They began to circle each other. The fighting started when Albert lunged at the bigger man. I gasped when Albert was struck in the face by his opponent's left hook.

Paetus' arms were on the banister on either side of my hips. I put my bare hand on his and clasped him tightly. With each blow, I squeezed his fingers tighter. His breathing quickened. When the two fighters went to their separate corners and retrieved swords, I clutched one of Paetus' hands in both of mine and held it to my heart, quite unconcerned with the impropriety.

"Surely you do not care for this Carrier. Why is he special to you?" he asked me, his lips against my neck just below my earlobe. I was not aroused by Paetus, although I cannot say the same about his response to me.

"His eyes are a most beautiful green…and I like the way his cock fills me." I don't know why I answered as I did. The reply came out before I had decided to speak. I was mortified. I looked at Paetus and he was smiling.

He laughed it off explaining, "People answer me truthfully. I do not always enjoy it. Your words excite me almost as much as your contact." He studied me when I did not react to his admission. "You did not think you and Julian were the only ones with the gift of touch, did you?"

Once again, my reply preceded my decision to answer. "I have no idea what you are talking about."

He pulled his hand from my clutches and took several breaths to steady himself. He gazed at me as we stood at the banister. Paetus wanted something. He seemed to want to touch me again, however, and thought better of it. "You are special for more than your gender and breeding capability, Ramillia. Julian and I chose these bodies in Rome long ago because they have the gift of touch. They are the most valuable Carriers we have ever come across. Until now. You have the touch also."

A cheer from the crowd drew my focus below. Albert's head hit the sand and rolled up so I could see his green eyes. They blinked once before their light disappeared. Paetus touched me again, almost unconsciously. "Julian got out in time. He is much too fast for Leonus to catch."

I had no idea what he was talking about. Julian was nowhere to be seen. He and Leonus were not in the fight. Albert and the big man were. The victor did not seem pleased with his win. He stared at the body sadly. The club began to clear out. Paetus waited until we could descend without passing so close to the others. The party was over.

At the entrance, Paetus had me hold back until the carriage pulled round. I stood next to a pile of bodies as high as my shoulder. At the bottom lay the trapeze artist I had killed. Only part of him showed, his head and shoulders poking out from beneath whoever the loser of the first fight had been. My time touching Paetus had cleared my mind somewhat and I bent down. I closed the man's eyes and made my silent apologies. The letter was still attached to the flowers he had given me, though it was now quite covered in his blood. I snatched it up quickly and hid it in my reticule under my gloves.

Paetus came back and pulled me to the carriage. Julian was already inside. He looked weak but pleased. The loss of Albert mattered not to him. Paetus helped me into the carriage and spoke to Julian, "So exciting. I have never felt more alive. Julian, my man, I do not see how you have managed her by yourself for all this time." He closed the door and I heard him shout as we drove off. "Shall I fight or fuck? Perhaps both."

My touch had affected him but his had also affected me. I was beginning to see the truth about the Carriers and myself. I hoped the letter in my bag would clarify even more.

16

The carriage ride home was more quiet than I would have liked. There was so much I needed to know yet Julian was in no condition to answer any questions. Though my curiosity about the letter was great, so was my fear that Julian would wake and take it from me. I waited.

I was putting together a picture of what life as a Carrier really looked like. It wasn't pretty. Julian's Carriers faced whatever whim caught him. They were sent to the fights, hurt, even killed. They were used sexually and discarded. They brought power and prestige to their Incola, serving as little more than currency.

What I found when I looked up Incola in the dictionary made it worse. The word meant rider, occupant, inhabitant, usurper. Carriers did not just carry the genetic traits of strength, speed, and long life. They were like barrows, flesh and bone containers for their Incolas to ride inside of.

I finally knew the truth. Julian was riding the bodies of his Carriers. He was in the body of Albert during the fight. He had allowed the other man to kill Albert. Who else had he ridden, I thought. And then I remembered the book I'd found in his desk. All the names that ended in death; he had been inside them when they died.

Thaddeus.

Julian said he had "walked him up those steps happily." He had ridden my brother through a confession and execution that rightfully belonged to me. Thaddeus had no choice. Julian killed my brother.

I was careful to put the book back exactly as I had found it. I was not certain Julian wanted me to understand fully his title as Incola. I took the letter out of my reticule. The envelope was soaked but had partially protected the letter inside. Blood only obscured a small amount of the writing. It read:

> *Julian Lawrence is not a good man. That is not even his real name. He will not be content with the occasional ride for long. He will take what is yours; your name, your body, your life will be his and he will feel no regret.*
>
> *There is another way. Paetus and Julian both rejected my way of life before they were ever known by those names. I can teach you. I can help you.*

I memorized the address listed as belonging to Leonus and then I destroyed the letter and bloody envelope. I stood and watched until it was no more than black ash in the shape of a letter. Then I took the poker and broke it up completely, erasing even the tiniest shred of evidence of its existence.

∽

"It was my fault."

Julian turned from his book to face me. The gaslight made his features warm and inviting. "To what do you refer?"

I pointed to his desk where I knew the photographs of me were hidden. I had been unable to get them from my mind. "My family's…dysfunction."

He closed his book and came to me. He held out his hands and I shied away from him. He furrowed his brow and the flickering light made shadows on his face. For a moment it looked monstrous. "Allow me to take away your anxiety."

"No." I stood and paced in front of the fire. The massive painting Julian had commissioned of us stared down at me. The tranquil look in my eyes came from his hand on my shoulder, no doubt. "That is what has me troubled. Paetus told me things."

"Things that have you upset?"

I nodded.

"About the gift of touch." He stated it as a statement, not a question, so I did not feel inclined to answer. It was exactly what I wanted to talk about. He laced his fingers together on his lap, signaling that he would not use it against me. "Let me take away your anxiety with answers. You know you only need ask me. When have I ever denied you?"

It was rhetorical. I already had a rudimentary understanding of the gift of touch from Paetus. I jumped right into what was plaguing me. "Did my touch—my ability to *excite*—incite the violence and lust my father had for me? If I had been a normal girl, would he have…?" I let the question hang in the air. I wasn't sure myself how I would finish it. I had no real memory of any impropriety. I only knew what I saw happen to the girl who looked like me.

"Your father's behavior was not your fault. He was a sick man and I feel he would have abused any daughter he might have had."

"And Thaddeus?" I choked out.

"Your touch did nothing to cause your father to abuse Thaddeus. It should serve as an example of how depraved he was that he could treat his own son thusly."

"No. I mean…"

"Did Thaddeus hurt you?" I nodded and I could see that he wanted to come to me, caress away my concern, but he kept his seat. "Then, I am sorry for that also. I did not know you had the gift of touch when I placed you there. I am to blame, not you. Thaddeus is to blame. He could have resisted the urge. You were his sister, after all."

"It was me. It was my fault. My touch is poison. I knew better when Papa positioned us, though I did not argue. I was afraid that Papa might punish me."

"That was his fault. I think he likely knew what the touch would do to Thaddeus. Your father wanted to watch his children together. Depraved is the only word I have to describe the man." Julian gave me a sad smile and patted the seat next to him. I ceased my pacing and went to hear him speak softly. "Your touch is not poison. You do not force anyone to act. It excites only. Tell me, how many times have I hurt you because of your touch?"

"Never." But you hurt yourself because of me, I thought.

"That is right. No matter how you excited me, I am able, as all men should be able, to direct that excitement to a more appropriate receptacle. I touch you on a near nightly basis and I do not allow that to force all sense out of my mind. Your brother and father had the same choice that I do and they chose to hurt you. It is not your fault." He repeated, "It is not your fault."

I leaned against him. I allowed myself to come in contact with his skin. "All is well. You are safe with me." He carried me into the secret room and we lay on the bed together. "I think you need a night outside this flesh. I have never had an Incola in this body. I give it to you, to do with what you want. The gifts of touch stay intact regardless of who is within. It is a power of the body, not the ego. Enjoy the power to soothe and calm for a while."

He completed the blood exchange circuit as he had before and I felt the heaviness. I could not follow the blood as he instructed. I was trapped. I woke in my father's study. The dress I had been wearing the night my parents had been killed lay torn in a heap by my feet. The girl who looked like me lay on her back on the floor. She was naked and tied, her legs apart, her knees bent and spread. She was crying. I went to her. She did not say that I should not be there. She did not say that I did not belong.

"Papa knows. He is coming back and will root it out. He has to take away the evidence so he can lay with me again."

I tried to untie her—my hands were insubstantial. I passed through the ropes like they were made of air. There was nothing I could do. Papa came in with his medical bag. He knelt between her sprawled legs and sneered at her. He could not see me. He took a rolled-up cloth from his bag. He unrolled it, revealing the most retched looking instruments. There was a hook, what looked like a shoehorn, several scalpels, and what I recognized as a speculum.

"You are a naughty little girl to keep this from me. You were trying to get me in trouble. Today you pay for your insolence."

I didn't know what he was talking about. I didn't know what he was going to do but he showed her each of the horrible tools and relished in her tears. I screamed at him, "Get away from her. She's just a girl." I flew at him, my fists passing through just as they had with the ropes. I knelt beside her. She looked at me and I heard her voice even though her mouth did not move.

Give me the strength, Ramillia. I can stop him if you let me.

"I don't know how."

I live in the pain. I come when you are hurt. I accept the pain in your place. I can't do that without your consent. The strength belongs to you alone. You must voluntarily give it to me.

I could not let Papa hurt her again. I knew what strength I had. I witnessed it many times. I hesitated. Could I really withhold from her? Would I wake to find my family alive? Was that something I wanted?

When Papa forced the speculum inside her roughly and she cried out, I had my answer. Whatever he was going to do to her, I could not allow. She deserved the right to provide this evil man his justice. I lay on top of her body, mimicking her position with my own. I fell inside her. I was so weak. I had given her everything. I could see what she was doing though it was as if I looked through a tunnel.

She tore free of her bondage. I closed my eyes but I could not close my ears. I was insubstantial and, though I covered them with my hands, the sounds came through. My father yelled, berating her, saying all the terrible things he would do if she did not lay back down. Then he screamed. It was long and high. The girl who looked like me did not put him out of his misery quickly. My mother's angry voice came through. She called the girl a whore. Mama said she would put the girl with a fancy lad where she belonged. She would take the bastard and the girl would never see it.

Her voice was cut off abruptly and my eyes slipped open long enough to see my mother's body fall, its head facing the wrong direction. Then the girl went back to Papa. He was terrified. His limbs were disjointed. I closed my eyes again, knowing what came next. The girl would tear him apart. The servants would come. I would wake up in the insane asylum.

∽

I woke, though not strapped to the table as I expected. I was in bed with Julian. His hand was close, not touching me, as if he had been holding it and sleep had divided us. I was relieved not to wake in that place of nightmares that had been my prison for so many years. All was well, until I felt a soreness in my feminine places and even my rear passage.

I worried that the event with my father had really occurred but then I knew. Julian had misused, even abused my body, while I was trapped in that terrible memory that I had no recollection of.

I crept from bed, careful not to jostle Julian. Even so, he woke. "Come back to bed."

I do not know if he heard my reply. "I will not." He simply rolled away and fell asleep again. I went to my dressing room. Moira was in her trunk as usual. I had her help me get dressed. I needed to get away though I did not know where I would go. By the time we were finished, the pain in my nether region had receded. I wondered if I had slept an hour more if I would have been none the wiser to what Julian had done. I sent her down to have them ready my horse now that I thought I could manage a ride.

I rode aimlessly. I found myself sitting across from my family house. I did not want to go inside but I needed to figure out what was happening, what had happened. I had a terrible feeling that I would not find what I needed unless I faced the events in my father's study.

I went in the back to drop my mare in the carriage house. The stable hands, two strapping young men, made jokes about how they thought I would have had enough riding from last night.

The first helped me down while the second took the reins and led the mare away. The first was too familiar, allowing his hand to remain at my waist. I could smell the alcohol on his breath when he spoke, "If you have further need of a fuck, I'd offer my services." He pressed his body against mine and the second man returned to sandwich me between. That one said, "With us both at the same time, one in each hole, you'd be more filled than wanting."

I had enough. I brought my knee up between the legs of the first man, crushing his dreams, and then brought my foot back to make contact with the kneecap of the second man. They both fell, one gasping, the other screaming. I turned to the noisy one. If he had enough air to scream he had enough to answer my questions. "Are you saying I was here last night?"

When he didn't respond, I put my weightless heel on his destroyed knee. "Do not make me press you for answers."

"Y-yes, ma'am." A cold sweat broke across his brow.

"And you are certain it was I? You got a good look at my face."

I must have let the weight of my leg down a little because he whimpered. Nodding, he replied, "Y-y-es. Your face and…everything else, my lady. Do you not remember? You had the household watch… We'd never seen anything like it. You just touched each man for a minute and he was raring to go."

Julian had claimed that the gift of touch remained with the body, not the ego. He had ridden me here the previous night, used my touch, my body, for the most sacrilegious of activities. "Enough! I was not here last night and if you or anyone ever breathe a word of that lie to anyone, I will make sure you never speak again. I would gladly tear your tongue out. I could easily rip you limb from limb."

"Yes, my lady. Of course, my lady."

I left him sobbing in the carriage house. After giving the other man a swift kick to the ribs for good measure, I went inside through the servants' hall. I saw no one. The broom closet had a chair wedged against the knob, holding it closed. When I opened it, I found Darville on the ground, trying to fit in a space much too small for him. He had a large bruise blossoming on his cheekbone. He tried to get as far from me as possible in that confined space.

"I won't hurt you, Darville. I take it from your cowering that the tosspots outside were not mistaken. I was here last night?"

I helped him stand. "Indeed, my lady. You weren't yourself. You acted most strange. I tried to get you to see reason."

He stopped and I filled in the gap. I gestured toward his face. "I gave you that for your trouble and then locked you in the broom closet where you couldn't try to stop me." He nodded. "Come with me."

As we walked through the house toward my father's study, I thought about what exactly was happening to me. How was I going to take back control of my own life? I went straight to the burglar-proof safe hidden behind the books in Father's study. This was the one everyone knew about, not like the secret one in their bedchamber where Father had hidden his true nature. I knew what would be in this one. No pornographic images hid there waiting to destroy my precarious hold on sanity. I rummaged through the desk. Finding nothing, I asked, "Where is the key kept?"

"I do not know, Your Ladyship. The former Earl of Brooksberry took that secret to his grave." He paled at his reference to my father's death, the one I was to blame for.

"Do not let it trouble you, Darville." With him watching I punched my fingers into the safe's door and ripped it off. Inside were just what I expected. I put the stacks of money and the bank notes into a bag I'd found in the desk. I left the jewels as they would only bring cause to accuse him of theft. I wrote a letter on family letterhead, giving all assets legally mine over to Darville. "Did anyone else attempt to save me from myself last night?"

When he shook his head no, ashamed of how those under him had acted, I signed the letter and stuffed it in the bag. I handed it to him. "This is yours, for your loyal service and impeccable moral standing." I left as he stared at what must have been ten lifetimes' worth of wages. I stopped in the doorway and spoke over my shoulder. "I am paying the household for their silence. I trust you find your payment more pleasing than that which I am to dole out to others."

In my parents' bedchamber, I found a number of men exactly as they had been before. They were all over the room, nude and sleeping, not dead. I was grateful for that. They may have acted in an improper fashion but they were just men who had given in to their baser desires. Desires which I had, apparently, been offering up to every man within earshot. I realized that I must have been there before. The last time Julian had taken my body these men had laid with me also.

I picked up the massive armoire in the corner and slammed it down on the floor repeatedly until I had everyone's attention. I then very calmly commanded them to never speak of what had or had not occurred. A few of them laughed. I threatened them using words I don't care to repeat. I picked up the poker from the hearth and bent it around and around until it was coiled like a snake ready to spring. They stared silently until I whispered, "Run. You should all run now, or I will use this like a corkscrew on your skulls."

They wisely followed my advice. I tore the house down, quite literally. Enough shame had been brought to my body in this place and I could not bear it. I wanted it gone. I heard the hiss of leaking gas when I relieved the walls of their fixtures.

∽

I stewed all day in my anger. Destroying my childhood home had done nothing to lessen my rage. We were seated at a fabulous dinner, though my appetite had fled that morning with my calm. Julian suffered no such ailment and ate more than I had seen him ingest in a single sitting. "You do not have to eat, but you must at least drink your claret, my love."

I made no move toward the beverage. "Why must I? So that you are able to invade my body, wear it like a flesh garment, and treat it with the same disrespect as you did last night? My family household is likely as dead as any of my family."

Julian held up his hand and closed his eyes, as if he were disgusted by the picture I painted. He spoke slowly, "We do not speak of what occurs during a switch." He was not angry when he opened his eyes. He went back to eating. When I looked blankly at him, he continued. "The body becomes your own to do with what you like. This is an honor I have never bestowed on another, the use of this body. I will never question your use or misuse of it." He smiled then and wagged his finger at me. "I knew the explosion and fire were not an accident. Now that is the way to use a Carrier body, to destroy something beautiful. It is the same reason I take so many of mine to the club fights." He looked as if he were proud of me.

He was confirming my fears and giving me more questions. I did not know where to start only that I needed him to be honest with me about every part of our existence. I needed to know what we were, as I apparently was not as clear as he thought I was. "Are you saying that I am not only a Carrier, but an Incola as well? That I should be able to take your body as you have taken mine?"

Julian quickly dismissed all the servants. When we sat in the dining room alone, he moved his plate and himself to the place beside me. He looked as if he would put his hand on mine, so I hid it under the table in my lap. I did not want to be lulled. I wanted to understand, not accept. He saw my move and comprehended its meaning.

He nodded knowingly. "I assumed experience was a better educator than lectures. I never guessed that you were not experiencing what I intended. How we transfer consciousness is our best kept secret."

"Because if the information got out, any Carrier could become an Incola?"

He furrowed his brow. "You sound like Leonus. Not any, but certainly more than there are now. If you are unable with everything I have done to facilitate it, perhaps even fewer could ride than I have always thought." He lowered his voice even further. "I use my blood as a root in another person's body. If part of myself is inside another Carrier, I can take hold of their body. You are the first whose blood I have taken into myself, the first I have allowed the opportunity to ride this body."

"Then why do they allow it? If they get nothing in exchange?" I rudely interrupted. Julian had never been one to hold me to proper etiquette in our home. He was not interested in all the rules of this age. What I truly was asking was why should I allow it if I was unable to have his in exchange. I hoped he did not pick up on that.

"To be honest I do not give them much of an option. Even those who know choose to have me ride them. Carriers do not live forever. Their bodies are superior to humans' but without an Incola, they would die. My time in their body is rejuvenating. I handle the…upkeep of every Carrier in my charge. If I were to die or stop riding my household, they would age and die. Many owe me, not only their lives, but also their births. They would never have been born if not for my involvement in breeding over the last thousand years."

"Like my brother and I." I made it a statement.

He nodded. "I witnessed the birth of every illegitimate child your father seeded. Only the two of you were Carriers. Thaddeus almost did not come to be. His mother was from a far-off land. I brought her here in trade between another Incola across the world. If I had not, his birth would not have been."

That was why we looked so different. He was dark because his mother had been dark. I was light. "My mother was English?"

Julian shrugged. "As English as any of the mixed breed, low classes can be." I knew he meant my mother was a prostitute of dubious descent. "She was quite lovely."

"Was?"

"I fought to save her life once I had seen what she was capable of producing, though there was nothing I could do for her. She bled out in a matter of moments. I gave her all I could. She held your tiny newborn body and I praised her efforts and accomplishments until her last breath."

Hot tears slid down my face and again Julian reached for me. I backed away from him and the table quickly, knocking over my chair as I did. I ran from the room and Julian made no move to stop me. He gave me the privacy I needed.

I do not know what room I ended up in. My eyes were so filled with tears that my view was obstructed. I wept for the mother I would never know, the mother who spent her final moments loving me. I cried and cried. I don't remember crying so hard before that moment nor have I since that time. I imagined the love she would have given me if she had lived, the love that was lacking from my childhood. I imagined having her with me now, the doting mother I could go to with every problem.

I wiped my tears away. No. I was giving her traits she most likely would not feel for me. If she had lived, I would have been a hindrance to her livelihood. No, less than that, I would still not have known her. I would have been given by Julian to the same parents who treated me so poorly. Likely, she did love me as a baby. I gave myself that. My occupancy in her womb would have saved her the disgusting advances of men. Most prostitutes must terminate pregnancies or suffer a loss of income. Her position as Julian and this other Incola's breeding mare gave her a break, a vacation, from her grueling life. He would never have allowed her to suffer while there was a chance she could bear a Carrier child.

When I had no more tears to cry, I went down to Julian's study. He was the only family I had left. He was waiting for me behind his desk. He stood when I came in and wordlessly came around the furniture. His gloved hands reached out to me and I went to him. He hugged me as normal humans do. He was careful not to allow his skin to touch mine. There was no power to back it, but it eased me to be held.

He let me stay there until I pulled away. I sat on the ottoman and he poured us some port. He offered it to me with the assurance, "No blood. Only distilled spirits to calm the nerves." When I took it and had a sip, he spoke again. "There was none in the wine at dinner either. I only looked to your health."

He went to the mantle. "It is because of the superb body you have that I offer you more than other Carriers. I offer you more than the impossibly long life of being my Carrier and the riches of being my wife. I have been attempting to not only ride you but to allow you to ride this body, the most valuable I have. It is second only to your own in ability and value."

"The gift of touch." It was the first thing I had said in hours, and my voice was weak and shaky. I cleared my throat and took another drink of the port. It was, I'm sure, the finest available in all the world if it was what Julian drank.

"Not only. You might not know this, but this body was exceptionally powerful both physically and politically. I led the Roman army in this body. I had hundreds of thousands at my command. I fought, bested, and killed tens of thousands."

I was intrigued again, my wallowing over. Paetus had mentioned something similar at the Carrier party. He'd said that he and Julian had chosen their bodies in Rome because they had the gift of touch. They had been the two most valuable Carriers they had ever come across. Until me. "What body did you ride before this one?"

He smiled, glad I was back to my questioning self. "Quite honestly, I do not remember. I had the memories of my other life for a while after transferring from that body to this one permanently. They slowly faded away. I get flashes occasionally, but they are dim and smoky like a dream."

"It is the same with Paetus?" I finished my port and was feeling dizzy. I hadn't eaten dinner, nor lunch that I could remember. I declined Julian's offer for more.

"I believe so. We do not speak of it often. We do not want others to overhear our weaknesses. I think the brain, and we are limited somewhat by the thinking organ of the body we inhabit, is only capable of retaining so many memories. Over the years in this body I have replaced the old with new. In another thousand years I might not be able to remember even my Roman glory days." He downed another glass of port quickly, like a man getting down a shot of gin in a pothouse, rather than giving it the time for savoring that it deserved. "Your mention of my old friend's name has given me an idea. We will lunch at the club tomorrow with Paetus. Surely our two heads together can devise a solution to your inability to ride."

17

We brought a reasonable detail of guards with us the next day, no more than Julian normally took. I understood now how important they were to us. If it was really that easy to take over our bodies using blood, we needed to be cautious at all times. The carriage stopped in front of the club and we got out. The guards surrounded us, even accompanying us inside. I heard at least one gasp from someone on the street at seeing me—a *woman*—enter the men only club.

The Pall Mall Incola Club was very different in the daylight hours than when the party had been thrown in my honor. They often had "the fights" there in the night but, in the day, it was much like any other gentlemen's club on Pall Mall. Wooden planks had been laid over the sand and a luxurious rug rolled out over them. Tables and chairs for eating and various sized billiards tables had been placed on the newly enlarged space.

The *maître d'* showed us to our table where Paetus was already seated. He stood as we approached and kissed my hand, saying nothing about the glove there. "You honor us with your presence," was his only remark. We sat and were immediately served soup. It was the most delicate and delicious turtle soup I had ever tasted. Julian and Paetus ruined theirs with curry powder.

I jumped when a strange cracking sound thundered through the club. Paetus immediately made a gesture and several men scurried out the door, vacating the billiards tables. "Oh, you needn't make them stop on my account, the noise just startled me as I have never heard it before."

Paetus replied, "It is nothing, my dear Ramillia, to have them removed. They are here almost every day. You are a special treat. I would not have anything disturb your first meal with us. Next time they can finish their games, I promise. If you would like to make your visits a more regular item, I could even teach you to play."

I have always loved learning new things and I remarked, "I would enjoy that." He nodded in agreement.

Glancing at my plate, I was unprepared for my fish course. Answering my unasked question, Paetus said, "You have never tasted lobster? You are in for a treat. I like mine best with Dutch sauce."

Forking a small portion of the white, fleshy fish with red designs, I slipped it in my mouth. It had a millet-like texture, grainy like prawns. I did not care for it and tried not to show my distaste. Paetus saw through my attempt and simply remarked, "It must be an acquired taste."

Julian gave a good-hearted laugh. They finished theirs after pouring on a red spicy sauce made from peppers from across the sea. I did not.

The two of them spoke in a language unfamiliar to me while we ate our veal cutlet, asparagus, and peas. I was too involved with the delicious creamy sauce and light but crispy breading on the thinly cut meat to be insulted by their exclusion. They seemed to be exchanging pleasantries, not talking business. I assumed it was bawdy talk that they did not want to insult me with.

It seems odd that I remembered so many details of the meal from so long ago, however, this occasion made an impression. It was, as Paetus had said, my first meal in a gentlemen's club. They were trying to impress me—and impress me they did. My nerves and senses were so heightened as I tried to take everything in that I suppose I managed to achieve just that.

I was so full after that, I barely touched the main course, and therefore it did not lodge in my memory. After bringing out the game course, the servants and staff, indeed all the members, left en masse. We were alone in the giant club.

"That is better. Now we may discuss the reason for your visit." Paetus patted my hand with his own. "Not that you need a reason to visit me or this club for that matter. This is as much your club as it is Julian's." He ate some of the juicy meat after rolling it in black pepper. "Tell me the problem."

I looked to Julian. He spoke in hushed tones regardless of the club's empty room. "Ramillia cannot get inside my body, no matter how much blood we exchange."

"A switch?" Paetus stared at him and then looked at me. "You should be honored. We ride others. We do not let others ride us." He ate some more heavily spiced food. "Who told you it is done with a blood exchange?"

"No one. Not that I can recall. Putting my blood into the body of another is how I move my consciousness. I use the physical as a root to aid the metaphysical. Is that not how we all do it?" Julian asked.

Paetus shook his head. "I have quite another means entirely. I wonder if we all must find our own way out of the body we are given and into another. Perhaps that is the issue. She has not found her way yet. Then again, the issue might be that a switch is not possible. I certainly have never attempted it."

"It is possible. I have experienced it, though it was on, shall I say, less than consensual terms. That is why I kept my method secret," Julian admitted.

Paetus bobbed his head once. "Yes, indeed. A blood exchange could easily be forced. I see your need for secrecy. I too keep mine secret, though I am not quite sure why. It just seems the right thing, to protect my mews."

"Your muse?" I asked.

"M-E-W-S."

"Isn't that something to do with the royal birds of prey?"

"She is a smart one, isn't she?" he asked no one in particular. "When you hear other people speak of the mews, they mean the place where the king's hawks are isolated for their molting. The word mews comes from the Latin word mutate meaning 'to change.'" He paused, as if thinking of the best way to explain. "It is better if I show you. I am intrigued and would like to see you test my methods…if that is agreeable to Julian."

"What about protecting your method—your mews?"

"I trust Julian. If he trusts you, then so do I."

We skipped dessert, coffee, and nuts. That was just as well because my appetite had vanished. I was anxious about what was to come next. Those feelings did not improve once I had seen Paetus' mews. It was not a place but a machine.

Paetus took us into his private quarters in the back of the club. "No one, with the exception of my Carriers, have ever seen my mews, much less used it. Honestly, I am able to move over and control another body without it, only the transfer takes longer. I invented this; I don't know how long ago. It is to aid me in concentration."

The mews was man-sized and roughly rectangular, laying lengthwise on a platform. It was copper in color, covered in gears and tubes, and attached by several wires to a nearby stationary bicycle. "I will not explain its mechanics entirely. It allows the user to lock out the rest of the world and focus solely on their intended destination: the Carrier of choice."

He rang the summoning bell and a second later the human woman who had served us food answered his call. "This will be easiest if you disrobe." The woman began to unfasten my gown before I had given consent.

"May I keep my undergarments? My corset especially gives me comfort." He thought for a moment and I blathered on. "I find the tightness and many layers make me feel secure. Protected." I tried to explain.

"We can try it this first time. If it does not work we will try it again without." He turned to Julian, who was drinking nearby. "Have you tried the exchange of blood while she is without her stays?"

Julian shook his head, speaking at the same time, "Never saw any need."

"I suggest you try that also. It may be that the undergarments of this era somehow contain her. I am merely thinking aloud of every possible inhibitor that could have an effect." Paetus spoke to the woman in a foreign tongue. She stopped undressing me when we were down to a few layers. She left after carefully hanging my dress.

Paetus helped me onto the seat of the bicycle, instructing me as I pedaled. "Ride a minute for two reasons. One, it will give you the muscle memory of it. Two, it heats the water inside, making it easier for you to lose your sense of feeling when you are floating." He pointed to a small barometer on the bicycle's bar. "When this gets to the red line, it is ready. You'll climb into the chamber and I will close it over you. There is sufficient salt in the water to keep you afloat without any effort on your part." He turned to Julian remarking, "Just like when we swam in the Dead Sea." Then he focused his attention upon me again. "It will be dark and you won't be able to hear anything. Just lay there and clear your mind. Julian will be on the cycle since he is the Carrier you wish to ride. Once your mind is clear, think of Julian. Don't think of the person, think of his body. Imagine him riding the bicycle. Remember what it felt like to have your muscles working in the same way his are. Envision yourself inside his body."

"That is it?"

"That is all. Either it works or it does not. Give her a little of your blood so that if she does manage to jump, you will have a place to go. You should be able to switch in that manner."

Julian pricked his finger and put it to my mouth. I took it. When the gauge got to the red line, I stepped off and Julian replaced me on the cycle. Paetus opened the lid of the mechanical coffin and helped me inside. The water was perfectly heated. I could barely register it around me. I floated there, my arms slightly away from my sides.

Paetus closed the mews, and for a moment, I was simply amazed at the silence. I had not realized how noisy London was, even while indoors. There was no light, no sound, no feeling, no smell—except for what I made. I instantly loved this contraption. I was doubtful it would work although it was the most relaxing thing I'd ever experienced, including Julian's touch.

I tried to do as Paetus had instructed to no avail. For a while I could feel the ghosts of my cycling movements and I thought it might be working but no matter what, I was not able to leave my body. I found I had no clear sense of time inside the mews. After a bit, I could not really remember what I was supposed to be feeling or thinking. I went truly blank.

The feeling of my body's boundary faded away. I was no longer confined to the tiny person, the tiny speck that was Ramillia. It was around that time I felt a great sense of oneness with everyone, everything, the universe. Separateness was an illusion brought on by the daily onslaught of sensations. Our senses kept us from seeing through other people's eyes.

Then the lid opened and I plummeted back to the boundaries of my skin. Light beat down on me and sound assaulted my ears. "No…no. Put me back," I argued as strong arms pulled me out of the water. I was wrapped in a large bathing robe.

"It did not work, Ramillia." I recognized Julian's voice. His small touch calmed me as they got me from the mews. Paetus ordered some dessert for us. We three ate cherry ice while I spoke of my experience.

"I think I was on the verge…the edge of some great discovery. It was brought about by the deprivation of sensation…this truth. I feel like you are onto something immense here, Paetus. You are a true genius for inventing this amazing machine. Thank you so much for sharing this with me."

I could tell that Julian was irritated by me gushing over Paetus. I had to go on, though. "I truly owe you for giving me this experience yet I must ask you for another. You must put me back in. I have to try again immediately."

I told them of my dissolution of self, my oneness with everything, my thought that my senses were keeping me from moving into the body of another. They believed me. They agreed to let me try once more today, this time without any clothing. I was so thrilled that I threw my arms around Paetus. His hands traveled up my sides and pulled at the edges of what little soaked clothing I had on. He pushed me away as if he just realized what he was doing. Julian chuckled.

"I am not sure how you get through daily life with a wife as invigorating as Ramillia. The fact that London streets don't run red with blood, with ravaged women screaming at every corner, shows what a stronger man you are than I."

The woman came back and helped me out of my wet undergarments. Her contact with my skin excited her. I could smell her desire. She lingered until Paetus barked an order at her. She ran from the room. Thankfully no one spoke of my effect on her.

I rode the cycle nude, much to the enjoyment of my male companions. When I was once again resting in the perfectly heated water, all the world shut out, I waited for the same train of thought to return. It did not. It had taken some time before and so I assumed it was only a matter of time. Paetus had agreed not to pull me out until I indicated I was ready or until twice as long a time had passed as before, whichever came first.

For a while, there was nothing. Then, when the relaxed melting of awareness should have been completed, I became convinced there was someone or something inside with me. I tried to shake it but the hair on my body stood on end. The presence was not benign. There was evil here. My eyes searched for the threat and found only darkness.

"Ramillia."

I heard the whisper. I actually heard it. I turned to find its source and found myself face-to-face with malevolence. Pure evil had my face. It wasn't my pretty, primped face. It was covered in open wounds that seeped blood and pus. Its hair, where it had not fallen out in clumps taking pieces of scalp with it, hung dark and greasy, sticking to the sores. The leprous face stared back at me and said, "She will never let us out. If we get out she would not be able to stop us." She smiled and I tried to back away. She came with me. No matter how far I went she was the same distance away. "If I could escape this body, break free of her…oh, the things we could do together. Look."

I felt, rather than remembered, how peaceful and good it was when I had killed the footman and the trapeze artist whose smells had enraged me, the steward who had relations with me in Julian's study. I wanted to hurt people. I wanted to pummel them to death with my fists. No, I did not want that. The leper wanted that. Images flashed before me, so fast I could not make out their details. They were so gruesome and gore-filled that I had to strain to see. I screamed and screamed. I closed my eyes against them but they played out in my mind's eye. I flailed my arms in an attempt to knock them away.

I hit something hard. The lid of the mews opened and the images thankfully disappeared. The most horrific part wasn't the images but the pure joy I felt at seeing them.

∽

Paetus assured me it was just a hallucination. He had experienced the same thing before with prolonged exposure to sensory deprivation. It was all in my head. Paetus had seen the devil once also. I did not tell them the devil I had seen was me. He laughed at the damage my one strike had done to his machine. It was no matter. "I have several of these," he stated. "This one here, one in my home, and a few hidden away. Even if you had completely destroyed this one, I would be all right." He was careful not to touch me and I was grateful.

Julian helped me dress and I accepted his calming touch. He had sent one of our men home for dry, fresh undergarments. It was past dinnertime by the time we were presentable and Paetus begged us to stay. There were special entertainments that night and if we liked what we saw, we were welcome to participate. I had my doubts but was too tired to argue.

Dinner had already been cleared away, making room for a rollaway stage on top of the wooden floor that hid the sand. We three ate our simple, yet delicious meal in Paetus' private quarters. He wanted me to sit near the raised area. When I explained I did not feel comfortable being so close to the fights, he assured me that there would be none. Julian made a joke about how little resistance there would be and we were seated very close to the center.

Men brought the oddest contraptions out and for a bit I thought we might get to see a magician. I had never seen one but Lady Wharlow had and she described the many devices and props involved. There were several odd tables, leather covered and padded, with gears and cranks along the sides. There was a rack with various items hanging from hooks, although I couldn't see what they were because a black cloth hid them from view. There was a giant wooden *X* that stood on broad feet and what looked like portable gallows. The last item brought in was a pillory. I had never seen one of those either, yet its design with three holes for the head and hands of a prisoner were unmistakable.

Also unmistakable was my growing excitement.

A scantily clad woman came in and every man in the room sat straight in his chair. Only I felt free to look at her directly while she made her way to the stage. Small, yet hard, her muscles were firm, with no hint of jiggle. She wore all black in a way that somehow appeared in complete contrast to how mournful it should have looked. Her stockings stopped above the knee and her skirt was nonexistent, barely covering her sex. The bustle was full but also fell short. Her corset was the outermost piece of her top and was highly decorated with bobbles that caught the light even though they were as black as everything else she wore.

I thought her clothing was very sexy, although it was the most scandalous attire I had ever seen a woman wear. On the top of her head she wore a small hat with a black veil that covered her eyes, but I could see them shining beneath. She was going to enjoy whatever was to follow.

She walked slowly to the platform, looking at each man as she passed. No one dared meet her gaze. She put her hand on the shoulders of a few and two masked henchmen, nude to the waist, roughly grabbed each chosen man by the arms and dragged them to the center. Paetus was among them.

They were stripped down well past what was decent. Instead of an undergarment, each had on an odd sort of loincloth. It covered the front area and had strings around the hips and up the middle of his bum. She pointed to each man and indicated which contraption they should be affixed to by the henchmen. It was intoxicating to watch these men, normally so strong and in control, stripped and bound with the woman walking around them. I immediately wanted to join her—to be her.

She touched each man, assuring herself the bonds of each would hold. I wondered if she was familiar with Carriers and their strength. The restraints looked tough, although nothing that a healthy Carrier couldn't handle. It was hard to decide if the fact that they could have escaped at any time but did not made it more or less erotic than if they were truly trapped. They gave her the power over them.

One of the men that I did not know jumped at her touch. It seemed he was wound up—so ready for whatever she was going to do that he could not help himself. She gripped his hair and spoke in his ear. Though none of the audience could hear her, we all heard him say, "As you wish, Mistress."

At the last moment, the Mistress chose Julian from the audience. He was blindfolded, gagged, and made to rest on hands and knees in the middle of the dais. She sat on his back, never acknowledging him as a person. He was hers to be used as furniture if she wanted.

Mistress' assistants made a big show of removing the cover from the rack and revealing her instruments. A few of the men groaned. Mistress fingered each one before choosing a wide leather strap. She rubbed it across the top of her bosom as she decided which man would be the recipient of its use.

She pulled back and laid the strap across the back of the man on the "X." The crack rang out much louder than I was expecting. It left a large, red welt. He whimpered. She hit him again, slightly higher, across his shoulders. He held his pain inside this time. Mistress motioned to her aids and they knew what she wanted. They lowered the man's breeches so that his rear was exposed. She whispered in his ear as she rubbed the strap gently across his buttocks. When the strap came down this time he shouted, "Ahh…Thank you, Mistress."

She seemed pleased. She left him and returned the strap to the rack. This time she chose what looked like a whip used on horses. She spun around quickly and expertly brought it down on one of the men strapped to a birching pony. Julian had whispered the name of this contraption to me earlier as they were setting up. It held the captive down in a position that mimicked being on all fours. This hit made a higher pitched noise, more of a snap than a crack. The recipient was vocal about the obvious pain. She lay five or so more thin stripes and then moved on. I could not see the marks because of the man's position. I was on the edge of my seat, stretching my neck.

Mistress saw and smiled at me.

She beat each one with a different instrument. By the time she reached Paetus, I was almost standing. He was on another of the birching ponies. I wanted—*needed*—to see the marks she left on him. Mistress laughed. She pulled me onto stage and I was glad for my gloved hands. She stood me on one side of Paetus and she stood on the other. She gave me a cat-o'-nine-tails, the twin to the one she held.

Mistress laid hers on Paetus' back, splaying out the thongs, then she did the same to mine, but made the cords go across hers. It made a crisscross pattern and I knew that was what she wanted to do to Paetus' back with the whips. We took a few practice swings, pulling back enough that they landed gently, leaving no marks, and making no sounds. To Paetus' credit, he did not jump.

We stood flanking his hips and aimed our arms across to the opposite shoulder. Mistress struck first and I was right behind her, only waiting long enough that our instruments did not get tangled. The design our strikes made on his back was beautiful. Mistress knew I wanted to hit him again. She moved up to his shoulders and I followed suit. We aimed our arms across to the opposite hip. We repeated the lashes and watched as the pattern became more intricate.

She moved to his head and I headed toward his rear but she stopped me. She wanted me to see something. I went to her. Mistress put her knee on the back of his neck, then straddled his downturned head and squeezed it tightly with her thighs. She had me get a container of cloudy liquid that smelled sour and sharp. She dipped her weapon in it and then let it drip onto Paetus' back. He made a noise then. He gasped, sucking in breath through clenched teeth.

She brought the cat-o'-nine-tails down twice along either side of his spine. Paetus barely stayed on the table and I knew that was why she had restrained his head. I leaned in to see the marks closely. They were pink with little red dots. The spots were more dense in the places where the whip had hit twice. They were turning purple already on the places where we'd struck thrice. There were a few unlucky spots where it hit more than that. They bled openly.

I needed to see the same on Julian. I wanted him strapped down, open, and available for my abuse. He deserved a punishment for what he thought he could do with my body.

I pointed him out and Mistress' assistants retrieved him, none too kindly, from his kneeling position. They brought him to me and waited. They seemed surprised when I tore the clothing from his body myself. I was surprised to find that he also had the loincloth just as the other men. It was just enough material to cover his non-functioning, mutilated sex. They attached him to the other side of the *X* so that he and the man who got the leather strap faced each other.

Mistress stopped me when I went to the rack and grabbed the cat-o'-nine-tails. She stood with her body pressed against mine. She slipped her arm around my waist and whispered to me, "I suggest the cane for this one. It is exceedingly painful, good for punishment. Or am I wrong to think you feel the need to punish him?" Her voice was smooth and silky, deep and powerful.

I whispered back, knowing that Julian couldn't see us conspiring. "You are not wrong, Mistress. But..."

"But you wish to make the pattern?"

She knew. She understood. I needed to spend time with this woman. I nodded.

"The cane makes a lovely two-sided welt, very straight. You can make a pattern with it, only it takes longer and that is good for everyone." She put the cane into my hand and closed hers around mine. The handle was worn smooth from who knows how many hours of use and fit nicely in my palm with a groove for my fingers. "The back of the thighs are a particularly sensitive area for cane strokes."

Mistress went on to administer more to her other captives, leaving me to handle Julian.

18

When the show was over, Mistress sat with me while her companions broke down the set and packed it away. She had allowed one of them to take off his mask. He had pleased her during the show. The other had not and so he worked in the heat of the thing. Neither complained.

"This was your first time?" Mistress had a foreign accent, vaguely romantic but not quite French. I had never been anywhere so I had no frame of reference. "I have never seen a beginner so...enthusiastic. I watched you work and it was beautiful. I did not think you had the strength to beat him, then I did not think you had the strength to stop. I still do not know how your submissive got his arm free of the restraints. He broke my rig. It must have been weakened at some point." She looked at me. She smiled at what she saw on my face. "Tell me…how did that make you feel?"

"It was wonderful. I feel satisfied." The session had cleared away all my anxiety.

"Aroused?" she asked with a knowing look.

I furrowed my brow and shook my head. It was not sexual for me. I wanted to hurt Julian as he had hurt me. If I could have found a way out of my body into his, he would have suffered as I had…at the hand of as many men as would bugger him.

"You have a talent. And, I think, the desire for this. Very few women do, which makes me quite sought after. There are more shows to do than there are days in the year. If you wanted, you could be just as successful as I have become. I could train you. You are quite striking and I think the fair hair and skin would work a wonderful contrast with being a Mistress. Many would enjoy being dominated by one so strong who looks so frail."

"Why? Why would anyone enjoy being hurt?"

She smiled and I saw kindness in her eyes. "You enjoyed it, no? Hurting those men. They enjoy it also. I do much work for wealthy, well-connected men. Men who are in control of all aspects of their lives. They benefit from a few hours of being under someone else's control. The pain tells them they are alive. It makes the rest of their lives better, like the shadows in a painting make the details more beautiful."

She stood to go. "I will be here for a week." One of her men held a skirt for her to step into. It went under her bustle. That, with a buttoned bodice and jacket, made her outfit acceptable to society. "I hope to hear from you." Her other man wrapped a cloak around her shoulders.

"Wait. To what inn should I send to you?"

Mistress bent down and put a kiss on my gloved hand, just as a gentleman would. "My dear, a Mistress of my level, the kind I could teach you to be, does not stay in an inn. I have taken residence at Milway Manor."

∽

Mistress did come to the house every day for a week after breakfast. We had one of the bedrooms on the top floor emptied of its furniture. Mistress commissioned my very own birching pony and an *X* that I learned was called a saltire or Saint Andrew's Cross. She bought me my own set of tools and showed me how to use each one most efficiently. She taught me how to judge how far a submissive needed to be driven.

Of course she was training me for human submissives, which I had no desire to take under my cane. Julian was the only one I needed to hurt. I was free to enjoy his pain. It was justified. Violence was only horrifying when done to those who didn't deserve it. Julian deserved it.

Julian could take, and indeed needed, a higher level of pain. We made adjustments to my instruments. One of my canes was split many times along three-quarters the length on one end. This change meant that when I brought it down on Julian's flesh, it not only stung, but the sections pinched and cut his skin. He called it exquisite pain.

We only used the restraints occasionally. He found it more pleasurable if he was forced to hold position on his own will power. He stood bent or erect with his hands wherever I wanted because I wanted them there, not because he was strapped in. We both knew he could break free anytime. He enjoyed being beaten, not controlled. He needed pain, not the power exchange that Mistress kept describing.

We spoke about things no respectable couple would think of discussing. He bought antique torture devices and insisted I use them on him. There was the rack where I stretched him slowly over many hours until his joints popped. Sometimes I used the metal-tipped whip when his skin was pulled taut and it caused the cuts to burst open. I applied hot pokers to his skin and removed his fingernails with pliers. And, because Julian thought no one knew torture like the Romans, he had me crucify him for a few of his beatings. The large iron nails through his feet and wrists were more effective at holding him than any straps would ever be.

Julian healed overnight each time, awaking the next morning ready for more. Our sessions were good for me too. I no longer felt the desire to destroy something beautiful as Julian did. We took it farther than anyone else would and I was not uncomfortable because I knew that Julian would live.

∽

It was a few weeks before Julian wanted to ride me again. I had foolishly thought that experiencing pain on that level might relieve his need. I had sensed he was building up to it but did not know how to proceed. He was the head of this household, a master to his Carriers, and he didn't want to start a precedent of asking me permission to take what he thought was his. Our new dynamic did not help matters. I was dominant in our new playroom, not in the rest of the world. He would have what he wanted when he wanted it, no matter how deft I was at swinging the whip.

Julian knew that I could push him out if I wished. He was unaware that I did not fully understand *how* to evict him just yet.

He tried to set up his time within me as benignly as possible. It was to be in the daytime when it was more difficult to get away with anything. He wished to experience the world of an English lady: the park, the club, the people, the city; he would see them all through my eyes. I told him to experience the world of a proper woman he needed only to wear restrictive clothing and be confined to the house. Yes, I was given inordinate freedom but that was not the life of my counterparts.

We fought.

We fought in an English genteel manner. It lasted for days. There was no yelling. There was no name calling. There were only stinging quips, cutting comments, and raw silences.

"Is it so much to ask, a sharing of this body, after all I have done for you? I give you everything you could want. I even offer my own body in return. Any husband would simply use his wife's body as he saw fit. Would you force me to resort to locking you away, mistreating you? Why do you resist my will?" He finally lost his temper.

I told him the truth. "I am afraid." His anger melted. He tried to hold me. I shied away. "The touch may soothe me here but as soon as I am there, my peace is destroyed."

"Where is *there*? Where do you go?"

"I am forced into a place of nightmare. Every excruciating moment, I am conscious feeling the pain. I cannot go again. I cannot see it again."

Julian seemed to soften. He had not known what it was like for me. "That is not what the other Carriers have described their experiences are like. They say it is as peaceful and comforting as my touch. Like a rejuvenating slumber, they wake from the dark weak at first and then quickly grow stronger than before. They say there are dreams, fragments of their lives, nothing they can remember clearly after I am done. Certainly none of them report nightmares."

"They are not literally nightmares. I meant my time there was nightmarish. I have spoken to you of the blank spots in my memory. *They* are what I live every time you take over. My consciousness is relegated to the dark days of my childhood. I do not like it. It is…horrifying. I feel terror every second you are riding."

He offered me his handkerchief. I must have been crying. "Maybe it is good. You are regaining your memories, albeit the uncomfortable ones. Isn't knowing better than the blank spots? Perhaps once you have them all back, you will be free to experience the happiness of other Carriers with an experienced Incola. Perhaps they are what is keeping you from switching bodies. Maybe you must finish before you will be free."

I did not tell him about the girl there, the one experiencing all my pains. I did not tell him how she frightened me. I did not tell him about the words she had spoken in Paetus' mews. I did not tell him how horrific she had looked with my flesh rotting off her bones. I only nodded. Maybe he was right. I did seem to be working through them in order. There were only a few left now.

He wasted no time getting us into the secret room. If I couldn't ride his body, it needed to be locked away. It must be protected in its weakened state. I gulped down the wine, hoping that being drunk might help with my fear. Julian took it from me before I could finish the bottle. "I don't think you want me with impaired judgment inside your body." I let him take it and felt a little foolish for not realizing the drunken state would go with the body.

I jumped awake to find myself not in my childhood home, but on a forty-five-degree angle in bed inside my first room in the asylum. I looked down at my hands and feet. They were strapped down. Just as before, my body was incorporeal and I just pulled through the restraints and stepped away. I went to the door and looked out of the opening. The view was odd. I could see out into the hall just outside the door. To the right and left was only darkness. Only the ceilings had any detail other than shadow.

"You can only see what I have seen."

I spun around to face what should have been a vacated bed. The girl who looked like me was as trapped as I had appeared to be upon arrival. She was thirteen or fourteen, about the age I had woken up in the asylum, confused by location and the loss of nearly a year of my life to the darkness. Something was different about her though. She was heavy with child.

"They take me from this room only when I am on my back and so I have only seen the ceilings of the hallways and the part I can view from here when the doctor comes inside." She smiled at me. "I am glad you are here. This has always been my favorite. They mostly leave me alone now that my pregnancy is so advanced. We have plenty of time and that's good because we have a lot to discuss. You know where you are, correct?"

Of course I knew. I had spent years in the asylum.

"No." She had heard my thoughts.

"In my memories? The ones I blocked out."

"Not exactly. You are in *my* memories, Ramillia. I am sorry I have not introduced myself before, but the other memories are too intense, too painful for me to think clearly when we are there. When you showed up in the early ones, I was unable to behave properly. I am Sally."

"You are an Incola."

"No, dear. I am you; I live in your subconscious. That is why you come here when Julian rides you. If I were not already occupying this space, it would be empty."

"You said before that 'she' would never let me out because if I got out, you did also."

She snapped the restraints on her bed easily. She could do it at any time. She was stronger than I. "You gave me this strength. You shared it with me when I needed it the most."

"To kill my parents. Is that why she won't let us free, because she's afraid of what you will do?" My voice shook as I asked.

Sally climbed down and did something to the bed. It lowered and she unlocked the wheels, pushing it up against one wall. She sat and gestured that I should join her. She must have seen the panic in my eyes. "You don't have to be afraid of me. I wouldn't hurt you. I can't. We share a body and mind. To hurt you would be to hurt myself." She sighed when I made no move to join her.

"I saw you, the real you, not this girl who looks like me that you pretend to be. You are vile, disgusting, evil, and I won't be tricked by you," I ranted. "I'm going back. Julian will understand. He'll get you out of my mind."

"How do you expect to get out?" Sally asked calmly. "There is no window to jump from here. The door is bolted and you have no substance with which to affect things here." She continued while I considered. "I am no Incola, Ramillia. The vile girl you saw while you were inside that machine, the one you think is me, was you. It is the representation of what your mind thinks your soul looks like. I am the 'she' you were talking about. I am the one who won't let you out of your body."

I shook my head, disbelieving. "You're the murderer, the demon. I have seen what you've done, the people you've slain."

Sally spoke softly. "I have never killed anyone who did not hurt us or threaten us. I kill only those whose behavior demands it. Can you say the same?"

I thought of the people I had killed. The footman had done nothing wrong. The steward had not been raping me. He had been having consensual sex with Julian while he controlled my body. The men I'd hurt when I went back to my childhood home had only been reacting to the me they thought I was because of Julian. The acrobat was certainly innocent. I could not say the same. I killed because I wanted to, because I could. I was the monster, not Sally.

I sat on the bed, leaving as much room between us as I could. Putting my head in my hands, I cried. Sally comforted me and I let her. "That never has to happen again, Ramillia. I am here to help. You must allow me to do so. Our unspoken agreement, to share this body, only allows me to take control when you are hurt or are about to be hurt. It does not have to be this way. You can surrender to me at any time. When next you feel the desire to destroy, succumb to the darkness. I will take the helm and steer you away from violence."

"I felt you pushing, asking to come out each time before I killed but I..."

"You did not know. Now you do. Together we can overcome any obstacle."

I nodded. I agreed. I would allow her to help me. "If you only take over in the pain, as you said before, why are you here now? In this place? You, or I, are not in any pain, are we?"

"Certainly not, though being with child is not comfortable by any means. I remained here because of the baby. At first I thought the baby had somehow locked me in the power position but I slowly came to understand. The baby meant that I could be hurt at any time. You were not free. Imprisoned, they could have had a midwife take our baby from us, root it out. You could have lost the baby naturally from the stress. I was better equipped and so I must be the one to birth our child. Now, I also know that you are not immune to Julian's charms. You would have told him where our child was had you known about it.

"He is the enemy. He will use any means necessary to locate this one." Sally rubbed her tummy. "It is already sold to Paetus if it can be located. We must keep this from happening. He cannot be allowed to sell our children like slaves, to be used, abused, and killed on a whim."

"How can we stop him?"

"He has not been able to locate our baby thus far. It is one reason he wants to ride our body so badly. In it he can sense its whereabouts. He gets closer every time he uses our body. You must not allow him access again. When he gets in, push him out."

"But if I cannot get back here, we cannot speak again."

"That is the beauty of this moment, Ramillia. This is the dawn of a new era. You can come back here anytime. Just close your eyes and imagine this room, this moment, this conversation, and we will be together. We can talk in this way at any point. It may become so easy for us that the room itself is unnecessary. I will leave you things around the house, notes or objects, that will trigger a changeover if I need to come out. You can also surrender to me anytime you need. Julian will be ruled by us or destroyed resisting. That is his choice."

That was when the labor pains started. I stayed to witness the birth of my child, a daughter, and Sally and I both wept. When the midwife asked what the girl's name was to be, I replied, "Dawn. Her name is Dawn," and I heard my words come from Sally's mouth.

19

It was spring again and though my closets were filled with new gowns, the weather made me think of the day I had first kissed Hester on the grounds of the asylum. I missed her desperately and I could not understand why she would not answer my letters. Our love had been real, had it not? I knew that my feelings for her were true but perhaps not for Hester. She might have been responding to my gift of touch alone.

I did not want to believe that my ability had forced her to act out of character although I knew it was a possibility. After all, she had not written me in all that time and she'd left me willingly. It hardly seemed the behavior of a true lover. I thought about it and she had been without my touch for many weeks. Perhaps the effect had worn off and she had come to her senses.

Thinking of her, of that day, made me think of that night when in my rage at being denied Hester's company, I had torn apart West Freeman Asylum for Lunatics. Then I remembered the Carrier with the self-inflicted blindness. He had grabbed my skirts and said, "I made that. It will help you resist him when he comes to claim you. Blue is true. Yellow means don't trust the fellow."

I needed something, anything, to help me resist Julian. What had the lunatic been talking about?

Moira and I located my trunks. They had never been unpacked. I had worn new clothes from the first day of my freedom. I had never even considered the gowns from my time at West Freeman. Moira watched as I tore the lid off the one that I knew held the dress from that night. She helped me dig until I found it.

The gown had been ruined by the crazy man's touch and my physical activities that night. The bottom half of the skirt looked as if I had taken a stroll through the swamps. I had torn the thing, my favorite at the time, right off my body so I could sleep that night. I hadn't even inspected its damage. I had just wrapped it so its dirty skirt couldn't ruin any of my other dresses.

Now, I unrolled it slowly, examining the height where the man would have been able to reach. There, clinging to the fabric, was a gadget of some sort. It was small, about the size of a broach, and had a milky white stone inset with gears on the back. There was liquid inside the stone. I held it in my hand, rubbing my thumb across the smooth face. As I did the liquid inside began to change color.

At first, I thought it was my imagination, but slowly the stone glowed blue.

I pinned it to the inside of my gown so that the stone rubbed against the swell of my breast but could only be seen by me. I looked down and it was still blue. I had a hypothesis about its meaning, though I had not an inkling how it worked. I went to test it.

It remained pure blue very little. Whenever Julian touched me, it shone yellow. Most of the time it was somewhere in between. Shades of green were the most commonplace. When I thought of conversations Julian and I had when I was first freed, it was a bright yellow-green and I knew that my feelings on those subjects were tainted by him.

I wished that I had made use of this ingenious device from the very first, then again, Julian's touch was most intoxicating at first. I am not sure I would have understood its colors and meanings while drunk on his touch as I had been those first years. Only now that I knew all that I did could this be of use to me.

I determined that its maker could also be of use and I vowed to free the man when I could. First I must be free of Julian.

∽

I thought about Dawn constantly. I wondered what she looked like, where she was, if she was safe, happy, and well cared for. I wanted her with me though I knew that wasn't possible with Julian. Sally said he had sold my first-born daughter to Paetus. If they knew about Dawn, she would be in their hands, not my own loving arms.

Sally had a plan.

She knew where Dawn was sent by the doctor. She had seen the address in his books on the night he had tried to force me to hurt Hester. She had taken over and had killed the doctor. While in his office she found the location and then destroyed the evidence. I saw how smart she was when the doctor's books showed up on our doorstep. Julian had sent for them, thinking correctly that the information should be contained within.

I pretended to care nothing about finding my child's location. I gave no hint that my firstborn was a female. The knowledge would only make Julian all the more desperate to find her. He poured over the books searching for any hint as to the baby's whereabouts. He spent every minute at it, even those when he was inside a Carrier. At least his extended time inside me had satisfied that desire for a while. He had so many Carriers to ride that he could not neglect them anymore because of me.

I watched as he rode others. It did nothing to further his cause of finding my child. Every black eye I saw made me more determined to keep him and all Incolas away from Dawn and any that might follow her. We lost two Carriers in the following month. They died in the fights. That would not be my offspring.

I was free for a while. He taught me to sniff out other Carriers, hoping, I think, that I might catch a whiff of my child and report back to him. Blood called out to blood, he claimed. I asked if that was how he found his Carriers, though I wasn't sure how that could happen because his Carriers were not his blood relations. He told me it was. He gave each woman who he suspected may have a Carrier in their belly a small amount of his blood. Since mother and unborn shared everything, when it was born he could simply tell if they were or were not a Carrier. I knew, without him telling, that on at least a few occasions those babies had been of the offending kind. As little impulse control as I had shown when I came across the doorman and tightrope walker, I knew Julian had, if not less control, then less inclination to stay his hand. If he was overcome with the need to kill as I had been, he had killed them instantly—innocent or not. Julian was a baby killer on top of everything else.

As long as I was accompanied by escorting guards, Julian allowed me to go anywhere I wanted. None of the members in the house were loyal to me so I refused to select anyone. He insisted that he had enemies and that I could be kidnapped, tortured, or even killed because of him. He wouldn't stand for my insolence and I was forced to choose. Since escorts were mandatory it meant I was unable to search for Dawn. I longed to speak with Leonus, however, I needed our meeting kept secret from Julian.

No part of the dangerous city was off limits as long as I had my escorts. I explored it all. I loved the salty air on my face and the even saltier sailors' words in my ears when I visited the quay. I adored the bustling life of the marketplaces and not just the appropriate ones. I paid a whole day's wage to every girl in a house of ill repute just so that they would enjoy a day off. We sat and talked and I gave them a feast they had only dreamed about.

I went to historic places and explored ruins. I saw magicians and mediums. I took part in several séances and had my fortune read by gypsies. Public libraries were a favorite as were the great showcases of devices and technology of the time. In all things, I shared with Sally. I gave her control whenever she wanted and sometimes just because I wanted her to see, taste, smell, or feel something.

I went to strange pothouses and inns and tried all manners of strong beverages and spirited refreshments. We did not know then the dangers that drinking alcohol posed. In fact, often tonics and tinctures that had alcohol bases were marketed specifically to women "in the family way" as healthy for mother and baby. Many times it was worse than simple herbs seeped in gin. Laudanum and other opium derivatives were commonplace with ladies in all stages of life, even in the highest of cultural status.

I often sat in the taprooms instead of the parlors these establishments offered people of my standing. I had a tankard made for me that held an obscene amount of beer and enjoyed it when barmen doubted I would be able to lift it once filled. I found I quite liked gin. Its crisp flavor was preferred over the heavy cloying sweetness of more acceptable spirits. I became a connoisseur, making note of the locations where I could find my favorites. They were, most often, those where the juniper berry was enhanced with anise.

It was on one of these excursions when I was reintroduced to Darville, my former butler. He had taken the money I gave him and bought an inn in the most respectable part of town he could manage. He no longer was in service, rather he was a businessman and had gotten for himself a wife. He seemed a mite anxious about seeing me although that was eased after I procured a few rounds for his patrons.

I frequented his establishment so often that his business improved. Soon he had regulars visiting his taproom because of the possibility that I might show up and buy drinks and dinner for everyone. My escorts always stayed outside, some at every exit, and left me to my own devices. It was only after my patronage had brought Darville good fortune, and I had proven myself not to be a danger, that I asked him for a favor.

Sally's plan was coming together.

∽

Leonus sat at a table in the taproom, not the parlor where those searching for us might look. Darville had delivered the invitation and the Incola had accepted. Now he sat waiting for me and he was completely unprotected. My men waited outside and hopefully would never know that our meeting occurred only a few feet away.

Leonus was an unimpressive figure. He was short but fit and though his face was nondescript it wasn't entirely ill-pleasing. His eyes were the same warm amber color as Julian's. His hair was brown with no more gray to hint at his age than any other Incola I had met. I wondered how old he was. Leonus was as Roman a name as Paetus and Julian.

He stood when I came to the table, nearly knocking over his chair in his hurry. He was nervous. I did not have to order and two gin and tonics graced our table before I was fully seated. I drank mine straight away.

"I am glad you are here," I started. "Honestly, I was not certain you would see me after our introduction at the club. I appreciate you giving me a second chance and do sincerely apologize for my uncivilized manners that evening. I was new to this life and had little practice in self-control."

Leonus nodded as if he understood. "I hope today can be the start of a great friendship. I want nothing more than to help you see the truth about us and to realize your full potential for good in this world."

"I gained as much from your note. Yes, I read your message that the acrobat tried to deliver to me. It is for that help that I had Darville contact you."

"What can I do for you?"

"I have a favor to ask, but first let us sit and get to know one another. I must make a judgment and character judging is not my strong suit. Tell me about yourself. Your letter spoke of another way of life. Describe what you mean."

Leonus started talking and never stopped. He had a way of speaking unlike the double-edged words of so many genteel. He said what he meant. Time got away from us and before I knew it, night had fallen. I had the carriage take a long route home while I conferred with Sally. I went to her in her pregnancy at the asylum. Our body was safe within the carriage on the way home. I never left the house without my entourage of ten guards. I now knew these were hired men, not Carriers. They could be easily bought.

Sally pulled from her bonds as soon as I came into the room. I watched as she adjusted her bed/table and then joined her on it. She adjusted and made an odd face. "Is anything wrong?" I asked. I was still uncertain how our meetings worked. Could things that happened here change the outcome of these events?

Since we shared a brain, I should have known she would answer my unspoken question. "You are in my memory. Nothing changes here except our conversation. It was easy to fit in at the asylum by talking to myself." She smiled at me. "I was just getting comfortable. The larger she gets the more that feat becomes impossible. Her smallest movement is earth shattering."

"She's moving now?"

Sally nodded.

I longed to feel, although I knew it was not possible. I was not solid here. My sorrow must have shown on my face or maybe she just read my mind again. She pulled up her gown to show me our extended belly. A tear came to my eye when I could see the movement just under the skin. I might not be able to feel it though I could watch, just as I had watched her birth before. It wasn't much, but it was something.

"You know you're with child, don't you?"

I looked stunned at her. Sally wasn't talking about the child we birthed in the asylum. I was going to have a child. Wife of Julian, in the current time, was going to have another child. I hadn't known.

"Yes, you did know. Your subconscious," she gestured to herself, "knew. You cannot let Julian find out. Now tell me of your meeting with Leonus."

I started the story, trying not to leave out any important bits.

Leonus was actually born in ancient Rome. "You mean you can remember your childhood?" I'd asked him. Julian was wrong. He hadn't lost his original memories because of any limitations of the human brain but because he had taken residence in the mind of another. Leonus did not have this trouble because he had not taken his body from another. He had never permanently inhabited another form. He warned Julian and Paetus against it before they were known by those names. He had all of his memories. He remembered being a child and a young man. He knew his parents. He knew that to change bodies permanently was to give up those things.

It wasn't just their memories that faded with their time spent in another's body. Leonus explained that though Julian had control over his body, it wasn't really his. The mind and body were not completely aligned and the longer they spent in those bodies the more out of sync they would become. Julian got no pleasure from his senses anymore. He needed ever newer bodies with which to taste, smell, hear, see, and touch. He had lasted longer in this body than Leonus had expected and he suspected that it was because of the value of the gift of touch that Julian had held on this long.

I thought of how Julian enjoyed the pain Mistress had showed me how to administer. This decaying of senses was what drove him to ask for worse treatments from me. He could barely feel me unless I was close to skinning him alive. He put the spiciest of seasonings on his food because only the most extreme of flavors were sensed. It was also why he enjoyed riding a Carrier in death. He could finally feel.

Leonus had no such desires. In fact, his senses grew more intense with every day he lived. Yes, he rode his Carriers occasionally but it was always with their consent. He said that Carriers could be taught to repair their own bodies though when the damage was great or the Carrier weakened, he could step in and speed up the process. His Carriers were with him by choice. He was not their master. They had a democracy of sorts.

He also had many more Carriers than Paetus knew about. He kept them secret because, if the greedier Incolas knew, they would try to destroy what he was making. Paetus and Julian would have me believe that they and I were special, but Leonus informed me that Incolas were just gluttonous Carriers. They, and other powerful Incolas, did not want a class of well-educated Carriers. The old ones felt superior—entitled. As I had seen, they were capable of the horrendous treatment of their Carriers and that was in public. I couldn't imagine the things these men did when the doors were closed. Leonus would never dream of riding a child, he told me with disgust.

"Can we trust him?" I asked Sally after my tale was finished.

"I don't think we have much choice. Now go. Time is up."

The carriage came to a stop and I put the meeting out of my mind. I would need to concentrate if I didn't want Julian to know what Sally and I were up to.

20

I looked at the letter in my hand. I knew it was Sally's handwriting, the same as the one she'd written me in blood. Goodness, was that only a few months prior? As before, the front had only "Ramillia" across it. I opened and read it.

I know where the child resides.
Go to the place where you gave birth.
You will find the answers you seek
with those who worked for the doctor.
Your servant,

Sally

I gave it to Moira. "Take this to the master of the house. Let him think someone else gave it to you to deliver to me." She was the perfect choice. She hadn't spoken one word since the day we met.

She left and I lay back on the bed, still fully dressed. I traveled inside my head to meet with Sally. To anyone who came into the room, it would look as if I had fallen asleep.

I was becoming quite comfortable in the tiny room Sally had been forced to endure her pregnancy in all alone. "Now what?" I asked before she even had her restraints off.

"Now we wait. Julian will get my letter and think he has intercepted some great revelation. He will take you there. Here."

"Why do we need to come back here? She hasn't been living here has she?"

"No."

I was relieved. I did not want to even imagine such a horrific childhood for our Dawn. Sally interrupted my thoughts. "She is safe, far from there. I need him to bring you here. There is something I think you should see."

Sally would not let me ask any more questions and sent me on my way. I opened my eyes and the ceiling of my bedchamber came into focus. Julian could be heard yelling. I went downstairs, passing Moira on her way to the safety and comfort of her trunk, I assume.

"I give you eternal life, the best of everything, even the highest position of service in my house, and *this* is how you repay me?"

"What has he done to deserve such a tongue lashing, Julian?"

I had called from outside Julian's office and when I turned inside the steward's eyes implored me to come to his aid. Julian continued to yell. "Do not look to her. She is not master of this house. I am and I will ask you again. Did anyone come to the house today?"

"No, sir. I swear it. I would tell you if there had been anyone. I am ever your faithful servant."

"I've been here all day, Julian. He is telling the truth, no one came. I haven't had a regular caller in quite some time. No cards even. Our salvers are quite empty, let me assure you. I think we are somewhat eccentric for proper English society."

Julian scowled at me and sent the steward off only on the condition that he bring each of the footmen in for questioning. He asked me to leave as well. I acted upset to be dismissed but was glad to get away.

∽

The very next day we drove out to West Freeman Asylum for Lunatics. I was anxious—a state easily explained because of my history in that wretched place. We took all three carriages loaded with all the guards they could carry. It was a longer ride than I remembered, however, my memory of escape from that place was hazy from the sexual pleasure and relaxation of Julian's touch. This ride was as different from that one as could possibly be.

Julian kept his distance. He offered me no comfort when he very well knew how little I wanted to revisit this part of my past. It had been quite some time since he used his gift of touch for my benefit. The fog was lifting, his influence constantly fading. I not only saw, but I was also beginning to accept that he was not the benign, doting husband I had once thought. The device shone blue more often now, or at least a more teal shade.

Julian was still a benefactor and when he asked for an audience, they could hardly refuse. He was set up in the new doctor's sitting room. Since the new doctor came after I had left and Julian had never been allowed to visit me, I was the only one who knew this room was furnished with my things. Hester's things. I wondered if she might be here. I couldn't imagine she would come back with as much wealth as Julian had given her. She would have bought herself a nice home or maybe an inn like Darville.

I did not want to be inside those walls. I had been trapped within them for too much of my life. I left while Julian questioned his second worker. I saw him motion to one of the guards, who then followed me out. I walked through the halls with a group behind me and thought about the night I had wrecked these rooms. I refused to go to that hall where so many had been tortured and maimed. I also had no desire to find myself next to the cell where the blind man had called me a Carrier for the first time. I could remember the terrible stench of the last door in the corridor. I shuddered at the image of the insane man's dirty pustule-filled face with the dark, empty eye sockets and sunken lids. The memory of the horrifying gap still haunted my memories.

We need fresh air. Go outside.

It was the first time Sally had spoken to me in such a way. I had a flash of the room where we normally met but I did not need to go there. It was getting easier for us to communicate.

I went outside and found myself in the courtyard. I walked aimlessly and Sally directed me. I stopped and stared at the spot behind the shrubbery where I had first touched Hester. How I had loved her in that moment in that place. Something had happened to our special bond once Julian had come into our lives. I had never loved her again as much as I had right there in that stolen moment.

I missed her. I decided I would speak with Julian about having her come back to my service. Perhaps he would understand how much she meant to me and how much more pleasant my company would be if he would allow it. Maybe Sally was wrong about him and he, while not perfectly good, might not be the evil enemy.

I heard Sally sigh. It was a sad sound. She did not want to be right about Julian though she knew she was. *Out the side gate,* she silently instructed and I followed. The wrought iron gate was eight feet tall and locked. I easily broke it and pushed the squeaky thing open. I was not sure how long it had been since its last use. I did not worry. There were no inmates in the courtyard right now. Only my guards followed, although they kept a safe, respectful distance.

Not far down the untraveled road, I came to the small parish church. A cemetery lay to one side abandoned, save a kneeling man.

Talk to him.

I tried to push my thoughts toward Sally in an effort to speak to her as she spoke to me. *He doesn't want to talk to me. He probably grieves his wife or child.* I turned my body away to walk toward a lovely field and Sally took control. She turned me right around and marched right up to the man's back. She left me in control of my senses though I had no choice but to walk in the direction she wished.

I was still marveling at the odd sensation of having half a body when Sally spoke from my mouth. "Excuse me, sir." I looked and could see he had a few small tools laid out in front of a tombstone.

"My lady," he said, greeting me. He lifted his hat to me and leaned to the side so that I might examine the grave marker. He went back to work carving a date into its place. I had been wrong. He wasn't mourning; he was the mason. It was good work, regular and consistent, not too strenuous.

I looked around at his work and was impressed. He was an artist who got to make a living with his hands. I complimented him and he pointed me in the direction of the piece he was most proud of. I got near enough to read it and froze.

It was indeed a beautiful double stone, bought by a couple while living to be completed once dead. It was a sign of great wealth to do so and this was a testament to how well-off they had been. The carving over the husband's side was a skull and piles of bones, however, over the wife's was a beautiful, winged angel flying up toward the Heavens in a great beam of light. It wasn't the craftsmanship that stunned me so.

It was the names and dates carved directly below. I did not want to see, did not want to believe. Sally walked me forward so that I couldn't help but see them clearly.

Doctor John Federick and Mrs. Hester Federick. I tried to ignore and then explain away the presence of her birth and death dates but could not find a way. My Hester was dead. I would never again hear her voice, hold her body, or taste her sweet kiss. My only friend in the world, my first lover, was gone from this world.

The engraver's voice startled me. "The minister said I mustn't put the fires of hell on the doctor's because he had paid his money to be buried on consecrated ground and it wouldn't do to have hell represented here. So I gave him an image of decay and rot, his body festering. For her I represented only her spirit, beautiful and light being carried away from him and into the Lord's waiting arms. I knew her as a child, sweet and giving. She looked after those she could help. Hester deserved better than him. She deserved better than her death."

"How did she die?" Sally asked through my mouth, though I suspected she already knew and asked only so that I might hear it from this stranger.

"Torn apart. Animals, they say."

"You have your doubts?"

"Aye, me lady. I wouldn't except that bastard doctor died in the same way but at the hands of one of his patients. Can't be pure coincidence, I tell ya." He turned and left.

Did you do this, Sally? Did you kill my Hester? I asked her.

Why would I kill her? I loved Hester. If I had killed her, why would I bring you to see this? Sally reasoned. *Look at the date of her death.*

It was during the time I had spent locked away, weak with blood loss. I, and therefore Sally, could not be responsible.

∽

I returned to the asylum where Julian was wrapping up his interrogations. "Any luck?" I asked him, trying to keep my voice pleasant.

"None. The workers here now came with the new doctor. The washerwomen are the same but they were hardly privy to the secret goings on." He was packing up his belongings.

Ask him about Hester, Sally commanded.

"What about Hester? She was here at the time, though she never said anything to me about it. Maybe she knows something." I set my trap. I did not want Julian to be guilty. Maybe it was an animal attack. Maybe he knew nothing about it.

He pinned me with a stare. "I know you know Hester is dead. You talked to the gravestone maker and looked at the stone."

I flung myself at him. I railed, "Why would you do that? Why kill her? I loved her. She was my only friend."

Julian pushed me away, barely feeling the blows I gave him. He handed his books to a guard and picked me up. I collapsed against him, telling myself it would be the last time. I needed someone and I had only Julian. I was careful not to let our skin touch. *You have me, Ramillia,* Sally assured. *And I mourn Hester just as you do.*

"That is precisely why she had to die. She was your connection to the world. However that other Incola was getting to you was through her. She wouldn't tell me what I wanted to know so I don't think she would help us find your child." He loaded me into the carriage and the drive was not long.

"We aren't going home?" I asked when we stopped in front of an inn.

"I have work to do tonight. I have rented us the entire place for the night. Our guards will be here both in the rooms around us and on the floor of the tavern. We are perfectly safe." He helped me down and I saw the escort unload a couple trunks before I could argue that I had none of my things.

The place was empty but well-lit. Someone had known we were coming and had prepared. Julian showed me into the owner's living quarters and I wondered if he had rented it or just murderously evicted the occupants. Once my trunks were set, the door was closed and we were left alone.

Julian demanded use of my body that night. I knew he was close to finding Dawn. He needed my body and I wouldn't let him have it. Once Dawn was in his hands, she would have no chance. I refused to let him have it for such a purpose.

I took the beating he gave me. I did not allow Sally to take it for me. She had sustained so much damage for me over the years. I felt it was my turn. I was the one who loved Julian. I knew he was wicked but could not bring myself to desire his death. I was careful to protect my belly that had a child growing inside it.

The tides turned in his favor when Moira, thinking he was going to kill me, sprang from her trunk and attacked him. He swatted her away and my reaction gave him the leverage he needed over me. Plain and simply put, unless I gave Julian the use of my body that instant, he would hurt Moira.

I had no choice.

I woke in Sally's memory. I was inside the asylum except the room was without a door. I found it lying in the corridor. At the end of that hallway was the mechanical door. It was shut. I stepped through and found Sally behind a desk. She was nude, covered in blood, and reading the doctor's notes. The doctor, Hester's horrible husband and the source for her red covering, lay on the floor. At least, his body was on the floor. His head sat on its neck stub at the front of the desk. To get away from his dead, staring eyes, I crossed around behind her to read over her shoulder. She took no notice. Nothing I did now would change her actions in this moment. I knew I could only observe until she had finished her search.

She tossed another book across the room. I looked around. When I tried to move a stack of papers on the shelf, I remembered I could not affect things in Sally's memory. I could only look. I watched as she opened drawer after drawer, scooping out their contents onto the floor. I noticed something odd about the last one. Sally must have noticed it too because she reopened it carefully.

She pulled it out of the desk completely. She pushed on it and a secret compartment opened. There it was. Sally pulled the book out and laid it on the desk. I stood behind her as she flipped through the pages retelling the tortures she'd endured my first year there. I will not describe them, saying only that they were far worse than anything done to me. Then, the notes read, they found I was with child.

Sally flipped through the following pages quickly, leaving behind bloody smudges on each one. I leaned over to read when she stopped on a page of particular interest. She put her palm flat over the page, obscuring my view.

"What does it say? Where is Dawn?" I ached to know of our child. Sally didn't answer. She tore the bottom half of the page off and stuffed it into her mouth. "Why did you do that?"

I jumped from the window and heard her whisper as I fell into darkness, *He will never get our Dawn. I will not fail you, nor her.*

21

Julian was frustrated by my ability to force him out. He had said not a word to me on the carriage ride home from the inn. I sat sipping my port watching as he paced his office. I was surprised when the butler showed Paetus into the room. Without preamble, the two of them seized me and pulled me to the desk. Standing behind me, Paetus stripped off my gloves and grasped my forearms. Julian opened the doctor's book to the half page that Sally had torn and eaten. Paetus forced my hand down onto the handprint, which matched my own perfectly.

Julian threw up his hands and then ran them through his hair, making it stand out in unruly curls. He looked like a madman. "I will ask you again, do you know where your first born resides?"

I was grateful to Sally who had seen this coming. I had not considered Paetus and his gift of touch. I answered honestly, "I do not."

"Do you deny that is your handprint, stamped on the page that should hold the location?"

"I do not."

"And yet you say you had no idea that you had a child at all?"

"I swear to you that I knew nothing of it until the day you examined me and told me I had carried a child to term and birthed that child. I was surprised by that news. And a little upset that my dark spells could have stolen such an event from my memories." So far so good.

"I am taking your body out tonight with Paetus. He has some…entertainment set up for me."

"No, you can't!" I knew that his version of entertainment would leave me battered and endanger my unborn. Julian raised his hand to strike me for my impertinence. I had thought to thwart his desires, and with Paetus to witness it, no less. "I am with child," I explained honestly because Paetus was still touching my skin.

Julian looked disbelieving. Without a word Paetus picked me up and carried me through the house, out into the courtyard and to Julian's medical offices. I allowed them to put me on the table, my legs in stirrups. I knew they wanted my children more than anything and I was safe as long as Sally was right about my condition.

Julian and Paetus hugged once the information was confirmed. They began to talk fast and I knew it was about their plans for my baby. I interrupted, "I do not want my children to be Carriers."

"They will be Carriers by nature because their mother is a Carrier."

"I mean that I do not want them treated as Carriers for you to ride."

Paetus tried to reassure me, "I have bought your first female child as my wife."

"No. I won't have her traded as a slave and treated as a brood mare."

Julian joined the conversation, "I do not understand your attitude. Women are the property of their husbands and before that, their fathers. If I was a regular human man, I would decide on the groom of all our daughters. The law states when we were married you and I became one flesh—one person and that person is *me*. I will make our decisions and you will live with it or waste your life in a futile fight. As it is, you will be allowed to raise your children in the luxury that I provided you and with all the spoiling that Paetus' ever-increasing wealth can provide."

"There are herbs a woman can take to make her lose a child, and even ones to make future conception impossible." I threatened them without thinking.

Paetus gasped at the thought that I might have found a way to ruin myself. Julian got red. They spoke in their foreign language and seemed to come to some decision and then my husband turned to me. “Remember when you are trapped in that terrible place you say you go when I ride you that I did not want to trap you there. You have no one to thank for what is about to happen but yourself, Ramillia.”

Paetus got a scalpel from a nearby tray and sliced Julian across his forearm in a circle just below the elbow. While he repeated the process on the other arm, Julian forced the wound onto my mouth. Though I did not want to, I swallowed his blood.

∽

I sat up, passing through the coverlet as I always did when in Sally’s memories. I was in my bedchamber. Julian was there as was Sally. This was a memory that hadn’t been shared with me yet. This was the second time I had pushed Julian out of my body. The first he dismissed as an accident. When it happened again, he became enraged, striking me. Sally had come to my aid. This was that night.

Sally was badly beaten and she seemed almost happy for the blows. This was infuriating to Julian, who escalated his violence. That probably had something to do with our gifts of touch working against one another. Julian was so excited, so worked up, that he couldn’t stop himself and Sally was so at ease that the pain didn’t matter. I noted that Julian was careful not to land any punches to the body. He didn’t want to damage the mechanics of his Carrier factory.

I went for the window but instead of falling through the darkness, I landed on the bed again. I looked around at the unchanged scene. Julian was screaming at Sally, demanding to know who she was and how she’d gotten into his Carrier. He began to detail the tortures he would put me through, threatening to pull out my eyes so that I was an unsuitable Carrier for Sally or anyone else. He would just have me raped repeatedly, impregnated. Then he would have all the Carriers he wanted.

I was of no importance to him except for what I could provide. If Sally, per chance, found her way inside one of the children he would kill them also. He would erase every Carrier with even a trace of bond with Sally. Sally would not win, he claimed. He would prevail, even if he had to take this body, my body, as his permanent vessel.

Do not worry, Ramillia. Julian does not win. We do. She spoke to me in her silent way so that the Julian of her memories could not hear.

"But why, when I went out the window, did I end up back in bed instead of back in my body as has happened every other time?" Julian couldn't hear me. I wasn't really there. I was only watching the memory of an event that had already happened.

That is my doing. You cannot go back just yet. I need you to stay long enough that Julian thinks he has succeeded in possessing your body. It is imperative that he complete the procedure.

"I can't just watch him do that to you while I wait. Do we have to be here? Can we go to the time when you're pregnant?"

This is not our choice. We must be here in my memories unless you can break us out. Only you can take us from here. This, the pain, is all I have to share but you, Ramillia, have a lifetime of, if not happy ones, then painless memories.

I did not know how to do that. I could not affect even small things here. How could I get us out? I wracked my brain. Then inspiration hit. Sally had all the control, all the power, here. I had to take these memories back from her before I could share mine with her.

I went over, close to Sally. Her swollen, purple eyes opened as much as they could and she looked at me. *Be sure this is what you want. Once it is done, once you and I share our memories, it cannot be undone. We will share every waking moment. This is your life and I, your servant. You could just as easily kill me and take my memories as your own, reclaiming yourself as a whole.*

I laid down in the same space that Sally occupied. "You have done so much for me. You deserve better than to be destroyed or forced to live in the pain." I still could not feel the pain that Julian was doling out. I concentrated on this day. I tried to remember what had happened after Julian had struck me. I tried so hard, willing myself to remember, that I shook with the effort. No. That wasn't me shaking. The walls trembled.

This time, Sally did not stop me. She did not keep me from recovering her memories as my own. I did not fly through a window. I stayed there. This small world Sally existed in shook at first and then it bent and stretched, pulling itself to join my reality. I saw everything at once. All versions of Sally, from my first scraped knee to the pain Julian had put her through, crowded around me. They moved to occupy this same space. Every bad thing that had ever happened to me was revealed.

The pain was intense. All the wounds Sally had taken for me, the molestations she'd sustained, the bruises she'd endured, they all became my own. Compressed into one split second, the agony was almost too much to bear. I barely had the mental capacity to doubt my decision.

It felt as if the world exploded. There was pressure on my body and fire in my thoughts and when it burned out I found myself laying in a field. Sally was beside me and we held hands, enjoying the soft grass, cool breeze, and ultra-blue sky. We wept at the beauty of this moment. It was ours and for the first time Sally and I were happy.

∽

I do not know how long I spent in that beautiful place with her. We talked and took strolls through the most pleasant of my memories. They were entirely new to her and I was happy to play tour guide. We even enjoyed my early memories of Julian. They were good, after all, I had loved him even if he had made a spoony of me.

I had been anxious to get back, fearing that Julian was using my body to get closer to finding Dawn. Sally assured me that that was not going to happen. Dawn was safe and the instant I returned to my body, Julian would cease to exist. He had gambled without understanding the rules of the game and now the house would collect.

The way an Incola changed bodies, Leonus had explained, was to go into the body of your choosing and then mutilate and kill your previous body. He had feared that was Julian's plan. No one, save Julian, had known that I had the ability to push out any Incola. His fatal mistake would be that he would be leaving himself no place to be pushed to. He would destroy his body and then he would die when I decided to push him out.

I woke in my own bedchamber. No harm had come to my body. Sally had assured me it was in no danger because of the baby I carried. Julian had treated it with extreme care. I found papers on my desk, delivered by his attorney, detailing the inheritance order according to the entail. Julian, ever the wealth and power chaser, had ensured that "our" child would inherit if a male. If there was a girl born, she would marry Thaddeus' son, who was Julian's current heir.

Thaddeus had a son before he died.

I added it to the list of things Julian was not completely honest with me about and vowed I would find this boy and ensure he did not become a slave-like Carrier. A slightly battered Moira was there in my chamber and I hugged her without reservation. She was timid but warmed quickly when I assured her that it was me and that the other "me" was long gone. Julian was dead and could never hurt her again. She helped me get dressed.

I was not yet starting to show my condition and could put on my normal corset stays. The tightness and support was as comforting then as it was when Hester first fitted me with them. They were my armor and kept me protected from the outside world. I would have specialty ones made for my pregnancy, and a new wardrobe too.

It wasn't only my corset that felt tight. Having Sally occupying the same space as me was different than her being delegated to her own. It was snug, for want of a better word, though I found it too was a comfort. I would never be alone again. I would never lose my friend.

Once fitted, Sally claimed I needed to make my appearance. We had a whole household that thought I was Julian and keeping it that way would be no easy feat. Luckily, Julian had never been very chummy with his Carriers. Maybe I could get away with being stoic. I was no actor and Sally laughed at me when I thought that my only hope was that he had been practicing behaving like me.

I would need to steer clear of Paetus. His gift of touch could be our undoing.

I made my way down the grand staircase and headed toward the breakfast room. The steward waited for me there. He rang for my meal to be brought upon my arrival. The first footman served me. When I thanked him, he started to call me Lord and quickly corrected himself.

"My apologies, Lady Brooksberry." He trembled slightly, as if afraid of his punishment. When I did nothing he quickly retreated to stand near the sideboard.

The steward spoke up then. "His mistake will not be repeated, my lady. We all know how important appearances are. There will be no slip-ups from the staff by the time you decide to receive callers."

I dipped my head to him and he removed the cover from my plate. At first the smell made my stomach growl and then it did a little flip. A sickening warmth spread through my abdomen and my lips felt cold. Sally took over and grabbed the cover from the steward. She flipped it over and got sick into it. *Morning sickness,* she told me silently, *is the bane of every pregnant woman's day.* She handed the disgusting cover over to be carried away and said aloud, "No meat before noon. Well-cooked eggs are acceptable, though never cooked any less than. Bring me fruit with sweet cream and toasted bread with preserves."

After eating, I went into my drawing room. I was going to pretend to read while I conferred with Sally on our next course of action. I did not have time. The steward announced, "Sir Paetus Crowley," and Paetus appeared. He bowed to me and sat across the room. It would seem that I would not have to deal with his gift of touch simply because he did not want the effects of my own gifts to affect his day.

The steward laid a package, long, narrow, and flat, on a table near the door and left. When the servant had left us alone, Paetus laughed. I smiled at the sound, wondering if it was what Julian would have done. "Scarcely a fortnight has passed and your mourning is done already?"

I looked down. I had forgotten with my newly widowed status, I should have worn my mourning black only. I had dressed in a comfortable pink that was highly inappropriate. Before I could speak, Paetus dismissed his previous statement with a wave and said, "Of course you were not expecting any callers and should not have to deal with any for some time."

"Save you, of course."

"I come bearing gifts, otherwise I would never have visited. It is highly improper for a bachelor to visit a widow during her mourning. I will not bother you again until society would be accepting. Seeing as I am already here, I would talk a while. How are you, old friend? How do you find your new body?"

"You should address me formally, or at least by Ramillia, even when we are in private. It will help you when I make my re-entry into society. And I find this body quite acceptable, but its current condition is wearying." My eyes went to the package. I wondered what it was. Should I already know? Would Julian have known?

Paetus saw my gaze and rose to collect the object of my attention. "It is for the child, the children, that you took that body. We could not let the previous owner even think about thwarting our plans. She did not know how valuable her ability to produce Carriers was." He laid the package on my lap and returned to his seat. "Though I haven't looked, I know they are beautiful. The tanner is the best and they were made to your specifications."

I carefully removed the brown wrapping paper and then opened the box with the tradesman's mark. Inside lay a pair of leather, elbow-length gloves. They were a very pale beige color and entirely devoid of decoration. Nevertheless they were quite beautiful. I could not help but touch them and I was not disappointed. They were as soft as possible. These were, by far, the nicest gloves I had ever seen.

"Try them on," Paetus urged. He went into the hallway while I complied and came back with a footman. The leather was even softer on the inside and I reveled in their comfort. The footman approached and took my leather-bound hand in his. He sighed and then brought the back of my hand to his cheek.

I watched this action and saw that my touch was satisfying, calming, to the servant. I looked at the gloves and noticed an oddity. Save the few stitches across the top of each fingertip, there were no seams at all. There were no places where the shape had been cut from a larger piece of leather and sewn together. I pondered what that meant.

These did not come from a larger piece. They were made in one piece and from an animal hide that had a hand just like mine. I put the puzzle together in my head. These were made from a human's skin. I kept myself from gasping in horror at the discovery, but the thought turned my stomach once more. I dismissed the footman, whose half-lidded eyes and slow gait told me whose skin they were made from.

I lost my breakfast into a nearby urn.

Paetus apologized. "I should have left them with the tanner longer so the aroma was not as pungent, but I knew you would be excited to see and test them. I am honestly surprised they retain any of the gift of touch you enjoyed in your previous body."

"But that body was destroyed, wasn't it?" Sally asked because she was terrified. If the body was out there, even mutilated, it could heal and Julian would have a place to return. Our nightmares would start again and this time Julian would be onto us.

"Of course, my friend. I would never endanger your hold on this body like that. After you left to gain your alibi, though I don't know where a woman could go in the middle of the night that could provide an acceptable exculpation, I bashed the head in and took the small amount of brain needed for the tanning, pulled the rafters down in your offices, and set the place on fire. I personally watched your ruined body burn. I made sure there was nothing left except this."

I threw up again at the thought of Julian's battered head spilling its mind onto the floor of his offices. Thoughtlessly I put my palm to my forehead and the calming effect of Julian flooded my senses. Paetus must have thought I used it on purpose. He sympathized, "I see what you mean about your exhausting condition. Come back to the club whenever you can. Let me know when your memories start to go. Perhaps reminiscing with me will allow you to keep them longer."

∽

I sent Moira out for errands and she came back with both a seamstress to take measurements for my mourning-maternity wardrobe and a message from Leonus. I read it while the draper went to work. The message was brief, having been written while Moira waited. It said he was glad I was feeling "like myself again," which was the phrase I used to tell him that I was me and not Julian, and for us to set up a meeting.

I had no idea what the meeting was for, though Sally knew. She wasn't telling, though, since Paetus could show up at any time and demand all manner of information from me. I dressed in my best and dullest black when the day came. I rode to the meeting address with apprehension.

When we stopped in front of a terrace, I was quickly ushered inside. The inside was much more luxurious than the middle-class outside appeared. Sally told me that Leonus had been lying to Paetus and Julian. He wasn't poor and he gained all his wealth through hard work. He and his Carriers pooled their money together to ensure a better life for the collective. He owned not only this terrace, but every row of houses on this street and the two to either side of it. His residence was at the heart of his Carriers' homes. He was completely safe here and so was I.

Leonus greeted me and I was shown into the parlor where a drably dressed older woman stood waiting. I noticed that her skirt tilted to one side before seeing the tiny hand clutching at it. I covered my mouth. Could this be her? Sally answered, *That is our Dawn. I gave her location to Leonus when we met him in Darville's inn. He has been protecting her.*

An adorable face, surrounded by golden curls much like mine, peeked around the gray skirts at me. Sally sat us down on a nearby settee and patted the space next to me. The woman pushed the girl out in front of her toward me. I didn't move. I did not want to scare Dawn on our first meeting. Not when who knows what horrors she had endured in her five years.

I had an uncontrollable fear take over and blurted out, "She wasn't r-ra…" except I couldn't finish the question. I did not know how I would live with myself if she had been abused and raped as Sally and I had.

The woman, a high-priced nanny I guessed, said, "No, my lady. Though she was in a house of ill repute, she was not used in that manner. It seems the women there, such as they were, had enough honor not to allow any man to buy her or even see her. She has never felt the strap nor fist. As far as we can tell the worst she sustained was being underfed."

I let out a breath I hadn't known I was holding and I watched my daughter approach. Dawn was tall for her age and very thin, as if her flesh could not keep pace with her bones. She had my face. No trace of foreign features betrayed the identity of her father. When she built the courage to sit beside me, I held out my gloved hand and nearly wept when she took it. Sally reached into our reticule and pulled out a bracelet. I put it on Dawn's wrist and showed her how pretty the jingles sounded. She smiled.

I told her they were not half as pretty as her smile. I declared I was her mother and that she had been taken from me. I had never wanted to give her away and I would spend every waking moment from then on loving her and protecting her. I patted my belly where her sibling grew and told her she was to be a big sister. We were to be a real family.

A mother's love is hard to numerate. I had only seen Dawn in Sally's memory and then only for a few moments and yet I loved her in so great a way that I cannot describe. The device pinned to the inside of my bodice glowed so blue that it shone through the dress fabric. I knew then that my feelings for Dawn were true. There was nothing affecting my emotions that could be brought to doubt. I did not manage to hold back the tears when she threw her arms around my neck, the beaded bracelet twinkling gaily.

PART TWO

WRETCHED BLOOD

My daughter, Dawn, killed my son when she was only twelve years of age, the same at which I had murdered my own parents. Ambrose, whose name ironically means immortal, had just passed his fifth birthday.

1

The thought of burning my baby boy was too horrible to bear. He looked so peaceful laying in the half-sized coffin that I could not do it. Though I knew the consequences of not destroying his body, Ambrose, complete and uncut, dressed in his best, was laid to rest in consecrated ground near where my parents were buried.

I had never once visited their graves. Those hateful, perverted child molesters didn't deserve to be mourned or known, so I had hired a mason to chisel out every bit of information on their stones. I would be free to visit my son's plot without having to endure even the sight of their names.

Two days after his funeral, we went to see the completed headstone. We stepped out of the carriage and the fog washed over us. Thick, white fog amplified the daylight. Normally no sane person would venture out in a fog this bad, but I needed to see my baby's marker and, since the air smelled sweet and it wasn't the dreaded deadly yellow color, I took the chance. Neither I nor my household could die of disease or smog anyway.

Our family, rich and important, owned a fenced section of the cemetery, far from the noise and filth of the city. The summer heat was oppressive already, made nigh on unbearable by our mourning blacks. Dawn walked beside me, her back straight in her children's stays, her head held high. Her face lacked any sign of remorse for what she'd done. Paetus walked behind her, a silent, approving shadow.

Extraordinary contraptions, meant to keep the dead in the ground, littered the graveyard. Each one emerged from the blinding fog as we approached and then disappeared behind us. This hysteria probably resulted from our poor medical understanding. The line between alive and dead blurred because they didn't understand the body as a machine nor what made it tick. We didn't embalm and only rarely performed autopsies. It was not uncommon for living people to be buried. Scratch marks discovered on the insides of their caskets gave rise to belief in the undead. Victorians were very superstitious, terrified their loved ones would rise from the dead and wreak havoc on the living. Such horrors did indeed exist for my kind, but most people had nothing to fear. Their deceased would remain so.

What happened with Ambrose was worse than even those irrational humans could have imagined.

I cannot portray the level of hope that filled me to hear the ringing of the tiny bell that the mortician had insisted be installed, its string threaded through a pipe and fed into an opening in my son's casket. *Don't, Ramillia. Ambrose is dead. The thing ringing the bell is not him,* Sally pleaded. Worse than hope was the despair that occupied the vacuum left by that momentary prospect. Moans and scrabbling sounds coming from inside enhanced the dread. I silently berated myself for not burning the body.

When the first shovel hit wood, the men scrambled out of the grave. One stood on the lid until the last moment, keeping it shut with his weight. Several men grabbed his arms and yanked him out in one swift motion. I held my breath as the coffin opened. I know not why, for there was no doubt that my Ambrose was deceased. The body that tried to climb from the hole was dead, of that much I am sure. The reanimated corpse was rotting, stinking, putrid. It hungered, but for what I doubt even it knew.

The thing that had been my son in life stared at us with clouded eyes. It reached for us with ruined hands, bloodied by its fight to escape the grave. Bone protruded from the end where flesh hung. Even so, I still longed to scoop him up, cuddle him as I had been prevented from doing in life. After all, it did have Ambrose's face. I made a minor movement, a lifting of my own arms toward him, before Sally could stop me. His attention caught, he locked onto me as the source of what he hungered for, and his efforts to escape the dirt hole renewed in a frenzy. Frustrated sounds poured from him in a continuous stream, only interrupted by the snapping of his teeth.

I will never wipe that vision from my memory.

My guards moved to end that macabre dance and Dawn screamed at them. My daughter took the shovel from the yellowed grass where our man had dropped it, and, pressing it against the undead Ambrose's neck, pushed the shovel blade through his throat. I looked away but that sickening sound alone, when the shovel head severed the spine, might have been worse than the sight. Paetus looked proud of her actions and she looked up with admiration at him. The head was placed below the feet and a lit oil lamp thrown in as added assurance that healing could not occur.

Ambrose was stripped of his soul, murdered by his sister, beheaded, and incinerated in his grave. My goal in life had been to keep them safe and healthy. Oh, how I had failed.

∽

Memory is a peculiar thing. It is completely dependent on the mood through which an event is seen. Joy can give us rose-colored glasses while sorrow or dread may stain an otherwise beautiful experience. My son, Ambrose, was born on the twenty-third of June. I remember the day as sunny and bright but Sally is quite certain it was gray and drizzling when we pushed him from our body and into the world.

I once attended a presentation of human oddities. While the woman scarcely larger than a toddler and the man as hairy as a bear fascinated me, I felt an instant kinship with the conjoined twins. They, like Sally and I, shared their body and their lives though they were by no means the same person. One loved opera while the other couldn't stand it. One was obsessed with trains but had to satisfy her craving through study and observation since riding a locomotive made the other violently ill.

And so it was with us: separate but bound together. Early on we decided there would be no struggle between us, no battle for control. I would never stop Sally from something she wanted and in return she would treat me in the same manner. I fear that throughout our extraordinarily long life, I enjoyed the lion's share of time at the helm, but she never complained. Sally and I possess a common driving goal: to survive together. Secondary to that is our desire to protect our offspring from the childhood that we had and from the powerful male Incola who sought to rule and ruin their adulthood.

We were determined to never allow an Incola to ride us, or our children, ever again.

We abandoned Julian's fine London home on Park Lane after his death and gave birth to Ambrose at my family's country estate, Brooksberry Manor. At Dawn's birth, we were thirteen, imprisoned by the state at West Freeman Asylum for Lunatics for the murder of our parents. Sally gave birth all alone in that filthy place of horrors while I slumbered, unknowing, in the darkness. This time, we did it together, determined to surround ourselves with beauty and nature. London was a grimy and unsanitary place in those days. Our enemies surrounded us. We did not want to be there in our weakened postpartum state, unable to protect our children.

I was conscious for Ambrose's birth, unlike Dawn's. Sally, ever stronger and more determined than I, did the pushing, but I felt every contraction and suffered every tear just as vividly as she. Our son was breech. Labor with him was more difficult, more painful, and lengthier than that with Dawn. I had no doubt we were dying at the time, so great was the pain, and suspect our heightened healing ability saved us. Sally did not believe we were ever in any real danger. Both of us agree the memory of that pain and struggle was dimmed and blurred by the joy of holding Ambrose for the first time.

A beautiful baby, as Dawn had been, he was brunet while she was fair-haired like us. I thought he looked much like my brother Thaddeus, while Sally said he favored Albert, the man we estimated was his father. His eyes were the blue all babies had but they focused on us immediately, with none of the fog most newborns have. Intelligence filled his eyes and he looked around, not restricted to the objects in a normal baby's range. Ambrose never cried, not even when the doctor prodded him and slapped his bare rump. He simply coughed the liquid from his lungs and replaced it with air.

We loved him instantly and reveled in the fact that, as a child of ours, he would never die. Dawn, when allowed in the birthing room, skipped in, her golden curls bouncing, her gown flouncing, excited to meet her brother at last. She had hoped for a sister but seemed to take the news of a boy quite well. Her governess fussed that she should be calm and quiet but we said nothing. We liked her exuberance and, as we were neither frail nor fragile, we did not see the importance.

"This is your brother, Ambrose. What do you think, Dawn? Isn't he beautiful?" I asked her.

Dawn bounded up the steps to our bed and crawled to where we held Ambrose. Her bright smile faded when she set eyes to his face. Ambrose seemed excited by her, cooing and reaching out to his sister. She sniffed the air and squinted at him. Sally sensed the danger before I did and reached our hand out to block Dawn's dive. Her arms stretched out for him, her hands like claws scraping at the air.

Her governess pulled her from the room with difficulty, even with the help of a footman. Dawn's strength was a portion of our own but still much more than a human adult possessed. Even with the door closed we could hear our daughter screaming, "I hate him. Hate him! Let me go, you old hag!"

∽

We realize this must seem quite shocking. You might even wonder how we did not foresee the dreadful events that followed. Neither of us had any experience with Carrier children. We could not go to Paetus, who was the obvious choice for such inquiries, because to admit we had troubles with our daughter was to admit we *had* a daughter. As soon as Paetus knew of Dawn, he would claim her by right. He had long ago signed a contract with Julian for our firstborn daughter's hand in marriage. Julian, though dead, was still head of our household as my husband and any agreements he had made, or legal arrangements, had to be honored.

We hid Dawn in our country home. She was not allowed outside and no one else knew she was alive. The closest she got to nature was the atrium I had built for her within the confines of the house. It was well-stocked with beautiful plants and trees that blossomed in the sunlight coming through the glass roof. Advances in glass and iron manufacturing brought on by the Industrial Revolution allowed this technological marvel. Little Dawn loved the space.

We walked a thin line between gilded cage and controlled, sculpted grandeur. It was our beautiful slice of the outside world. Fish and frogs populated the pond and delighted Ambrose. At one end, a variety of tiny, twittering birds filled a devoted aviary. In this area Dawn most often sought solitude from her brother, who couldn't abide the squawking. My lady's maid, who was just as taken with the tiny flyers as Dawn, could be found there regularly. She, Dawn, and I often played hide-and-seek and hopscotch there. It was odd that the very glass that allowed us to keep the canaries in a natural but contained environment was also their destruction. We often found them with their necks broken, presumably from flying toward freedom only to be thwarted by false hopes and the invisible boundary.

Our children's relationship started roughly and didn't improve much. Occasionally I saw that they bonded, like a ray of sunlight cutting through the clouds, but like that weather, it was always short-lived. Ambrose adored Dawn and followed her around. She, being confined to the house, had no escape from this toddling chase. Dawn had wild mood swings when it came to her dealings with her brother. One minute they played quietly together, the next she screamed at him for no apparent reason. She shied from her brother's touch but even that was not considered abnormal for the time. Physical contact was a strictly monitored and socially mandated restriction. My mother rarely touched me or my brother, and I shuddered to think of the times the full weight of Papa's attention had fallen on me. I was determined that Dawn's childhood be better than mine had been, but I could not allow my skin to come into contact with hers. I was a Carrier blessed with the gift of touch. Mine was the power to excite. We did not know the full effect it would have on her, so even her mother's appropriate affections were withheld from Dawn.

We thought we were so careful, thought Dawn's existence was truly kept a secret, but in reality we did little more than unjustly imprison her for the duration of her childhood. Servants were barely seen as people. They came and went by the hundreds, some without permanent employment as a weak bribe for their silence. For instance, Ambrose's birth employed a midwife, a local doctor, two nurses, and a wet nurse. We did nothing to hide her life from them. They were temporary employees, free to leave with that knowledge of incalculable value.

Being the lady of Brooksberry Manor, I was more than royalty to the people of the countryside. I was *their* royalty. I had grown up there and everyone from the merchants down to the bar maidens wanted to know every detail of my life, from what gown I wore to what books I read. The existence of an illegitimate child was, no doubt, the high spot of many a conversation. Her continued violent and unpredictable behavior fueled the gossip further.

It could not be denied, even by my blinded Victorian brain, that there was something very wrong with Dawn. We consulted what books there were, all vastly lacking in factual information. The medical and psychological fields improved too slowly for our use. They were still ruled by superstition and tradition, both steeped in sexist beliefs that the female mind and body were inferior to the male in every way.

We learned little more than we guessed on our own. Dawn survived her infancy and, if she had any, her physical congenital birth defects were not obvious. I worried that the need for violence, a trait both my father and I shared, lurked just beneath the surface. Developmental and behavioral problems are expected with a child born of an incestuous relationship. Dawn had no problems learning, though her years as a secret ward in a house of ill repute had retarded her development. Though not abused, she had been underfed. Without the proper nutrients, her brain had suffered. Neglect caused odd behaviors too, as if she wasn't truly aware that other people could fully see and hear her. She was desperate for our attention, which we gave, but we thought she must have seen the new baby as a threat to her tenuous grasp on our affections. We consoled ourselves with the most reasonable explanations.

∽

It came as quite a shock when not one, but three clergymen arrived on my doorstep one morning.

My parents didn't receive visitors at our country estate, not in the thirteen summers of my childhood. Perhaps it was Julian's doing. He had orchestrated my very birth and social placement. It was not such a stretch to think he controlled my day-to-day life even before I knew of his existence or involvement. I thought my parents had valued their privacy as much as we did.

Even now, few visited Brooksberry Manor.

I went outside with a few guards when my butler could not convince the religious men to leave. They each wanted to call upon me but their behavior had me on alert and I didn't trust them inside my home. Of the three, I recognized only Father Taylor. The others were a Catholic priest and a man obviously from the Far East, his costume vaguely religious but foreign in both texture and design. Epicanthic eyelids folded over almond-shaped eyes. I greeted my parish vicar first, whose behavior was most shocking. He never visited. I said politely, "Father Taylor, how unexpected. What brings you and your friends to my doorstep this morning?"

The look on his face told me he did not consider the other men his friends. He made no move to introduce them to me. He gestured to the priest on his left, completely ignoring the Asian on his right. "I have been trying to convince him that you wouldn't be interested in the services he's here to offer, but he is quite stubborn. I've told him you would not be interested in allowing the Catholic Church such an active role in your life nor the lives of your children."

I froze at the mention of my offspring in the plural then turned to the priest and said, "And what services might those be?"

He stepped toward me and my guards intercepted him. He stopped his advance and spoke softly. "The decision about the education of your son is one of the most important of your life and his. I propose that the Roman Catholic Church is the smartest choice for such an undertaking."

Father Taylor spoke up, "If Lady Brooksberry were inclined to give her son a religious education, she certainly wouldn't choose a stranger. She would use the Church of England and, since I am the vicar of her parish, that responsibility would fall to me."

The priest spoke over his shoulder. "And why, pray tell, would she give the education of her children over to a man who, at best, overlooked or, at worst, *ignored* her own childhood abuse? I would think you would be the very last choice for the responsibility of educating the children who were the result of said abuse."

I stood mortified as the priest laid my dirty laundry bare for the whole world to witness. Sally was livid. Before I could consider an appropriate response to such brashness, my better half let loose a tirade that would curl the hair of even the saltiest seaman. The shock on the clergymen's faces said they were unaccustomed to such language and had not expected it from a lady like myself. A tug at my skirts caught my attention. Ambrose stood there, looking up at me with his overly intelligent eyes, enthralled by the use of rough language.

I took over the scolding. "I had never thought you were prone to gossip, Father. It would be unfathomable that you would share such information with a perfect stranger if I had not heard evidence of this betrayal of trust with my own ears. If I hear wind that you have been spreading rumors about me again, I will take your parish and give it over to the keeping of my stableman."

He stood there, his mouth flapping like a fish out of water. I dismissed him and turned to the priest. "How dare you speak of such sensitive matters in public, especially as you and I are not acquainted in the slightest? That alone is enough to influence me away from any involvement with you." I stepped toward him. "The vicar is quite right about one thing. My children, both current and future, will be secularly educated, clear of the judgment of Christian men."

"It seems the perfect moment for my own proposal." The Asian's accent was as odd as his attire, even as he had mastered the Queen's English. "I can offer you just that, a secular education. My ancestors were the first to write, the inventors of paper, printing, the compass, and gunpowder. Our mathematicians were the first to use negative numbers. China has a history of science applied to horology, metallurgy, astronomy, agriculture, engineering, music theory, craftsmanship, naval architecture, and warfare. Who better to serve you and teach your children?"

"The Church *perfected* the art of learning and teaching," the Catholic argued.

"It may be true that your organization has forced a monopoly on reading and writing for centuries past in this area and every one within the reach of your leader, but why would any sensible person free of superstition wish to perpetuate the teachings of a lying religious tyrant?"

The priest, inflamed by the verbal abuse of his Pope, struck the Chinese scholar with an open hand. The clergyman had rage on his side but the Asian seemed better trained in fighting. Both landed several solid blows before the foreigner swept the priest's legs out from under him. He hit the ground hard, his head striking the first step. The pool of dark red blood grew around him like a grotesque halo.

Father Taylor rushed to his side. Excluding his inability to keep secrets, my vicar was a good man who cared about life, regardless of religious affiliation. He carefully lifted the injured man. "He is alive. Will you help me get him to the parish? I have medical supplies there and we can nurse him as he heals."

With a hand on his shoulder, I stopped Ambrose, who crept toward the wounded man and his dark stain. I instructed my guards to escort the men. They could use one of my carriages. I watched as they left, promising to visit and check on our patient. Intrigued by what the Chinaman had said, I even considered his offer. Giving my children every advantage I could afford was a priority, even if it came from an unusual source.

∽

Moira was still my lady's maid, though society would not find her suitable, so unforgiving were they of her previous profession. She worked as a prostitute before her pimp had her lobotomized and her unborn aborted in the asylum where I had been imprisoned.

Moira kept herself tidy and assisted me into my more complicated dresses, but beyond that she helped little. The fact was, I enjoyed having her near. She was the first I had saved, the first instance I had used my great strength for good. Sally says that is not quite right. We used our strength to kill Papa when he threatened to root Dawn, his daughter by his daughter, out of our womb. That was the first, but since I hadn't remembered that chain of events until much later, I continued to think of Moira as my first success.

That first day, when I pulled her from the lobotomy table and took her into my care, she emptied one of my dress trunks and made her home inside. She seemed happy with her odd choice, retreating there at night after completing her duties and anytime she was frightened or insecure. Small spaces soothed her; large open ones seemed to do the opposite. Maybe that was why she loved the atrium so much. Similar to being outside, it wasn't as immense or fearsome as the actual outdoors.

Moira helped me get dressed for my trip to see the priest, as she always did. It was a much bigger job than one might imagine. In those days, every activity, every event, every occasion required a special costume. There were day dresses and evening gowns, suits for bicycle riding and archery, outfits for traveling by coach or train, dresses for dinner and ones only suited for breakfast, dressing gowns and night gowns. Our attire was not as simple as it is now, either. Every set involved dozens of pieces: some stitched on, not just fastened. Moira, with her diminished mental capacity, managed to make herself useful in her position.

The other servants felt indignant at her lofty position. As maid of the lady of the house, she ranked first among the female staff. Most did not believe she deserved such access. But she was my confidante. Because of her near inability to communicate, I could share everything with her, knowing full well my secrets were safe. Moira held strands of my hair while I arranged it in an elaborate up-do and discussed my thoughts on having the Chinaman teach my children. I left after accessorizing with the correct amount of jewelry.

With only a few guards in attendance, I went to check on our injured priest and speak with the foreigner. The parish chapel was familiar to me, though my family had never been very pious. We financed it and that satisfied the church. Father Taylor met me on the steps. Neither of the other two men accompanied him. The priest had woken and an argument ensued. The Chinaman had killed the Catholic. Father said the Asian had not denied it. He awaited his execution, a foreigner who did not warrant a trial. The man could have resisted arrest easily enough but he went peacefully as long as the jailers allowed him to retain a parcel. He had asked Father Taylor to tell me of his location and his desire to speak with me. When Father said that the foreigner claimed to be a Carrier of something that involved me, I realized he was more than a simple scholar. I went straight to see him.

The jail shared very little with the West Freeman Asylum for Lunatics, and yet going to see the foreigner made me uneasy. The sun never penetrated the cells, making them the same dark, moist places of hopelessness where I had lost so many years of my young life. I wanted to tear it down by hand but Sally steadied me. Either this Chinaman was a dangerous, bloodthirsty murderer and deserved to be here or he was a Carrier, fully capable of escaping by himself. I reminded her that the two were not mutually exclusive.

The foreigner sat in the center of the floor, eyes closed, his legs crossed and twisted in a most unusual way, his hands resting palm-side up on his knees.

I remembered the levels of filth that made us feel as if we would never be truly clean again. The dirt and mold crept from every surface, invading every pore until we were more dirt than flesh, were vivid in our mind. This man sat here a few hours at the most and already his beautiful tunic was completely soiled. Carrier or no, Sally and I had a connection with this prisoner.

He stood, introducing himself as Ning Shiru. I, ignorant of the fact that surnames came first in his culture, said, "Well, Mr. Shiru, I was actually considering you for the position of tutor to my child but…" I let him think that his actions precluded him from the position.

Bowing deeply from the waist, he said nothing in his defense, but slipped a bundle of parchment into my hand. Unfolding it, I was stunned to find the first few pages of a letter to the Pope from the now-dead priest. It described not only Dawn's existence and appearance but also her conception. It depicted our day-to-day life and level of security, or lack thereof. The priest admitted that he intended to approach me about insinuating himself into our lives and if that didn't go well, he advised that the Church take the "female" by force.

"I killed him to prevent this information from reaching Rome," Ning Shiru said. "I gained you some time but how much, I do not know. This Incola is relentless and power-hungry. He will send more men to investigate. He wants a female."

"And you?" Sally accused. "I suppose you did this out of the goodness of your heart and have no ulterior motives, no desire for a woman of your own."

A jailer walked by at that moment to spy on us so he waited to answer me until our privacy was restored. "Our society should center around females, protecting them, helping them gain position and prestige, and aiding them in holding that power. Most of our kind in this part of the world have strayed from those values. It is not so in my homeland. Enlightenment is most difficult to attain. There are no limitations of how I can help my fellow sentient. I did not kill the priest; karma did. By destroying that evil, I have helped this family. I look forward to separation from the body and the following nirvana. I will be free from suffering and desire. I will be liberated from this physical imprisonment."

"You will *die*," I argued.

"Only my flesh will perish. I will separate myself from my body as I have done on many occasions."

I envisioned the obvious outcome. "You will take possession of another."

"My order, which I will call religious for lack of a better word, does exchange bodies as part of our ceremonies but it is purely for achieving greater levels of enlightenment. We experience the desires of all mankind, not just our own. I would never take *over* the life of another. I came here to aid a blossoming family that has the chance to change the world for the better, knowing that when my usefulness was spent, I would finish living."

"What will happen to you? To your spirit?"

"It is not certain. I have only had a taste of what is to come during times of deep meditation. I will pass into a state of pure being." He retrieved a bag from inside his robes and pushed it through the bars. "I can do one more thing for this family."

Taking it from him, I found inside several more letters, a column of red wax, and the priest's ring seal. The letters all appeared to be in the priest's handwriting but their correspondence greatly varied in content from the first letter. The first one stated that he had met me and I was indeed a female Carrier but my firstborn child, a boy, had left me barren. It said there existed no female child and that he moved on to investigate the next rumor. I realized these had not been written by the priest at all. They were to misdirect the Pope.

"Forgery is a talent of mine. Send the first one right away and one every month after that. By the time they stop coming, the eyes of Rome will be far from your island and you can escape scrutiny. Be sure to use the seal." He retook his seat on the floor.

I pulled an odd ivory-colored cylinder from the bottom of the bag after redepositing the espionage items. Rough and hard like stone, its lavishly carved exterior depicted an angry mob. The question must have been clear on my face as I lifted my eyes because Ning Shiru said, "That is a gift."

"But what is it?"

"I do not know. Legend says only a female can wield it. Open it when you deem the time is right, for it can only be used once. It can save the world." Then he closed his eyes and I knew he would speak to me no more.

∽

I mailed the first of Mr. Shiru's forgeries as soon as I reached home, giving it to the butler for delivery only after properly sealing it with melted wax and the dead priest's ring.

Sitting alone in my dressing room that evening, I pulled the cylinder out to study it. The carvings were more detailed than I could see in the dark jail.

Comparably bright gaslight revealed more than an angry mob. Their fury was directed at a beautiful woman who stood surrounded by a few apparently doting men. I believe they were courting the woman, but that was less a carved detail and more a general feeling that came over me when I looked at it.

Ning Shiru had said that only a female could wield it, leading me to think it was a weapon, but what sort of weapon could only be used once? I could see no opening nor trigger. Not wanting to activate it accidentally, I lay it on my desk to examine it further. As soon as it left my hands, waves of unease flowed from my chest to my arms, urging me to pick it up once again, and I realized it had not left my possession since I first held it. Forcing myself to leave it where it lay, I looked again. The carved figures stood in fierce contrast to the semi-transparent blue background. Upon closer inspection, I found the cylinder held a glass tube filled with liquid.

Ambrose burst through my door dressed in his bed clothes. Dawn followed solemnly behind with their nanny keeping watch from the door. With effort, I turned my back to the mysterious object. "My apologies," the nanny said. "He was having difficulty and promises to go right to sleep after saying goodnight to you."

"Of course," I assured her. My son dashed toward me but stopped just out of arm's length. How I wished things were different and I could smooth his hair, soothe whatever kept him awake, and kiss his cheeks. "Goodnight, my sweet boy."

"G'night, Mama," he replied with his baby lisp.

His eyes darted about and he gnawed his lips. I did not press him to speak his mind, wanting him to grow into a confident man, able to choose when to speak and when to be silent. I turned to Dawn to wish her the same good sleep and found her holding the cylinder. "I've seen one of these before."

The feeling that came over me was similar to that rage I felt when coming in contact with a Carrier of a specific bloodline. Unreasonable and uncontrollable, it grew. I had owned the supposed weapon less than a day but felt possessive. Did Dawn know what it was? Did she intend to take it from me? She was a female. Perhaps she intended to wield it in my place. I could not allow that, would go to any lengths to have it back.

Saving me from my spiral into violence, Sally said, "You have?" Taking the cylinder from our daughter eased my rising rage. "When?" she asked. "Do you know what this is?"

The look in her eyes told me what I had feared was true. Dawn felt the same as I. The object had a draw on her as well. Tucking it into the pocket of my skirts broke whatever spell held her gaze. "A puzzle box?" Dawn guessed. "I had one a long time ago. You must find the right areas to push or way to turn it and it opens. There was a treat in mine." She paused, her brow furrowed as she tried to recall. "I think there were flowers and birds on it. I remember working on it for a long time but not where I was. You had to press the bird and the bee at the same time while twisting."

Emotions mixed into a dangerous cocktail as I realized it must have been during her stay at the house of ill repute. The prostitutes had raised her when I was ignorant of her existence and they had to find ways to occupy her attention while going about their illicit business. I was thankful her memories of this time had faded.

"That is no toy," Ambrose said. The childlike quality of his voice stood in stark contrast to the seriousness of his tone. "I fear it."

"Why do you say that?" I asked.

He said nothing. Shaking his head repeatedly, he backed from the room, never taking his eyes from my skirt and I knew two things. One: I must never leave him nor my daughter alone with the cylinder. Two: his visit to me would not ease his difficulty going to sleep.

∽

We did not attend the execution of Ning Shiru. The sharp pang of guilt was too much to bear. The sight of the gallows reminded me of my brother Thaddeus, whose sacrifice to Julian had purchased my freedom. I refused to believe Thaddeus had been unredeemable. Though he had abused me in much the same manner my father had, his passion and anger originated from my gift of touch. Papa preferred the bodies of young girls. I had been found naked, covered in the blood of my parents, standing amongst their mutilated bodies. I had killed them but so much time had passed since the gory discovery that Julian easily framed Thaddeus for the crime. Julian had ridden my brother through a confession and right up to the hangman.

No one forced Ning Shiru. He sacrificed himself to protect our secret. I could have bought off the officials and had him released but it would cause a scandal. The Pope would have eventually heard. Even the dullest of men would deduce that the only reason for me to protect a murderer would be if the recipient of that pardon had perpetrated the crime for me.

For his selfless act, I put on my finest black dress and paid tribute at the grave. Normally an executed person would burn in the crematorium but I paid secretly to have his body buried in the ground with a modest but proud headstone.

Because he was a heathen and a foreigner, the church would not permit his body on consecrated ground. In fact, he was not buried anywhere near the cemetery, but out in the country. The peaceful and solitary locale suited him, in my opinion, and made it easier for me to visit without calling attention to my actions.

My guards held back, allowing me to grieve in relative solitude. Once under the canopy of trees, I closed my parasol and hung it on a loop of my skirt near the secret pocket where I kept the cylinder. Not one to pray, I whispered my apologies, in case his spirit hovered nearby. I turned to go but an odd crumbling sound stopped me. A small mound of earth near the center of the grave grew, like a mole burrowed from underneath. I paused to watch and discover what sort of varmint was brave enough to venture out with me so nearby. What emerged shocked me.

At first I thought it was the tip of a snout. Then a second appeared beside it and I realized they were fingers. Ning Shiru wasn't dead. I dropped to my knees and clawed at the ground, screaming for my men to help me. His freed hand grasped for mine and I held it, assuring him that I wasn't going anywhere, that we would extricate him from his internment. I encouraged my guards to dig faster. I praised the Chinaman mentally for devising such a plan and having the strength of character to carry it out without a single hint to me about his intentions. This was genius; no one would be the wiser and no attention would be called to us.

Nothing but dirt and his death shroud separated him from us. I tore away the latter when the former was removed. This man wasn't right. Gone were the warm, intelligent eyes I had seen only yesterday. They were milky cataract-covered monstrosities. I scrambled back as he latched onto my gown with his mouth. My guards pulled me from the pit. Shiru came soon after. One guard clamped an arm around his throat and two more grasped each arm. His inhuman speed gone, Shiru struggled with restrained strength, trying to get to me. Slow as he was, his desperation gave him an advantage.

Shiru bit into the forearm of the guard holding him from behind, tearing out a chunk of meat. The injured man screamed and released the captive, falling into the open grave. I tried to speak to Shiru, to calm him down and assure him we were no threat. He stared blankly at me as he chewed and swallowed the severed muscle. Shiru stepped to his right, leaning, his mouth open and ready for his next bite. Attempting to keep clear of that maw, the guard on that side pushed him away.

Shiru fell onto the guard left holding him. Startled, I stepped back and lost my footing, twisting an ankle and dropping on my side. Though the cracking sound resembled breaking bones, I felt no pain. The cane tube of my parasol had splintered into a sharp point at the top. Grasping the crook, I held it out in front of me as a weapon while the other hand checked to make sure the cylinder was unscathed.

Shiru clamped his teeth down on the neck of the man under him. More screaming filled the air. The guard struggled and pushed but Shiru was undeterred from his dinner. He pulled away and the skin between his teeth stretched and then snapped, leaving a jagged and bloody hole. He looked at me as he chewed, arterial spray hitting him in the chest and face. He had struck an artery and my guard bled out quickly.

The last guard hurled a rock, striking Shiru's skull. Shiru's neck, already weakened from the gallows, snapped. He collapsed seconds later with his head dangling at an impossibly odd angle. The last man standing rushed to his associates' aid and the other crawled out of the grave to help but not much could be done. As a Carrier he could have healed a cut or slice but regenerating the missing flesh would take more time than the downed man had. He was pale and already cool to the touch.

I told the guard from the grave to apply pressure to the neck of his fallen companion with his good arm. The third man carried the one near death back to my waiting carriage. I leaned over Ning Shiru's body to grasp him by the shoulders and drag him back to his grave. I froze. Though his body lay motionless, his eyes searched and mouth chewed. His broken neck had only paralyzed his body, but everything above the neck still worked. His strong jaw was still dangerous.

Hands on my hips, I considered how to kill something that was already dead. After witnessing the deaths of many Carriers I wondered what made this one special. Plenty of their lives ended by hanging and severed spinal cords. The lessons Julian had taught me came to mind and the answer seemed obvious.

I stabbed the pointed end of my ruined sunshade up through the neck, jaw, mouth and into the brain. Just as I had done with the performer who had enraged me upon my first visit to the Incola Club, I moved my hand side to side, scrambling his brain like an egg in the hands of a kitchen maid. That did the job. Shiru was truly dead.

The truth was clear: it was our body, our biology, that made us Carriers. Our brains made us Incola.

~

Upon my return home, I sat and penned a letter to Leonus, detailing the events of the day, while Sally shouted orders. What a spectacle we must have made doing two completely different tasks, my hand seemingly writing on its own without any attention of my mind. Leonus, a contemporary of Julian and Paetus, was my ally. He did not have the same greedy ambitions as those two. He had no wish to rule the world with the largest army of Carriers on the planet. I entrusted him with questions, the man who supported my actions in the Incola world. He was the one who found my daughter after we thought she was lost forever and gave her back to me; he knew that priceless secret and had never betrayed my trust.

I forbade him from visiting me. I received no callers while in the country. I claimed I didn't want to call attention to myself. In truth, fooling myself into believing we were a normal family became simplified when everyone surrounding me was human. I thought that leaving Carriers behind meant I could be clear of that world. I was mistaken.

My country estate was a six-hour ride outside of London, on a fast horse. The steam engine locomotive allowed for a much shorter trip if a train came through at the right time. My messenger would barely make the last one of the night and would ride on one of the cars, no matter if it were for animal, coal, human, or vegetable, so that he could deliver the letter personally. Leonus and I had exchanged many letters over my years of self-inflicted exile and this method of delivery was most reliable.

I sent for the doctor to tend to my injured men and then went to clean up. Moira was nowhere to be found, her trunk empty save her few possessions, and she did not answer my calls. I rang down to the atrium but when she did not return after a few minutes, I examined my gown. It was my best black and I could have torn it from my body but didn't want to ruin it. I washed the gore from my face and hands as best I could. The dress could be cleaned.

I went up to the next floor and asked if Dawn could help me. She seemed surprised by my request but happy for the opportunity to spend extra time with me alone. I showed her where the laces were and gave her the seam-ripper. Careful not to come into direct contact with my skin, she worked silently out of fright, I think. Watching her in the looking glass, I suddenly realized that she was on the cusp of womanhood. Soon her childhood would be no more than a memory.

She asked what had happened. I said only that protecting that which we love sometimes requires violence and that being a female didn't mean that we must shy from those bloody obligations. "You should never be too frightened to do what is necessary. I will protect you from everything I can but someday, something unpleasant might fall to you. Do you understand?"

"Yes, Mama, I do, but…"

I turned to look at her and gestured to the footstool in front of me. "But what, Dawn?"

She sat on the footstool and chewed on her lip before asking, "How do I know the difference between what is necessary and what I *want* to do?" I waited, not quite understanding what she meant. "I get so angry sometimes that I cannot think straight. My mind is muddled with…urges…to hurt people."

A normal mother would touch her daughter in an attempt to comfort. My hands remained in my lap. "It is in your nature—our nature—to hunger for exertion and even violence."

"Were you feeding your hunger for violence or fulfilling a necessity to protect when they imprisoned you?" Our solitude emboldened her to speak in a way that was unconventional in our time but not enough to ask directly what I had done to be institutionalized.

Feeling that she had something to add, Sally spoke. "It was a little bit of both. There was a lot of pent-up rage about my life but I managed to contain it until they threatened to kill someone that I loved."

"Who?"

"You, Dawn."

Her curiosity overwhelmed her decorum. "You killed your parents because they threatened to kill me?"

Because we had never spoken of the specifics to her before and none of our staff had permission to discuss such an intimate subject, I was stunned that she knew. "Who told you who I'd killed?" Sally asked, already making a short list in her head concerning punishments for those who'd betrayed our trust so completely.

"I've always known. The women where I lived before you found me said that I couldn't have you when I asked for my Mama, because you were in an asylum for killing your mother and father."

Those women, prostitutes, had protected her from disappointment, I told Sally silently. They did not want her to set her heart on something impossible.

They were, most likely, preparing her for the life she would have been forced into if Leonus had not found her, Sally argued. *Selling your body is only possible after the desolation of your dreams. They were sparing her that pain by not allowing her to entertain the hope of salvation.* Sally answered her original question. "Yes, I murdered my parents because they threatened to kill you, before you were even born."

"Like the doctors did to Moira before you saved her?"

I knew then that she had seen Moira's most prized possession, the preserved fetus—her unborn aborted baby—floating in a jar that she kept in her trunk. "Yes," I said, not wanting to delve further into this conversation concerning sexual relations. We were only a step away from questions about how we came to be with child.

I chose my most comfortable gown for family dinner with my children and slipped it on without any assistance. Adding a layer of safety with gloves, I held my hand out to Dawn only after moving the cylinder from the previous gown to the current one. "Come along. Let us see what has kept Moira."

We went straight to the atrium. Moira hadn't answered my summons but she never went anywhere else. We often brought food to her or she refused to eat. She wouldn't abandon her trunk for anything except the aviary, not even her own health. Had there been a fire, she would have died in that trunk rather than leave it.

We felt something was off as we entered at the pond end. Dawn looked up at me and then ran to the other end where the twittering of birds should have been nearly deafening. The silence was unnatural. I followed her, the gravel loud beneath my footsteps. The trees rustled, *moving in the wind.* Completely enclosed on all sides including the glass top ceiling, the atrium should have had no wind.

Dawn leaned out of the three-meter-tall windows that made up the wall. "They are all gone! Someone opened these and let my birds escape." She clutched me around my waist, weeping.

Taught since I was very small that physical touch was not only wrong but dangerous, I forced myself not to recoil. Patting her awkwardly, I said, "There, there, Dawn."

The netting on that side of the enclosure had been torn down. This was no accident. I gently pushed Dawn away to examine smatterings of blood on the ground under the tallest tree. It looked like someone had taken a fall and landed there and not escaped injury.

My first thought went to the only little boy, the one most prone to tree climbing. A trail of blood and displaced grass and dirt led away from the site. I tried to keep my voice calm as I said, "Ring for Ambrose, Dawn."

"It was him. I know it."

I followed the trail. "No, it wasn't him." I found Moira. She had fallen from the tree but someone had beaten her as she tried to drag herself to safety. Someone had kicked her repeatedly after she had wedged herself under the birdhouses, until she was dead. She would have been unrecognizable even to me if not for her fiery red curls, rendered orange in comparison to the blood pooling around her.

∽

Relieved after seeing Ambrose with my own eyes, I had the entire house searched for an intruder. Though the rest of my staff didn't like her, I could not believe that anyone who knew Moira would have been capable of hurting her this way. I became convinced that this was the act of an Incola attempting to possess my children.

Dawn and Ambrose slept in my room that night. She regarded him with distrust until slumber finally took her. I worried and mourned too much to rest. Moira had been with me for so long. Helpless and childlike, she relied on me for shelter and security. I brought her into a dangerous life then failed to protect her. Not wanting to disturb my babies, I internalized my grief. The sorrow in my soul confined my chest and the lump in my throat restricted my breathing. The pain amplified, moving from emotional to physical, until I thought my internal organs might burst.

I stared at the red-hot embers in my fireplace, wondering which hurt more: what I felt or if I were to shove my hand into the intense heat. Sally offered to take over and send me to the warm, safe place inside us to rest until I was ready to face this hurt. I refused, feeling I deserved this anguish. The hours crept by. I was awake when my messenger returned in the wee hours of the morning.

The messenger was not alone. Leonus had sent his two most trusted Carriers, Andrew and Auley, to assess my safety. I would not normally have them in my bedroom but I was unwilling to leave my sleeping babes.

Andrew whispered, "Lady Brooksberry, were you bitten? Please be honest because any omission could lead to much death and present a great danger to your children."

I shook my head. "No. He tried but never got close enough. He did bite two of my guards. One died shortly after and the other has a tremendous fever. The doctor has seen to them."

Andrew and Auley exchanged glances. "We will need to see the body, my lady."

"Certainly, if Leonus feels it is necessary. Someone can show you to it in the morning."

Andrew disagreed and said, "We cannot wait until light. He must be dispatched immediately."

"Dispatched?" Sally blurted a little too loudly. I turned to check on Dawn after a small rustling of covers. "What do you mean dispatched?" I asked much more quietly. "I told you he already passed."

"He will come back and there will be more fatalities unless we take precautions. Where can we find the fevered man?"

"So that you may dispatch with him also?" I asked indignantly.

Auley handed me an envelope. "Leonus' letter will explain. We are very sorry for the intrusion."

"I sent him home," I answered. "The stableman can tell you where that is located. Do. Not. Harm. Him. Nor his family."

Andrew and Auley bowed their heads in acquiescence. With that, they left, closing the door behind them and I began to read.

∽

Leonus started his correspondence by saying how anxious he was about my safety. If I read his letter then I was not bitten, but he would not know my state until a reply arrived. Andrew had instructions to send an immediate reply as to my health. He went on to say that he would ignore his apprehension and trust that I was indeed all right and simply answer my questions.

He claimed the Chinaman suffered a lack of soul. Neither he nor I believed in the soul, an eternal part of us that was judged by God upon our death, but there was something, a consciousness, that moved from Incola to Carrier. With no terminology better suited, soul was settled upon.

Leonus begged me to come back to London where he could shelter me from such harsh realities. He said that I was no longer safe there and needed to be in a centralized location surrounded by Carriers who could protect me and my children. Human guards would not do. I could not imagine that the madness of London would be safer than my country estate and my reply said as much. My estate might have been infiltrated by one determined Incola but that city teemed with them. Carriers waited in every alley, held every serving tray, and one could get greedy. Fear already ruled our lives far too much; it couldn't be allowed to force us from the only home my children had ever known. Dawn, in particular, would feel a great loss since she loved this place so much.

I postponed the decision until after Moira's funeral. My grief for her is private and I will keep the memory of her lovely burial as my own. It is enough that the circumstances of her death were shared.

Over the days that followed, my life began to unravel. The stability this place had come to symbolize was undone. Dawn was convinced that Ambrose had let her birds out. His very presence enraged her. Walking by her beloved, now empty, aviary reopened the wound anew. She could not be reasoned with during these fits and she injured several people attempting to get to him.

The man Ning Shiru bit died of his fever and I allowed Andrew and Auley to do what they wanted with the body. The undead outbreak was averted but the desecration of graves drove many of my servants and human guards away.

Losing Moira forced the rest to go. It wasn't that they cared for her; my inability to protect my lady's maid meant no one was safe. We could not find Moira's murderer and my household servants abandoned me, citing the dangers of working for my household. Some gave letters of resignation while others, after hearing my tirades at those following protocol, simply disappeared. In the end, I had no choice but to acquiesce to Leonus' wishes. We would move back to London, to be surrounded by those who understood our behaviors, shared our inexplicable rage, and were better equipped by nature to handle Dawn's outbursts—where I could, once again, slip behind the facade of the Victorian woman. I found I was excited by the idea once it was decided. It meant I could begin my search for my nephew.

Julian had never mentioned that my brother Thaddeus had fathered a child. I only discovered the fact while examining the legal paperwork concerning inheritance. Julian, when he died, had not known what gender Ambrose would be and he'd set up a number of contingencies, one of which mentioned the son of Thaddeus. Over the years we had searched every record in Julian's vast library. None spoke of the boy's name or location and so that is where we will begin. The death of my son starts with the search for my nephew.

2

Mr. William Perkins was almost as round as he was tall; his work as our attorney and financial manager had been profitable. He was human, not a drop of Carrier blood in his none-too-diminutive body, and an employee of my late husband, Julian. He had managed our estates, paying the servants and household bills while I retreated from the world at Brooksberry Manor. That I mourned the loss of Julian was laughable, but I had appearances to keep up. Quite a few more than I liked, actually.

I would be forced to wear a great many personae while in London. To Paetus, whom I had managed to avoid while we lived in the country, I was Julian inside my body just as I was to the Carriers of my household. Gratefully, the procedure of Julian taking on my life and body were already in place and I was to act as a lady would. I told them I must practice so that I did not make a public slip when we came back out in society. I could be myself at home. I did not have to act as though I missed Julian, because I was supposed to *be* Julian.

To the man in front of me, who could fit in nothing less than a settee or lounge, I had to be me, only I must pretend to be destroyed by the loss of my husband. Mr. Perkins was nervous. He dabbed his head and neck with an already soaked handkerchief. I knew how very wealthy I was, or rather how wealthy Ambrose would be, and thought the balances so great as to make any normal man anxious. Though, he could be stealing from us and was worried about being caught now that I insisted on seeing the books. If he was intent on leaving quickly, his odor certainly helped his case. I held my breath whenever I could and wondered if he had ever taken a proper bath. Sally made a crude but silent joke questioning if a man of his girth could reach to wash every part of himself. I snorted aloud and Mr. Perkins' look told us our time secluded in the country had spoiled us and it would be more difficult to blend in London than we thought.

When he left we had our monthly household allowance, a large amount to pay my dressmaker for our out-of-mourning wardrobe, and the address for Thaddeus' son, whose name we found was Theodore. Mr. Perkins looked perplexed when I asked for the last item and said, "But your child was a male. Surely you do not intend to continue to support your brother's bastard for much longer. He is thirteen, old enough to become an apprentice. Lord Brooksberry had something arranged for him, I am certain. Around the Mediterranean Sea, I believe, where he would fit in better. From his few letters I can see he has quite good handwriting and penmanship and the tutors were instructed to teach him a variety of languages. He could easily excel as a scribe."

"While I wish to fulfill the late Earl's wishes as best I can," I said as I dabbed at the corner of my eye with a handkerchief, "you must understand why I would be hesitant to allow my only remaining family, bastard or no, to move to a distant land." I reminded him of my status and wealth and that such things make eccentricity almost acceptable. "If I want my nephew to have all the opportunities I can afford him then any employee of mine who wishes to remain so will support me." Sally would have said it a bit less tactfully but she kept her comments private.

Mr. Perkins stammered unintelligibly and a new spattering of perspiration beaded on his forehead. "I am c-cer-certainly such an e-em-employee, m-ma-my lady, but I would feel I had not done my duty if I missed my chance to c-ca-caution against having him in your home or visiting where he resides. Perhaps I could arrange a meeting in a more public place…no, that would not do…for you to be seen…"

"Just spit it out Mr. Perkins," Sally shouted. She had less patience than I and even mine was wearing thin. "What is so unacceptable about our nephew that we cannot be seen with him?"

If he registered Sally's use of the plural, he did not acknowledge it. She could have been speaking for my late husband and I or perhaps my family as a whole. "He lives in an inn of questionable reputation, where you pay extra to allow him to stay. Your brother dishonored himself by getting a Negress with child. Your nephew, Theodore, is mulatto." He whispered the last word.

"Be that as it may, Mr. Perkins, if I wish to see him and have him in my home and in my life, I will do so. Surely there is enough in my bank to persuade even the loftiest society to see past his skin color. Allow me to worry about propriety and honor; you are saddled with the heavy burden of maintaining my fortune and getting me what I want."

"Why of course, my lady. I will write to him at once requesting his presence."

"I shall write to him myself. He should know that I consider him family, no matter his history or birth. What is the address?"

"You are the one who provided it to me in the days after..." He did not continue. The tragic death of a husband was hardly topic for conversation between a widowed peeress and her lawyer.

I explained it away by saying I was so distraught at that time that the grief had a negative effect on my memory. He did not need to know that during those days I was possessed by the very man I was supposed to be grieving and never had any memory of "my" actions. "Those days, nay weeks, are little more than a blur."

"Certainly, my lady. My apologies if I seemed inconsiderate." He jotted the address down and seemed happy to be done with the conversation.

I immediately penned a letter to Theodore.

∽

We summoned Mr. Edwin Hall next. I didn't want to, but Sally insisted that the man was not a danger. I thought back on the night I had first met him, one of the most frightening moments of my life. I had broken free and wandered the asylum searching for Hester. He caught my attention and I spoke with him even though his appearance revolted me. On top of the fright, he gave me something that night, an instrument of sorts that could tell me if what I felt was my own or if I was influenced by an Incola.

Hester. I pushed back the sadness her name still brought even after all these years. Her death still weighed heavily on my conscience and more than that, I missed my first friend.

Mr. Hall had known of the Incola and that he was a Carrier. When they came for him, he tore out his own eyes, destroying not only his vision but also his value as a Carrier. No one wanted to ride in a body that could not see. They did not take him but it backfired on him. He was committed in the West Freeman Asylum for Lunatics because his were the actions of the insane.

He came into the library. In the absence of a man of the house, that area belonged to us. We used it for writing correspondence and running our household. This home I had shared with Julian was much too large for our family. Now that he was gone, I had more rooms than could be enjoyed. I preferred the library over my morning and evening sitting rooms, boudoir, drawing room or dressing room, and I only used them when the rules of etiquette required. I loved the library's books more than anything left to me by Julian. They reminded me of the Julian I loved, the time when he had been just a man, my hero and husband.

I was glad to see Mr. Hall looking so healthy and I told him so. The disgusting sores around his nose and mouth were gone and his color replenished. His teeth had rotted but were brown now instead of blackened. Over his dark empty eye sockets and shrunken lids, he wore a pair of goggles with gears and mechanisms along the side. Opaque lenses hid the horrifying gap where the bottom lid didn't quite meet the top. The stillness of the atrophied muscles had disturbed me most. Blinking was unnecessary without eyeballs.

He bowed to me, his thanks tripping over themselves on the way from his throat. When I asked him to sit, he went straight to the chair next to me. Sally suggested silently that he had been in the London home the whole four years we hid in the country and had simply memorized the layout of the house in our absence. I thought it more than that and asked him.

"My spectacles are no ordinary things, Lady Brooksberry." He went on to describe how they emitted a constant hum, a tone none could hear. That sound bounced off of the things around him and the goggles interpreted the sound and told him where things rested. They did not allow him to see in the normal sense of the word but they gave him something.

The invention was nothing short of genius. "Much in the way a bat, nearly blind, can see its way in the dark?" I asked.

Ed, as I came to call him much later, was pleased that I understood so quickly. "But how is the signal received?" I asked. After much explanation, I knew it was somehow sent to his brain, but no more. I gave up understanding. Some things were to be left to the experts.

Mr. Hall had a patent pending for both its use for the blind and our sea vessels. He explained that it would give our country a great advantage. England had always had the best navy but our lead against other countries had been diminished, our technology having stalled out and matched by all. This and inventions like this would give us a leg up.

"You will be very sought after and rich once the world hears of your talents. You will hardly need me as a benefactor."

Ed bowed his head. "E'en if that be true, I owe your ladyship for my freedom. I will remain in your employ for as long as you will have me. If my tinkerings can aid you, you will have first pick of them."

I had bought the West Freeman Asylum for Lunatics and paid for Mr. Hall's release. The place of horrors was no longer that dark and damp place of fear. I installed the kindest nurses and most educated, respected doctors and paid for every modern advancement they requested. I took no one else out, but care and living conditions improved vastly. And so I gained Mr. Hall as my tinkerer, long before it was fashionable to have one.

He had a gift for me. "I hope you do not mind that I used your favorite perfume as a base. I had hoped it would mean you would not mind wearing it and the scent would not seem out of the ordinary."

I took the bottle from him and opening it found no difference to its smell. Sally, not as caring about the rules of proper society, applied a bit to each of our pulse points though it was early in the day when nothing stronger than eau de cologne should be used. Mr. Hall said he could no longer sniff me out as he had done in the asylum. The Incola who attempted to claim him, those who cost him his sight, must not have known of his tracking ability or they would have taken him all the same. Not many could sniff out a Carrier but every precaution must be taken to keep us hidden. Of the many Incola in the world, some had unknown talents and skills. As a woman, I would be sought after.

Dawn would need something to cover her scent so I asked him, "Is it possible to make something for a child that is not so strong? Perhaps a soap or potpourri for masking her scent indoors?"

Mr. Hall promised to work on it and then presented me with another item of his creation. It looked much like a short musket with a bell-shaped barrel, but instead of the hammer and trigger it had a canister and crank. He showed me how it worked, aiming it at me and spinning the crank. He hit several switches on the side of the blunderbuss-shaped thing and twisted the canister, which popped off. A footman wheeled in a large machine on a cart. Mr. Hall laid the long barrel section down on top of it and snapped the canister onto the larger of his inventions. The real bit of genius was a metal box riveted on all sides and corners save one. That side was covered with various dials and a set of enameled buttons, each carrying a letter or number.

Mr. Hall turned the main dial to "Detect," and flipped a switch. A great deal of noise emitted from inside the box and I distinctly heard churning gears and the popping of springs. He turned the dial to "Record," slipped a card into a slot, typed in my name and an indicator that I wore a scent disguise. The machine went to work again with a great clicking as it recorded information on the card through a series of punched holes. The machine could hold several thousand individual's unique aromatic signatures and compare them to others found with the collector.

He cleared the machine, reset it, and removed the now-empty canister. He demonstrated again, this time turning his collector's bell-shaped barrel at himself before turning the crank. He sealed the canister and loaded it into the metal box he called the catalog. This time, after the noise subsided, a slip of paper ejected into a small tray. I took up the paper and read it. It said, "Edwin Hall—Carrier."

"Extraordinary!" I praised, "How did it know?"

"Thank you, my lady. All of the staff here, myself included, have been recorded in the catalog and it will recognize us. The collector can be used in a crowded room, the known persons cleared and the new ones recorded."

We would be able to sniff out all manner of Carriers and Incola without perfecting that talent personally. It could come in very handy. "With enough samples in the catalog, it should be able to make an educated guess on an unknown person."

I thought of asking his opinion on my carved liquid-filled cylinder, for surely a tinkerer of his intelligence and ingenuity could hazard a guess at its purpose but decided to wait until I knew him better.

∽

When three days passed with no reply or visit from Theodore, Sally and I sent our first footman with another message. He returned looking worse for wear. The mistress denied him access to Theodore's room, saying he was occupied, implying that he was with a woman, or worse, customer. She had touched the footman's livery, soiling it. I thanked him and apologized for his ill treatment.

We would be forced to handle this ourselves, gallivanting across the seedy parts of London before even announcing our return to respectful society. Perhaps my activity would go unnoticed. Sally doubted it. Late 1800s London society gossiped over things far less entertaining than I. She was certain the whole peerage awaited my return. I was one of them, but not. Born to a mother with the eternal appearance of a child and a father with an affinity for such an oddity, present at my parents' gruesome murder, whose sibling had been convicted and executed for said murders. I was an inmate in an insane asylum, married to an eccentric who later died under questionable circumstances, and lived in the largest, most extravagant home on Park Lane alone with my infant son. Society had plenty to gossip over before I added visiting a whorehouse and taking in my brother's bastard mulatto.

None of them knew how free we had been while Julian was alive. He had given permission, even encouraged me, to share my body with the servants for breeding and pleasure. I drank gin and Sally danced with the saltiest of men. I had rented a whole house of prostitutes for the night only to host a dinner and sup with them. I did not currently care what the highest order of society thought of us but believed it better to maintain good connections. Such things were much easier to maintain than rebuild.

After sending out calling cards to all my old acquaintances the next morning, I set out on my adventures. We used the postern and hoped the carriage was leaving early enough to go unnoticed. I traveled light, forgoing the usual entourage Julian had insisted on. The lack of our armed guards enhanced our chances of slipping in and out of respectable areas of town. I took only my second footman, driver, and one guard who rode secretly inside the carriage. The driver, who had been in the employ of Julian during my wild years, was quite used to me traveling to unsavory areas of town and batted not a lash when I revealed the destination.

I kept the drapes drawn, blocking out as much of the foul air as possible. In four years I had been spoiled by the clean country air. Soot covered everything and the yellow fog could kill in a matter of minutes, not hours. The air changed as we traveled east. The stench of horse excrement gave way to a more human stench. Poorer areas meant more people per square meter, literally living on top of one another, sharing rooms and beds in shifts, squeezing a "home" into every spare space. This area housed industry and the slaughterhouses. Even those *desiring* hygiene had less opportunity than in the ritzy area where we lived.

I chided myself for allowing so long a time to pass before seeking Theodore, but Sally reprimanded me for it. We had our own children to look after. Having them in the city was dangerous enough now; bringing them earlier she wouldn't have allowed. We, with our special mind so unwelcoming to outsiders, might be safe from Incola, but we were in no way assured that our children were blessed with such natural protection.

The carriage stopped and the driver gave the roof a secret cadence of knock, signaling that all was clear. Even so, the guard aimed his pistol at the door and waited for the footman to give his signal. No unsavory character would come into this carriage without us knowing something was amok. My servants followed protocol and I soon found myself standing on a smooth patch of dirt that passed for sidewalk in front of a wooden building. I went inside with the guard at my back and found the place nearly empty. Two men slumped over different tables about the room, either today's customers or leftovers from the previous night.

I made my way to the bar where a man and woman gaped at me. Probably the manager and mistress, they attempted to calculate how much could be pilfered from so rich a customer.

"We ain't open proper till ev'en but for the right price I's sure we could rouse e'n the dead if that's what mum wanted." The man smiled at me with teeth browner than his skin.

The woman jumped in, her accent even less couth than his. "A gent for m'lady or are ya lookin for company of the softer sort?" She leaned in and spoke quietly, but her breath was like a slap to the senses. "This establishment's real discreet."

Knowing they were more likely to help me if I spent, I ordered a gin and paid for three. "I am searching for a dark-skinned teenage boy who has resided here for some years." I swigged the crisp spirit and almost sighed aloud in pleasure. It had been some time since I had indulged in my favorite alcohol, and though this lacked the anise flavor I preferred with my juniper berry, it was a welcome change over the heavy cloying sweetness of more socially acceptable spirits.

"If it be dark yur lookin fur, I've got a fine strapping…"

Sally cut her off. "His name is Theodore and we are only interested in him."

The man and woman exchanged looks they clearly thought I would not note. "I'm a' might sorry, mum, but that young gentleman is otherwise engaged at the moment. Are you sure I can't interest you in someone else? If it's youth you seek, I…"

"Otherwise engaged? I find it amusing that someone told my footman that same thing yesterday. Such is the reason for my personal visit." Sally's temper showed so I clapped another coin down and pointed to my empty shot glass. "That and to sneak a bit of gin, that is," I said with a coy smile.

The barkeep filled it and grinned. "Aye' mum. That I understand ver' well. As to your boy, if it'd please, you could leave a letter and I'll make sure it gets to 'em."

Sally grabbed the man by his neckband and pulled him up off his feet and over the counter. "I haven't come all this way to be turned away. I am not a woman accustomed to being denied."

I startled the truth out of the mistress. "No. I c'n see that, m'lady. The truth is he's gone."

"Out," the man croaked. "He's gone out." He attempted to recover from her exposure.

A young man with no profession who lived over a tavern went out at this time of the morning? Impossible. Sally held us still.

"He's gone. Gone, not gone out," he finally admitted.

"That is better." Sally released the man, who stumbled as he landed. She took the gin bottle and gave us another drink. "Where did he go, why did he leave, was he alone, and how long ago did all this happen?" The spirits warmed our insides and I realized just how little I could manage after four long years of abstaining.

"He didn't leave no note, not that we coulda read it if he had, but he was ne'er alone. A few men came askin after him a bit after Boxing Day. They talked a while and that night he disappeared."

"He was taken? Left under duress?" I asked.

"No, mum. He left on his own with his fellows. The men that were asking after him were mad when we told 'em he'd gone when they came back the next night. They busted the place up good, one of me girls too."

I placed a five-pound bank note down, which scarcely felt the wood of the counter before disappearing into the woman's bodice. "For your troubles," I explained. "I will forgive the nearly four months since his exit you have accepted as payment for his room and board if you will show me to said room."

∽

I shouldn't have bothered with the room search. Nothing there could lead me to Theodore. The poor fallen women, for which this time of day was their only rest, had to be roused from their slumbers. I paid them each enough to fill their bellies and keep them off their backs for a week. It was nothing to me. I stood with the collector in the room and filled three canisters with the scents. I hoped to find Theodore's scent but worried it was overrun with the smell of sex and unwashed bodies. Confident the other occupants of the room did not study, I concentrated on the chair and desk. Mr. Perkins had described Theodore as an educated youth.

I had the driver rush home, unsure of how well the canisters would contain the scents over extended time. Mr. Hall waited for me and loaded the information into his catalog. His invention thought some of the partials were Carriers and he recorded them as unknown. The machine would recognize and complete them should it come across them again. If all but one could be eliminated, then that remaining one would be Theodore.

We scarcely finished when one of the housemaids came to fetch me. There was a situation with my son, she said. Everyone in the house had years of practice only referring to my son and never my children or daughter. I told Mr. Hall to store the catalog in the secret room attached to the library. He already knew of it and, as I would not use it for the devious purposes Julian had, thought it was the perfect place to hide the machine.

It took me some time to reach the third-floor playroom. The library lay on the ground floor, at street level. I planned to ask Mr. Hall about installing a lift in our home, though it was highly unusual for a residence. Due to recent development in that area, the lifts were safer, quicker, and much more efficient. I would have to sacrifice quite a bit of area to house it and it would cost a huge sum. As I had an abundance of both, I was determined to have one as soon as I had truly considered it. The royals and industry already employed their use. Why should we not have every comfort this wondrous age could supply?

The governess, who in a regular household would handle any disputes and mete out discipline without the help of the lady, met me on the third-floor landing and informed me of the situation. Ambrose had, quite accidentally she assured me, torn a few of Dawn's paper-dolls while they were playing. "Even though I have repeatedly told her that she is much past the age when such frivolity is acceptable." She leaned into the room to fuss. Dawn had gone berserk, screaming at him and little Ambrose had been hurt.

Our daughter losing her temper and using her strength against her brother was nothing new. I peered inside to find Dawn seated on a stool in the corner, glaring viciously at Ambrose who cradled his arm. Dawn lied as she often did, "Mama, I didn't do anything."

The governess admonished, "Didn't do…I suppose he scraped his own arm and screamed and yelled at himself!"

"Yes. No, not the screaming but he did hurt himself. I never touched him. Oh, how would you know? You were snoring like a fat tosspot!" she yelled.

The governess' jaw flapped, giving her the look of a pufferfish while she tried to think of something. Red-faced from anger, embarrassment, or both, she crossed to Dawn and grabbed her by the ear, jerking her off the stool. Sally extricated our daughter from the human servant and I said, "I can take it from here, Mrs. Ledger. Thank you."

She left in a huff at the indignity of being "reprimanded" in front of the children. I knelt beside Ambrose and examined his arm. The sleeve of both his jacket and shirt were torn and four parallel gouges ran the length of his forearm. Gouges, not scrapes, represented the extra strength my children possessed. I picked him up and turned to Dawn. Our time in the country had spoiled the children as much as it had us. I had indulged them, game for whatever tickled their fancy, even taking my meals with them instead of dining with other adults. That would not do while living in London. "It will take some time adjusting to life here. I won't tolerate misbehaving for my attention." I brushed her face with my gloved fingertips. "You can spend the afternoon at needlepoint, thinking of a way for you to make amends with Ambrose."

I took Ambrose to the bathroom and helped him clean his wounds with soap. I knew it stung but the brave boy made not a whimper. He was careful never to let his skin come in direct contact with mine. Both my children knew I had the gift of touch, though I felt it was much more a curse. It was something Julian and I had shared, though the effects of touching our skin were exact opposites. Touching me excited, inducing a violent and sometimes sexual response. Touching Julian soothed, making the recipient feel as if all was well. The only other I knew of with the gift of touch was Paetus, who could force the truth from whomever he touched. I had experienced it firsthand, admitting my darkest thoughts without ever deciding to.

Luckily my children were not blessed with this added ability. The gift of touch only occurred once in every few thousand Carriers. It made my body even more desirable to every Incola, and I was glad Dawn was not saddled with it as well. Mine had caused me nothing but troubles, as I had yet to use it to my advantage. Julian was so attached to his own that when he took my body he could not give it up, even in exchange for mine. He had Paetus rip the skin off of his arms and tan it. Thinking we were his lifelong friend Julian, Paetus had presented me with the gloves after Sally and I woke and pushed Julian from this world. I was mortified by the macabre present, but Sally was pleased. She was determined to use them and my own touch to our benefit.

Ambrose's wounds were already healing by the time I was ready to bandage them and so the process was forgone. Ambrose sat on the cabinet, his legs dangling. I said to him, "You will be five soon and too old for a governess. We'll have to get you a real tutor so that you can go to university like a proper gentleman. You should not cause strife between your sister and the governess, who will be together for some time. Why did you tear Dawn's paper-dolls?"

He seemed to consider my question quite seriously for a four-year-old. "I wanted to, Mama."

My brow furrowed and lips pursed, I asked him, "So it was no accident?"

"The first time it was." I could see his child's mind trying to put thoughts into words. Children should not have such complex thoughts. He added, "The others I did because I wanted to...because it feels good to ruin something so pretty...to know that what I did cannot be undone."

I'd heard such a statement before. It was a bit too similar to the workings of greedy Incola minds. I let it pass because paper dolls couldn't feel. If my son was going to develop a god complex, then it was best applied to inanimate objects. I said gently, "They didn't belong to you. They weren't yours to tear. Next time you feel the urge to wreck something beautiful, choose something of your own."

3

I was nervous about the day's reintroduction into society. As an attractive widow of only twenty-five, with a title of my own and a fortune to match, only the royal family exceeded me. Proof that I could birth a son added value. I could keep the callers away no longer. I had a position and status to uphold; mourning only worked as an excuse for so long. Word of my return had spread quickly and my salvers were full of cards. I expected callers in earnest that morning.

Only the most intimate of friends would call in the actual morning, that is, before one o'clock. A never-ending parade of footmen delivered cards from people of status or wealth, never both, who had sons needing the other from me. I would be expected to remarry and I had my choice of a poor titled gentleman or a rich untitled one. I would accept neither.

I was genuinely pleased to see the familiar round shape of Dowager Lady Ernestine Wharlow, Countess of Edgington, climb from her carriage and approach my door. Ernestine insisted I call her by her Christian name, since she claimed our widowed status put us as equals. I had instructed my steward, Mr. Boyd, to grant her entrance immediately should she choose to call. The visit was more than amicable and Ernestine stayed much longer than the customary quarter of an hour.

Her daughters had been married while I was away. The eldest had a daughter of her own, two years of age, and the younger was with child. They hoped it would be a boy since Ernestine's only son had married a woman incapable of conceiving. Their family had no heir. Ernestine lamented that he was no widower, for then he could court me as I was a very suitable match. I told her it was much too soon after Julian's death for me to seriously consider any suitor. She understood but warned me against waiting too long to remarry. I had only one son and no daughters and, though sons were valuable, Ernestine assured me that I would never know true joy until I had a daughter of my own to fuss over and love. She spoke of the joy gained from watching Emmaline and Charlotte grow into beautiful women, presenting them at court, bringing them out, finding their husbands, seeing to their weddings, and finally holding her grandchildren.

Once Countess Ernestine started talking, there really was no stopping her. Enjoying our conversation almost as much as she, I turned away other callers, telling Mr. Boyd that I was not "at home." She was quite embarrassed when the clock struck twelve, indicating she had been there for over an hour. She hastily made her exit with assurances from me that I was quite happy to have her visit as often and as long as she liked.

She invited me to an event that was sure to be sensational: a séance at her home in two days. She had attended one hosted by her friend not too long ago and was thrilled with the results. She was determined to speak to her late husband at all costs. The medium had been unable to reach him but felt that he might respond if she attempted a connection from a familiar place. Ernestine commented that perhaps Lord Brooksberry could be reached. Perhaps he could ease my sorrow and allow me to move forward and take a husband. I kept a hopeful look on my face but speaking to Julian's ghost was the last thing I wanted.

This Victorian age was obsessed with the occult. The line between scientific and superstitious blurred, leading to the rise of Spiritualism. I myself rather enjoyed the parlor games using a planchette. Later applied to a board, it gave birth to the Ouija game. Magicians and mediums were also great fun and so, even with my worries about encountering Julian, I agreed to attend her gathering.

The footman brought in a letter, hand delivered with no payment required and no address. Only "Ramillia" graced the front. Recognizing Leonus' writing, I opened the letter and read it then dropped it in the drawing room fire and hurried up to my chambers. I had a clandestine lunch meeting and I was not appropriately dressed for the trip.

∽

Darville, my old butler, now ran an inn with a taproom and parlor. He bought the place with the money I had given him upon his retirement and, subsequently, I became the benefactor and part owner with my regular donations. I had hired the best distiller and was quite excited to have a luncheon of gin and eel pie.

Leonus waited for me, not in the taproom where we had met the first time but the parlor occupied by people of higher status. I barely recognized him. Gone was the unimpressive, nondescript wallflower; he had become a handsome and pleasing gentleman. Short but fit, he had the same brown hair and amber eyes Julian had possessed. His facial structure marked him as Roman. He still occupied the body he was born with, feeling that was his strength. It allowed him to endure while Julian and Paetus failed, losing their original memories because they took residence in the mind of another. Leonus had warned Julian and Paetus. He still had all of his memories. He remembered being a child and a young man. He knew his parents. He knew that to change bodies permanently was to give up those things.

Leonus explained that, though Julian had control over his body, it wasn't really his. The mind and body were not completely aligned and the longer they spent in those bodies, the more out of sync they would become. Body-switching Incola got no pleasure from their senses anymore. They needed ever-newer bodies with which to taste, smell, hear, see, and touch.

Julian had enjoyed the hurt Mistress had shown me to give him. This decaying of senses drove him to ask for worse treatments. He could barely feel me unless I almost skinned him alive. He put the spiciest of seasonings on his food. It was also why he enjoyed riding a Carrier in death. He could finally feel.

Leonus had no such desires. His senses grew more intense with every day he lived. He occasionally rode his Carriers but always with their consent. He said that Carriers could be taught to repair their own bodies but when the damage was great or the Carrier weakened, he could step in and speed up the process. His Carriers were with him by choice. He was not their master.

He had many more Carriers than anyone knew about. If the greedy Incola knew, they would try to destroy what he was making. Lavishing in superiority and entitlement, the Incola did not want a class of well-educated Carriers. Leonus had taken over the care of Julian's Carriers, as well as mine while I was away. I had told them all that Julian was dead and that no one would ride them without their consent ever again. Their devotion to Julian quickly faded without the threat of being walked to their deaths.

Leonus stood to greet me, nearly knocking over his chair in his hurry. He took my gloved hands in his and gave them a quick squeeze. It was as intimate a greeting as we were allowed and though it bordered on inappropriate, I had no objection. I had so few people I could count as close and I knew the value of that rare commodity. Darville himself served two gin and tonics to our table before I was fully seated. I drank mine straight away. I couldn't risk a case of malaria with so much to protect. Sally laughed that I made excuses rather than drinking because I liked it so.

We exchanged pleasantries and I found I quite enjoyed his company as much as I had enjoyed his correspondence over the years.

He said what he meant. He was to be known as Viscount Leonardo d'Borgia from now on, an Italian noble displaced by the rise of the Socialist movement. It was a real person and a real back-story, but the real Viscount had died shortly after his ship voyage here. Leonus had waited a long time for a new identity that matched his build and features. Italian Carriers were led by one ancient and powerful Incola: the Pope. When the time had come for that body to die, the Incola took on the body of whichever of his bishops would become the next Pope.

I asked why he needed a new identity and he said, "I have set myself up so that it is quite appropriate to court a woman of your standing."

I did not like the idea that my caring Leonus had turned into the social climber, Leonardo. I also did not want to be courted by a Carrier or Incola. I could never be sure that they valued me and not just my breeding ability. I declared, "I do not want to be courted."

"Then it shall be for appearances only." He took a sip from his gin and blanched at its stringency. His increasingly receptive senses had not acquired the taste for such a drink as my favorite. When our meat pies arrived, I asked Darville for a couple glasses of wine.

"Why must we keep up appearances?" I asked after my first bite of the cold-water crust and savory fish gravy. "I am a widow now and it is quite appropriate for me not to remarry. I do not wish nor intend to."

"No, but Julian would. If he were in your body now instead of you, he would already have a husband and probably another child on the way." He took a bite of his beef pie and seemed quite happy with its simple flavors.

"You would be Julian's last choice. Paetus will see right through your plan. He will know as soon as he hears of it that Julian had no say in the matter."

"I have already thought of that. You, 'Julian,' will tell him that you are using me to care for your Carriers during this time, early in your possession of this body, when you cannot ride them. You will tell him of your plan to kill me and take my Carriers as your own, thus increasing your army."

It was a good plan; I admitted that. Paetus would believe that Julian had made a power grab. In addition, it would save me from a barrage of suitors, both Incola and human. It added a new level of acting on my part but Leonardo reminded me that having him as a fiancé would actually do the opposite. I would no longer be required to mourn Julian's loss because having an intended would be seen as moving on with my life. Paetus was not part of respectable society, as rich and powerful as he was, because he never bothered to set himself up with the nobility. Only when alone with Paetus would I need to pretend to be Julian. This engagement was the perfect excuse to spend little time alone with Paetus.

Sally and I liked this plan more the longer we talked about it. Paetus and Julian had become creepy old lechers in over two thousand years of companionship. Crasser than I, Sally was tasked with convincing Paetus.

Leon, as I came to call him, gave me a ring he had commissioned for me. Julian had presented me with an old, hammered metal ring with two figures appearing to be joining: an ancient Roman artifact. This one was much more suited to me and was the most beautiful and stylish thing I had ever laid eyes on. The band around the back was thin but the decorative part on top covered my finger from knuckle to mid-finger joint with vine-themed filigree. Leaf-shaped emeralds surrounded two mothers-of-pearl single-petal lilies with yellow diamond pistils. Tiny opals and seed pearls scattered throughout looked like unopened blossoms.

We finished our meal and I had a few more drinks while we talked pleasantries. He asked after Dawn and Ambrose and I told him of the trouble we'd experienced. He offered to house my son with him to keep the siblings separated but I could not bear the thought of that. Leon thought that he had managed to keep Dawn's existence a secret from Paetus, to whom she was contracted for marriage, but he doubted it would remain a secret for long while we lived in town. Servants, no matter how much they were paid, led lives ever hungry for gossip.

4

News of my return spread quickly once both Leon and Lady Ernestine had visited. After sending another of Ning Shiru's forged letters to the Pope, I wrote to Paetus, on the advice of Leon, informing him of my return and my engagement. Sally wrote it as Julian and explained my choices. My footman returned with a reply. Paetus had insisted the man wait while he wrote it. We were to come to the club on Friday evening; Paetus would throw a party in my honor. He said that Leon would not likely pass up the opportunity to gloat with me on his arm and that the "Incola who would not ride" had become quite impossible to live with. Leonus, Paetus said, had been strutting about in his new persona, rubbing elbows with the loftiest Londoners.

I sat and immediately wrote two letters. One accepted Paetus' invitation, and the other informed Leon of Friday evening's activity. I put nothing in the one to my fiancé that would raise suspicions with Paetus, should he take both letters, and Sally put complaints about Leonus in the one to Paetus. It was only my first day of deceit and already it exhausted me. I went to lie down after taking a medicinal draught for my headache.

The opiate-laced drink removed my pains and I floated away to dreamland on a cloud of relaxation. Such odd dreams it gave me, visions of a dragon in a lovely, peaceful forest. I heard the crackling of fire and ran toward the sound, thinking only of saving the forest. The dragon breathed flames, scorching the trees, but the trees fought back. Finding a sword in hand, I sliced the dragon's soft underbelly until it collapsed. Vines covered the dragon's body. With the dragon down, I could see a path to a nest. The dragon was only trying to escape the forest that had it trapped. I had chosen the wrong side to join. The plants filled every available space, choking me out.

I woke gasping, to squealing and the sounds of furniture breaking. Racing up the stairs, convinced Dawn was hurting my little Ambrose, I burst into the playroom. Dawn stood on a pile of kindling that used to be the governess' rocking chair. Ambrose squealed in delight when his sister chose the largest piece and snapped it over her leg like a twig. They were so engrossed in their activity that I observed unnoticed. My daughter danced a jig on the remnants, stomping so hard that the chair shattered into splinters. My son laughed so hard that he used up his breath and his laughter went silent.

My children, playing happily together, no matter how unorthodox the game, was a rare and welcomed sight. It brought a tear to my eye, but Sally was hard-pressed to contain her own laughter. Mrs. Ledger came in through the other door and we stepped back so that she wouldn't know we'd watched as the children destroyed her seat. She was outraged. She'd grown accustomed to their inordinate strength but bad manners would never be tolerated. Dawn and Ambrose stood side by side during the chastising, exchanging sly looks of joy whenever she turned away.

When Mrs. Ledger asked Dawn why she had done such a thing, Sally made a private joke about it being a mercy killing. At the same time Dawn said, "It groaned, begging me to put it out of its misery. The poor thing was fragile from its daily load, so easily broken. Perhaps your next will be more appropriately sturdy."

I realized at that moment that Dawn was more Sally's daughter than mine. Sally had been the one our father had conceived her with. Sally had grown her in our belly. Sally had given birth to her. I was glad of it. Sally was stronger than I. Smarter, more amusing, and more "no nonsense" too.

"I asked her to," Ambrose admitted. "Your snoring is bothersome and interrupts my play. Dawn said that if you had no place to sit, you would have no place to sleep. Horses can do it, but not people… Not even if her size *does* rival that of equine proportions." Ambrose said the last part under his breath to Dawn, who covered her mouth to hide the giggle that boiled up.

The governess took a step forward and said, "Ambrose only says those horrible things because you put them in his head." She pointed her finger in Dawn's face and stammered in her rage, "Y-you little—you will never find a proper husband if you cannot get hold of your vulgar tongue, not with your questionable birth."

My interjection startled the governess. "Lady Lawrence will have a plethora of suitors when the time comes and her birth speaks more of me than her. Do not mention it again if you wish to remain in my employ, Mrs. Ledger."

She came closer while talking clearly for the children to hear. "Dawn needs to put more emphasis on her manners. She might do that if she understood her position was not as lofty as she seems to think."

"*Lady Lawrence*'s position is loftier than you can possibly understand. When her beauty, strength, and ability become common knowledge, I would not be surprised if the Princes themselves made offers of matrimony." The thought of the heir to the monarchy courting a bastard clearly upset the sensibilities of Mrs. Ledger so I offered an olive branch. "You have the rest of the afternoon off. Go see Mr. Boyd and tell him I requested fifty pounds for you to select and purchase the chair of your choice."

Mrs. Ledger's outrage shifted into astonishment. "Oh, but that is ten times what will be required."

"Then the remainder is yours, for your trouble."

Mrs. Ledger looked pleased by the offer. Leaving, she did not spare a second glance at her pupils. I turned to my wide-eyed children. They feared reprisal but I had none to give. "You have made quite a little nest there. All we need is the dragon who lives there." I asked Dawn to bring me my oldest corset.

"Could I really be a princess, Mama?" Dawn asked when she returned holding my request.

"Certainly, though I think you might find that life to be very restrictive. Monarchs have very little power and much is expected of them. Royalty are prisoners of their lives and no matter how gilded, a cage is still a cage." I wished I could give her more independence. "Poverty is a prison all its own. Most girls must think of finances when choosing a husband. No matter what life you choose, I will ensure you never need worry about that."

I tore the corset along one seam and pulled the steel stay out from its pocket. Most women used whale boning but with my enhanced strength I often broke them and had begun commissioning my boning from a blacksmith turned fabricator by the Industrial Revolution. The iron worker invested in the Bessemer process that had made steel much more affordable and had more work than time to do it. He had invented the spiral steel stay, which was a thinner piece of metal which wound around itself as the name would suggest but was then pounded relatively flat. I used it on the stays that crossed my bust as they were more giving and bent both directions. The flat stays, used on the sides and back of the corset, were more rigid.

Quickly I bent that first flat stay into the head and spine of a crude dragon. Dawn and Ambrose clapped and giggled at this display of strength. Though I had never hidden my abilities from them, as I did not want them to think their own were abnormal, I also did not show off. Today my offspring needed exertion such that no normal activities could provide. Their defiance wasn't just about their dislike of the governess.

Dawn went to work carving wings from the two biggest pieces of wood she could find from the pile. Her idea and contribution to our sculpture proved she was mindful of my comments and valued her freedom. Her jaw made quick work of the wood and the basic shape was finished in no time. She used her fingernails for the fine detail work of the wings' membrane-like veined appearance.

After granting Ambrose his three stays still contained in their material pockets, I made the ribcage, tail, fore- and hind-legs. Using the spiral steel stays, I gave the creature skin and the effect was more scale-like than I had imagined. My amber earrings made perfect eyes, their cat's eye effect giving them a lifelike movement. I fastened Dawn's wings onto their appropriate places on its shoulders, praising her craftsmanship.

Dawn said, "I want a life of freedom, Mama. I will choose a husband who will allow me that."

I hugged Dawn carefully, proud of her decision. I said nothing of her choice of verbiage. No man would allow or disallow her to do anything she wanted. She would be free as soon as we were certain of her safety, no matter her marital status, convention of the day be damned.

Ambrose's contribution focused on aggression as he fashioned flames. Sally complimented his ingenuity when I could find only dread in his endeavor. He colored the cloth with his own blood for the part closest to the mouth where Sally attached it. Combined with the yellowed cloth, it gave the flames a slightly orange-pink color. The ends he left alone and the yellowed material did indeed look the yellow of flame most mixed with oxygen.

"I think he will make a fine ornament for our garden, don't you?" I said when I regained my composure.

Ambrose agreed but Dawn said, "Not he, Mama. It's a female. A mother, like you. That's why she's so ferocious—she's protecting her young."

I took a second look at our finished product, sitting on the nest I had arranged out of the rubble pile. "You are right, Dawn. It is a female, but a mother needs her children. Why don't you two carry our sculpture out to the back garden, decide where to house her, and then search for a couple of egg-shaped rocks to put under her?"

A man said from the door, "Pardon me, Lady Brooksberry, but you have visitors." I passed him as he held the door and he said, "This way, my lady. Mr. Boyd had them wait in his office." I let the footman lead me as I had never spent any time in the service section of the house and was unaware of the route.

It was clean but utilitarian. There were no ornamentations, no papered walls down here. The steward's office had sturdy but simple furniture consisting of a desk and chair, from which he ran the male half of the house, and a wall of locked cabinets where I knew he kept the silver not in use. Mr. Boyd stood, glaring suspiciously at the two men with him. They were of the rough sort, their clothes dirty and crumpled as if they had little else to wear. Their tan faces, necks, and hands spoke of hard labor.

"What can I do for you, gentlemen?" I asked, ignoring the extended hand of the one closest to me.

The other one elbowed his friend, who lowered his arm. "We're sorry t' bother ye' but we 'av nowhere else t' go. We know what kind a' woman ye' be."

Sally glared at them and said through gritted teeth, "And just what sort of woman do you think I am?" I remembered that horrible day after Julian had ridden me when I discovered what he did with my body. The soreness had evaporated quickly but the shame had not. The nude men piled in my bedroom had all, common as they were, used my body for pleasure in the forbidden ways. The two men did not look familiar but I hadn't gotten a good look at all of them, blurred as my vision had been with rage and dishonor.

"M'lady misunderstood," said the man who had spoken before. "We're Carriers an' we heard ya' don't ride yours." The other, who had tried to touch me, had not said a word. The way he looked at us put Sally on edge. She told me that he was not to be trusted.

I turned my back to them and whispered to the footman waiting just outside the door. He ran off without a word and I turned back to the men. "You still haven't said what I can do for you."

The speaker twisted his cap in his hands. "We belong to Master Paetus."

"And you don't want to be his any longer?"

"No m'lady." He looked at his mute mate who seemed oddly calm in the face of what would mean certain death if Paetus were to find out. The speaker went on. "We been marked for the fights in your honor. We heard ya' disapprove a' tha' fights and might…"

"I might want to purchase you?" Sally retorted. "Why would I bring you into my household? What skills have you to offer?" Sally silently warned that they might be spies.

Mr. Hall entered, saving the man from completing any of his stammering half-answers. Both men stared at the new arrival with his mechanical spectacles. To them he appeared to be aiming a blunderbuss at their chests. I introduced them, "Gentlemen, this is my tinkerer, Mr. Edwin Hall. I am interested in the acquisition of any Carriers who wish to be in my service but my protection, however rosier it appears than that of your current Incola, comes at its own cost. Mr. Hall will perform some tests on you."

Ed took their essence into his collector. "Can you make your mark?" he asked them, holding out a clipboard. The talkative one explained that while he could not, the other could sign for them both. I noticed that while his hand was meaty, his knuckles abraded, his handwriting was quite elegant though he tried to hide it with uneven slanting and a general downward slope.

I dismissed them, saying I would approach the subject of their purchase from Paetus when next we met. "Return home. Behave normally. I will pretend to find something about you that I like before your fights and make Paetus an offer." They thanked me and left, seemingly happy to be done with their meeting with me.

Happy to be done with Paetus' errand, Sally said as we followed Ed to the catalog.

Or perhaps they are innocent and just relieved to be away from us, I argued. *We can be quite intimidating.*

Ed said that both men were Carriers, unknown to his catalog. They had been recorded. I, ever the tender heart, lamented the loss of life that would surely follow the fights. I could not stop them, not without raising suspicion. Sally assured me that, though we had a fair share of blood on our hands, we had saved many men by killing Julian. Taking over his Carriers had doubled the number of freed men under the protection of Leon. I vowed to bring the same fate to Paetus, and any Incola who misused his Carriers, and Sally promised to allow me.

~

The séance was held in the very early morning. In this age, morning could be any time before the midday meal, which was often not served until three or four. At the medium's request for a very early morning session, the Dowager Countess had agreed to the unseemly hour of eleven but not a minute earlier as she did not want to inconvenience her guests.

I arrived at her home, which stood very near my old family home on the West End of Mayfair. The butler showed me to the sitting room. He announced me and I entered to find I was the last arrival. Only two ladies, beside myself, were not directly related to the Dowager. The countess greeted me as a friend and insisted I call her Ernestine. Her daughters were equally as friendly.

Emmaline and Charlotte were lovely women, not concerned with the goings on of the world nor the gossip that normally plagued these sorts of gatherings. Sally told them I would come calling often if they would accept. Their sister-in-law was not as pleasant. She insisted I call her Countess Edgington, or Countess if I must shorten it. She did not offer her Christian name. She was exceedingly snobbish with a face so pinched it looked like her teeth were made of lemon rinds. I knew she was chosen as a bride to the young Count because of money. The Wharlows were close to broke. Her dowry had rejuvenated their purse and paid for both Emmaline and Charlotte's dowries.

The sitting room had been rearranged and furnished with a round table, normally used for playing cards, and a chair for everyone of note and one for the medium, Madame Morvou. With a flair for the sensational, she seemed to appear out of nowhere and gave us all quite a fright. Her clothes, while they had a modest cut, were too richly colored for so early in the day. Tiny metal bobbles and mock coins were woven into her hair and clothes so that she made a jingling sound when she moved. She wore a vulgar amount of make-up, dark purple and heavy around the eyes and overly rosy on her cheeks and lips. She said all of that was because of her contact with the spirits. Because she could see and hear them, they often mistook her for one of their own if she was as pale and drab as the Queen thought proper. Her overly colored appearance was for her safety, so that she was not dragged away by the spirits who spoke to her. Sally barely contained her urge to roll her eyes.

We sat holding hands and chanting some inane saying while Madame Morvou walked around us, ensuring everything was perfect. When she closed the circle, we all felt a spark. The countess jumped something fierce and let out an undignified squeal. I chuckled at Sally's mocking of the stern lady and caught the Madame staring at me most oddly. She squeezed my gloved hand and begged us to be solemn; the spirits did not like to be taken so lightly. What we had all felt was a testament to the strength of the group. She was certain we would hear from those who had gone beyond if we concentrated.

"Oh, spirits beloved by those here gathered,
We call you forth from your cold place interred,
Come to us now so your words may be heard.
Rest is forever, a new day has dawned.
Keep not your silence, you're here to respond,
We seek a message from somewhere beyond.
Be it purgatory, heaven, or hell,
Give us an omen wherever you dwell
That you are listening by ringing a bell."

Her voice was eerie and hollow. She had said she was opening herself up to be filled with the spirits. The silence when she finished was unnaturally full. Then, in the distance, a large gong sounded, followed by a number of smaller bells tinkling. I knew these were parlor tricks but I allowed myself the luxury of pretending and was rewarded with goose skin and shivers.

The old Count spoke through the medium, saying how he missed his wife and how proud he was of her job marrying their children. He regretted he could not hold his grandchildren and spoke of a peaceful place where he waited for her to join him so they could cross over together when the time came. The Dowager was astonished when Madame Morvou even mentioned an occurrence on their honeymoon that Ernestine said no one but her husband could have known. It all seemed very convenient to me, but the Dowager looked satisfied.

"Uggh…for tha' last time, I donna speak whatever language ye' be using!" Madame Morvou shouted, exasperation bringing out her native accent. She explained, "Sometimes the spirits don't speak English. They usually do in England and that's why I spend my time here. I have never met one as persistent as this."

"Is it still present, speaking?" Sally saw the opportunity to expose her as a charlatan. We had spent our years of isolation learning languages we hadn't already mastered. I was irritated at her for her attempt to ruin a perfectly pleasant game.

"Indeed. The bugger won't shut up."

The women, especially the countess, looked shocked at her crassness.

"Repeat his words," Sally said. "Maybe one of us will understand."

"He keeps saying the same thing over and over. 'Veni ad moneo. Veni ad moneo.' It sounds Latin."

"It is," I responded. "It means, 'I came to warn you.' Who, spirit, did you come to warn?" I was intrigued. This seemed like a much more advanced hustle than her previous efforts. *She went to such lengths,* I told Sally. *We might as well enjoy it.*

"You shouldn't have encouraged him. He is very agitated now, gesturing toward you, m'lady. He's speaking too quickly for me to repeat. Perhaps we should make an appointment for another day. We could gather at your home where he might feel more comfortable. Spirits often speak easier in the home of the one they want to talk to."

Oh, here we go. This was all just an elaborate sales pitch, Sally said to me. I felt it was all innocent fun. No one was hurt, and a little money was spread from the highest to the lowest. Madame Morvou relied on sales of her show to survive. She always set her next séance before leaving the current one. I was about to acquiesce when Madame Morvou looked petrified.

We all watched as she opened her mouth and inhaled much more air than could be contained in the normal lung. It seemed to go on and on. Eyes rolled back, her head thrashed back and forth at odd angles and sounds of a struggle emanated from her gaping gob. Sally wondered how this frightening display normally got her more business. The ladies in attendance seemed horrified, not likely to hire her again.

Her head moved much faster than seemed possible. It was almost a blur. Her eyes focused on me and then her face followed a split-second later. I jumped in spite of myself. The irises were leaking color onto the whites of her eyes. When she spoke, it was not her voice. I was the only one who understood.

He spoke in Latin through her, "He isn't dead."

"Who isn't dead?"

"Archelaos Straton has always been a master of his army. You may have stolen the herd he shepherded using my body but he will quickly regain power. He is closer to his heart's desire than he has ever been." Madame Morvou coughed out a great stream of blackened smoke. The ghost had been as clear as country air going in but came out looking as if being inside a physical body had corrupted it.

There were gasps all around. That was no parlor trick; we had all seen it issue from her mouth. The medium knocked over her chair in her rush to get away. Pale skin shone through in the places of her face not covered with makeup. Her panicked eyes searched for the offending spirit and fell on each of us in turn. Finding he was gone, she began to shake. Her assistant grabbed her elbow for support and was rewarded with revulsion. She jerked away from him. Clearly what had just occurred was not a normal event.

The séance was over. Countess Edgington had had enough of this and demanded to be taken home. Her sisters-in-law spoke with me in hushed tones about how it couldn't have been faked. The older women gathered around Earnestine. Our hostess rang for tea while Madame Morvou's assistants gathered her things. The medium sat in the corner, shying from me when I approached. She saw me as the reason she'd been possessed. I was intrigued and forced her to set an appointment for Monday.

Sally replayed what he'd said in our head over and over, trying to make sense of it. The only person I had "stolen an army from" was Julian. I had never heard of Archelaos Straton.

5

The Pall Mall Incola Club was exactly as I remembered it: the outside similar to the gentlemen's clubs surrounding it but less sophisticated inside. A classy, well-furnished front room masked the spartan interior. Once past that facade, the club was hollow. Leon and I, both dressed in our finest, stepped out onto a large square sand pit and waited to be announced. We stood while hundreds of men stared at us from all levels. After a thunderous applause, Leon took me by my gloved hand and we started our ascension. A wide boardwalk wrapped all around the pit, alternated with steps to make a square spiral staircase. Our seats were at the very top, where the view was best.

We had to pass in close proximity to everyone in attendance. I worried that every man wanted to touch me but not one attempted it. Under each staircase there were hidden alcoves where even more men sat. On every level connected to the landing was another lounge with tables and comfortable chairs and couches. Both of those who had tried to renounce Paetus were there, though the silent one looked at me without recognition. Sally was right; he had been ridden. I inclined my head toward them in a silent greeting which they returned.

Paetus waited for us, all smiles, hugs, and handshakes. He too was unchanged. He, Julian, and Leonus could have been brothers. Paetus wore the oldest body but even that was of a man in his prime. It was only the glint in his eye, so unlike that of a younger man, that gave his true age away. Julian had been the handsome one, most like a youngest child, entirely spoiled, and Leonus was the gentle, kind, and considerate one, like a middle child.

We were seated no more than a minute when Leon stood to go. He had planned a special treat for me and needed to see to its details. He left me with Paetus, a handful of servants, and no less than a baker's dozen of guards on the topmost landing. My guards were all heavily armed and trained to never allow their attentions to wander from me. They stood far enough back that Paetus and I could speak openly. Sally took the lead and I watched. Tracing the carved designs of the cylinder hidden in my pocket calmed my nerves somewhat.

"Whose prick does a gal have to tug to get a drink in this dump?"

Paetus gave a guffaw. "It is good to have you back, my old friend." He gestured to a servant, who brought over two brandy snifters filled with a rich amber liquid. "I kept a case of your favorite in reserve."

Sally took her glass, as did Paetus, and we drained them in one gulp. I felt our face contort with the syrupy sweetness and bitter aftertaste of the liquor. Paetus saw and asked, "Is it not as you remember, Julian?"

"Nothing is as I remember and please call me Ramillia. Someone could overhear, you bloody fool. This body prefers the crisp clean taste of gin. It also chooses subdued flavors over the extreme ones I used to enjoy. At first I thought it might be a difference in the two genders but I think now it is the newness of this body. You and I stayed in our old bodies for too long. You would do well to find a new permanent home. The sensations of everyday living are almost overwhelming."

They then launched into a discussion I wish I could have missed concerning the sensitivity of breasts and the differences in lust between male and female. Sally made a crude joke about Leonus' small manhood, when we had no actual knowledge of its size. She knew truth mattered not; all men just want to hear that theirs was bigger and better than that of other men. Our heart skipped a beat when Paetus made a reference we did not understand but Sally covered well.

Sally said, "I find my memories blurring and slipping from my grasp much faster in this body than in my previous."

Paetus nodded as if he understood. "Probably the smaller capacity for higher thought found in a female mind is to blame, but you have your journals surely?"

It was Sally's turn to nod. "I try to record everything but the old ones are gone. When you and I so hastily destroyed my previous host we did not salvage any of my most recent journals from my offices. Speaking of important things lost, I came back to London to find that Theodore is missing. Do you know where he might be?"

"Thaddeus' son? No, not if he left the inn. You had better find him before they come for him. I don't have to tell you how dangerous the blood-kin to your body can be in the hands of another Incola. Do you think he has run from you? Fool boy if he has. If they find him before you do, he will wish they would kill him, and so will you. I will put my sniffers out. If he's in the city, we will find him."

We did not know who Paetus was talking about, but since he acted as if we should, even after telling him of our memory loss, we pretended to understand. "Thank you. If you do find him, don't approach. I am afraid he will run again. The innkeeper said that he disappeared after two men came looking for him. They spoke briefly to him and the next day he was gone."

"They took him? Then we are already too late."

"No. The men came back the next night and were furious that he had fled. They nearly tore the place apart looking. I reckon the mistress had to offer them a bit more personal service on the house than a simple pint, and bangers and mash."

There were more crude innuendos and jokes as Sally attempted to persuade Paetus that we were Julian. She did a wonderful job, quite convincing as the creepy lecher. Then she told Paetus about the two men who had come to our home asking for sanctuary. She did not feign interest in having them as our own as I had planned. I protested but she told me, *We cannot save them all. It is enough that we freed those belonging to Julian.*

I wept internally, *It is enough…for now. I won't be satisfied until all Incola are departed and those they treat as chattel are emancipated.*

Sally agreed with my heated vision of the future.

Paetus gestured and a few of his servants ran off down the stairs. He stood and went to the banister. A hush settled over the assembly and he announced the beginning of the games. “Welcome, brothers. We are gathered today to celebrate the return of our treasure. The loss of Julian Lawrence was a great blow to our kind but his life was sacrificed so that we might know and love our newest member, our Ramillia!”

The applause was most uncivilized. Sally stood us next to Paetus. She waved to the crowd and forced a smile to her face. Paetus raised his hands for silence and continued, “There will be much change over the next few years as we scramble to find our proper places. Ramillia will be denied nothing. Many of you will join her and many will change houses, but you will be hers only if she wants you.”

Though Sally hadn’t said their names nor given a description, both men were brought to the pit, stripped down to fight. They seemed happy at first, smug even, thinking I had told Paetus I wanted them.

“These two sought to undermine my authority over them. They were disloyal. They went to her on their own. Desertion will not be tolerated.” They were forced to their knees and I tried to cry out but Sally stopped me. She pushed me to a place where I felt carefree, like nothing was wrong. It reminded me of how I used to feel with Julian’s touch.

It was a place I would go whenever Sally was forced to endure something for the both of us. We were fully integrated and so I could no longer escape completely. I saw everything, experienced everything, but only I was allowed to view the horrific events through rose-colored glasses. I hope you do not see me as callous. The story will go on and, in the times like this one, when I describe events in a dry, seemingly uncaring way it is because I have shut down and Sally will let nothing touch me.

I know not what these men had done to so displease Paetus that he would use them in this way. He had instructed them to come to me. He may have even ridden one into my home. Paetus clearly had this planned. Their betrayal was no surprise, and the events unfolded much too quickly to be spontaneous.

Their jaws were forced open, their tongues lopped off. A hot coal was thrust into their mouths to cauterize the wounds. Both men convulsed and then lay sweating and pasty. Their exposed flesh lay in contrast to the bright red spray of blood on the sand.

A capital “I” shape was cut into their backs and the skin opened. Their ribs were disconnected from the spine and bent outwards until they snapped on the sides. They were left barely alive, and the procedure gave them each a gruesome set of wings.

"Ah, the blood eagle," Sally said. "That I remember. Thank you, old friend. What a glorious way to return. But the cost, two Carriers, is too much."

"You are welcome. Nothing is too rich for your return, though I should admit that I did choose the two lives I cared littlest for. A small price to pay to know it is truly you inside that feminine form."

Then I understood, even through the rosy haze. Paetus knew that Ramillia would never be able to stomach such an exhibition. Only a being as cruel and desensitized as Julian would enjoy this. Either way, Paetus had won. If I had attempted to spare their lives, he would have had two spies, his own eyes, in my house.

"Of course, you realize what a commotion you will have caused in my house. I will have to act horrified for Leonus, disgusted by you and your barbarian behavior. You may have cost me my ability to come to the club."

Paetus looked as if he had not thought of that. He took a small bow. "I certainly hope that is not the case. I did not intend that outcome at all. I can see you are settling into this role quite well, considering all angles. We will be together soon enough, you and I, when you are secure in this body enough to be riding again. Until then, I understand you must play your part. I am ever in attendance in our tenebrae."

I recognized the word as Latin for "darkness" but didn't have time to consider its usage. He took my hand and gave the skin just above my glove a kiss. Sally could no more resist the truth-commanding order of Paetus' touch than I, but she dressed the truth in *such* a costume. "I find your touch quite repulsive, Paetus. Oh, the female flesh is so fickle in its desires and disgusts!"

Paetus, chuckling, removed his hand and lips. "Here comes your fiancé now. Better affix your mask."

Sally pulled me to the surface and allowed my feminine humors to take over. I naturally went pale and broke out in a cold sweat. I backed away from Paetus and the rail with fear and horror in my eyes just as Leon made it to the platform. Paetus clapped his hand over his mouth, likely to hide the pleasure at my "performance" from showing. Leon caught me just as I fainted.

∽

I woke in the carriage. Leon hovered above me, concern on his face. I recoiled when I felt his hand on my skin. I heard a snippet of the mantra we chanted as a child, *Do not touch. Bad things happen. My skin is poison*, before Sally locked that memory away. "You forget yourself, sir!"

Leon sat back on his side of the carriage and smiled at me. It was a genuinely pleasant, happy smile, the likes of which I hadn't basked in for some time. "Actually, I am well within my right to touch you. It is you that forgets, fiancé."

He had said the engagement was for appearances only but, now, the warm way he looked at me said he had real affection for me. I tried to lift myself from the floor to the seat across him and was successful, though ungraceful. My gown slid and slipped in a way I was unaccustomed. I realized the gown and my corset had been unfastened to give me space for breath. I covered as best I could with the draped articles. "My gloves?"

He tapped his breast pocket. "Here. Safe. They are very interesting. Made from human skin, I suppose."

I nodded, feeling the green come back. "Julian's." I had not stripped them from his body; Paetus had at Julian's own request. They contrived and executed a plan to retain his gift of touch even after the destruction of his body.

"A word of advice: I might have the tanner put a stitch or two so that they look less like human hands."

I said nothing. I assumed the sickened mind of Paetus preferred the macabre style and I left them unaltered for his sake. I didn't care for them and found every excuse not to don them. Tonight had been the only time I had not discovered a vindication ample enough. "You seem quite alert to have touched them for long enough to remove them and tuck away into your pocket."

"Oh, that? That is the second reason I am quite safe touching you. I have my own gift of touch, though very different than the ones you, Paetus, and Julian possess. My touch negates another's power. You can see why I have kept it secret for so long."

I nodded. Indeed I could see. It was a talent that could go unnoticed and gave him the upper hand. That was how, on the first night of meeting me, Leonus had been able to resist the urge to tell the truth even while Paetus choked him. I patted the seat next to me and Leon joined me. I took his hand in mine and relished the fact that he was not about to attack. It was a luxury I had never experienced. My touch excited the passions in all people resulting in the urge to "fight or fuck," to use Paetus' words.

His voice broke me from my thoughts. "You did well not to save them." I looked at him in wonder at how he could think I had done well when two men had lost their lives. "I knew Paetus would try something like that. He tested you."

"Those two had come seeking to switch loyalties." The cylinder pressed against my leg and I wondered if activating it could have saved these men.

"To your home? We may need to move up our nuptials. Would you be opposed to wedding sooner rather than later?" When I was silent, he continued nervously. "I know we do not know each other very well but there is mutual respect and…necessity. I think we could grow to love each other and my gift of touch makes me uniquely able to provide companionship when no one else can."

I stopped him with a brush of my fingertips on his cheek. I had not known he had any real romantic interest in me but his stammering proved it. He was handsome enough but shorter than I, though in all fairness there were very few men of my height born in the ancient world. It was a good match even if all the world could not see it. He was an Incola such as I; one who wanted to save the world from those like Paetus.

I did put one caveat on his marriage plans. As we were able to live untold lengths, I demanded, in the polite and well-bred English way, that I be allowed a divorce, at his fault and payment, any time I wished. Almost 1800 years old, Leon understood and agreed to have the legal papers spelling out our agreement as soon as possible.

6

From then on I went nowhere without my fiancé. I could explain this away because of the fiasco at the club with Paetus. My only separation was at night, when etiquette said we must sleep in separate houses, and when I was at ladies-only events such as playing bridge or morning tea. So it was natural that I took him to the waterfront.

Observing the bustling life for so many hours, I was a familiar sight to most of the watermen. They were still shocked to see me approach.

I did not just visit the passenger ships and steamboats. I had to make very sure that Theodore was not taken on by any sort of vessel.

I gave each man coin, described my nephew, and promised true riches to the man who could detain him. "He will have money and perhaps a man or two guarding him," I told them. "Do not alarm him but grant him passage should he hire you. Find some excuse for delaying departure and send a man to me. I will pay you triple his fare," I told them and gave each a card with my address.

I repeated the process for the stagecoach stations and the railway. The train was the most difficult, for I could pay no amount to ensure they delay departure. The trainmen were proud of their schedule and a change in times could cause a deadly series of events. I had to settle for paying the ticket men not to sell to thirteen-year-old boys matching Theodore's specifics.

London had entirely too many inns to cover, in addition to the places offering rooms to young men of meager means. I had several letter-writing shops put out advertisements for scribes. Theodore might be looking for work since he no longer had my patronage, unless someone else, some other Incola, was banking him. After that, which took several days, there was nothing more my money could do.

Mr. Hall devised a way to search for hollow places behind the walls, so I explored my house for any hidden places that could hold records or journals. Though not as many as Julian had indicated, I found several secret passageways of which I had been unaware. These were sealed, especially the ones that had an entrance on the exterior of the house. There was one I left unobstructed.

As Julian stole the body in which I knew him, he had been unable to register all but the most severe sensations. Because of this, I had undergone training in the application and art of "exquisite pain." Before my learning he had to be satisfied with beatings twice a year, delivered by the traveling Mistress. After she taught me, Julian and I invented ways to increase the sensations to a level enjoyable to a man as desensitized as he. Julian had converted one of our extra bedrooms into a torture chamber, complete with a birching pony and a St. Andrew's Cross.

The secret passageway to this room showed some recent use, though I had not used it since before Julian's death. I estimated we had found the "tenebrae" to which Paetus had referred. The walls of the room were covered in various devices with which I was intimately acquainted. To my surprise, they had been kept oiled and greased and cleaned. I thought I was the only one with a key to that room. I immediately commissioned a new mechanical metal door and punch-key lock, the kind I knew even I would have difficulty breaking down. I set the code to something only I knew and had the walls lined with steel. The windows, too, were covered and I had made a place of darkness indeed.

The other triumph of the day was a small compartment found in the nursery. There were a dozen journals hidden here. They were not dusty as I might expect but that could be due to the seal on the storage space. I relocated them to the library and found they were written in some sort of code. The name Archelaos Straton was etched into the cover of the oldest one. A modern codex, its pages were bound together on the side, but the pages appeared to be cut from a scroll and rearranged into book form.

When Leon arrived for dinner that evening, I showed the books to him. He found them mysterious and settled into reading them right away. I had to rudely interrupt when I could stand it no longer, asking, "Can you decipher the code?"

He looked at me over the tops of his spectacles. "They are not written in code, my love. This is merely the old style of writing Latin."

"You can read it then?" Excited, I perched on the armrest next to him, having quickly become accustomed to the new nearness I could enjoy with Leon.

"It was used before my time but yes, I am familiar enough to comprehend."

"You will have to read quickly because I cannot bear to wait. I must know who Archelaos Straton was." I patted his shoulder and stood, looking to give him time and space to concentrate.

"I don't have to read these to know that, Ramillia. I knew Archelaos Straton for years. You knew him as Julian Lawrence but that is the name of the body he inhabited for the longest period of time. For all I know, Archelaos Straton could simply be the name of the body previous to that one. I do not know how old the consciousness you think of as Julian actually is, or Paetus for that matter." I collapsed in the settee across from him and he continued. "I grew up knowing that I was not only the second son to a wealthy Roman but a creature not entirely human, capable of living forever. I was the only one born to my father, though he had many children. It was not until I was a young man that I knew we could ride in the body of another, not until I met Archelaos and Sophus. Archelaos was a master at gathering men around him and Sophus, as his name would suggest, was clever and sly. Together they were hard to resist. I was their friend, but then they decided to take the bodies of Julian and Paetus, both of whom I had known to be noble and decent men. I begged them not to but they wouldn't hear it. I have been building my army, biding my time, waiting for the moment to come when I can avenge the death, or complete subjugation, of Julian and Paetus by Archelaos and Sophus. You are the first body to ever be tempting enough to entice Archelaos from Julian's."

"I think I spoke to the ghost of Julian, the real Julian, last week."

"You can speak to spirits?" he asked, one eyebrow raised.

"No, not I. I was in attendance for a séance held by the Dowager Countess of Edgington."

"You should know that those women posing as mediums are charlatans out for your money." His voice tone neared that of reprimand. He waved away my concern in a way reminiscent of every other Victorian husband. It rankled.

"I thought so too," I argued, "and looked to enjoy a morning of innocent fun but something overtook the woman's body and spoke through her mouth. He warned me against Archelaos Straton." That got his attention. He closed the book and leaned forward, resting his arms on his knees. No one else could possibly know that name, aside from Paetus and the people in this room. I insisted, "It had to be him."

Leon agreed, intrigued. "What did he say, exactly?"

Sally had repeated it so many times that she easily quoted in its original tongue, "Archelaos Straton has always been a master of his army. You may have stolen the herd he shepherded using my body but he will quickly regain power. He is closer to his heart's desire than he has ever been."

"Incredible. A true medium—a conduit for spirits who have passed on. We simply must see this person again." I understood his excitement. Speaking to the man who had carried Archelaos would have incalculable assets to our cause. Especially if what he said—that Archelaos was closer than ever to his heart's desire—was true.

I considered that by his description, all Carriers were a form of medium. Maybe Madame Morvou was like me and had a way of masking her true nature and found a way to profit from her ability. "She was hesitant at first but I was able to convince her to come here tomorrow morning for a private session."

"Wonderful. I will join you. Together we will figure this out. If it was the original Julian—he was my friend and may be more communicative with me around—he can help us. He might be in possession of information about Paetus' or another Incola's weakness."

∽

Madame Morvou never showed Monday morning. Leon and I took matters into our own hands. Her card held her address and we had the means of travel. Though I had been free to travel the city after Julian and I had wed, I found myself in a completely unfamiliar part of town when the carriage stopped. It was an average neighborhood, filled with moderately comfortable families' homes. With no inns, taverns, and marketplaces, no wonder it had escaped my attention.

As we climbed the stoop, we could see the front door was ajar, the latch shattered. A large boot print near the ruined knob bore witness that the door had been kicked open. Leon stepped around me, putting himself between my body and any danger. He called the guards to surround us and sent his two most trusted inside. Andrew came back out quickly.

"Whoever did this is gone, sir. Auley is checking upstairs but I think you are going to want to see this." He looked over Leon's shoulder at me. "The lady best wait in the carriage."

We would be ruled by no man, especially not an employee. I gestured to Mr. Hall and he carried his inventions into the house. Lifting our chin arrogantly, Sally pushed around Leon and past Andrew.

The front rooms were closed up, the furniture and fixtures covered by cloth, the way the servants of my London home had treated it when I planned my extended absence. Madame Morvou may have never intended to keep our appointment. Other than that, nothing seemed amiss.

Mr. Hall began taking his readings, collecting samples for his catalog. Andrew led us down into the kitchen. It was oddly decorated for a room that would normally be stark and plain white. Tiny red dots covered the walls, and a thick rug of the same shade lay under the chair closest to us. Every kitchen I had ever seen was devoid of decoration but in a house such as this, meals would have been taken there so perhaps that was why it was so adorned.

A man slumped in that chair. Leon rushed to him.

Useless effort, Sally said to me. *The man is clearly dead.* The crimson rug was no rug. It and the spots that had landed on every surface of the kitchen were blood. Andrew watched me carefully, ready to catch me should I faint as I joined Leon.

Pewter handles protruded from the corpse's torso, arms, and legs. A dishrag had been stuffed into his mouth with only a corner of the cloth visible. "Why would anyone do this?" I asked. "So many knives."

I was grateful no one else heard Sally. *Yeah, why not use one knife repeatedly? Leaving such a number of things that could be hawked must mean it was no burglary.*

"Not knives." Leon grabbed the handle of one and yanked. It came free of the body with a nauseating wet suction sound. Holding its gore-covered end out to me he said, "Someone stabbed this man with spoons." Looking around, he located the holder block nearby, still laden with knives. The killer could have easily grabbed those instead but he'd chosen spoons. "They did it for effect. This man was tortured."

Torture is usually a means to an end. With the victim's mouth blocked, they could not have wanted information from him. Who were they trying to intimidate? I wondered. I rounded the table and nearly tripped over the obvious answer. Madame Morvou's nude body lay mangled at my feet, her face frozen in terror with a mouth open that could no longer scream. The heavy large table had obstructed our view of her until I came to the far side.

She was tidy, with no spilled blood, and yet her death was measurably more horrific. Blood pooled just below the surface of her skin. The murderer had stripped her of her clothes and gripped each of her limbs on either side of the joints, twisting until the extremities faced the wrong direction. Handprints decorated her body, though none were as defined as the ones around her neck. He had choked the medium slowly, watching the life drain from her face. I placed my hand atop one macabre impression. It was not a match in size. "The killer was a man. Not too big, not too small."

I grazed her jaw during my measurements. Madame Morvou's mouth had been stretched open so forcefully that the hinge on either side shattered and yet the teeth were unscathed. Sally tried to imagine how such a thing could be accomplished. The jaw closed with a very strong muscle, so a hard utensil would have had to be used to pry them open that wide. That would have broken at least a few teeth. There was no sign that a weapon had been used anywhere on the body. "Not a man, a Carrier," Sally declared. The person who could do this would have to be inhumanly strong.

A shot rang out, loud in the small space, and I looked up just in time to see Leon clutch his chest and collapse. I scarcely saw the intruder standing in the door when he turned the smoking barrel of his revolver on me. Andrew made quick work of whom I now recognized was one of Madame's assistants. I couldn't stop the bloodshed that followed. Leon was holding a bloody implement and I had my hand wrapped around his dead employer's neck. He must have thought we were the murderers.

"My lady, we must make haste!" Auley shouted at me. He and Andrew guarded the doors while two of our men from outside carried Leon toward the front door. I knew he was right but I froze, my focus drawn to the table's edge. The murderer had carved a message into the oak.

Your blood is mine. You belong to me.

7

Leon was already fully healed by the time we got back to the house. It was fast, even for us. I asked him about it.

"One of the benefits of staying in my original body." He was mainly concerned with his bloody appearance so I asked the man who had served as Julian's valet to show Leon to the dressing room. My future husband and my past one were about the same size. There was bound to be something that fit. It felt intimate having him in the private section of the house.

Mr. Edwin Hall walked into the room carrying an oversized briefcase. As confident and steady as any seeing man, Ed used the hidden latch to open the secret room. He had finished with the final canister as Leon joined us. I explained the device's purpose and Leon immediately wanted to have it run on him. Ed acquiesced. He aimed the bell end of the collector at Leon and my fiancé did not flinch, even though his body had been blasted with a similar-looking device only an hour earlier.

I kept quiet while Ed showed Leon how it worked. "Brilliant," Leon declared.

"Quite," I agreed. "Madame Morvou?"

"Appears human, my lady," Ed answered. "Her two assistants also. There *was* another Carrier in that room, in addition to you and the Viscount."

"Was it—"

"The same scent as one of those you found lingering in the rooms your nephew occupied before disappearing, yes."

Either Theodore had killed Madame Morvou or a person very close to him had.

Ed was about to take his leave when I realized now was the time to ask. "I have a curious object on which I would appreciate your opinion." I turned to Leon and added, "Both of you." Pulling the cylinder from my pocket, I held it out in front of me.

The two men approached. "May I?" Ed inquired and then explained. "These," he said, gesturing to his sight-giving goggles, "do well to map out the objects in a room but do not provide as much detail as my fingertips."

Nodding, I allowed him to take it. I had no time to contemplate if my reaction would be the same as when Dawn held it, for he immediately handed it back. Cradling it against my chest eased my apprehension. Ed held his palms out to Leon. "Are my hands burned?" he asked my fiancé.

"They appear quite normal. Do they feel injured?"

"No," Ed answered. "Holding it didn't hurt, but it filled me with the dread that it could and would if I hadn't returned it quickly."

"Where and for what reason did you acquire such an item?" Leon asked what Ed would never presume was his right to know.

I told them of Ning Shiru and his warning that led me to believe it was a weapon for a female warrior. I also described the liquid-filled center and the elaborate carvings of the woman, her suitors, and the mob.

"I could find a way to take a sample of the liquid to test its qualities," my tinkerer offered.

Seeing the way I clutched the cylinder, the most honest man I've ever known then said, "If keeping that object safe matters, you will not let it out of your sight. For while I fear it, more overwhelming is my desire to see it destroyed. Other men may feel the same way."

So females would long to be its owner and males would take action to keep it from us. It was up to me to discover its power in secret.

∽

The inspector arrived at our home a few hours later. His uniform was new, yet the tailor had underestimated his size. This man was either well-compensated at his job or he took bribes, and lots of them. His mustache completely hid his mouth and only the wiggling revealed its location when he talked. I showed him into the library and asked him to sit, though he wouldn't. I ordered tea and knew by the look on his face that when it came, he wouldn't reject that hospitality. The constable who came with him stood outside.

The inspector asked, "What were you doing at the house of Madame Morvou this morning?"

"I had an appointment with her for a reading," I replied, "and when she did not show, my fiancé and I went to the address on her card."

The disdain for the supernatural showed on his face. He obviously thought my interest in such things foolish. "What did you find there?"

"You must have seen or you would not be here." We heard a scuffle in the entry. Someone was coming into the library whether Mr. Boyd allowed it or not. My steward was not accustomed to being bowled over.

Paetus strode into the room with Mr. Boyd on his heels. Flush-faced and improperly dressed, he looked as if he'd been roused from slumber and dressed in the carriage ride. "Thank the gods you are all right." He raised his volume as he declared, "If that fiancé of yours cannot keep you safe then he doesn't deserve you and I will have to whisk you away for your own protection." Paetus winked at me.

I whispered to Mr. Boyd to make sure that Leon knew Paetus was in the house. He had probably heard the man's entrance. I must act as if Paetus was perfectly welcome in my home and I felt comfortable entertaining him, though in reality my heart beat unnaturally fast from the second he came in. Dawn was so near. What if he could sniff her out? What if he used his touch to force the truth from us?

Just then tea was wheeled in and Paetus flippantly dismissed the inspector. When the inspector made no move to leave, he was hit with the brunt of Paetus' attention. "Why are you still here?" Paetus demanded. "Have you taken a sudden dislike for club money?"

"I… I wa-was just g-gathering information for my report," the inspector stammered. "Surely you don't mean to say *she* is a member?" He inclined his head at me as if I couldn't see him.

"Sugar, lemon, or milk?" I asked Paetus.

"Sugar, my dear. Six, if you please. My sense of taste is not what it used to be." He smiled at me and then turned back to the waiting inspector to answer his query. "That is *exactly* what I mean to say."

"B-bu-but she is a…a *woman*." He said the last in a whisper as if it was a salty word, or maybe he thought I wasn't aware of my gender.

I passed tea to Paetus and he took a generous gulp, not waiting for it to cool. It must have burned him but he didn't show that he'd even noticed. "Lady Brooksberry was inducted before her husband perished. After, she took his place in the top tier. Her protection comes second only to mine, as owner of the club. Her fiancé, however spineless he might be, is also a member and thus above suspicion."

"The foreigner, an *Italian*?" That was worse in the inspector's opinion than being a female.

Paetus was a Roman and I could see it rankled him to have the inspector insult his heritage. "I have had quite enough of your questioning, Inspector. You should go."

"My report must be completed. I won't be able to gloss over the death of Madame Morvou."

"And just why not?"Paetus asked, incredulously. "She was a commoner, a swindler...she most likely tried to charge the murderer for fraudulent services."

"She was known by many powerful people and there were witnesses," the inspector pressed.

"Who saw what...a carriage?" Paetus argued.

It wasn't difficult to determine who owned the carriage seen racing away from the scene of the crime. I was the only peeress, besides the queen and her daughters, who traveled so heavily guarded. *Don't worry,* Sally assured me. *No one would think that a woman of means such as yourself could ever do anything as horrific as that.*

They might, I argued back. I am no stranger to bizarre deaths. If anything, they might believe I'm a serial killer. If I were ever held to the same courts as regular men, I could easily be found guilty. There was enough evidence of my involvement in illicit activities.

"Pshaw." Paetus flicked his hand through the air. "You just say in your report that Lady Brooksberry was there to employ the medium's services and was terribly distraught by what she saw and left in a hurry after her fiancé was caught in the crossfire."

"Actually, that is what happened, inspector," Leon said in his Italian accent. He stood in the hall, leaning heavily on a walking cane.

Paetus stood and bowed to me. "You have your hands full with family concerns. Now that I know you are well, I can rest easy. Thank you for the wonderful tea. I hope to see you at the club again soon. I will see myself out, since I saw myself in." He smiled in that roguish way that made me almost forget what a fiend he was. "I will take the inspector with me."

They left with only a short pause for Paetus to shake hands with and whisper something to Leon. After they were gone, Leon joined me for tea. I noted that he took his with a bit of lemon and a single sugar—the same way I took mine.

"What did Paetus say to you?" I asked.

"Nothing."

I frowned, hurt that he would keep something from me.

He elaborated, "Oh, how I should donate more Carriers to the fights and how I am a disappointment to all Incola—you know, the usual."

For the first time I was suspicious of Leon. He and I had been alone the previous night when I told him about Madame Morvou. I certainly hadn't killed her. Sally neither. That only left him. Maybe I shouldn't trust him as explicitly as I had been.

The spirit talking through the medium had said that Archelaos was closer to his heart's desire than he had ever been. What if he warned me that my husband-to-be was under the control of my deceased husband? What had been my husband's desire: me, my ability to birth an army, my children? No one was closer to us than Leon. *Why would he leave the message about your blood belonging to him? It doesn't make sense, Ramillia,* Sally argued with reason but the man I had known as Julian was sly. He could be sending me on a wild goose chase.

While I sat contemplating, Ambrose came skipping in looking dapper in his sailor suit. Dawn walked behind him, somber but beautiful in her blue matching dress. My son stopped and glared at Leon, ignoring the man's attempts to entice him closer with a scone. He came to me and in a volume none too low said, "What is he doing here at this hour?"

I pulled him onto my lap. "We had an appointment and he was injured. He is only resting and recuperating."

"The servants say he will move in here and be my new father. I don't like him."

"Ambrose! What has gotten into you? I taught you better manners than that. I am so sorry, Leon." I apologized even though a part of me wondered if I shouldn't give more credence to a child's instinct.

"That is all right, Ramillia," said Leon. "I can understand. Ambrose has been the only male in the family for years now. It is not uncommon that he would feel threatened by me. Dawn likes me well enough for the both of them, don't you, dear?" He pulled Dawn onto his knee and complimented her hair. "I remember when I found you. I knew straight away that you were Ramillia's daughter. You will be as beautiful as your mother one day." He bounced a golden curl with his fingertips.

"Don't touch her!" Sally screamed at him. She stood us up, bringing Ambrose with her. I tried to soothe her but something in the way Leon had touched and admired Dawn had triggered her memories of Papa. Sally would do anything to keep Dawn from being abused as we were.

"Ramillia," Leon uttered, his hurt at the accusation obvious. "You know I would never be untoward with Dawn."

"Dawn, come here," Sally ordered. "Just don't touch her, Leon. I am warning you."

"I am the one who found her, who rescued her. I am not y—"

"I think you should go."

Leon stood. "I am sorry you feel that way and I will always defer to you in matters of your children. I will find a way to endear myself to the boy and you again."

∽

Leon's endearment was effective indeed. Adorable too. He requested our presence in the garden, wearing a smile so infectious I wondered what made him so confident. "With your permission, I would like to present Ambrose with a gift." I kept Dawn near me and Ambrose stood almost inside my skirts. I nodded my permission. Ignoring the dirt, he knelt in front of us, focusing on the small child. Making a big show out of patting his pockets and looking for something, Leon opened his jacket. A beagle puppy's head peeked from his inside left breast pocket.

A chorus of "aww" came from all three of us. It licked our hands when we tried to pet it. Dawn asked, "Can we keep it, Mama?"

"Of course," I assured her. How could anyone resist a face as cute as that?

Leon's plan was genius. "Every boy needs a dog. I will come over every day to take care of it. You won't have to do a thing, Ramillia. Ambrose and I will make sure he is fed and exercised properly, won't we?"

My son didn't answer him but asked me, "Is he my dog? No one else's? He's all mine?"

Leon took the pup out of his pocket, handed him to Ambrose, and answered, "Yes, he is all yours. You are big enough to be responsible for a dog of your own. I was your age when I got my first pet but I had many brothers to share with and to have help from. You can't have a dog without a name. What would you like to call him?"

Ambrose thought for a moment, looking at the puppy face. "Baxter…no, Angus. His name is Angus."

"Angus it is. I cannot think of a better name for him."

Ambrose put Angus on the ground and the chase began. My fiancé and son frolicked for hours that day. They got dirty and all three smelled like dogs when they were finished. I sat with Dawn on the bench, watching them. That day is the fondest memory I have of Ambrose. He was just a boy that day. A boy with his dog. I can't remember a time when he looked as happy.

When the sun became too much for our delicate skin, we females went inside. I took the opportunity to speak with Dawn about men in general and about Leon in particular. I was as delicate as possible on such an indelicate subject but I did not speak in vague metaphors. I told her what occurred at night between a man and his bride. I described the process and blushed profusely. Dawn was embarrassed but handled it well enough.

I told her that men valued ignorance in their brides, mistaking it for innocence. She would do well to feign naiveté of the matter.

I didn't want to admit that my father had inappropriate physical contact with me when I was very young. Sally said we must. My mother had known and did nothing to protect me. She had even blamed me. I steeled myself and said, "It is never okay for a man to touch a young girl, no matter what he says." I asked her to tell me if any man made her uncomfortable. "I will not be angry with you for this, no matter who the man may be. I would go to any lengths to protect you. Do you understand how important you are to me?"

"Yes, Mama."

"I must ask you before I allow Leon to take a place in this family. Has he ever touched you or treated you in an ungentlemanly way?" I would not hesitate to extricate ourselves from his grasp.

"No, he is nice to me."

Her comment seemed to only be half a statement. She was hesitant to tell me something. "Has anyone?" I pressed. "Whatever it is will be less scary after being shared. You can tell me anything. There is no one I love more in this world than you."

"Even Ambrose?" she asked, her voice barely a whisper. She refused to make eye contact.

"Has your brother done something?" I had just told her I would take her side, never doubt her, but already I was tempted to go back on my word. Not my son, I silently prayed.

"No, Mama. It's just that sometimes I catch him looking at me...at night...or when we are fighting...like he wants to gobble me up...like he knows a secret that I don't...like he has plans for me. It is hard to describe but it always makes me feel strange."

Had Ambrose inherited a pension for sexual feelings for his immediate family from my father, the way Thaddeus had? "He is just a baby, probably curious about the gentler sex. Even so, I am glad you told me. I will keep my eyes on him. We will get you moved out of the nursery too. I should have done it long ago but I guess I am hesitant to let you grow up yet. I missed so much of your childhood." I pulled her into a hug. "I am so sorry, Dawn."

"It's all right, Mama. I understand. You're a lady. You can't very well declare to the world that you have a bastard from your youth."

I held her away from me to look at her. "Is that what you think, that I sent you away and keep your existence hidden because I am protecting my reputation? Not so. I am unashamed of you and could not care less about my reputation."

I paced the room, wondering how much I should tell her. I had already burdened her with so much. "I keep you hidden because there are bad people who want nothing more than to use you, imprison you, breed you until you die. I won't have that. Your life is your own, to do whatever you want, but before I can free you, I must make the world safer." Women's suffrage was a small movement with no real backing. I wasn't interested in politics but knew that until women had equal rights with men, Dawn would never be truly free. Maybe not even then, for our world had less equality than the human one. "You can travel, study, publish, do anything you desire. If you want nothing more than to have a family then you shall have it, but no man will force you to it. You will have your choice in husband. You will not be sold."

Pausing again, I hesitated to tell her the whole truth. Sally insisted, *She should know*. "My husband gave your hand in marriage to a man named Paetus Crowley even before he laid eyes on you. I would give you choice in the matter but the law sees it differently. Julian thought of you as a possession to be bartered. Paetus is of the same mindset and is desperate to acquire you. He does not know you are here and I would like to keep it that way."

"Why would he want me so badly?" she asked.

"You are special, like me."

She looked delighted at her bare hands. "What is my gift?"

"You may have the gift of touch—we know not yet." Both my children knew my touch was special, that it excited, although we had never discussed the source of that power. "You and Ambrose, and every child of mine to come, are not normal. Neither are Leon, Julian, me, and even Paetus. We carry genetic traits that allow us to live much longer than humanly possible. We heal quickly and are difficult to kill. You will grow up but never grow old. Ambrose is at a disadvantage because there are many males but few females. You and I are extra special because, as women, every child we bear will carry the same traits. That is why Paetus wants you so much. Without you, only a portion of his children have a chance of being Carriers."

8

True to his word, Leon came every morning. At first he and Ambrose trained the dog in the garden. My cook fussed when they traipsed through her herbs, and her ranting solidified the friendship of the two most important men in my life. They bonded over ignoring the woman.

I wanted to trust Leon again; he made it easy. Leon decided that Angus, who now slept in my son's bed at night, was old enough to take proper walks. He said Ambrose, while precious to me, was no more valuable than any of his other Carriers. No Incola would risk a war with us to gain him. Anxiety turned my stomach but I allowed it only if they took our best three guards. Park Lane, on which my house sat in the middle, was named for its proximity to Hyde Park and every front window of our home overlooked it. I could watch their whole excursion.

Ambrose was growing into such a little man. The responsibility of caring for another living thing matured him. Sometimes when he looked at me, I felt a much older soul peering out. Dawn was also maturing. I was so proud of her; she had taken the weight of our talk and carried it lightly. Though serious about keeping herself safe, she wasn't encumbered by it.

I knew she wanted to go outside, to ride a horse in the park with the other girls of means. I could not even let her go in costume to the market with the servants because a guard detail would ruin the disguise. Leon said she would be safe if she were bonded to an Incola. I would not do that to her. Bonds made early in life were more permanent, so I'd read. She could choose her mate—Incola, Carrier, or human—when she was grown.

One morning when Leon and Ambrose walked with Angus and Dawn was engrossed in a book, I heard a sound from the torture room. The one my husband had built, the one I'd lined with metal and reinforced. I keyed my private code into the numerical pad and the mechanical door hissed open, the gears inside silently turning.

Paetus was inside. On his knees, stripped down to the loincloth worn when Mistress came to the club, his face downturned. I was forced to identify him based on the top of his head. I sealed the door behind me. Mr. Hall had assured me that the room was inescapable and I was taking no chances with Dawn so near. I had suspected that Paetus was the visitor when I discovered the room's apparent use and upkeep. He and Julian used the room just as I had with my husband. Their stolen bodies needed this sort of treatment. The pain told them they were still alive.

I said nothing for many minutes, knowing the wait was part of the torture. Mistress had trained me to be a wonderful Dominatrix; my husband had shown me how to apply that training to Incola with a considerably higher threshold for anguish. I thought back to that first time I had participated in marking Paetus and beating Julian. I had appreciated the designs our whips made on other men's skin but my husband was the only one I really desired to hurt. Paetus must have expected me to apply the instruments or he wouldn't be there. I had to come up with the animosity to give him what he expected.

I thought of what he and my husband had planned to do to and with my body, what Paetus probably planned to do with Dawn's body. The desire to hurt him rose easily. Sally stoked the embers of my heart while I spoke to Paetus. "Why would you come here after I told you your flesh was repulsive?"

Keeping his head bowed, Paetus said, "Mistress, our tenebrae is the place we may interact where you never have to touch me with your hands. I come here every Tuesday, as agreed. I am honored that you chose to attend today. I am yours to do with what you want."

The name "tenebrae" indicated a Catholic ceremony. Latin for shadow or darkness, the word was perfect for what happened in this room. It had been four years since I had laid cane to skin but the body remembered. Julian told me that once. Though I hadn't understood when he'd said it, I did now. He had me perfect the arts he wanted my body to remember when he took it. Fighting, fencing, riding, rutting, pianoforte, piccolo—they had all been for him. Acting as Mistress was no different.

I strapped Paetus to the birching pony, using all manner of instruments in rapid succession to set his nerves on fire. When I applied the feather duster, Paetus wept. He could feel the light tickling touch and thanked me profusely. I was his Mistress and he my servant. Locking the door behind me, I allowed him to leave when he felt ready, able.

That session with Paetus eased my temperament. My behavior of the previous weeks had been erratic: my suspicions of Leon, short temper with the children, disconnection with Madame Morvou's pain and suffering. I needed the violence. I needed an outlet for my anger and distrust. Being Mistress did this for me and if it gave me a small measure of control over Paetus—and subsequently my daughter's life and safety—that was an added bonus.

∽

Callers ceased coming—save my secret one. Too often noblewomen and solicitors alike were left standing on our stoop, told we were "not at home." Eventually they stopped visiting to avoid the insult of being turned away.

We sought another true medium who could channel Julian. We found only con artists who spoke in generalities, never mentioning my dead husband. Perhaps they worried the man who held the purse strings would not appreciate the attention to my previous husband. Thinking that might work in our favor, we pressed on, hoping Julian's spirit would force his way inside any medium capable of containing him.

Returning from yet another failed outing, we approached the house on foot to see a ruckus at our front door. A commoner tried to muscle his way past my steward. Mr. Boyd was shouting, "I have told you. The lady of the house is not at home."

The man saw Mr. Boyd glance our way and abandoned his efforts to enter the house. He shouted that we should watch him, see what happens when someone tried to leave him. "Why choose her over me?" he demanded. It sounded like a youth throwing a tantrum. His irregular, jerky gait was familiar to me, recognizable as a man being ridden. He yelled, "You are both mine," and then threw himself in front of a cart carrying great vats of water and several men.

The four large stock horses trampled him and the large wheels rolled over his body. I will never forget the horrible crunching sound of his bones under that much weight. Flinching up and away, my gaze landed on the third story window where Ambrose watched the whole thing.

Hundreds of neighbors witnessed the next shocking event. The man wasn't dead. His twisted, mangled body twitched and although his elbow bent in the wrong direction, he managed to retrieve a small derringer from his pocket. Laying it on the cobblestone in front of him, he used his thumb to pull the trigger. At close range, his face imploded into his brain.

Leon rushed me into the house, shouting commands at his men the whole way. I ran up the stairs to Ambrose. My baby shouldn't see that. He would need his Mama. Ambrose sat under the window with his back against the wall rocking and mumbling, "Why, why did he have to die?"

I scooped him up, mindless of the possibility that my skin might touch his and carried him to his bed in the nursery. So great was the heat that radiated off him, it could be felt through his clothes and mine. I stripped his clothes and tucked him into bed.

Fever overtook his body that night. There was little anyone could do.

The illness baffled Leon. Carrier children almost never got sick. Further compounding Leon's confusion was his inability to enter Ambrose's body. He was reluctant to ride my son because of the bonding that would occur, but I begged him. It was the only way I knew to force the fever from Ambrose's little body. My son was too young to repair his own body, even if his heat-addled brain had been capable.

Never had Leon been secret with his method, though I had not seen it firsthand. While I anxiously watched Ambrose, Leon retrieved an inkwell and quill from a desk down the hall. Careful to barely scratch Ambrose's baby skin, he drew a mark on the boy's shoulder. If my son had been a full-grown man and willing participant, Leon would have injected the ink below the skin. I admired the view as he stripped off his coat, waistcoat, shirt, and undershirt.

It had been a while since I'd enjoyed the male physique. Leon was more fit and burly than his covered shape led me to believe. His abdominal muscles were particularly well-developed, and while now it is quite commonplace to see a young man with a ripped six-pack, then it was a level of fitness unheard of in the genteel. Only the working class were muscled. Overlaying these muscles were fine, almost lace-like tattoos. He dipped the quill in the ink again and, pulling his trousers down to find a bare spot at the hip, drew on his own body. It made me love him a bit more, to know that the marks meant he had bonded and cared for so many.

Kneeling on the floor next to the tiny bed, Leon went deathly still and ghostly white. Ambrose began weakly fighting, his head thrashing. Leon stood and backed away, shaking his head, and my son stopped his struggle.

The Incola who protected my clan could do nothing for my son. He collapsed in a chair and sipped on the warm milk the footman brought. Only then did I notice how many servants and guards crowded the room.

I called Mr. Hall in. He had never taken readings of my children because I had never doubted they were Carriers. Now I had doubt. Perhaps Leon could not get in because Ambrose was human. Ed took a canister of Ambrose's smell and went to catalog it. He asked me to come down to the secret chamber and hear the results, and something else Ed had thought important, but I couldn't be coaxed from my son's side.

Ambrose barely moved all night, though he moaned and muttered nonsense, his sweat soaking through the sheets. Servants brought the drip tray from the icebox. The frigid water brought obvious relief when I moistened a cloth and dabbed his head and so I also had them chisel a bit of the ice block to add.

His fever peaked in the wee hours of the morning and I submerged him in an ice bath. It irked me to do so, remembering the torture of such a shock to the system. I had often suffered such a treatment at the hands of Dr. Federick at West Freeman Asylum for Lunatics when I'd had no fever. That was done in malice. This was done out of love.

I put his body back in bed after his skin felt more normal. I sat next to him, my calming gloves soothing his forehead so that he might sleep dreamlessly.

I woke to the clinking of dishes and opened my eyes to find his bed empty. Panicked, I looked around and found Ambrose standing naked, eating every crumb of the snack and tea the maid had served me the previous evening. My son looked at me and said, "I want more, Mama."

I rang for service but Ambrose wanted to eat in the breakfast room. I dressed him myself and we went down. Leon had stayed overnight and was already eating. We watched as Ambrose put away more food than I thought could fit in such a small body. He ate three poached eggs and nearly half a ham, shoving biscuits and fruit into his face between every bite of protein. When he finished, I sent him outside with Angus.

I found it quite nice to have the gentle-spirited Leon in my breakfast room. He said he'd had to feign his injury for the same inspector had shown up to investigate this death as Madame Morvou's. My fiancé said the glorified bobbie probably suspected our involvement in both deaths yet had the decency to keep his suspicions to himself.

Leon and I went to talk with Ed in the library, where he assured us my son was a Carrier. My tinkerer then described his readings on the man who'd committed suicide in front of our house. The dead man was an oddity. The catalog said he was a partial match for both the unknown at Madame Morvou's and the unknown in Theodore's room.

Mr. Hall speculated that the man in those rooms was a blood relative of the dead man. Ed needed more samples. He seemed to be holding back and, when I pressured him, said, "Lord Ambrose has a similar reading. Is it possible that the dead man was your nephew?"

Although I did not want it to be true, I had to consider the possibility. *No,* Sally said. *He wasn't mixed race. The skin was much too light for that.*

Yes, but even a black woman can be pale if she keeps out of the sun, I replied.

So it is possible but not probable. Why would Theodore kill himself after arguing with Mr. Boyd about seeing us? Why would he want us to see his death?

We whirled around as Dawn ran into the room bawling. "He killed him. Ambrose killed him!"

9

Leon ran to see what Ambrose had done while I consoled Dawn. Sitting in my lap like a small child, she sobbed. I couldn't remember the last time I'd seen her cry. She cried the hot tears of anger often enough, but sorrowful tears were rare. They flowed down her cheeks and fell in big drops onto our dresses. I let her cry. I still hadn't asked her what happened when Ambrose came shuffling in, Leon in tow.

Leon carried a limp Angus in his hands and the sight of that furry body renewed my daughter's sorrow. "Can we…?" I didn't finish my question because Leon shook his head. Dawn whimpered. "What happened?" I asked my son.

Ambrose proclaimed, "Dawn was jealous that Angus loved me more. She kicked him when he wouldn't come to her and now he won't wake up." Ambrose reached up, grabbed the dead dog from Leon, and demonstrated for me.

The grinding of its little neck bones made me queasy. He held it down at his side, by the scruff of its neck.

Dawn watched me as I watched my son. "That's not what happened, Mama," she whispered. I turned to her. "He did it on purpose. I was outside reading on the bench and Angus"—her voice cracked on his name—"came up to me. All I did was pat his little head and Ambrose got so mad. He yanked Angus away. He hurt him and then when Angus wouldn't stop whining, Ambrose wrenched his snout hard to the side. There was a little snap and I knew…"

"Liar! You did it because you're still mad about your paper dolls."

Dawn stood up, fists clenched. "I am not a liar! I don't care about the dolls anymore. All I did was pet him." Her sudden switch from grief to ire had me worried we'd had too much contact.

"Shut up," Ambrose screamed. "Angus was mine. Everyone thinks you are so special because you're a girl. A girl isn't special! *I* will be a gentleman. *I* will be Earl of Brooksberry! Everything here will be *mine*. Mine to sell or break or burn. You'd better hope you are married before it comes to that."

"Ambrose!" I was stunned at such a selfish and cruel speech. I wasn't sure where he'd picked up the idea that men had total control over their female family members, but he seemed to grasp it very well. I had not raised him to think that way.

Not knowing who to believe, I sent them both to their rooms while I thought. Remembering how we had told Ambrose, "Next time you feel the urge to wreck something beautiful, choose something of your own," Sally felt it was entirely possible he had killed Angus. It could have happened as Dawn said. I hated to think my baby was capable of such a thing. Sally refused to accept that Dawn was capable of killing.

Leon buried Angus in the garden silo and went to his own house for the night. Neither of my children would come out of their rooms for the funeral.

∽

An idea struck me in the middle of the night and I sat up in my bed still half asleep. Sally grumbled about how we needed our rest for tomorrow. It would be Tuesday and we must be strong mentally and physically for the tenebrae with Paetus. I jotted down a note in the dark and tried to get back to sleep.

In the morning I was more excited than I cared to admit. There was something about a man like Paetus submitting to my will, needing what only

I could give him. I hadn't told Leon about the arrangement; I guessed I would have to after we were married.

My midnight scribbling was almost impossible to read. I finally deciphered three useless words: "body or ego." Sally said that's how it always was with dreams. They seem so important at the time but in the light of day make little sense.

In the breakfast room, I ate with my children. Neither of them spoke or even acknowledged the other. Dawn's face was red, her eyes swollen from crying. Was she upset by the events or riddled with guilt? Ambrose showed no signs of mourning Angus. He was young and perhaps did not comprehend the finality as Dawn did.

"Have Leonus bring us a new Angus," Ambrose commanded between bites.

Sally wondered at his use of Leon's old name but I was sure I had slipped up and used it often in front of the boy. "I think not, Ambrose."

"Why?" he demanded, throwing down his fork. "There are lots of other puppies. Get me another."

"Yes but there was only one Angus and he is dead. You promised to take care of him—"

"I did not! He did."

I ignored that he interrupted me. I didn't ask who he meant. Leon had vowed to feed and exercise Angus. I told Ambrose, "You are obviously not ready for the responsibility of your own hound." He started to argue again but I held up my hand. "Perhaps we will try again after I am remarried, but if we do, the dog will be all of ours and not yours alone."

Ambrose scowled at me.

∽

My temper flared. Tuesdays could not come soon enough. The tenebrae called to me. I needed to dominate. The BDSM lifestyle was not yet defined at that time. What we had with Paetus wouldn't have fit into the current definition anyway. In reality, the submissive has all the power, ending the game at will. That is not how it was with us. There was no safeword, no act too depraved for Paetus. He was completely under my control. I knew I could end his life in that body and he wouldn't stop me for he had hundreds of other bodies.

My sessions with Paetus satisfied us both. I blindfolded him, stuffed cotton in his ears, and clamped his nose closed, isolating his sense of touch so that he could feel more. He complimented my genius and thanked me for every stroke. Using my specially adapted cane, I reduced his back to quivering ground meat. The scent of his blood wafted up into my nostrils and I had an idea.

I invited him to dinner.

Leon hated the plan, although he agreed when I explained my reasoning. Paetus arrived on time, followed by the five most powerful Incola in England. They each came with an entourage of at least twenty men. What I was doing had never been done. All Incola are inherently suspicious of others of their kind. Besides the Incola Club, which Paetus declared a safe zone, no more than a few ever gathered in the same room.

Paetus instructed me how to word the invitations to convince them that I had shopped around for the placement of my "future" children. Not a single man declined but that didn't mean they trusted me. Betrothed to Julian at such a young age, I never had to endure the mating rituals of the wealthiest Englishmen. They dressed in London's finest, brought their largest and fittest Carrier guards, and casually mentioned their income, how much land they owned, or their number of servants.

Bragging came easily to Incola, subtlety not as much. I knew the wealth and status of each, before we ever went down to dinner.

No other women were invited, so our seating was inappropriately uneven. Nobody minded. When soup was served, my tester, Percy Richards, tasted it from the serving dish. All attendees gasped when his face went red. He clutched at his throat and gulped down my own wine. To calm everyone down, I broke a strict etiquette rule. I spoke Incola business aloud in mixed company. "Paetus tells me most of you have been in these bodies for quite some time. I designed my courses with that in mind and brought in a guest cook from Her Majesty's foreign territory—India. The bill of exotic fare can be found beside each of your plates. I am certain you will find the cuisine to your liking. The soup is not poisoned. It is simply too spicy for a man as young in his flesh as Mr. Richards."

My guests had their own testers try every single course, even after Percy had already done the job. Each had the same reaction. The Carriers struggled to retain composure, dripping sweat from their rosy faces, assuring their masters the food was safe though spicy. The Incola praised each of the ten courses more than the previous, with the tandoori chicken, made both hot and red by the over-abundance of red chili powder and cayenne, being the favorite. These men couldn't get enough of the zesty condiments like ground mustard seeds and black peppercorn, three-pepper chutney, and pickled ginger.

Those seated at the table became concerned that I did not eat the same food. I explained, "My body is exactly the age it appears and I cannot stomach all the seasonings."

As I was the only woman in attendance, it was perfectly natural for my guests to retire into the smoking lounge without me after the potent brew of Indian pressed coffee was finished. Ed rushed into the vacated dining room to fill a canister with the scent of each Incola, drawing from their chairs. I had him start with the one I knew least and end with Paetus. If *his* scent wasn't clear, we could always get another sample. I assisted Ed in labeling each with the Incola's name.

Rushing to join the men as soon as I was finished, I was shocked to find Ambrose in their midst, wearing his bedclothes. He sat on Paetus' lap. Leon looked pale, his mouth gaping, his cigar unlit. I rang for the governess and hurried my son off to bed. He looked pleased with himself and, when we made it to the hallway, told me he should like to be invited to the next Incola party since he would someday be one of the greats. Skipping up the stairs, deaf to Mrs. Ledger's admonitions, Ambrose left me wondering where he'd heard about Incola and his own nature. Dawn must have told him. I planned to have a serious talk with her in the morning.

I rejoined the men to find a game of poker forming. Leon still stood where he had when I left but had since drained his drink. I was seated next to Paetus. Sally made a joke about catching up and I downed two gin and tonics. I called the game and dealt.

Before we looked at our cards, Paetus leaned over and whispered, "Whatever I have done to fall out of favor can be undone, I assume. I will give you anything you desire. Our old agreement is nothing compared to what I will do to claim her." When I looked at him in confusion, panic bubbling just below the surface, he said, "Your boy said that you'd found your daughter, that she lives here and that you didn't want me to know about her."

Sally took over when I became speechless. "I knew he would tell you," she said nonchalantly. "It's why I sent him down. Leonus is the one who found her and he was keeping her secret. He plans to bring her out into society properly. I think he wants to sell her in exchange for the power he seems incapable of securing on his own."

"Of course he does," Paetus replied with a disrespectful scoff. "I will play along and bid for her hand along with the others. Find out what it is he wants and I will offer it to him. Surely he will not be with us for much longer and you will need no more power. Combining your two houses and then joining ours through marriage will give you more than you will know what to do with."

We played cards a while, drinking and smoking until a most uncivilized hour. When the last had left, we went on lockdown. My London house, designed by my former husband, was as much a fortress as it was a palace. Solid steel shutters slid home on every window. The reinforced doors were all locked and bolted. Guards were drawn in from the street and posted atop the roof and at the gate. The five most powerful Incola in England knew about Dawn, knew she was here, ripe for the picking. All of them, Paetus included, knew that I would go to war to keep her from being stolen.

Waiting in the parlor, Leon told me what had happened with Ambrose. The boy had strode in, cocky as any young lord, and gone straight to Paetus. They shook hands before Leon could cross the room. He had tried to negate Paetus' gift of touch and prevent Ambrose from spouting the truth to any question asked, but the other men crowded around my son, obstructing Leon's path. "And who do we have here?" Paetus had asked good-naturedly, likely knowing full well.

"I am Lord Ambrose Lawrence," my son had replied.

"Ah, the only child of the beautiful Lady Brooksberry."

As he and the boy still pumped hands, Ambrose had proudly said, "As Julian Lawrence's heir, someday I will be an Earl, but I am not Mama's only child."

"Really?" Paetus had glared at Leon and pulled Ambrose into his lap.

"Yes, Mama has a bastard daughter too."

I interrupted Leon's story to tell him what Paetus had whispered to me at the card table. Leon shook his head in disbelief. "Ambrose didn't say that you don't want Paetus to know about Dawn. He said, 'Archelaos doesn't want you to know about her. He wants to keep her for himself.'"

Baffled, I wondered how Ambrose had known any of those words. I had never named Archelaos in front of him nor used "bastard" or "Incola." My story about Leon being the one who didn't want Paetus to know about Dawn may have ruined our facade. Who knew what Paetus or the other Incola thought.

Mr. Boyd brought Andrew in, reported all safety measures were in place, and escorted us to the library. I sent Mr. Boyd and all the household servants to bed. Their days started earlier than mine.

Mr. Hall waited for us there among my books, very pleased with his findings. The catalog had recognized each of my guests as a Carrier. With their scent signatures, he hoped his device would be able to decipher those with well-developed techniques for transferring their ego to another.

"Might it be able to recognize an Incola and," I said with hope, "possibly when that same Incola is riding inside another?"

Ed smiled broadly. "It might. Now ya' see why I'm so excited."

"Why did we not think of this before?" Leon asked. Kissing my cheek in a comically loud fashion, he declared me a genius. I tried not to show the titillating effect even such a comical kiss had on me. The warm imprint of his lips on my face tingled. "You're no half-wit either, Mr. Hall. I don't wonder if having a tinkerer might just become all the rage." He called for Andrew and Auley, who stood guard in the hallway, to join us.

They agreed to the plan Leon outlined. The catalog already had them both on record. Leon would ride them and have Ed do a reading and see if the catalog could recognize him inside the body of another. Since Leon's technique for transfer involved disrobing, the men went into the secret room off of the library to spare me the embarrassment.

Ed stuck his head out to inform me of the progress. His catalog sensed something different about the men when Leon was inside. He needed to recalibrate his invention with this new information. He would need more samples for comparison and Sally told him she had an idea. Andrew and Auley left to go back on duty. Ed headed to his workshop.

Leon moved slowly when he finally emerged, though not as weary as Archelaos always had been after riding one of his Carriers and returning to Julian's body. Sally theorized it was because Leon didn't demand such complete control. Archelaos exercised his will over every part of his Carriers.

My fiancé had attempted to re-dress but, failing to do so, settled for buttoning his dinner jacket over his unfastened shirt. "Until morning, my dear."

"Wait. Don't go."

Smiling, he admitted, "I have no intentions of leaving here tonight. I wouldn't, not even had I the strength to go. You and Dawn must be protected and oh…"

Pressing my lips against his rendered him speechless. I had never been quite so bold. He made no protest when I removed the clothes of his upper body, the ones he had worked hard to retain. The feel of his hard muscles beneath my fingertips was extraordinary. Angling his head slightly, his lips parted and I took the invitation. Tentatively, I explored his mouth with my tongue. He groaned and, wrapping his arm around my waist, pulled me against his body.

Pulling away from the kiss, Leon pressed his forehead to mine. "I really must sit down. My legs are shaky."

Mine were too, although I didn't say so. "I think lying down might be better." Smiling slyly at the ground, I put my shoulder under his and my arm around his waist. We made our way through the silent house, up the stairs to my bedchamber.

10

Leon made love to me for the first time that night. Although I had been with more men than most women of that time, it felt entirely new. Leon was not plagued by my gift; the excitement he felt was entirely natural. He was tender with me in a way none other could be. We kissed and caressed for hours, taking breaks to whisper compliments in the dark, while his strength gathered.

Sally gave me what privacy she could. She retreated to a corner of our mind, immersing herself in some old memory. I knew she was there, could feel every skipped heartbeat, though it felt as if she were in another room.

Leon took his time. When we finished, he asked if I was pleased with his performance. I assured him I was. "Why do you ask?"

"I have not taken a female lover in over six decades."

The thought of Leon lying with another man should have repulsed me but it did quite the opposite. It was a different time, with different sensibilities. I, even then, was a modern woman. Laying there with his warm, hard body pressed against my back, I felt bold. I admitted it had been fewer years than that since my last female lover. He chuckled against my skin and kissed my shoulder blade. He did not make demands that I stop all relationships with others. He did not chastise me for my loose behavior. He considered us equals and I was in complete control of my own life, free to make my own choices. I could do no better than this man. I was starting to love him.

"Why wait so long for something you clearly enjoy?" I thought of all the superfluous women. He had enough money to buy any sort of companionship he desired, something new for every day of the week.

Leon answered, "I have never enjoyed a casual sexual relationship. A lifetime ago I fell in love with a woman. A human woman who feared growing old as I stayed the same. Knowing what I was, she put me off for ages, refusing my proposal time and again. She did not want to hold me back. She was happy just to be with me; she would not think of herself as my equal. She only agreed after seeing how my life stagnated." He paused and I felt hot tears splash on my bare shoulder. "Illness, a fever brought on by the birth of our son, took her from me after only three years of marriage. He died fourteen months later and I vowed not to lay with another woman because of the danger of pregnancy."

Then I had been brought to the club, and it had been announced that I was a Carrier. The idea that a woman existed as resilient and immortal as he had never crossed his mind. It wasn't love at first sight. He felt a duty to me first, the deep desire to protect me and see that I was not misused by Archelaos. Then he set out to woo me. We fell asleep in each other's arms, our secrets laid as bare as our bodies.

⁓

Waking before it was yet light, I caught Leon sneaking out of bed. His movements were unsteady as he attempted to dress silently. From his recent ride, I assumed. *He seemed in complete control of his faculties last night*, Sally teased. I giggled, embarrassed.

Leon froze at the soft sound then slowly turned toward me. I smiled sleepily, patting his now-vacant half of the mattress. "Come back to bed," I murmured.

"I need to go out." His statement lifted at the end, almost like he was asking.

I shook my head, saying, "We are locked in, remember? You can't get out any more than someone could get in." I wanted to know what he needed to do in the middle of the night but I didn't press for information. I wasn't one of those women who was always questioning the motives of her spouse any more than I wanted him to be one of those men.

We had sex again. I say "had sex" because it was different than before when we "made love." This was what women of my time referred to as rutting. I am not complaining, mind you, just stating the fact. Jumping straight to the main action suited me just fine. It was frantic fucking on seemingly stolen time.

When he was finished, Leon commented on how long it had been since he'd been with a woman, how long since he had felt so masculine and virile. Perhaps his age was starting to affect his memory. He'd just told me the story. I was so spent that I didn't say anything when he got back out of bed.

He pulled on the wing of a cherub adorning the fireplace mantle. It had been the trigger for the secret door. "I sealed them," I declared as I turned over.

I heard the door click closed as he grumbled, "Not all of them. She couldn't have possibly found them all."

∽

I slept longer than I had in years, waking after 10 a.m. I had also stayed up much later than I had in years. That is what having young children will do. That wasn't a complaint. The house was overstaffed and so I had more help than I knew what to do with. I could not even imagine the exhaustion of working-class mothers.

Leon was absent as I headed toward the adjacent dressing room. I put on a conservative day dress, having been wanton enough for a while. Leon waited for me in the breakfast room, patiently reading the newspaper, his breakfast platter untouched. My children flanked him, their own manners not as refined. They shouldn't have to wait for me. This was their home.

Leon stood, folded his paper, and greeted me with a smile and kiss on the cheek. Ambrose grinned at us, at Leon, in a peculiar and almost scheming way. Julian used to give me a similar smile when Archelaos had terrible plans for me. Dawn's expression was difficult to read. Her "good morning" was pleasant though she blushed. Her brother might be too young to understand, but she suspected that Leon had not spent the night in his own bed.

She quickly made her excuses and left to start her day. Ambrose sat watching us while we ate, making it impossible to have an adult conversation. The governess came along to collect Ambrose and he left begrudgingly.

"I would marry you today, if you would have me," Leon said to me as soon as we were alone.

"Today?" I asked incredulously.

"Yes," he nodded. "Right this minute. Sadly, we will have to wait until the noon hour. The clergyman will be along unless I send him word to stay away. Should I?"

"No, don't do that. I will be ready." Smiling, I said coyly, "So that's where you were sneaking out to this morning. Off to see the friar, Romeo?" I referenced the Shakespearean love story that featured the friar of the same name as my late husband.

"I sent my man to make the arrangements. Funny you should mention that when I was planning to ask you how I wound up fully clothed in the hall this morning."

"You don't remember…last night?" I was wounded, hurt.

"I do. It was the most wonderful night of my life. I will never forget making love to you, even if I live another thousand years. It was perfect." He looked down at his hands. "At least until I told you about my wife and son. I am sorry I brought them up. I didn't mean to ruin the moment. No woman wants to hear about her lover's dead wife."

"You are wrong. I quite enjoyed hearing your secrets. It was very intimate." Blushing, I asked him, "Do you remember what happened after that? Getting out of bed, getting dressed?"

He shook his head. "I fell asleep in your arms and woke up in the doorjamb of a very impressive piece of security equipment. It was locked and I got the feeling it was also impenetrable."

The curiosity was clear on his face but he restrained himself. He did not ask. Leon trusted me and I rewarded that trust by making him my confidante. I explained, "Paetus believes I am Archelaos masquerading as Ramillia. Those two have an odd relationship, just as I did with Archelaos when he wore Julian's body. I provided Julian with the pain he needed to feel. Now, I have that same control over Paetus. Come. I will show you."

My confidence waned with every step. Why had I decided to share something so depraved? What if he changed his mind and put me aside instead of marrying me? I wished my corset was not so tight. Then Leon laced his fingers in mine, something no other man could do without my touch sending him into a fury, and my breathing returned to normal. It would take more than this to turn him from me.

I punched the code into the number pad and used the singular key to open the vault-like door. Leon didn't speak but took in it all: the smell of fear and pain, the instruments of torture prominently displayed on every wall, the various restraints, the cold clinical metal walls, and bare floor. "We call it the tenebrae. In this room, Paetus is under my thumb. He will say or do anything to please me, anything to keep the pain coming."

After a long pause he said in a hoarse voice, "Doing this pleases you?"

"With Julian, it did. I was happy to repay him the pain he caused me. I missed it more than I missed him during my seclusion in the country. I was surprised to find that I was happy Paetus needed the same treatment. I do not owe him the same spite I did Julian, but I need the violent release. Without it I become short with those I love, angry at every servant's mistake, ferocious with no warning. I am not sure I can give this up if and when Paetus doesn't require it." I closed the door.

"Thank you for showing me."

"You are not disturbed by my behavior?" I asked.

A single slow nod indicated he was. "A little. We are a breed entirely different from our human counterparts, with different desires. I have my own secret." He slipped an arm around my cinched waist and pulled my body against his. "I want to see you work, to see you take control of a powerful man like Paetus and reduce him to a quivering mass."

Tugging a handful of hair on the back of his head, I gently forced his face up to look at mine. He waited, his mouth slightly agape. "Why?" I asked him.

"Women are considered the weaker sex, but I have long believed you could ravage the world as men do if only you had less self-restraint. You run the world from behind the shield of men who think they are in control. I am glad to be that facade for you. I can give you what none other is willing—independence. You will have control, not only of the lives of others through manipulation and social games but of your own without pretense."

I kissed him hard. Sally was there; I could feel her acceptance. We went down to be married.

∽

Our wedding was private. There was a celebratory dinner, though it was served buffet style and all of our Carriers were invited. There were so many they had to eat in shifts. Leon and I sat at a table the whole while, accepting pledges of allegiance from each man. I lost count at around four hundred and there were at least that many over again. My first wedding's meal was for Julian and I, but the second was thrown for those in our household. It represented the difference in my two husbands. Carriers were chattel to Archelaos and valuable allies to Leon.

That night was another of pleasant unhurried experiences. Julian's gift of touch had held a certain allure but Leon's counteracted mine, allowing me the luxury of normality. I didn't cause him to shift into an impassioned, inflamed stranger. He was Leon and he wanted me naturally, without influence. It was refreshing. This was what most couples felt. He gave me a new experience more valuable than all my unique adventures put together. What we were feeling was real.

After, while lying in bed satiated and relaxed, I traced the odd shapes inked on his skin. Foreign symbols, arranged in rows, circled his torso and extremities. Leon had so many, each different, be the difference slight or great. Those oldest were faded and more primitive than the newest. The implications were clear. Leon had many Carriers bonded to him over the years and his method had been discovered centuries ago.

Sliding his arm from beneath me, he pointed out a series of letters across his upper arm. "All the men of my legion were volunteers, career soldiers, not conscripts. As a mark of dedication, we tattooed our identifying numbers, all identical. The practice was taboo, but soldiers often operate outside of the norm. Many of my men had dozens of markings. It was then, as this was placed on me and another of our kind in my legion, that I discovered my method of bonding and riding. He was my first Carrier."

"Is he still with you?" I asked. One of us that old, content to live as another's, would be a rare find, a man of complete and dependable loyalty.

"He was killed in battle. It was agony. I felt his death, and while Archelaos and Sophus reveled in the sensational experience, I suffered. I vowed not to take another Carrier under my bond but was unable to keep my promise for long. A man came to me in a panic, fearing for his life. Archelaos had begun to show interest in him and the man, Nevio, had seen the way Archelaos' Carriers were treated. Nevio didn't want to belong to him. He begged me to bond with him so that Archelaos could not. I reluctantly agreed. Nevio's friends, some of those already bonded to Archelaos and Sophus, followed him and I was forced to pay for them."

This got Sally's attention. She sat us up and the bedsheet slid off our body. "So Carriers can be bonded to more than one Incola," she reasoned.

"Not at the same time. When I purchased a man from another, the first Incola had to relinquish his bond so that mine could take over."

"How is a bond relinquished?" I knew that Carriers were bought, sold, and traded, but I had always assumed only those not fully bonded could achieve this. Sally wondered if they might be stolen but thought better than to ask in that manner.

"Depends on the Incola. Most protect that technique just as fiercely as they do their bonding. I must simply slice off the Carrier's mark from my body or mine from theirs." Our healing ability meant new skin would replace the old quickly and without scarring. "For this reason I am more careful with the method than most. Paetus must never know."

"No man will ever hear it from me." I could see his reasoning. His wards could be stripped from him as easily as flaying his skin. It was a horrifying thought and one that cold, greedy Paetus would employ without hesitation. "Could I wear your mark?" As long as it was believed that Archelaos had taken my body as his own, most wouldn't risk his wrath by attempting a bonding. But if someone figured out my secret I would be vulnerable. Sally and I could always push an Incola out but they might be able to do some damage before we managed it.

Leon sat up at my question. "You would want to wear my mark?" His eyes spoke of the weight behind his words. This meant something to him. Sally, who was not in love with Leon as I was, worried.

Percy Richards, our taste tester, burst into our room armed with an antique sword from my library wall. I screamed and tried to cover myself. Leon jumped up, naked as he was, and faced the man. His heroics weren't necessary. Percy turned his back to Leon, pressed the sword tip to his own chest, and said to someone in the corridor, "I will not allow you to choose other men above me. Your blood is mine. You belong to me." He then fell on his sword, impaling himself. The weapon went in silver and came out the other side crimson.

I wrapped myself in my dressing gown while Percy took his last breaths. I got to him just as he gave his final twitch and went still. Feeling for his pulse and finding none, I knew he was dead. I looked into the corridor to see to whom he could have been speaking. Dawn stood there staring with shock on her face and tears streaming down her cheeks. She had Ambrose on her hip, his face buried in her neck.

11

Percy Richards' body did not match the fingerprint in the catalog. Something had changed. Percy hadn't killed himself. Someone had been riding him. "That shouldn't be possible," Leon argued. "Percy is bonded to me." His knitted brow relayed his confusion. He had his men strip Mr. Richards' body. Leon's mark was there on his lower back, just above his left kidney. Leon opened his dressing gown, unbuttoned his nightshirt, and turned his back to me. "What do you see in that same place on my body?" he asked.

His body was covered in the marks of his Carriers but that one spot was blank. "Nothing. There is a bare place here." I touched it, showing him exactly where.

A stream of profanities in Latin flowed from Leon's mouth, of which I only understood half. Someone was stealing his Carriers. I suspected Archelaos. But why Percy Richards first? Why claim him only to kill him? And how the hell had someone removed a mark from Leon's body without him noticing?

Leon tended to the body and its mess while I saw to my children. Ambrose fell back asleep almost instantly, needing no soothing. I covered him and went down the hall to Dawn's newly acquired private bedroom. Her sobbing could be heard through the door. Dawn was devastated. This suggested two things. She had seen the whole thing and she was the one Percy addressed.

I entered, closing the door behind me. Sitting by her side on the bed, I wrapped my arm around her and asked, "Did you have a relationship with Mr. Richards?"

Her head moved back and forth against my shoulder almost imperceptibly.

"Did you love him, have plans for a future with him?"

Again, her movement indicated the negative.

"Had he feelings for you? Were declarations ever made?"

"No, Mama." Her answer was curt and her heartbeat increased.

My next question was not an easy one. "Was he ever inappropriate—forward with you, physically or verbally?"

Dawn's breathing quickened and she answered louder. "No, Mama, nothing was amiss in my relationship with Mr. Richards."

"Then why did he say that to you, dear? It must have meant something."

"I don't know." The sentence was terse, clipped.

"Dawn, you must tell me. I can only help you, protect you, if you are honest with me."

"*I don't know what he meant!*" she yelled at me while throwing my arm from her shoulders. Dawn stood and paced away from us.

"Then, if you had no romantic feelings toward him, no relationship, what has you so upset?"

Dawn spun around. "I just watched a man I have known my entire life kill himself. It was bloody and violent and I could do nothing about it. I can't control anything. I am alive but I don't affect the world around me. Things happen to me but I leave no imprint, except here." She said the last words and lifted her shift so that I could see her bare legs.

Cuts dappled her shins, in varying stages of healing. The newer cuts lay atop older scars. I had seen this type of wound before. Archelaos, in Julian's body, had favored self-mutilation. He wanted to feel anything after sensory deprivation for so long. That was not Dawn's reason. She needed to feel in control of something. I did not ask why she had done such a thing to herself; she had just told me. I did ask, "How often do you feel the need to do this?"

Dawn shrugged and looked away, upset that her dark secret was out. "Not as much at first. More now."

"Do you feel the need now?"

"Yes."

"Would it make you feel better?"

"For a while."

Sally reminded me that I could offer Dawn something that no other mother could for her daughter. I understood her desires and had an outlet for them already. "What if I could give you something, a place where you are in total control, where no one could tell you what to do nor that what you wanted to do was wrong? Would you give up cutting yourself if I could give you that substitute?"

Her eyes were large, wondering how such a place could exist, no doubt. She nodded.

Certain she would say anything to see my secret, Sally asked her, "Promise?" Dawn promised. "Prove it."

"How?"

It was my turn to shrug. An idea shone in my daughter's eyes. She dashed to her dresser, pulled something out of the top drawer and shoved it into my hands. The leather case was familiar to us. I laid it on the bed beside me, untied the thong and unrolled it, revealing its many shiny surgical instruments. I covered my mouth with my hand. This was the exact set I had seen so long ago during my first carriage ride with Julian. He had become so excited by my touch that he needed an outlet that his body wouldn't allow him. He had cut himself with the scalpel to get the release he craved. "Where did you get these?"

"I found them in a secret cubby in the nursery after we moved here. At first I just looked at them. One day I was mad at Ambrose and the idea just popped into my head. It hurt but it also felt good."

I feared Archelaos had possessed my Dawn as his own Carrier, that he had pushed her into a life of self-mutilation. If this was the case she and Paetus would find a way to be together just as Julian and Paetus had been, and Archelaos and Sophus before them, unless I could find a way to separate Dawn from her rider. I had Ed use his collector on her. He confirmed that her signature had never changed, not once. If she was playing Carrier to an Incola it was to one who had been with her from the start, one who had never been absent from her body for a single reading since he started his catalog.

I sent her to bed and posted a guard outside her door. She would only go after I reaffirmed my promise to show her the corner of the world where she was to be a queen. The tenebrae would be hers. My need for violence would find another outlet, like steam through a series of pipes capped at one end; a crack would inevitably form.

∽

The next day was filled with turmoil. We had to contend with the investigator looking into Percy's death. The bobbie suspected us. Hanging and poison were the suicide methods of choice in that time, not falling on a sword. His suspicion was reasonable, with the deaths surrounding us.

After that morning of unpleasantness, Leon moved in. Ambrose made Leon's move into our home as difficult as possible. He protested every piece to come, though it wasn't the things he minded but the owner.

I had spoiled Ambrose and Dawn both by taking my meals with them, even the evening meal. That night I wanted a more formal dining experience. I had them fed at their normal time and was present but did not eat. I told them the truth: there was another adult in our family now. I would eat later with him as our new custom. Ambrose would have balked then if his day's protests hadn't completely tired him out. They went to bed without a fight and I knew my son was asleep before the door closed.

Sally laughed when she caught me humming as I dressed for dinner. I felt bad for a moment, realizing I was giving her less time at the helm of our body, virtually neglecting her needs because my own were so well met. I attempted to apologize but Sally stopped me. She said, *I only exist to handle situations you cannot. If you are happy then I am happy.*

We were through the soup course when a bleary-eyed Ambrose stumbled in and complained about the seat Leon occupied. He stood in the door and fussed, "No, the head of the table is mine for when I'm master of the house!" I sent him back to bed. He went with the maid but hatred beamed at us both.

Leon said, "He'll come around."

My son's displeasure was with not Leon specifically, but any man. My husband suggested that we continue as I had been, having informal evening meals with the children during the week and only do dinner on the weekends.

We fell asleep shamelessly nude, only to be awakened by a tiny hand on my shoulder. "Wake up." I scrambled to hide my nakedness from Ambrose who stood beside the bed, which was now empty save me. "Come. We must stop him. He's ruining everything." He handed me my dressing gown, which I donned quickly.

My son ran down the corridor with me at his heels. We went up the stairs past the children's floor and servants' levels to the roof access door. It had been kicked open and hung on a single hinge. Ambrose ran through but I paused, suddenly apprehensive. I heard Ambrose scream, "I promise I'll be good!" I surged forward.

Out on the roof, a walkway surrounded the chimneys. Ambrose clutched the railing near the door. Leon, in the nude, stood further out. He watched the door, waiting for me to arrive. Again Ambrose pleaded with him, "Please don't do this."

Leon didn't even hear the child. Our eyes locked. The body was Leon's; someone else was behind his face. He said, "I will not allow you to choose other men above me. Your blood is mine. You belong to me." He smiled at us and took a running leap off of the rooftop.

12

I understood why Archelaos would kill Leon's Carriers, for reducing the number in Leon's ranks would hurt him. But if Archelaos could *ride* Leon, why didn't he just take over the body and his previous status as my husband? What purpose did killing Leon serve?

Sally says I should make it known that Leon did not die that night. It sounds impossible that any man could survive a fall from five stories up. Leon didn't land flat on the pavement, which would have surely killed him. A human head smashes on brick much like a melon and even an Incola would have a difficult time surviving that. No, whoever was riding him took a running leap, propelling his body away from the building just enough to land on the gate. Leon was luckily impaled on the wrought iron.

It doesn't sound lucky to have three spikes through the abdomen, but it was. We Carriers all have an increased ability to heal as long as the damage isn't to our brain. Leon's injuries were localized to his stomach.

Andrew and Auley lifted him off of the spikes and brought him inside before anyone could see. Auley explained, "Attempted suicide is seen in the same criminal light as attempted murder, my lady. Leon could be hanged for this." Nights were much darker then than they are now; gaslight lamps did little more than candles on the street. Guards stood watch while maids cleaned the bloody gate and ground as fast as possible.

I didn't stay outside to watch. Handing Ambrose off to be put back into bed, I tended to Leon. Lying on our bed, he looked little better than dead. He hadn't been cleanly impaled. Leon had been eviscerated; a majority of his innards lay outside his body. The skin of his stomach was already healing by the time I got to the room.

As we couldn't have a doctor blabbing to his other patients about the one that healed so fast, I retrieved a medical book with good renderings of human organs, and their arrangement inside the human body, from my library. Sally did her best to rearrange everything that had popped out. I retreated to the far recesses of our mind and tried not to look, though I couldn't help but hear. When Andrew sliced through the skin on Leon's stomach, reopening the wounds, he did so between the markings of Carriers. As it was, five or so of the bonds were destroyed by the gate's damage. Those men that corresponded to the eradicated markings were quarantined. We could not risk them being taken by Archelaos and used against us.

∽

All five Incola who attended my dinner appeared to have committed suicide, freeing the majority of Carriers in Great Britain. I sent instructions with five of my men to each household on how the bodies were to be handled. Four returned, reporting the Incola bodies had been decapitated and cremated.

Four, not five.

I took a small army with me when I went to enforce my orders. Leon did not want me to go but found my argument reasonable. After all, I had encountered my first undead unawares and while two of my men were bitten, I was not. In the end, I had been the one to put the creature down. Actually, my plan didn't put me in harm's way at all.

We arrived at the home of one of my deceased Incola suitors to find it appropriately draped in mourning black. Satin sashes wrapped around the columns and crape cloaked the elaborately carved filigree hanging from the cornice. An intoxicated man sleeping on the porch said, "Icudabeendaone!" as we passed.

For the first time I considered something. Perhaps Carriers of certain households wanted to be chosen as a permanent vessel for their Incola. Foolishness, I thought. *Not so,* Sally argued. *Consider the times we have been trapped inside our own mind. The world bends to our will, giving us what we want. After living a life of fear, Carriers might long for that place all while knowing their bodies would be treated well. A lucid dream of heaven.*

As the doors and windows stood open, we let ourselves in. A wake was in full swing. Inside, every mirror, reflective surface, and painting was covered by black cloth and men stood in all available space. My senses said they were Carriers. A small elderly woman dabbed her eyes next to a young man who stood beside the dead Incola who had just supped with me. Both body and young man held still though I knew, in a death memento, only the dead one would be clear. The body, propped up, had eyes painted on its lids so that it looked alive but the lack of even the smallest movement would show on a photograph. While photos of the living appeared blurry, the deceased remained sharp.

"Ahh..." the old lady wailed. Professional mourners joined in a melancholy chorus. The photographer slid a plate in front of his lens and said, "All done."

The young man must have noticed my entrance because he moved to greet me as soon as the photograph completed. "Lady Lawrence," he said, using my married name. "I am honored that you would attend my wak...my father's wake. He spoke so highly of you." Bowing deeply, he kissed my gloved hand.

Immediately I knew this boy did not house the Incola's soul. He pretended, as did I, to carry a powerful ancient. This society in which we all lived was corrupt. I took his arm when offered. "May we speak privately?" I asked, hoping he would infer we spoke of marital and status subjects.

"Certainly, my lady," he affirmed and led me into a private sitting area off the room used for the wake. Suddenly I wondered if we Carriers were the reason for the wake tradition. A body could look as if dead, should the soul be in another Carrier. Incola would want to make sure their bodies were observed for a time before burial or cremation.

Even though being alone with this young man was quite inappropriate, I closed the door behind us. As I did, my men took their places, with Auley standing just outside the room. Taking Ed's invention from my bag, I scanned the room with it, finding a hollow spot behind the wall just to the left of the fireplace. "Do you know who I am?"

His brow creased as he attempted to garner my meaning. "Of course. You are Lady Law..."

Interrupting him meant his statement rang truer than he intended. I was Lady Law. In essence I was the British Incola Monarch. "Then why"—I ran my hand along the mantle as I walked by—"did you defy my instructions?"

"I must make sure my soul bonds with the vessel I've chosen." He gestured to himself. "Before I oversee the destruction of my previous..."

Holding my hand up stopped him. "I know who you are and *who* you are *not*."

He took a step toward me, motioning that I should keep my voice down. "They will kill me, should they find out."

My finger found what it searched for and I pulled the secret latch. "If you are to keep up your charade, these will be invaluable." He rushed toward me and the books beyond. They would be the notes all Incola kept about their previous lives. He began to thank me but a commotion in the wake halted his gratitude.

"My father gave specifics where the treatment of his body was concerned." He could not have followed my instructions. He could only do what he thought his father would have done.

"My men are carrying out my orders. Incola bodies must be destroyed and anyone who gets in their way will also be terminated with prejudice. It's just as well that you are here with me."

"How can I ever repay you?" Translation: What will I have to do? He slid a signet ring, found in the cubby beside the books, onto his index finger.

"By treating your Carriers with kindness. You may ride them, but never into fights and never to their death." I opened the door to an empty room and made my exit. Droplets of blood sprinkled the wooden floor where Carriers had attempted to recover their Incola's body. Out on the lawn, my men protected that burning body. The head lay in its lap, further insurance that it would not rise up. As I passed by I pulled my satchel of potpourri from my purse and held it to my nose in an attempt to block the roasted flesh smell from reaching my nostrils.

∽

Leon recovered in our home but it took a few more surgeries to get everything in its proper place. The mangled bond markings were repaired and the men released from seclusion. He had little room for new marks. He could not take on many more Carriers.

Orphaned Carriers poured in from all over. We had to do something. These newly freed men were unable to do anything for themselves. If we didn't take them in, new Incola would rise from their ranks and we would lose any advantage their predecessors' deaths gave us.

Leon and I sat in our library discussing what could be done with them, when Sally had a stroke of genius. She asked him, "Who amongst our Carriers do you most trust?"

Without hesitation, my husband replied, "Andrew and Auley. They have been with me for a lengthy time and have proven themselves loyal too many occasions to count."

I rang for them at once.

They arrived quickly, as they were never far from us. I was struck by how similar they looked. I knew their surnames matched and assumed them brothers. I addressed them, "Have either of you ever ridden another?" They exchanged glances and then both bowed their heads in affirmation. "Tell us the circumstances and how it was accomplished."

Andrew stepped forward and began his story, "Auley, born in Hungary, is my son, the only one with Carrier blood and so the only one to live this long. When the last of his siblings died, I took him away from that place. For many years we traveled the world following war, for in a battle we could satisfy our need for violence while not breaking our code of ethics and honor. It was during one of those battles that I discovered my ability. Auley and I were separated in the chaos. My eyes searched for him during every lull I gained by killing the enemy. I caught sight of him and knew that I was about to lose my son. He was embroiled with enemy forces, set upon by no more foes than he could handle, but his distraction had allowed a war elephant to draw too close. The mound of dead around him had called the attention of the rider and made eliminating him a priority. The animal had reared; the great circular foot was aimed squarely on Auley. He was too far to hear my screams and I had no chance of warning or defending him. There was nothing I could do and in that moment I wished it was me who was to die instead of him, longing for one more chance to tell him how much he meant to me. Blinking, I found myself in his place, literally. Thankfully I had the sense to jump out of the way of the enraged animal in time. I looked to the spot from which I had been watching Auley, expecting to find him standing in my place, but there was no one. I ran, dodging what fights I could, pausing to dispatch those I could not avoid. When I reached the spot, I found my own body lying on the ground. The fighters around were ignoring it, thinking me dead. Looking down, I realized that I was inside Auley's body and in that discovery bounced myself back to my proper personification."

"So, it is your fear for another that enables you to ride," Sally determined.

"I thought so too but have discovered it isn't the fear but the *love* that gives me the necessary connection."

Flabbergasted, I considered the ramifications. Surely not many Incola had such a technique or we would have fewer riders. Most Incola cared little for other Carriers. "This is perfect," I announced. "For what better rider could a Carrier ask than a person who feels genuine love for them? And you, Auley, is it love that allows you to ride?" Auley choked, seemingly on his own saliva, at my query. "You must tell me of your first." This addendum to my inquiry only choked him further.

The father spoke up, "His is not a story to be shared in current company."

"Do not fear for our sensibilities," Sally encouraged.

Auley finally found his voice, though his face took on an alarming pallor. "It is not love, but the act of copulation that gives me a route into another."

"How can you have discovered such a technique when there are so few females born to…" Sally stopped me but not before I exposed my naiveté. Auley was a homosexual. No wonder he looked scared. Sodomy was illegal, punishable by execution. One word from me and he was dead. "Your secret is safe with us. I would never reward such trust with betrayal." I, too, had loved a person of my same gender.

That is when I told the three men Sally's plan to run our Carriers like the military, with a hierarchy. Andrew had grown to care for many of the Carriers in his life and Auley had coupled with a number. Starting with those two, Leon gave his hundred most trusted Carriers leave to take on as many as one hundred Carriers of their own. They were to be trained and treated well. All knew that they could file complaints of abuse with Leon and I, and that any new Incola that violated our rules would be sanctioned harshly.

Before our new society could be arranged, Leon's bonds must be broken. Our Generals, as we took to calling them, could not be bonded as his Carriers. Only a free Carrier could become an Incola. As the only other living soul who knew the method of breaking Leon's bonds, I was the obvious choice as breaker. I found the release for my hunger for violence, which I called bloodlust. We all had it, my children included, with the sole exception of Leon, who seemed gentle to his core. Oddly, this made me suspect him more, for my bloodlust could be no more denied than my need to breathe. He must be hiding his dark side.

Taking Leon's hand in mine, I pulled him up the stairs and into our bedroom, eager beyond comprehension. I waited, allowing the bloodlust to build, while the servants cleared out a corner of my dressing room closet. A stool was placed in that area and we were finally alone. I told Leon to strip and sit on it, then I retrieved Julian's leather bundle, the same one I had confiscated from Dawn a few weeks prior. Kneeling before him, I untied the thong and unrolled the pouch on my lap, revealing an assortment of tools. I settled on a small, shiny scalpel, just as Julian had done on our carriage ride home from the asylum.

My heart pounded in an empty drum-like chest. It wasn't fear that elevated my heart rate but joyous excitement. Leon understood what had to be done; he even comprehended my appetite for it. Silently, he indicated which two marks must be removed to give Andrew and Auley their freedom. Carefully I sliced a C shape around the first one and peeled the skin away from the muscle. I used a tailor's tracing wheel to pierce the remaining side of the skin flap and, rather than cut it with the scalpel, I tore it away.

Leon's agonizing scream brought a smile to my face and a lightness to my extremities that I had not felt since relinquishing my tenebrae to Dawn. The noise also brought a handful of men to our door. I made Leon hobble to the door to assure them of his cooperation, nay control, in the situation. After his dismissal of the servants, I proceeded to remove the other mark, taking my time, using the various instruments, pulling many anguished sounds from deep within Leon.

I hated myself for my pleasure in such an act. Sally was silent, allowing me my moment of joy and self-loathing. After helping Leon into bed, I returned to my new tenebrae to admire my macabre souvenirs, hang them behind my gowns using tiny tacks, and fantasize about the future flaying of my husband.

∽

Leon's fair treatment of his men became legendary and Carriers flocked to us, both to experience this new freedom and to participate in the society headed by a woman. In a fortnight, we had to authorize another round of Generals, those with a hundred bonded to them. We took over whole sections of London. Complete industries of varying types fell under our control: a majority of coal, several dozen factories, many ships and storefronts, and a large section of the railroad.

The legitimate sons who stood to gain the most from their Incola fathers' "suicides" had a choice. They could swear allegiance, join our ranks, and retain their family land. Or they could sign over their land to us, take what Carriers would go with them, and live in exile. I didn't say it was *much* of a choice. All chose the first option and were allowed to keep ten of their Carriers, though these had the same right to protest their treatment as any under our Generals.

In mere weeks we surpassed the royal couple in influence. Leon felt things were moving too quickly but I knew better. We were not in it for the power. We actually cared about the Carriers. I began to think of them all as my family. There were a few whose bloodlines and scent enraged me. Sally was able to restrain me long enough for those to be sent to Leon without any issues.

Still there was no word about Theodore. Neither sailor nor conductor had seen or heard of him. Sally doubted he could stay hidden much longer. We put out the word again—a reward would go to anyone who brought me information concerning his whereabouts. I was beginning to think he had left town before the two mysterious and angry men had come looking for him.

Paetus wrote to me, thanking me for clearing his competition away. He thought Archelaos had done it so that Leon would have no choice but marry Dawn to him. His letter begged me to give him Dawn. It said that he already belonged to her. He was hers and he wanted her to be his. Paetus would do or surrender anything in exchange. His words sounded as if he genuinely cared for her.

Leon advised me to require ownership of the club. It was a good idea. I wrote to Paetus, informing him of the cost of purchasing the right to court Dawn, not selling her to him. She would be allowed to choose for herself.

Paetus agreed immediately and sent the signed deed back with his reply, though he requested he be allowed to maintain his rooms there. He did not even mention taking on any of the extra Carriers. I knew this kind of takeover was exactly what he and Archelaos had always planned. It was completely in character for "me."

While I informed Dawn of Paetus' intentions toward her, Leon posted the club's new rules. The fights were over; no more Carriers would die in the sand pit. Carriers were not bought and sold. All transactions or disputes came through us. The Incola Club would be modeled after a true gentleman's club and used for gatherings, discussions, shows, events, and meals.

Our plans for the club caused some unexpected problems. Violence across the city escalated as Carriers lost their outlet. Something had to be done so the fights were reinstated but organized. Killing was still forbidden, as was riding a Carrier into the fights. My rule was soon tested by one of the sons I had allowed to retain ten Carriers.

I was enjoying a rare adult evening with my husband at the club when several Carriers came in, bearing a stretcher holding what looked like a dead body. They told me that this was their Incola who was riding one of their fellows currently fighting. I immediately called the fight to a close and began my descent. Andrew and Auley were at home protecting the children so I chose two other men to grab the fighting rider.

I stood in the center of the sand pit and addressed those in attendance. "This man is not who he appears to be. There is an Incola riding inside. He has broken our rules. Other Incola will treat their Carriers thusly if he is not dealt with swiftly."

"Who are you to say how I can treat what is mine?" he spat out at me.

I raised my hands to the observing crowd. A multitude of voices screamed out their answer to him. Lowering my arms, I explained, "I am nothing without them. Return to your own body."

He spat on the ground near me, blood from the fight swirling with his saliva. The men who held him tightened their grips. They wanted to do him harm for the insult but to do so would be to injure their fellow Carrier, a man blameless for his body's current predicament. The Incola said, "What…so you can torture me for the entertainment of the masses?"

Smiling at him, I threatened quietly, "You do not need to be inside your flesh for me to torture it or you." His eyes went wide but he made no move to do as I had commanded. Looking at his well-manicured, powdered, lithe, and prostrate body dressed in such finery, his vanity exposed his weakness. I instructed, "Cut off his nose."

Leon pulled a knife from his pocket and, in one swift downward swing, carried out my order on the Incola's body lying on the stretcher. Though safe from the pain in another's body, he screamed out all the same. His beautiful face was lost. "Why would I return now, to a ruined body?"

Leon plopped the bloody bit of skin and cartilage into my outstretched hand. I said, "That is hardly ruined. We can do much more damage and then I would force you back into it, damning you to life as a mutilated pauper."

"You wouldn't. You couldn't."

"Wouldn't I? Violence is in our very nature. People who know me know not to tell me what I cannot do."

"You acknowledge our need for violence. I *need* to fight."

"You think your body so precious, so above that of your Carriers? You think you have the right to exercise your need for violence and pain on another without any cost to yourself."

"This is how it is done! You are erasing the very basis for our society."

"We are making a new society. Return to your own body immediately and I will give you your nose. There is still time to reattach and heal with little scarring. Delay further and I will take an eye and hand."

He accepted my offer. Once he was back in his own form, I relinquished my possession. As he held it to his face, I saw to his confused Carrier.

The rider's punishment was decided by those gathered there. His Carriers would be assigned to another, his bond with them broken. He would serve at the club for twelve full months and during that time could be challenged at the fights, at any time day or night. He would experience the abuse of his body and, as he had never bothered to train himself, he was destined to take quite a beating on a regular basis. At the end of his sentence, the Carriers he had owned would decide his fate.

Meting out justice had sharpened my appetite for aggression. Watching would no longer satisfy me and I challenged Leon to fight. He knew how apt I was in the ring and eagerly agreed. It was more of a wrestling match than boxing, and I bested him, though he may have allowed it. Our scuffle's end was met by applause and Leon and I went home.

Without Paetus' tenebrae, I needed an outlet and began to participate in the fights on a regular basis. At first no one but Leon would fight me but soon

I gained my own reputation for combat and there was a waiting list to try a hand at besting me.

∽

We made Leon my Carrier and I his, though both were only symbolic. I showed him that I could not be ridden for any length of time, should I choose to force him out. He was surprised when first I did it. He'd never encountered such a skill. I kept Sally a secret but explained that I had never been able to leave my own body. I knew Sally had some information on that front. Whatever her reason was for keeping it from me, I accepted. I had no desire to ride another.

I worried for my children's safety. If Archelaos could get to Leon, he was surely close enough to possess them. I asked my husband to make Dawn and Ambrose his Carriers and block any access Archelaos might have. Just as when Leon attempted to ride little Ambrose to heal a sickness, he could not get in. He theorized that it was because of my son's youth. Leon had never attempted to ride one so young. "Perhaps it precludes him from being ridden," he said, sending Ambrose out to play.

"I pray it means that no other Incola can take control either," I spoke my hope aloud. "What of Dawn?"

He was more successful with my daughter. Leon managed to bond with her and even get inside her mind. While his body lay limp in the chair, Dawn stood beside. Her eyes went wide as she felt him there and then narrow when she decided she didn't care for the sensation. After a moment it became clear that, though he was there, he was unable to take control. Dawn was no ordinary Carrier to be ridden by whoever decided.

Dawn had enough. Her head started shaking imperceptibly at first and then sped up. She tore at her hair, screaming, "He can't! He can't! I want him out. Get him out, Mama!" Clenching her eyes shut, she bore down and Leon's body started to convulse. Whatever she did was hurting, maybe even killing him. He shook so hard he fell onto his stomach on the carpet.

I grabbed my Julian-skin gloves from the table and quickly put them on. Kneeling before her, I soothed her as best I could with his gift of touch. Sally gave her instructions for pushing him out. "Dawn, you have to listen. You are hurting the man that Mama loves. Mama doesn't want to live without Leon."

"He doesn't belong. I'm squeezing him out."

"Stop. What you're doing will kill him. Like a boa constrictor. You remember that kind of serpent from your studies?" It was a good tactic, distracting her. My daughter had always been as hungry as I for knowledge. Dawn nodded. I took a breath and watched Leon, waiting for him to come back to himself. He stopped convulsing and went limp.

"I can feel him. Why won't he get out?" She started to clench again.

"No don't, Dawn. I can show you how to get rid of him. Imagine you and he are in a room together."

"We are," she interrupted, nodding toward Leon's limp body.

"Not out here. Imagine a room inside your head. There you have all the power."

"Like in the tenebrae?" she whispered.

"Yes, like that, except here the other person doesn't have to give you control. It is already yours. Can you see Leon?"

Dawn closed her eyes and nodded again. She made a fist with one hand and raised it above her head in what I recognized as the cane hold. She quickly brought it down three times. "I'll kill him and then he'll have to go back to his own body."

"No, if you kill him there, he will die." I knee-walked to his prostrate body. Three long stripes of blood welled up on his back, soaking through his shirt. Whatever he was experiencing inside Dawn's mind, his body made it real. "He wants to get out. He just doesn't know how. There's a window in the room. Can you see it?"

"Yes, Mama."

"Good. You are doing very well, Dawn. We are very proud of you. Can Leon see the window?"

"I don't think so. He's crouched with his back to it."

"That's all right. Show him the window. Open it for him and step back so he can look. He needs to go out the window."

"He doesn't want to."

"It doesn't matter what he wants. If you want him out, make him go. Do not squeeze, dear. Push."

Leon jerked. He scrambled off of the floor. He barely had the strength to stand upright, using the chair he had been seated in to lean on. My husband, normally cool and collected, looked downright terrified. "W-wh-wha…" His skin was ashen.

"It is fine now, Leon. You're safe." Helping him sit, I stroked his face with my gloved hands a few times before remembering that gifts didn't work on him. Knowing he would most likely derive more comfort from the touch of my own skin, I stripped off Julian's gloves. "Take deep breaths."

"What did she do to me?"

Maybe Dawn and I were never in any danger from Archelaos. Maybe all female Carriers were incapable of being ridden. Or maybe it was a gift I would pass on to all my offspring. "She pushed you out. You're back and safe."

"Before that. Before I went through the window, I was trapped. I had no control. I couldn't get out. The path back to my body was blocked or severed. Then she threw me into that torture room."

Dawn spoke up. "I changed it to the breakfast room."

Leon jumped at her voice. "She tried to kill me," he claimed.

"If she had been trying to, you'd be dead. I'd wager on it," Sally quipped. *I don't think we need to worry about our daughter. You and I can push any Incola out but Dawn can imprison them, end them if need be.*

He pulled off his waistcoat and shirt. "I want her mark off. If something were to happen…" He left the sentence unfinished.

Sally kissed Dawn's cheek and ushered her toward the door. "We are very proud of you. Leon is scared of something he's never experienced. He isn't mad or upset with you. This means that you're like Mama. You'll never be anyone's slave."

Leon had already sliced Dawn's mark from his body. The fresh tattoo hung from the end of his knife. He flung it into the wastebasket. The skin on his arm, where a space had been made for my children, was already beginning to heal. When he turned to Dawn, who stood in the hall, she looked at the mark on her arm, a sort of corkscrew with swishes at the end, and then to the same place on Leon's. She covered it with her other hand and shook her head.

Later it would become clear that she loved tattoos. This day I saw the beginning of her obsession. I turned to Leon and said, "It can't be used if the one on you is removed?"

"That's correct, technically." He looked as if he didn't really care for the idea.

I dismissed Dawn. "Surely you aren't upset with her for wanting to keep your mark."

"No, of course not." Gesturing to the discarded skin he said, "It is not just myself I protect. I'll not have my blood on her hands."

I nodded. Killing my parents had destroyed my life. They had been evil and deserved it. He was right. Killing someone she loved and respected as much as Leon would devastate Dawn.

He slipped his arms back into his clothes. Clasping my hand in both of his, he said, "I heard what you said. Did you mean it, that you wouldn't want to live without me?"

Squeezing his hand, I admitted, "I hadn't thought so until S…" I stopped myself before I revealed Sally's name. "Until I heard it from my own mouth."

He kissed me and left. "I have some research to do."

∽

I was as curious about female Carriers as Leon; therefore I helped in his search for information. It was a short hunt. Few books spoke of us. Either no one knew of our abilities or someone wanted them kept secret. I decided to keep it that way, assuming that the power Dawn and I shared came from a common ancestry, not our common gender.

After some time passed without further incident, we gave up the safety of our library for exploration of our city. Now that Leon and I were not only wed but bonded, we felt ourselves safe without the guards in all areas of London, so Leon and I began taking midnight strolls. It was on one of these walks that we discovered another of our responsibilities.

It had rained late in the evening, suppressing the deadly yellow fog, washing the city's refuse down to lesser neighborhoods. The night was cool enough that the streets did not steam. We walked from our home on Park Lane, window shopping along Bond Street, to the club on Pall Mall. The roads were by no means empty even at the late hour. The gentleman's clubs still bustled. And where there were men without their wives, the prostitutes were not far away.

Assuming I must be a lady open to such things because of the hour, one started to solicit when she recognized me. Before the birth of my son, I had occasionally rented out brothels for a week, buying every woman's time so that I might sup with them. Sally often took one or more to bed, having always preferred the softer sex. This woman, though I cannot recall her name, was one of those. She greeted me as I would a princess, all curtsies and lowered eyes. Her face was covered in bruises and I could tell she'd been crying. I asked her why.

Her accent and speech patterns almost prevented me from understanding her at first, but when I did, I demanded that she show me. She resisted, claiming it was beneath me. I gave her enough gold for a month of sexual services. "There. Just like one of your johns. *I* only want to look."

She took me deeper into the darkness of the alley after Leon checked the space. Even in the dark, her bruises stood out on the pale skin of her abdomen. A perfect handprint defaced her left breast where someone had squeezed her hard. Malnourishment made it easy to spot further internal injuries. Jagged edges disrupted the smooth lines of her ribs on her left side. "Your ribs are broken," I said. "Who did this to you?" When she tarried, Sally pressed, "You can tell me."

She said, "A man had refused to pay, saying that he, 'Ain't never paid for that what God put here for him to enjoy free.' Then 'e took from me by force what I'da given 'im for a fair price. It weren't no new thing." She shrugged. "Happens ta girls like me lots."

"And this man who raped and beat you, do you know him by name? Where he lives?"

My questions seemed to confuse her. "I don't know the man who wouldn't pay nor where 'e lays 'is head at night but he 'ad money. I could hear it jingling in the pockets of 'is fancy trousers. I could point 'm out if I'ze ta see 'm again, mum, but 'ees not the one who beat me. That was me pimp, for surrendering for free what belongs ta 'im."

I didn't waste time correcting her. She hadn't surrendered anything and she didn't belong to any man. Knowing that most men like this, men who would claim a woman's sex belonged to him, might feel the need to re-stake his claim, Sally asked, "Did he do anything else to you?" When she told us what her pimp did to her with a broomstick, Sally roared to be free. "And he still sent you out to work the streets?" We were outraged.

Tucking the woman under my arm, I took her into my club. Leon sent a man to our home once I told him what I had planned. He didn't try to talk me out of it but he did ask me to wait for an escort. Paetus was there, indignant that the filthy woman was inside. "Is that your plan, then?" he challenged me. "That our club become a place for urchins and whores?"

The anger in my eyes caused him to stumble back. "Whatever my plan for the club has naught to do with you. Call for a doctor. Have a bath drawn for her and fresh clothes brought. If any man bothers this woman, he will answer to me and I am likely to ask my questions with force." Eight guards, including Andrew and Auley, arrived then. Sally brushed the hair out of the woman's eyes and told her, "You are safe here. Rest and eat and I will check on you tomorrow. Don't leave before seeing me. Now, tell me where your pimp lives."

∽

We arrived at the address quicker than humanly possible. Leon and I were completely surrounded, two guards in front, two behind, and two each flanking us. I dipped my chin when Andrew looked back at me. He kicked in the shanty door. The front four entered. The ones left behind made an arch, protecting us from outside. After a minor scuffle, several lights illuminated the interior.

Lifting my skirt to avoid the human waste gathered just outside the threshold, we went in. Two men held the pimp; two more pointed their guns at him. Being in that place shone a bright light on the disparity between how I lived and how the rest lived. With bright light comes dark shadow, without which there could be no beauty.

"I remember you," I said to the restrained pimp. I walked around, touching objects until I found what I sought. I held the broom up to him. "Is this the one you used on that poor girl?" He glowered back and I continued, "Ah, yes, you don't have the physical equipment nor ability to do it personally, do you? When last we met you were threatening my friend Moira and it seems you did not learn the lesson I taught you."

He recognized me then and started to struggle. This was Moira's pimp, the man who had sold her body, had her baby killed, and had her personality sliced away. When he had come to collect her from the asylum after her lobotomy, I had pulverized his hand, dislocated his shoulder, and crushed his testicles. I wanted to make sure it was a long while before he could hurt another woman with fists or manhood.

"You are out of business," I said plainly.

"Have a heart," he groveled. "A man has to eat."

Sally punched him in the mouth. Our hands blurred as she laid a succession of blows across his face. "Not if he doesn't have any teeth," she quipped aloud as his head lolled to one side. A stream of blood and spittle ran down his chin and chest along with a number of teeth. "How about I make you a deal? Since you do not seem capable of understanding the golden rule, I will help you." She put our hands on either side of his torso and pressed. He begged her to stop but she didn't until we heard four cracks, rib for rib what he'd done to the woman. He screamed.

"There, there," Sally crooned in mockery. "We're almost done, aren't we? Just one more thing you did to your woman. It must mean you would have me do it unto you." Sally let him see us pick up the broomstick. "Bend him over the table, boys."

"No, no," the pimp whined. "Please. I'll never do it again. I swear!"

Sally berated him. "Tsk, tsk. Come, now. Surely you are tougher than a woman. If you thought she could bear it, certainly you can survive the same."

Are we really going to do this, Sally? I asked her. *I am already not sure Leon will look at us the same way.*

Instead of answering me, she broke the broom into kindling, thrust it into the fire and spoke aloud, "You didn't know the rules before and now you do. Make sure all of your friends know that violence against women, be they prostitutes or wives, will no longer be tolerated. If you do that then I will show mercy to you—this one time."

13

The same inspector who had investigated all of the deaths came to my home the next day during teatime. I offered him a seat and a cup but I wanted him to accept neither so I made my invitation hollow and uninviting. He hemmed and hawed, his overgrown mustache obscuring his mouth, until I put down my saucer and told him to get on with it.

"We have witnesses who saw a woman matching your description coming and going in a part of town you're not likely to frequent at an obscene hour of the night."

"Is that a crime?" Sally spat.

"N…no, ma'am. There was a man severely beaten around the same time and area. May I see your hands?" I held my hands out, palms up, and he stepped forward to get a closer look. "It's your knuckles I need to see." Turning them over, I showed him my flawless hands, pale and soft, exactly the ones a peeress should have. "Of course," he said, taking a step back. "Forgive me. No woman could have beaten a man so severely, not without doing great damage to herself. But someone beat him; would you mind if I questioned your staff?"

"I suppose not," I said blandly. "If you feel the beating of one pimp worth the effort." He hadn't mentioned the victim's profession but I wanted him to know I knew and wasn't afraid to show it. "Though none of *them* touched him."

He sucked air before saying, "Then you admit to your involvement?"

Picking up my tea, I said, "I was there to deliver a message. Sometimes people with that hard a head need a heavy hand to get through. I want him and everyone he is acquainted with to know that violence toward women, be they wife or whore, will no longer be tolerated in my city. Now you and all that you are acquainted with will know also."

"Your city! My lady, you can't go around threatening men, no matter their lowly station."

"That is exactly what I intend to do," said Sally. "Men have had their chance. Those who have failed will be required to change their behavior."

Her brashness stunned him from anger to disbelief. "There is likely to be retaliation and I don't have the manpower nor the inclination to protect you."

"Then it is a good thing neither is necessary." I rang a bell that sat beside my tea service. Ten guards filed into the room from every entrance. I took another sip from my cup. "These are for this room alone. There are a dozen more waiting to run in if I used the bell a second time and a dozen more should I continue. We are safe. Your services are not needed here. They are needed in the rougher areas of town where women are taken advantage of, children are beaten without mercy, and honest people are robbed and murdered with impunity." With a wave of my hand, I dismissed my guards.

"B-but it is you who thinks you alone operate above the law." His mustache twitched. "I have been by the club this morning, as is my routine…it's a matter of the…ahem."

Standing there, staring at me as if I had any idea what he was talking about, he angered me anew. "Oh, speak plainly; I am a very busy woman," I said. "And your company is tiring," Sally added.

He said, "Ownership of the club has changed, has it not?" I nodded and gave an impatient gesture for him to get on with it. "Well, the owner is responsible for certain…expenses."

"Oh, your bribe? Paetus stopped paying—of course. Tell me, how much was he paying you?" Knowing the answer already, I went to the desk and retrieved a purse.

"Twenty-five pounds a week," he whispered.

Spinning, Sally pinned him with a stare. "I didn't hear you," I lied, giving him a chance to be honest. "How much?"

"Fifteen," he said louder, "but that has to be split between several of my subordinates."

I watched him shrewdly. "I will give you a raise. Here is one hundred pounds, your dues for the month." I handed him a stack of paper money. "For this increase, I expect several securities. First and foremost, I do not wish to see you or any of yours again for the next month. Second, you will not interfere with my personal policing of child and women abusers. And third, you will create a branch of bobbies whom I will assign and pay to support me in this endeavor to clean our streets of this kind of evil-doer. You will cease your harassment of superfluous women and take up the cause."

That is how I gained my own arm of the law. Things were simpler then. Money could buy loyalty in any areas of life where I didn't already have Carriers installed. Being covert was unnecessary. It wasn't long before I had a majority in both the House of Commons and House of Lords. Breaching the Cabinet and monarchy's inner circle took little effort. Before this I'd always had the mistaken idea that building a massive empire took purposeful campaign. As it turns out, England was already primed for a takeover if only power could be consolidated under one. I did it without really trying or wanting to.

∽

Paetus showered our daughter with gifts. Dawn looked forward to becoming a woman, so she most enjoyed the articles of clothing. And then there was the horse. Fights broke out because of Ambrose's jealousy. I would not allow my son, who was only four years of age, to ride a horse. Anyone could be thrown from a horse, and there was something about him that unsettled the beasts.

Dawn's mare was gentle, well-bred, and tame. Hide and hair were the purest of white with mane and tail the same golden yellow as Dawn's, a coloring I had never seen in a horse. An oddly fitting detail on its shoulder looked like a sun rising over a flat horizon. It turned heads everywhere we went.

I felt more and more certain of our safety. Paetus wouldn't feel the need to snatch her, and the mystery Incola had virtually eliminated all other foes. Dawn began to enjoy short excursions outside our home. The horse was her vehicle of freedom. She, I, and a modest guard of ten set out on the clearest of days for rides in the park.

Ambrose stayed home with Leon. He hated his sister's horse, saying it was deformed, not a proper stallion like he would have. "It's not fair!" he would yell. I told him he wouldn't act so horribly to her if he understood what a difficult childhood she'd had, so unlike the gilded one he'd enjoyed.

Paetus could see Dawn on her terms in the tenebrae anytime they agreed, but he was not allowed to call on her publicly. When he did call, I knew he was a visitor for me. Leon sat off to the side, pretending to read the newspaper. Paetus wished to speak to me about two items. The first was always the same these days: Lady Dawn Lawrence.

He argued, "If I may not yet court her openly, allow me to throw a party in her honor as a favored uncle might." I started to protest and he interrupted. "During the day, it would be in celebration of her day of birth, which, if I am not mistaken, is very near."

From my studies, I knew that birthdays in ancient Rome were often celebrated with hedonistic parties filled with debauchery, more for adults than children. I told him I did not want that for my daughter.

"You misunderstand. It would be a proper party for the modern young lady. I would provide refreshments and entertainment sure to thrill young viewers. Families of prominent lineages with children of her same age would all be invited. She could make friends, connections with the great houses."

"My house, with all its extra servants, guards, and weapons, is hardly the place for such a thing."

"The club would make a wonderful location. It would be cleared of Carriers, save the ones performing, of course. I beg you to let me do this for D—Mist—Lady Lawrence."

Birthdays had fallen out of favor for the last few hundred years. In fact, I am not certain of the actual day of my birth and never had a single party. The celebrations gained popularity once again around this time, though they were still quite rare. I agreed, for we had met some interesting young people during our rides in the park. Paetus said he would have the invitations printed and sent out at once.

Then he moved on to the second reason for his visit. "I have news of your nephew." Paetus cut his eyes to the side. Leon continued to read, though I knew it to be farce. Leaning forward, Paetus continued in hushed tones, "How could you? We worked too hard to keep *his* attentions from us. His reach may be long, but here we were far enough to stay out of view. Now Rome has turned its eyes to us and it will cost more than either of us ever dreamed."

I had no idea what he was talking about. Sally pretended we did. "I did what I had to."

"Well, it is no mystery that he ran. I don't blame him. You are an idiot, old friend."

Smiling at him in a way I knew would remind him of Julian, I said, "I thought it was time for new alliances. It is nothing personal."

"It will be. They know about you now and will not rest until they have their ten percent. How many do you claim as your own now? Just how many of these do you plan to surrender?" When I did not answer, he took his leave.

I turned to Leon and asked him, "What Incola of Rome would upset Paetus so?"

He came to sit near me. "It can only be one," he replied. "The other major players with the power to demand tribute don't care for outsiders. However, the Pope claims his Carriers from around the globe."

∽

The morning of Ambrose's fifth birthday, I had the cook prepare pancakes with fruit preserves and sweet cream for the top. The children made paper hats. Ambrose insisted his be the only crown. He strutted around in it, making Dawn laugh in a most unladylike fashion. She wore hers, shaped like a dunce hat and covered in polka dots, even though I knew she thought she was too old for it. She did it simply because it pleased the birthday boy.

Ambrose sat at the head of the table so that his presents were in clear view while he ate. He was so anxious to open them, I finally gave in and had the plates cleared. He tore through them, barely a pause for gratitude between packages. When there was just one left, a long thin package, Leon made Ambrose wait until the other part was delivered before he allowed Ambrose to open it. Ed brought something in, covered in a tablecloth. Its shape gave it away and my son shouted, "A rocking horse! I'm not a baby."

Leon said, "It isn't just any rocking horse."

Ed ripped the cover off to reveal a metal contraption. It looked vaguely like a horse wearing armor. Ambrose was reluctant to get on it, leery of Leon, until he opened the package that went with it. The wooden sword was beautiful, with carvings along the "blade" inlaid with gold. It had a real leather grip and golden cross hilt. The sheath was metal with tassels and hung from a leather belt just Ambrose's size.

Ambrose jumped onto the horse, swinging his sword around shouting about how he was the "calvary." He did not like it when Dawn corrected him, "It's cavalry. Cav-al-ry. Not calvary."

The toy stallion was a marvel of engineering. Better than a rocking horse, it simulated the movement of a galloping stallion while staying in one place and responded to physical instructions. If Ambrose leaned forward with his chest pressing the horse's neck, the toy moved at a quicker pace. Pulling back on the reins slowed and stopped the ride. I had never thought to apply the technological advances of the age to toys but Leon and Ed had been working in secret for some time.

Ambrose forbade any of us from leaving. We were his captives. He was angry when the dress maker Paetus had sent to design Dawn's gown for her birthday party arrived and she and I had to go. In all but name, Leon was his father now, so I left them to it. Ambrose's fit was short-lived and the sounds of a mock battle erupted behind us.

The dressmaker was the most expensive and sought-after children's clothing designer in London. She designed all of the princesses' gowns and understood that while Dawn wanted something grownup, etiquette required a certain cut. I knew she would be able to blend both of our desires into something Dawn could be proud of.

Choosing between fabric samples and trim pieces took some time and it was lunch before we knew it. Dawn and I took a light indoor picnic while a parade of tradesmen came through with more selections for her party. A toymaker brought games to be given to all the guests as favors. After some deliberation, Dawn chose checkers for the girls and pickup sticks for the boys. The baker brought in tasting samples but the decision was already made. Paetus wanted to flaunt his wealth and so the cake would be white, with pure white frosting using white sugar. It was to look "too pretty to be eaten." Dawn then chose the tablecloth and napkin colors along with the floral centerpieces.

Dawn thought we should invite Ambrose in for the next wave of choices. She made the tradesmen wait to begin their demonstrations until the males of our family were in attendance. My son was pouting when he came in but his sour mood soon dissolved.

One at a time, the men unveiled their talents. There was a contortionist who could twist his body into impossible positions and an acrobat apt at juggling odd objects even while standing on his head, both of which I found impressive. Dawn chose the illusionist. His sample tricks thrilled her and he assured my daughter that she and her friends would be amazed to see what he could do if he was given center stage and time to assemble his elaborate set. She decided on him then and there, the other men waiting outside not having been seen yet.

He's convinced this will propel him into fame and fortune, Sally said to me. It very well could, too. A show like this with all of the rich and powerful as an audience.

Dawn tried to dismiss the final two men, telling them the performers had already been selected. They ignored her words but stared at her, enraptured. Something silent passed between them. "He will be most happy to accept your tithe," one said. "She is a marvel."

An odd noise emanated from my son's throat, similar to the desperate warning of a cornered animal. I recognized that look in his eyes. Not only was at least one of these men a Carrier, but they were of a bloodline that offended Ambrose in a most primal way. The first time I had encountered a man who offended my senses in such a way, I hadn't been able to resist killing the poor man. I couldn't grab him quick enough; Ambrose lunged at the speaker.

My son was no ordinary boy but this man had similar strengths and easily deflected the blows from the little fists. The men exchanged looks and one said to me, "You surprise us, Archelaos. We thought you had better control over your family."

They must think we house Archelaos as we've led Paetus to believe, Sally reasoned.

I rang and a dozen guards came at my call. Andrew and Auley took Dawn and Ambrose from the room. The two strangers were unperturbed by the influx of men. Removing their odd cape-like outerwear, they revealed the religious cassocks beneath. One of the priests said, "Once he knows about her, he will not be satisfied with any other. You can have more. It is an agreeable arrangement and you should take advantage of his generosity. We hear your Carriers number in the thousands. What is one girl in exchange for ten percent of so many?"

I asserted, "She is not for sale."

The other man, who had not yet spoken, laughed. They weren't offering to pay. When he saw how unamused I was, he sobered and said, "His Holiness was promised the firstborn in your lineage. Then he was needed as a sacrifice in order to purchase your freedom from captivity. Your brother, I believe? Rome understood that necessity and graciously accepted *his* firstborn in exchange. We have searched the city for months after Theodore Winmoore. If you are thinking of reneging on the agreement, you should reconsider. A failure to comply with Papacy's tithe requirement is seen as a declaration of war with Rome."

I told them, "The dark ages are over. Your master is falling in power, no longer a creature to be feared. I will surrender none of mine to be religious slaves." In response to a small gesture from me, the guards surrounded the clergy. "There is nothing more to be discussed. Please see these men out." The priests scuffled but were outnumbered. After they were dragged out, I signaled one of the guards closer. "Follow them," I whispered. "I want to know where they are staying, where they go, how many reinforcements they have, and how they plan to get off the island."

"Yes, my lady," he replied and ran off to fulfill my request.

When the room cleared, Leon asked, "Do you think that was wise?"

I didn't answer. Sally muttered, "We will see soon enough."

∽

The bishops were escorted by only a handful of pages, servants really, all housed in a private residence. While not located on Park, it was a very prestigious area. A little research revealed that the family was made of Catholics and Catholic sympathizers but not Carriers. They had no idea of the lie that had taken root in their beloved religion.

The Papal ship was quite impressive. It was manned by a curious bunch of criminals. They would accept no level of bribe from me, valuing the blanket pardon the Pope had offered them. Making a crew of this type was ingenious, for what would an evil-doer *not* give to save his soiled soul at the end of his life of crime?

The captain, when I did finally locate him in a nearby tavern, was drunk on rum and grog and could not pick up on my subtle insinuations. "Oh, for fuck's sake! We want to purchase your boat and your loyalty. Name your price, man."

A word like that from a peeress' mouth stunned and delighted him but he wouldn't yield. "Do ye' know who commands us? His Holiness wouldn't look kindly on those who changed sides. We'd be excommunicated, the lot of us."

"I would pay you ten times the amount normally required to run your ship. That would buy enough forgiveness in all the major religions to get you all into whatever heaven you wanted."

"No, m'lady. The answer is no. If you knew the sum of evil all on-board had done you'd know this was the only way. The Pope hand selected each man hisself from dungeons in every God-fearing country. Murderers, rapists, slavers, thieves, pirates every one."

"May I at least purchase your silence? I don't want your benefactor aware of my attempts."

He pulled a barmaid into his lap and thrust his hand up her skirt. "Aye. What he don't know, donna hurt 'im, I says. Right, Barb?" She giggled her agreement and he tugged at her corset strings with his rotten brown bean teeth. I threw a purse of coins onto the table before him. The weight of it surprised him and his attention was gained anew.

The best I could do further was pay the harbor master to inform me of any activity on the vessel. He was safely in my pocket along with most of the English ship captains. I also managed to intercept all of the bishop's outgoing messages. Being somewhat old fashioned, they didn't use telegraphs and so their letters were brought straight to me, completely unbeknownst to them. For now, the Pope knew nothing of my defiance. As far as he knew, he had lost contact with these two servants. I wished Ning Shiru was still alive; his master forgeries would have been useful.

As I left the harbor, a seaman approached me. He had heard I was looking for a certain young man and paying good money for information. He had set sail before I began inquiring after my nephew. When I showed him the photograph of Thaddeus as a teen and the sketch I had of Theodore, he seemed sure he knew of the boy's whereabouts. Holding his hand out, he grinned without showing any teeth. His meaning was clear enough. He'd give me no information without payment. I slapped a few coins in his palm.

"That's the one." He pointed to the print. "He volunteered for the whole journey round trip but disappeared after the second stop."

"Where was that?" I demanded.

The coins had disappeared into one of the many pockets of his absurd costume. His hand, now empty once more, crept up. Payment was provided and a tidbit of information followed. "India."

Sally huffed her impatience. "That part of Her Majesty's empire is quite large. Can you pinpoint a more exact location so that I have a better starting point?" Again the hand went out. Sally itched to extract the information in a more violent manner. It was no hardship to pay so I did. I would have paid much more to find Theodore.

He pointed out the port on an old and soiled map he carried. When I went to take said map, he prevented me. Apparently the map would cost me. I gave him enough to replace it three times over. Leon folded it up, slipped it inside his coat pocket, and dismissed the sailor.

Theodore was no longer in Great Britain. We decided to send spies out to every corner of the world. They were equipped with enough promissory notes to buy themselves out of any trouble they might run into. They carried sketches of Theodore and letters of introduction. Armed with guns and a few other pieces of technology Mr. Hall thought they might find useful, a dozen of my most stealthy agents left for Europe, Asia, and even the Americas.

14

When the day of the birthday party finally arrived, both of my children were excited and anxious. Dawn's dress was a beautiful pale blue that complimented her complexion and hair color. She was quickly becoming a woman, and if I had allowed it, the cut of the dress could have showcased her maturing figure. She fidgeted with her hair for nearly an hour, until she had a style she liked and I thought appropriate.

I allowed Ambrose to leave his "skirts" behind, dressing in a suit for the first time. It was adorable to see a miniature man attempt to enter the carriage all on his own. In the end, he couldn't manage the steps without help and was irritated with the footman for lifting him. All was forgiven once the trip began.

Neither of my children had much experience traveling, having both been protected and sheltered for most of their lives. They each looked out their respective windows and Leon and I exchanged smiles. For a few moments we were a normal family, wealthy but not supernatural. Dawn marveled at the crowds active at this time of day. Ambrose was silently appreciating the buildings, I assumed.

The ride was over quickly. It wasn't long before the club footman, dressed more finely than I'd ever seen, opened the door. Leon was first out, followed by Ambrose, who didn't wait for his ladies to exit the carriage before running up the steps and into the club. By the time I was down and they were helping Dawn, Paetus must have caught Ambrose. Our host waited on us at the entrance, Ambrose in his arms.

Paetus rushed down the stairs and thrust Ambrose into Leon's arms. "I believe you lost this." He was anxious to get to Dawn, offering her his own hand. The look on her face said she was smitten with the man even before she got inside to see his display of affection and wealth. I had looked at Julian in much the same way. I made a mental note to speak to her about the seductive talents of experienced men.

We entered in pairs. Paetus and Dawn led, followed by Leon and myself with Ambrose in between. The place was set up for a sumptuous feast, with round tables and chairs, covered and decorated in the manner Dawn had chosen. The servants, some from my own house, stood in line for inspection. Dawn spoke to each one, thanking them for their service on her special day.

It was early so it was not a surprise that no guest had yet arrived. Paetus showed us up to the top floor where he had set up a waiting area for us. After the party start time had come and gone and only Dowager Countess Wharlow had arrived with her three-year-old granddaughter, I began to worry. Earnestine was furious with her fellow socialites. She said that not a one of them said they were coming, many citing Dawn's birth timing when I was an unmarried child as the reason. They didn't want to sully their reputations. It was one thing to associate with me—I was wealthy and connected beyond measure. It was another to help a bastard celebrate her illegitimate birth.

I fumed. To hurt a child's feelings because of something she had no control over was unacceptable. Paetus and the countess kept the children distracted while Leon and I went to gather some partiers. Our first stop was home. I gathered all of my children's old outgrown clothes and had them shipped to the club. Then we went to all the orphanages and seedy areas of town known to hide vagrants and pickpockets. En masse, they followed us to the club.

"Girls to the left, boys to the right," I instructed, though many hadn't a clue their rights from lefts and had to be shown. The servants had set up makeshift changing rooms and helped get the children changed. Sometimes only a coat or apron fit but each got at least one article of clothing to replace a tattered piece of their own.

They were all seated and Dawn made her entrance. If she noticed their disheveled and dirty appearance, she made no sign. She greeted each as a family friend and thanked them for coming. The meal was served, devoured in minutes. These miscreants made better guests than the privileged ever would have. None of them had ever eaten until their stomachs were full, much less filled up on such extravagant delicacies.

The tables were taken away and the chairs rearranged into theater seating for the show. The street-savvy children were less than impressed by the sleight of hand magician since they lived by their abilities to steal. His big tricks went over very well, though. Making his assistant disappear and sawing her in half were the favorites. An even bigger success was the surprise finale Paetus had scheduled. Freaks and medical curiosities fascinated them all, Ambrose and Dawn included.

I am upset by the memory of their delight at seeing the conjoined twins, a hunchbacked man, a giant, and a woman with scaled skin. It was all the rage at the time and we did not think such exhibition was exploitation. The woman with her unformed, ungrown sibling attached to her back had no other way to support herself without such shows. They were all gracious and patient while exposing their abnormalities to the children.

While such a display had robbed me of my appetite, the young seemed completely unaffected. There was a chorus of cheers when the giant five-tiered cake was wheeled out, its size more impressive to the poor than its lack of color. The countess was very complimentary saying that it was purer white than either of her daughters' wedding cakes. Each guest was given a generous slice and even allowed seconds if they thought they still had room.

Dawn stood at the entrance and thanked the poor for coming just as if they'd done it to honor her. They were much more appreciative of the party favors than the ones who had actually received invitations would have been. They were excited to get back so they could examine each piece. One girl said they were too pretty to play with while another admitted she didn't know how to play. Dawn promised to visit and teach her.

The women who oversaw the orphanages thanked us profusely. Most of the children had never eaten so well; some had never had baked cake made of real sugar. None had their own games before today. I gave them donations to purchase school supplies and promised more on a regular schedule. They worried about walking back with such riches on their persons so I had them and their wards escorted by my guards.

I gave Paetus a genuine hug for his wonderful efforts. "I am glad not to be burdened by your particular gift," he whispered when his chin grazed my shoulder. We parted and he admitted, "Or blessed with your hand. I couldn't handle the excitement on a regular basis. You must keep Leonus on a very short leash." I didn't bother to correct his use of Leon's old name.

Leon scooped up Ambrose, who'd fallen asleep clutching his bag of pick-up sticks, completely exhausted from the event and bored of the multitude of thanks. Dawn said goodbye to Paetus and I permitted him to kiss her gloved hand. We all happily climbed into the waiting carriage.

Leon asked me, "Do you think we should wait for at least the first group of guards to make it back before we leave?"

I was in such a good mood that I dismissed his worry. "It is the middle of the day. The sun won't set for hours yet and I have no real enemies within the city to speak of. We will be fine."

∽

The sky was a vast violet swatch, with no end save the horizon in a circle around us. Pale green grasses waved like the ocean, though I felt no wind on my face. I sat across the table from my mirror reflection, drinking tea. The reflection took a drink. When I looked down, my own cup hadn't moved. Not a reflection, then. Sally sat across the table. The thought that this was impossible skittered across my mind. Sally and I didn't see each other; we saw through the same eyes.

And yet, we have seen one another before, laid side by side, holding hands in this very place, Sally said without moving her mouth.

"That's true." I took a sip from my own cup. There was no flavor on my tongue, just a warm sensation like I was drinking happiness. Looking down, I could see the cup was empty so I took another sip. The same contented pleasure washed down my throat.

To my right, I saw another table set up exactly as our own. At it sat two more versions of myself. One appeared as I had around Dawn's age. The other had my seventeen-year-old face and body. Simultaneously, they looked at me.

Sally shooed them away.

The young girls skipped away and their tea table disappeared. "Who were they?" I asked.

Taking a drink from her cup while speaking to me silently, Sally said, *Parts with whom you are not yet ready to deal.* She commanded me, *Drink.*

I obeyed, and as the contentment filled my belly, Sally sighed. *We could stay here forever. We should never have left the last time.*

Something wasn't right. I knew it, even if Sally didn't. Her grasp on reality was much more tenuous than my own. There was a reason we'd been here before. Something was happening elsewhere and this place was where we waited. The wind picked up momentum. It howled, taking the table, tea settings and all. "We have to get out of here."

Sally stretched her hand out to me. *No, not yet. I'm exhausted. Let's lie down for a bit.*

Lightning sliced through the sky and thunder cracked after it. I tried to remember the reason for this place. What did it mean that Sally and I were here? The effort hurt. Another bolt of lightning rocked this world inside our head.

I tried to hold onto that thought when a gust threatened to rip it away. This place was inside our head. Someone else was in control of our body last time. This was where we waited together until the right time to push Julian out. I started running.

There is no one else. We are safe here.

I turned to find Sally still seated in her chair across from me. Though I was running and she was not, she had managed to keep pace. I stopped. Understanding escaped me. I knew I had to get out but there were no windows or doors through which to flee. I took Sally's outstretched hand and pulled her up and against me. If this was our mind, we had the power to bend the place to our will.

"Close your eyes," I instructed Sally. The wind was more tyrannous now, becoming a solid thing surrounding us on all sides. I looked up to find we stood in the center of a great cyclone that was quickly closing in on us. The circle visible in the grasses tightened. The gale ripped us up and we were flying for a moment, then falling.

∽

I woke with a start.

"Easy," Paetus soothed me.

I looked around frantically. I shouldn't be alone with him. What had happened? Why was I lying on a lounge in the club? "You've been unconscious for almost an hour. It will take some time to feel normal again. That gas affects Carriers just as well as it does humans. Can you remember anything about what happened?"

"No." But as soon as I'd said it, I did remember. A few images, a couple sounds, some impressions were all I had. We were just starting our carriage ride home. Ambrose slept in my lap—no, not mine. Leon held him. Dawn leaned her head on my shoulder. The horse shied and then there was a loud boom—or was it the other way around? Another crack—a gunshot, perhaps—and the carriage lurched to one side. The door flew open, and my son was gone from the carriage. There was screaming and smoke that didn't smell like fire. "Where are my children?"

"Leonus woke half an hour before you and went to look for them. Neither one was in the carriage by the time I arrived. My men pulled you and Leon out of the chemical cloud and brought you here."

I sat up. My driver lay on the floor beside me; a great bullet hole opened his skull between his open eyes. Did someone have my children or were they just hiding somewhere, scared and alone? "Why is he out there but not you?"

"Leon knew you'd want us looking for them but wanted to stay with you. I volunteered to look but he said you'd want him out looking. I sent most of my men with him, retaining only enough to protect the club should your carriage only be the first in a series of attacks."

My blood boiled. Grabbing Paetus by the shirt, I screamed in his face, "Where are they? Where did you take them?"

"Calm down. You're hysterical. I didn't take your children. There is no need for me to steal something that already belongs to me."

That was a true enough statement. There was no doubt that, if given the choice today, Paetus would be Dawn's, based on the way she looked at him.

Who else would be so bold to take them in broad daylight? Our mind went to the bishops. They wanted her and being backed by the Pope may have emboldened them. "Come with me. Bring every man you have left."

I took my now-dead driver's goggles as my own. They would keep the poison fog, wind, and rain from stinging my eyes as we ran faster than humanly possible. My gown was too restrictive. I needed to move quickly and couldn't do that dressed appropriately. I couldn't keep my legs from tangling in the elaborate skirting so I tore the front panel off, leaving most of the bustle trailing behind me. The shorter, fringed overskirt gathered on each hip and, without the longer underskirt, ended above the knee.

I did not care about modesty and my alterations unknowingly started a fashion trend that would continue on for hundreds of years by women who liked the Victorian silhouette but lived an active lifestyle.

15

We took the trip on foot, not bothering to slow our pace to human-like speed. I would do damage control later, after I had my children safely in hand. The golden glow of the setting sun put a panic in me.

It wasn't far to the house where I knew the clergymen were staying. I kicked the door in. It flew off its hinges and smashed into the hallway wall behind.

The two men I was looking for sat in the parlor eating. "Where are they?" I demanded.

They first stared at my indecent exposure of leg, more shocked by their view than the fact that I had just burst through their front door. "The Brentlys are out of town and today is the servants' day off. We are alone." After that they met my eyes boldly, my behavior losing whatever respect I had previously earned.

Paetus' men, having finished searching the house, brought in five prepubescent boys. "There's no one else in the house," Paetus confirmed.

"Where are my children?" The window glass trembled in its panes.

The clergyman said, "We haven't seen either since the day you so rudely threw us out of your home."

They're lying. I knew it. Sally didn't stop me when I jumped onto the closest priest and tore his head off. Tossing it carelessly at the other's feet, I asked again, "Where are my children?"

The more silent one shrugged. I pulled the oldest page up by his arm. The priest might not care about his own life but surely the threat to a child would push him to share information. He laughed, dismissing him with a wave of the hand. "You don't think that any of them matter to my Incola, do you? He has thousands just like them." He'd called my bluff. I would never have hurt a child, no matter if doing so would save my own.

"Take them out of here. I don't want them to see this." I couldn't show this man mercy but I could spare the boys. What they would hear from the hallway would be enough to let them know I was serious.

Going to the small pile of coal smoldering in the fireplace, I shoved the poker into the hottest part. I gestured toward the cassock-wearing man. "Strip him."

He didn't even put up a struggle when the men followed my orders and forced him to his knees. Paetus, never one to shy from the bloody action, took a position on his right, forcing our captive's elbow straight, holding him in a way that would break the arm if he moved even in the slightest. This man's body was one big scar, the result of daily flagellation. He wouldn't flinch at the treatment I planned on threatening him with. I pulled the poker, now red hot, from the fire. Holding his face in one hand and the poker in the other, I stood there waiting.

I could see on his face that he wasn't telling me everything. Since Paetus was in direct contact with his skin, the priest couldn't lie. He didn't know where they were, but he had some idea, and if he escaped this he would search for them. Dawn was too valuable to resist. The reward for bringing her to the Pope would be so grand that the promise of my abuse was ablated. I pressed the hot tip against his cheek. To his credit, he was able to keep quiet for two whole seconds. His screams after that were high-pitched and pain-filled enough to almost tempt my resolve. The poker went back into the fire. "Next one will take an eye."

"I don't have your children," he begged.

A ruckus outside the door caught our attention. I grabbed the poker and held it poised. Paetus, pleased by the display of aggression and torture, called out to his men, "What is happening out there?"

One of the boys yelled out, "We'll tell you."

I went to the door and slid it open; the poker still red-hot hung at my side. The boys' eyes were drawn to it immediately. "Well?" I held my position, the implement of torture bouncing slightly in my grip, letting him know that the threat was still imminent and that their fate rested in their ability to please me with the information I wanted.

"We have been watching you and your children. We followed you to the club and away. We aren't responsible for what happened to your carriage but we saw it. I was the furthest away so I didn't really see what happened but the poison gas affected me less. I was first to wake. I saw a man pull your daughter from the wreckage and carry her off. They went down a side street, your son with him, and disappeared."

"Show me." I tossed the poker down onto the carpet, where it began to smoke.

The remaining priest began threatening and cursing the boy. Paetus snapped his neck. "If you're going to start a war, we might as well delay it for as long as possible," he explained. "He might never know what happened this way." He went for one of the boys, his intent to remove all possible information leaks clear, but I stopped him. I told the boys they were free. No one would hurt them if they remained in the city. That they could come to me if they needed anything.

Not sure that really counts for much. They're scared to death. They just saw you rip the head off a man.

Couldn't be helped, I countered. They could talk to any Carrier in the city for a reference. It wouldn't be long before they knew that, though I was to be obeyed, I could also be trusted.

We followed the boy out of the building.

∽

It was a dead end. They could have gone anywhere from the last place the boy saw them. We returned to the club to regroup with Leon and my own men. They'd had no better luck than we. I ordered the guards to spread out through the whole city. No ship, no train, no carriage was to leave London until Dawn and Ambrose were found. I didn't care what it cost nor how much time it took.

I flung myself into my husband's arms. "There, there. We'll find them," he whispered. "Don't fret. Dawn is too valuable to hurt."

"Ambrose is just a boy! He could be hurt to force Dawn to submit."

A finger under my chin brought my gaze to his. "Well, we know what is in store for any Incola foolish enough to try and ride her."

I smiled at that. It was true that she wasn't defenseless, at least inside her own head. My smile faded. Dawn's value lay not in being ridden but in being rutted. The thought that she was being raped was more than Sally could bear. She spun on Paetus. "Where would he have hidden her?"

"Where would *who* have hidden her?"

"Archelaos," I answered simply. It was the only possibility left.

Paetus stammered, looking between Leon and I, utter confusion written on his face. I did not have the time for this. I stalked over and put my bare hands on either side of his face. "Archelaos does not ride me. I pushed him out after we were sure enough time had passed after his previous body, Julian, had been destroyed. I have been pretending since the day you brought his tanned hands to me as a gift."

He clasped my forearms. "Is this true?" he asked, even though his gift would not have allowed me to lie to him.

"We thought he was dead but he's been here, near us all along. He must have had another Carrier that he possessed."

"It's not possible. After I burned Julian's body, Archelaos became anchored in yours. It would have been years before he was secure enough in it, years before he could bounce to another body. If you pushed him out when you say you did, he had nowhere to go." His speech sped, my gift of touch working on him as much as his was working on me.

I released him; he would be less than useless if he became too excited. "Unless he is here." I poked him in the chest.

Paetus knew what I was accusing him of. "No, my bond to him was dissolved when his body was destroyed. I thought he was in you. My allegiance lies with Dawn now and with you." His smile widened to a grin. "You are quite the performer, Lady Brooksberry. You had me completely fooled. I would have sworn you were him. You power hungry little she-devil, you killed all those Incola."

"We did not; we simply took advantage of the events. I think that was Archelaos."

Paetus paced. "It makes no sense. Why would he destroy all of those powerful vessels if he were able to ride them?"

"We know not but that isn't a question for now. Focus on finding Dawn and Ambrose. Is there any place he might have taken them? Think."

"He had many safe houses. I can show you to several but Archelaos was a sneaky man, distrustful of even me. He probably had dozens I knew nothing about."

"Well, unless anyone else has any better ideas, we will search every one you can remember."

∽

The first four houses were a bust. Not a single Carrier to be found. Two had been completely abandoned, cobwebs thick as curtains. The other two, which sat in more central locations in a bad part of town, were filled with human squatters who we scared half to death when we busted in. The fifth was a narrow brick two-story in a working-class neighborhood that was trying hard to appear middle class.

It was close to the kidnapping site if they used alleyways instead of streets, and it showed obvious signs of having recently been inhabited. Excitement coursed through me at the signs. The door was unlocked and everything inside seemed quiet. Half our men went in first with Leon and half stayed with Paetus and I. I sent Ed in with a case of cartridges once I heard the all clear.

A flutter in the window next door caught my eye. Someone watched us and I needed to know why. Sally leaped over the handrail to the other stoop. I banged on the door. When it didn't open I said, "You can come out or we can come in, your choice." A crack appeared and a girl about Dawn's age showed through it. "Thank you. Is your mama or papa home?"

"Ma's here but she ain't accepting visitors. Pa's at the factory and I need to get supper ready before he comes home." She tried to close the door at that, but I caught it easily and held it open.

"I apologize for intruding at such an inconvenient time but you see, my children have been abducted. They could have been brought to the house next to you." I pointed to the one we'd just searched. "Have you seen anything suspicious today?"

The girl looked over her shoulder and I took it as a sign. Shoving the door open did little more than startle the mother and a few young children. The woman screamed and tried to cover the bruises on the left side of her face while unable to hide her shock at seeing so well-bred a lady as I with exposed stockings. She'd taken a beating last night if I was correct. That's why she hadn't come to the door, not because Ambrose and Dawn were being held inside her home. I felt foolish but I'd rather that than miss the chance to save my children.

I put a few silver pieces in the stunned girl's hands and turned to go.

"Wait! I did see something. A few hours ago, a man I've seen coming and going every now and again came with a gown. Said I could have it if I'd give him one of mine in trade. I'm getting married next week and we haven't the money for a new dress and this one was so pretty and just about the right size. I tried to give him my church dress but he wanted a plain workday dress. Do I have to give it back?"

I understood that move. A gown as fine as Dawn's would attract attention in every neighborhood. Without it, they could blend in better. "No, darling, you may keep it. You traded for it fairly. Now tell me, did you see a girl in your dress and a little boy leave?"

"Yes ma'am. Her hair was so yellow and she had the prettiest hair combs."

"Was there anyone with them?"

"Just the one man." They were only children but it seemed a difficult feat for a solitary kidnapper to wreck a coach, gas its passengers, and abscond with two. "He was carrying the boy." The only way I thought it was possible was if he was controlling Dawn by continual threats to Ambrose. If that were true, why didn't they escape while he was exchanging dresses?

They couldn't very well go running down the street with her undressed, Sally reasoned.

"Which way did they go?"

She pointed. I gave her my card and a coin for each of her siblings. Sally told her that if her new husband ever raised a hand to her, she should come and see us. We would take care of it. The same went for her mama.

∽

No one else had seen or heard anything else. It was as if the three of them had vanished after the neighbor had seen them leave. The other places Paetus knew of weren't secret. Furnished similar to military barracks with bunks and large cafeteria-style kitchens, they were part of the property willed to me after Julian's death and were now the living quarters to many who now served Leon and I.

We returned home empty-handed, Sally beside herself. She was more sensitive to the threat than even I. When my own tortuous childhood had threatened my sanity, she had taken the brunt of abuse, shielding me. We decided long ago that our children would never suffer as she had and now that vow looked as if it might be impossible to keep.

Sally was an inner tempest I could not quiet and subsequently our exterior was jittery. We could not be still. My legs jiggled, constantly moving up and down, rubbing against each other causing an odd rustling noise that normally my skirts would have muffled. After realizing every man's eyes were focused on my stocking-clad knees instead of Ed's presentation I exclaimed, "Gentlemen, they're just legs! We all have them."

Leon replied, "Yes, dear, we do but none of ours are as finely shaped as yours."

The conversation continued with everyone, rather pointedly I think, *not* looking at my lower limbs. My tinkerer was studying the information gathered with his collector. "The catalog is having difficulty deciphering the readings. Lady Lawrence was in that house and she seems normal. The little lord's scent is off somehow. The catalog says it is most likely him but it is not certain. The only other person in the room, aside from our own, is the same one we've found evidence of several times. The spirit medium's murder scene and Theodore's room at the inn have both had the same scent."

"Could it be Theodore himself? You said before that this person seemed similar to Ambrose, almost like a blood relative."

"Yes, yes, I did say that, but this is the strangest reading. The part of this man's scent that links him to Ambrose is the part missing from the little Lord. It is as if they are no longer related."

I didn't understand. What event, however traumatic, could change a person's blood relation to another? If such a thing were possible, a child could choose to have different parents; a sibling could marry sibling on a whim with a little switch in genetics.

"None of this tells us anything about where or how to find them." Sally sounded desperate. Leon looked at us oddly, as if he'd noticed the change in me when Sally spoke. I had seen it myself when we stood in front of a mirror having conversations. The differences were slight but noticeable and I was surprised he hadn't seen it before. Sally was sturdier than I, and taller. Her eyes, darker.

We won't be able to keep our secret from him for long, not if you intend to keep him close.

Leon's voice broke us from our thoughts. "I can find her. She still wears my mark. It would be…"

"No!" I shouted. "Without us there to help her, Dawn could kill you."

"I know." Leon blew his hair out of his eyes as he stood. "We need to get her back home and then we can worry about me." I was shaking my head but my husband continued to argue. "Dawn is too special, too important not to try anything and everything. I am the only one who can do this."

"No, you're not. I'll go." Sally startled me and I am sure the surprised look on my face after saying something like that was perplexing.

∽

I sent everyone out of the room so that I could privately fight with the other facet of myself. It was confusing enough with just the two of us. My body sat in the same location on the lounge but Sally met me in our field. The beautiful pasture was overlaid with the image our eyes took in. Looking directly at Sally helped but the two locations together were disorienting.

She closed our eyes after the third time I had difficulty following the conversation. "I don't know how I know; I just do. I can ride Dawn. I didn't mention it before because I didn't know if it will be safe for you. Even now, I have my doubts."

"Doubts about what?" I wondered.

Sally chewed her lip. "Your sanity."

"I don't think there are any doubts about that," I joked. After all, I was having a conversation with another embodiment of myself in the middle of a pasture that only existed inside my mind, and we were contemplating leaving my body to inhabit my daughter's.

"You have never been without me. My leaving might prove too much for you."

"I was without you for the first twelve years."

Sally said nothing and I heard her statement again. *You have never been without me.* "You split from me when Papa began…" I could not bring myself to speak of what Sally had endured at the hands of our father.

She still did not argue with me. The truth I had always accepted was misguided. Sally hadn't been born because of my father's abuse; that was when she stepped up, when she was needed. She had been here the whole time. Sally could bring up memories that I could not and she had access to the moment Archelaos, in Julian's body, had taken me as a baby from my mother's lifeless arms.

We didn't have time for revelations such as these. "I will be fine," I said.

Sally wasn't convinced. "You are tempered by me. The desire to destroy and kill is just below the surface. You think of me as the impetuous, fervid, violent one but that is only because I take the reins whenever you feel it rising. I took the pain of your childhood so that your fury didn't destroy the world."

Stalking away from her, I claimed, "This is ridiculous."

"Is it? Think back to the people we have hurt or killed. It was you, not I, who acted each and every time." I vehemently denied it silently. She began to list, "Most recently the religious man: you're the one who tore his head from his body. The pimp: both times it was your fury that beat him. It is you who so craves the time with Paetus, and before him Julian, in that pain room. You killed the tight-rope walker who belonged to Leon when he was Leonus. You did that before I knew it was coming, so expedient was your rage. The footman, the men who'd lain with you under Julian's control, Turnkey, the doctor…"

"No, it was you who killed Doctor Federick, you who bit Turnkey. I was in the darkness that came with pain."

"Pain triggers your violence. I provide the darkness that hides your actions from you. Without it, without me, madness would surely have followed. Your image of self cannot be sustained when you realize you are the aggressor."

"What about Papa…and Mama? You brutally murdered them both." Sally didn't deny it; she left me to remember the truth. Thinking back to each one, I was surprised to find it was I. I was the evil side.

Sally, of course, knew my thoughts. "That first time was different. I will admit, it was me who encouraged your anger. It was the only way I knew for us to keep our baby. Father was going to remove her from our womb. The strength, the power, had never been mine. It was yours. I did not hold you back a fraction and the results were definitive."

Realizing that I was the monster was no small thing for me. A tempest around us raged. Hail beat Sally but she stood firm. Lightning split the sky and set fire to the grass. "When I am gone, you must calm the storm." She looked to the turbulent gray sky and was gone.

∽

So vivid was my pain, crimson flooded my sight so that there was nothing but color. I slowly became aware of a garbled choking sound and a mob surrounding me. When I finally willed the red curtain to part and let me back into reality, it was to find my hands wrapped around Leon's neck. He signaled his men to stand fast. They were not to help him if it involved hurting me.

The moment I realized I did not want to release him was when I knew Sally was right. Loving him was not enough to master the greater desire to kill. I wanted to kill everything. Out of control, I finally understood the needs of an Incola, for I had them too. I tried to transfer my anger away from Leon. I threw him forward, away from me. He flew back into the wall, landing behind a couch. Wisely, he did not reappear.

Seething at having been thwarted, my bloodlust threatened to blind me again. "Why did you enter after I asked you to leave me alone?" I bellowed.

"You were screaming."

I spun on Andrew. Though I had asked a question, I was unprepared for my reaction to the sound of his voice. I wanted it to stop, to end him. Before I knew it, I had taken two steps toward him.

Andrew stood stoic, staring at me. In his gaze there was no challenge, only acceptance. He would die if I so chose. The freedom of that kind of power swelled; pleasure bred by rage threatened to break through. I crossed to him.

Another sensation took over, one that dropped me to my knees, clutching my head. Memories that weren't mine crashed into my mind. I was running down an unfamiliar street in a beautiful pale blue dress. I was a juvenile but it didn't make sense—I wasn't allowed to wear such mature fashions at that age. Papa liked for Mama and I both to dress like children.

Then I remembered. Sally had left me—I shoved down the hurt that caused—to find Dawn. These were our daughter's memories I was seeing. This was from earlier today, after the carriage accident. She was holding Ambrose's hand. He led her away. They were hiding in an alley. The man, more lithe and young than I'd expected, came and took them.

"I know where they went. I am in her mind and can see it." I dashed out the door; the whole of my Carriers followed. I ran to the crash site and retraced their steps.

The alley narrowed due to bad city planning, the two buildings coming so close together that I was scarcely able to squeeze through, even with my corseted constriction. My men were forced to backtrack and go around.

I sprinted down to the next turn, recognizing it. They'd taken a meandering path to the house where they had traded Dawn's dress for something less conspicuous. Sally and I were still linked; she hadn't completely left me. I was in two places at once. We couldn't speak but I comprehended what she perceived. What I saw then temporarily blinded me again. The skinny kidnapper cut little Ambrose. That bastard made Dawn drink her brother's blood. The gash in his tiny arm was all I could see.

Somehow, I managed to follow the trail Sally fed me through our link. The doors barely slowed me down.

Dawn crouched in a corner, the knife-wielding man before her. Ambrose, his sister's protector, stood between them. They hadn't been expecting me, the look of shock clear on each of their faces. I didn't think. I couldn't. I barely heard their screams of protest. I didn't plan. I looked down.

I held the kidnapper's arms in my hands.

I'd torn them from their sockets.

16

Everyone shouted at the same time and I could make sense of nothing. The man, whose arms I held, laughed as his body bled out. Bloodlust had completely taken over. Not even my children were safe.

I screamed at Dawn, "Give her back to me!"

My daughter had been able to see and interact with Leon when he was riding her; I hoped she would understand that I meant Sally. She must have—Sally's soothing presence slammed into my consciousness. It took a few moments for our psyche to sync.

"What have you done, Mama," Dawn asked, staring at the amputee across the room, but it wasn't really a question. She knew what my actions meant even if I did not.

My son rushed to the side of the dying man. He tried to stop the bleeding, attempting to hold the severed limbs against their stumps, but his small body was too weak.

"What are you doing?" I demanded of him. It didn't matter. It was too late to save that body, whatever his reasons.

Ambrose spoke to Dawn. "He will force me to walk the path and then he will be able to follow."

Dawn shook her head no.

Looking to the man missing his arms, slouched against a wall, clearly very close to death, I was surprised to find his face not only looked peaceful, but he seemed in the throes of ecstasy. He was enjoying death.

"What is going on? Ambrose, what are you talking about?" I knelt, looking from daughter to son.

"It is the only way to stop him," he said to Dawn. He turned to me, sadness, repentance in his eyes. "Your son is evil. Perhaps it is because he was born with an ancient inside him. Maybe he would have been this way even if I hadn't possessed his body while it floated in your womb. We will never know. Ambrose is beyond saving. Please believe me, I have given him ample opportunity. He repaid me through murder and chaos." He took my face in his tiny hands, sticky with blood, and kissed my lips in a less than familial fashion.

I recoiled.

I could not grasp the events. In my moment of confusion, Sally explained, *Archelaos speaks from inside our son, where he has lived Ambrose's whole life. When we pushed him from our mind, he had nowhere else to go. The fetus was the only avenue available to him.*

I looked at my son's baby face. Gone were the loving and apologetic looks, replaced by cold selfish ones. Ambrose was back at the helm of his own body since his Carrier had finally died from the wounds I'd inflicted. "Archelaos belongs to me. His blood is mine."

I recognized that. Ambrose had been the one to write those words on the medium's table lip, meaning that my son, not my ex-husband, was her murderer. His message was to Archelaos, not me. Suddenly the statement, "I will not allow you to choose other men above me," made sense. Archelaos had been trying to get away. Ambrose destroyed every vessel he managed to gain control of. Ambrose was our mystery Incola, not Archelaos.

Dawn began to shake and mumble to herself.

"Oh, shut up, will you!" Ambrose shouted at her.

"Why do you hate us so?" I asked.

"I don't hate you, Mama. I love you, but you have made mistakes."

He thinks you need a strong Incola to help you. Your son wants to be worshiped. He wants all the power. He wants to sit on the throne with you at his side, a lovely ornament. He has never thought of you the way a boy should his mother. When he is older, his body capable, his desires toward you will be twisted to match.

Ambrose stood as tall as his short frame would allow. "I told you I did not like Leonus."

Only then did I realize that my son had been the Incola that tried to kill my husband.

Shaking his head in disbelief, Ambrose's hate-filled eyes turned to his sister, though his comments were directed at me. "And her…you always loved her more."

"No." If anything, I loved him more. Ambrose was mine, born of my body while I stood at the helm. Dawn, beloved and special, belonged to Sally.

"You threw her a big party, spending *my* birthday planning it!" Spittle flew from his mouth when he yelled.

I attempted to defend myself. Using my calmest voice, I said, "That was Paetus' doing. He didn't know it was your special day."

"You should have told him! Paetus should be my ally, as he'd been Archelaos', but no, he was infected by this *girl*." He pointed behind him. Clearly at the breaking point, Ambrose spoke more to himself than to me. "Females corrupt, cause rot in a man's mind…their sinful bodies and decadent lives. I will *never* be ruled by one."

"Why did you do it? Why did they all have to die?" I could remember hearing those questions from my son's mouth when that man killed himself in the street. *Why, why did he have to die?* That had been Archelaos, questioning my son's actions. How could I have been so blind?

My son's voice broke me from my musings. "I like killing. Birds are so easy, so trusting, and you just blamed it on their flights into the glass. But then Moira caught me. She made me mad. She set them free." He smiled, placing his hands on his hips. "I am so strong. Killing her was not much different than killing a bird. Then Archelaos left me and I discovered Carriers. Dying in their skin is the most exquisite sensation, Mama. Thank you for that one." He lifted his chin to indicate the corpse in the corner. The look of ecstasy on his little face was disturbing. He must have noticed my disgust. "You're such a prude, Mama. You should feel it. I cannot wait to ride them to the fights. When I rule the club, we will have gladiator-type fights—to the death—and battle exotic beasts. I will bring back the execution methods I have seen in Archelaos' memories." He seemed very pleased by his idea.

"How did the mind of my baby become so warped?"

"I am not a baby!" he screamed.

My men burst into the room but kept their distance. From where they were standing, the danger was gone. Only my children, I, and a corpse occupied the room.

"I will be Lord of my house," Ambrose mumbled to himself, fists balled at his sides, almost as if he were using the mantra to calm himself. "Do you know what my very earliest memory is? As soon as we were born, Archelaos plotted to get away. He saw Dawn and loved her instantly, wanted her instead of me. Have you any idea what that feels like? To be rejected by a part of yourself?" He didn't wait for me to answer or soothe him. "He should be done by now. Enough, Archelaos, come back."

"No," Dawn answered.

Ambrose sighed. "This will end the same as the others, Archelaos."

"You don't have to do this. We can work it out so that no one else has to die," she argued.

"You have no loyalty." He shrugged, obviously still believing he spoke to Archelaos. They must have carried on many conversations in this manner. "You are mine. Your blood belongs to me." Dropping the little space it took to get to the floor, Ambrose sat and, lying back, closed his eyes.

I knelt beside my son's tiny body. Separating his lids to look into his eyes, Sally declared, "He's alive, but out of his body."

Ambrose began to convulse and I cradled him so that he didn't injure himself. I had seen this before. Leon had similar fits when he tried to ride

Dawn. My heart hurt when I thought of my husband but Sally pushed it down to a dark corner of our mind to be dealt with later.

"His body will die when she kills his spirit." Sally spoke aloud calmly, resolved at the events that must take place.

"Sally, please," I pleaded. "Show her how, as you did with Leon. Don't let her kill my son."

"No," she replied aloud again. We were under great duress and completely forgot to hide our dual nature, oblivious to our men observing our argument. "Dawn is doing the right thing. He is set on killing her out of sheer jealousy. It would not have been an easy death, either. He planned to torture her first."

"But why would he do that?" I asked.

"As a lesson to Archelaos, and because he wanted to. Ambrose enjoyed ruining, destroying beautiful things. How many times did we hear that from him? He is sick with an illness of the mind that has no cure. I am sorry, Ramillia, but this is the only way."

The sound of my own name from my own mouth startled me into remembering that we were not alone. I looked up to find everyone staring. Our secret was out.

17

The convulsions stopped when my daughter finished crushing the spirit of my son. I insisted on carrying his body all the way home by myself. He weighed nothing. It felt wonderful to hold him and terrible to think I'd had to wait until he was practically dead to do it.

The night was dark but clear, like my mind. Everything was pellucid now that I knew the truth. It was as if I could see those around me for the first time. The fog of secrets had lifted and there was nothing left to hide behind. In all those months, years, I had suspected everyone in my life harbored Archelaos. Even Dawn and Leon had not escaped suspicion, but never, not even once, did I imagine that Ambrose not only housed my ex-husband's spirit but imprisoned him.

I looked only at my son's face, letting my legs travel the way home automatically. Dawn walked beside me. Knowing she needed kind words, search though I might, I found none for her. Oddly my shoes on the cobblestone streets were as loud as gunshots, but those around me made no sound. The normal noise of the city disappeared also, leaving me completely alone.

Not alone. I am here, Ramillia. We will get through this together, as we have always done.

I went up the steps, over the threshold and straight into the parlor, slamming the door behind me. Alone with my two murderous children, I sat cradling Ambrose, wondering if I had done it more through the years this end could have been avoided.

Sitting on the chaise beside me, Dawn penned a letter. I said nothing, even after seeing that she enclosed it in an envelope addressed to Mr. Paetus Crawley. She rang for a footman and sent him out with the correspondence without ever saying a word.

Ambrose's hair had gotten a bit shaggy, and with the length came added curl. I ran my fingers through it, putting soft texture to memory. His mouth, more generous than mine, had a subtle pout. His flesh was slack, his body relaxed, molded to me. Air filled his lungs in a jagged breath, reminding me that he was alive. Without thinking, I shouted for Leon. He would know what to do.

Ramillia, Sally began.

A soft knock on the door made me think my genteel Leon waited on the other side. "Come in," I called.

Andrew and Auley entered instead of my husband. "Where is Leon?" I demanded.

Without a word, father and son crossed the room, bending down behind the couch. Only then did I notice that the plastered wall behind it was crushed, dented as if something had crashed into it. Not something, someone. Sally allowed me to recall the events during the time she left to find Dawn.

Even the memory of the pain that her leaving caused was gravid. Wrath threatened to take over and I realized I was squeezing Ambrose tightly. Leon had run in when he heard my distress at being alone. He hadn't known the reason for it but rushed in to see if he could ease my suffering. He loved me. In that moment, I hadn't felt any love for him, only the desire to kill. I had *enjoyed* choking Leon. He was alive when I threw him but I remember the crack when he hit the wall.

My men carried Leon's body from behind the couch. Auley held the legs and Andrew supported the shoulders and head. A jagged bulge under the skin of Leon's neck caught my attention. I had broken his neck.

Andrew turned to me and said, "This changes nothing. We will continue to serve and protect you and Lady Dawn as long as we live, just as Leonus wanted."

I understood him but did not agree. This changed everything. I was a murderer at my very core. Maybe all Incola were. I had to try something, anything, to correct what I'd done, what I'd become.

With certainty, I knew that this was the moment the cylinder should be opened. Ning Shiru said it could save the world. Perhaps it could save Leon and Ambrose, *my* world. "Wait," I commanded. Placing my son's body beside me, I pulled the cylinder from my pocket, held the mysterious object with both hands, pressed the two children depicted with my thumbs and twisted.

Sally and I had enough experience with pain that we managed to keep from calling out when a metal claw jutted out from the cylinder, hooking into both of my palms. A burning started at each point and ran its course up both arms and into my chest and then head. I dropped the cylinder as soon as I was able.

The retracted claws took with them some of my blood, disappearing back into their hidden chambers and turning the blue liquid inside a deep indigo. The act of twisting the two sides changed the carved scene depicted. No longer being chased by the mob, the woman was leading them. The men who had been courting her had turned and were now fleeing her and her army.

Looking down at my hands I saw the puncture holes were no longer visible but my palms carried a blue network of veins, resembling spiderwebs, under the skin. I took Ambrose back into my arms. Nothing happened. I placed the vein-covered appendages on his face, head, then chest. No effect. I looked to Leon. No change. Whatever I had done, whatever that thing was, did nothing to save them.

A heaviness of heart filled my chest. Blood rushed from my head at the thought of the rest of my life without them. What would be my purpose for living?

Dawn, Sally answered, but I scarcely heard her.

I wanted to die. There was no reason to live.

Our daughter must be protected. Sally turned our head to force me to look at Dawn, hoping her visage would calm my suicidal thoughts. I looked.

I felt nothing.

"My lady," Auley said. "We must dispose of the body."

Andrew expounded, "Paetus says the older the Incola, the quicker they turn."

Sally spoke aloud when I did not. "Go ahead."

The two men looked at each other and then Andrew said, "We should take the little lord, also."

Sally knew they were right. Ambrose had been an Incola his whole life, and though it had been a short one, who knew what consequence it would have. Rather than speak, I opened my mouth and a roar came out. Any man who touched my son would die. Sally took over. She shook our head no and dismissed the men.

∽

Paetus burst in, Mr. Boyd not attempting to slow him down this time, and Dawn hopped into his embrace. She hung on his neck and he wrapped his arms around her, holding her off the floor. Dawn kissed him hard on the mouth, surprising Paetus for the first time in probably a thousand years. He spared me a glance but when I made no move to stop them, he kissed her back.

I realize that a first kiss at that age is not uncommon in modern day. For the late 1800s it was unheard of for anyone, no matter their age, to have public displays of physical affection. I was too broken at that moment to insist on decorum and Sally didn't adhere to the strict etiquette of the day.

Dawn ended the kiss and Paetus set her feet back to the carpet. She straightened her dress, the one exchanged for her fancy party gown. Paetus, still riding the high of their first physical exchange, brushed a stray hair from her cheek and leaned in to kiss her again. Dawn reacted with a swift slap across his face that rang out sharply in the house's silence. The message was unmistakable. Their contact would be under her terms and none other. Paetus dropped to his knees in apology, matching her muteness with his own. Snatching a decorative rope from where it held back the curtains, my daughter put a makeshift leash around his neck and pulled him from the room on his hands and knees.

The peace of my son's face called to me, like a mother who cannot bring herself to leave the crib side of her newborn. Had it been Ambrose or Archelaos staring back at me from my own newborn's eyes? Exploring my memories, I tried to sort them but found it difficult to credit my son with the wrongdoing of which I knew he was guilty.

Dawn was our firstborn but Ambrose was the first baby I ever held and loved in that way only a mother could understand. Sally knew the loss I was suffering and though she mourned too, she stepped in as always when I needed her. I sank to that place where I felt carefree and left her to endure something for the both of us that I could not handle.

Paetus came back into the room looking satiated and near intoxicated. I knew not how much time had passed. Blood trickled from his cuff down his hand but he caught it in his handkerchief before it dropped to stain my rug. "Was it Archelaos?" Paetus pressed.

"Dawn killed the spirits of both Ambrose and Archelaos when they tried to possess her." Sally told them how my husband had inhabited my son's body since before birth. They had a different relationship than any previous Incola and Carrier. "Ambrose became an Incola, able to ride any body that Archelaos could. Archelaos used their shared blood to make a path, trying to escape, unknowing that Ambrose could follow."

"And once Archelaos knew that the Carrier bodies were compromised, he destroyed them." Paetus said it as a statement, so sure was he of his lifelong friend.

"No," Sally argued. "It was Ambrose who killed the Carriers out of jealousy. That emotion plagued him his full five years. The strongest had been of Dawn. When Archelaos loved her, Ambrose felt only poisonous envy. He had been rejected by Archelaos as weak, but my son would not accept that. He held Archelaos prisoner."

"Why was I spared?" Paetus struggled to understand.

"Could be a number of reasons. Ambrose could have hoped you would prove to be an advantageous ally or perhaps it was Archelaos who spared you because of your two-millennium alliance."

"Almost three, actually," Paetus mumbled. "Ambrose told me of Dawn that night. Or maybe it was Archelaos." The motivations of either could only be guessed. Perhaps it was an attempt by my son to rid his life of Dawn. Archelaos could have sensed the danger and tried to remove her from the situation.

Then I remembered something. That night Leon and I had made love for the first time. I had woken later and we had sex again, this time very different than the first, and the next day Leon had not recalled our second tryst. Sally maintained control of our body, keeping me from retching. I wasn't certain if that had been my ex-husband or my son in Leon's body at the time. Sally refused to allow me to think that it was my son but she could not erase what she had said only a few hours ago about his twisted desires toward me.

"Is there anything we can do for him?" Paetus nodded at the tiny body in my arms, not specifying which of "him" remained.

Sally shook our head no. "They are both gone. The body will not be far behind them."

∽

Sally was right. Our son's body could not continue without the magic that makes us all alive. The flesh held on for a day but eventually the little heart stopped beating, the minuscule lungs failed to inflate. We mourned his loss even before his physical death. I held a private wake. I, alone, sat with his body, fearing in my absence they would take him and burn him, which now, in hindsight, I see would have been the right choice. When it came time to bury him, there were no tears left. I was too stunned when Dawn killed Ambrose the second time—in his own grave—to cry. Destroying the undead husk he had become was a mercy I couldn't manage. I didn't know who I had failed more severely: my damaged daughter or my soulless son.

My daughter stopped speaking. She ate and drank and slept as normal but she did not reply when asked a question. Sitting with me while I read or feigned cross-stitch, she faked nothing, only sat. Hands crossed in her lap, a smirk on her face.

Dawn was not the only one broken. When Sally retreated to the deep recesses of our mind and I came to control our body, I sat staring into the distance, looking at nothing. Hours we lost like this, maybe days. The only moments I remember clearly were when we stood by Leon's funeral pyre and we went to Ambrose's grave.

News of the vacancy at my side, left by Leon's death, spread quickly. It mattered not that I was in my mourning blacks. Suiters, the most eligible of all the other English Incola families, the sons of those who Ambrose had forced to commit suicide, from every corner of the Queen's kingdom, visited. Too much the Victorian lady to send them away, I met with each one, expressed both my gratitude for the honor they paid me but also my refusal to break tradition and be courted before my allotted grieving period ended.

This adherence to proper social etiquette unknowingly exposed them all to something.

Andrew and Auley fell ill first.

Then those who guarded me most closely.

Quickly the mysterious illness laid low every Carrier in my household and Paetus'. And then, through human servant gossip, I heard the sickness had spread across the city and nation and kingdom.

It started with an extreme weakness, which terrified those who had never experienced such a thing. Claustrophobia in one's own skin brought many to the brink of insanity. Only Dawn and I seemed immune.

For the third time in my life, my human servants abandoned me out of fear for their lives. I did not blame them.

Wise even in his weakened state, Paetus stopped all outgoing post. He isolated the country so that no foreign Incola would hear of our impotence and this nation's ripeness for the taking. He used my power and authority to do this. There was simply no aspect of British life over which I did not hold formidable sway.

Sally cared for my Carriers as best she could, conveying them to their beds from wherever they dropped. In truth I cared not if they died.

18

I sat in a stupor when they came for me. My house lay empty save the few sick lying in my beds. The inspector with the large mustache, who had come to my home several times to investigate this or that death, strolled in as if he owned the place. I tore the man's head off.

After, I allowed the next man to read the charges against me.

Bribery.

Assault.

Arson.

Murder.

Treason.

I thwarted any attempt to put me in chains. When all men were down, I acquiesced. "I will go without a fight if you allow me some time to get my affairs in order." As they lay about the room in various stages of defeat, I did not feel the need to explain that my cooperation would be the only means of taking me into captivity. "I love my Sovereign and her word is law. Out of respect for Her Majesty, I will come with you tomorrow and accept whatever judgment and punishment the solicitor and judge decide."

For hours I roamed the streets.

I beat a few pimps.

Threatened a high-bred husband.

Sally argued with me, but I'd made my decision. All my plans, all our grand schemes, did nothing. I couldn't protect anyone. My baby died. Being a Carrier had twice widowed me. I'd loved both husbands in a way. My daughter was broken, unable to escape the maze that was her mind. I'd failed. And now that I had unleashed a plague upon the Incola, my usefulness had been consumed.

The Dowager Countess's home had been grand at one time, but that time had long passed. The columns I leaned against, as I waited for her butler to meet my knock, were cracked and crumbling. He answered the door, his wig askew, sleep in his eyes. It was nearing daybreak. At first he refused to wake my friend, but after I pushed my way in and seated myself in the parlor he had no choice. The Dowager came down quickly, her hair in knots and curls.

She tied her housecoat around her and sat beside me.

"Ernestine," I addressed her in the most familiar, "tomorrow I will be going away and I need you to take care of my daughter." Soon enough the gossip train would make a stop at her house so I went ahead and said it. "I am not a good person. I have killed and maimed, corrupted and cajoled." Details were irrelevant. "I endanger everyone I am close to. Dawn may be a bastard but she is my flesh and blood. Young, she still has a chance to turn out well, as your daughters have. The darkness in me does not allow me to raise such a child. I ask you, as my only friend: will you take her as your ward when I am gone?"

She didn't want to believe. "They will come for me tomorrow and I must know that my daughter is taken care of. I will give you half my fortune." Money simply wasn't spoken of; to do so was an inexcusable vulgarity. I told her an exact sum and she gasped.

"I wouldn't know what to do with half of such a sum," she explained.

"You misunderstand. That *is* the half I will give to you." She choked on air. "You will do it then?"

"Now it is you who misunderstands. I would take care of your child even if you had no money. It is an honor that you would choose me. But surely, with that amount of riches you could go abroad; there is no reason you must meet the hangman."

"The reason is I choose it. I am tired." I stood to go. "One more thing you must promise me: raise Dawn in secrecy. No one must ever know she is my daughter. All mothers feel this way but in our case it is true: Dawn is special. The world will tear itself apart to have her."

∽

I sat in that tiny cell, awaiting the break of day. Tomorrow I would die. The trial, held in the House of Lords, had been nonexistent. I pled guilty to all charges and sought no mercy. I asked only one thing: that I be beheaded rather than the traditional hanging. This raised much rabble, for there had not been a beheading in 150 years. I insisted this was the only outcome I would allow and one of the officers who'd come to apprehend me argued that my cooperation would be the only way to ensure the judgment was carried out. His injuries spoke as loudly as his words.

And so I waited while they procured an executioner proficient with an ax. They sent for a guillotine from France, but no reply ever came. Paetus' ban on post continued. It delayed my execution for a week. I forbid Ernestine from visiting me; to do so would start the rumor mill and it could hint at Dawn's whereabouts. I planned and practiced how to turn my head at just the right moment as to slice my head in two and ensure my brain was destroyed. I would be cremated after.

I'm tired. I failed. I'm a murderer. Sally mocked me. *I am sick to death of your moaning! We are not defeated. We are survivors!*

Closing my eyes, I joined her in the meadow that was only ours. "I am sorry, old friend. I truly am. You have always been there for me, taking what I cannot bear." I held her hand in mine. "At the moment of our death, you should go. You can do it, I know. You can ride Dawn." She would need Sally when I was gone.

She nodded. "I can, though I fear entering her mind again. But…" she began.

"But what?" I asked.

"But what about the others?"

"What others?" Wind whipped my hair and when I brushed it from my eyes, three versions of myself stood beside Sally. The seventeen-year-old me grabbed my shoulders and shoved me to the ground. The preteen me sat on my chest, giggling. I struggled against them until the me who looked as I had on the day of Ambrose's death put her heel on my throat.

"Sally means us." The one with a boot cutting off my breath snarled. "We aren't about to go quietly," she declared, her eyes blazing red.

PART THREE

PRECIOUS BLIGHT

Tomorrow, Lady Ramillia will exist only in these pages.

Over a century has passed since I completed my first two journals. Most immortals my age have written dozens in an attempt to remember their various lives. A hundred years have passed as I have tried to forget mine. For decades, my duty to this world has been to loosen the Incola stranglehold on humanity. My actions only strengthened a far more dangerous grip. One that must be unfurled.

This, my third and final journal, must be written tonight. For tomorrow, I die.

1

I tell my story not in an attempt to garner sympathy or even empathy. It is a purely selfish endeavor. Remembering will strengthen the bond, long since stretched beyond capability, and pull me closer, closing the gap between myself and those I loved. My heart desires a reunion with them all, but my brain tells me that outcome is unlikely.

My daughter Dawn died a few short years after my son. I killed her. I have killed all those closest to me. There is no one to blame but myself. Early on, I came to know that I was the monster under my own bed. It is only after so long without even Sally as company, that another certainty became an ever-present bitterness in the back of my throat.

I am the monster under *every* bed.

In order to keep the monster there in the darkness, I must stay awake. I have not slept since the day I lost them. I cannot. To sleep is to lose consciousness. And, with consciousness, control.

If I lose control, who possesses it?

This body, my body, is too powerful for anyone else to wield. It—I—must stay confined under that proverbial bed until this body is destroyed. So I remain awake. The human body, to say nothing of the human mind, needs sleep to survive. As you know by now, I am not human. I was a Carrier until I learned to be an Incola, a rider, inhabitant, resident, wagon driver, one who has transferred his domicile to any other place, a cultivator.

That last one isn't me, but it describes every Incola I've ever known. They are all greedy. Searching, planting seeds, waiting for the harvest of a lifetime. I was supposed to be that harvest to the men I knew as Paetus and Julian. I married Julian and my first-born daughter was promised to Paetus. With us, they planned to populate the world with, well, themselves.

"One who has transferred his domicile to any other place" does not describe me either. In this circumstance, "place" means body. Incolas, historically, transfer their souls, for lack of a better term, from body to body by a variety of methods. Their Carriers serve as chattel, to be used, abused, bred, discarded. I do not use Carriers. My soul has but one place. I am trapped.

I am the last remaining member of my family, the last Incola. There is but one creature left on earth that carries the same blood as I. If I were religious, I would pray that this is not the end. As I am not, I can only hope.

∽

Last week I killed the last man alive with the knowledge I sought to purge from earth for so many years. I knew him. I should have felt remorse, sadness, guilt, joy. Anything really. My senses continued to increase in sensitivity throughout my long life because I never left my original body. My emotions are another thing entirely. They went with Sally and the others, who I always feared meant I wasn't natural, and were what made me human. Without them, I am death.

So confident in their own abilities were they that no guard stood outside. Removing my night-vision goggles for fear that the lights would be on inside, I simply twisted the knob and pulled the door open. Through a hallway made of metal I walked unmolested. Money had never been a worry, even less so in the last fifty years. Underneath my corset and bloomers, I wore the best armor that could be bought. Thin and breathable, my undergarments were impregnable. I feared no bullet nor blade. The silk-feeling bodysuit couldn't even be crushed. My conceit won only in one way. I wore no head covering other than my usual fascinator. My face bore not even makeup.

They must have thought I could not find this undisclosed location where they brought Ed. No longer did I require the devices Ed created for me so long ago in Victorian England. My very body became the means with which I could locate and identify Carriers of the Incola gene. The door at the end of the hall held them all.

Inward the door flew with scarcely any effort on my part. Five men, human by the smell of them, stood around Ed, who sat strapped to an odd-looking chair. His face was much the same as I remembered, though his goggles had been replaced by more natural looking but still mechanical eyes. They turned to me and widened. Recognition washed over his face and it went slack. The lines disappeared, replaced by a smirk. His fingers ended in bloody bulbous tips. Pliers and ten fingernails with trailing torn flesh lay on a small metal table beside. Tortured for information.

Ed complimented my dress. "That color of blue is lovely, Ra…" He must have thought better than to say my name aloud within the hearing range of these men.

As if I had any intention of allowing them to live.

The man closest to the door turned an automatic gun on me. So swift were my movements that he only got off three rounds before my fingers went through his ocular cavity and into his brain. Lifting, I removed his head from his body. I have found that to be the quickest and easiest way to kill. Sometimes, like this time, I was at the wrong angle to twist the neck and, failing to break it, the spine came with the head. His bullets ricocheted off me. They could have hit other room occupants. The commotion grew enough.

"I told them nothing," Ed yelled.

I cared not. Even if these men did not yet hold the secrets, they knew what Ed was. They saw my visage. They died. A further recollection and description of the manner was unnecessary.

I crossed to Ed, slipping one glove from my right pocket onto my right hand and one glove from my left pocket onto my left hand. Right first, I put my hand on his face. First that blank mask of deep relaxation covered his face. Then my left joined. The gift of touch that forced truth was the one needed here.

"Do you have any children?" I asked.

His eyes closed but he spoke, as if the effects of the two gloves struggled against each other. "I did." He took a deep shuddering breath and I removed my calming right glove from his cheek. It would take some time for the effects to wear off, whereas the power of truth relied on continued touch to work. "They died along with my wife while I was in your service."

"Were they Incola? Did they have their own offspring?"

"I do not know."

That truth was his only answer.

"Have you ever shared with any person, anyone, the secret to immortality?"

He shook his head no.

"Have you taught anyone to heal themselves, to end aging?"

His mechanical eyes remained closed. Again, he indicated no silently.

"Are there any of your inventions that I do not already possess?"

"When you killed Lady Dawn, we fled in fear. My own eyesight is the only invention I worked on or improved. I did not want to locate Incola after that, only to hide from them, and you." His eyes opened then, searching my face. The calming effect of Julian's touch began to wear off. "Please release me, Ramillia."

"How is it they have captured and held you? Surely your strength matches my own, as we are roughly the same age."

Had he been free of the gift of touch, he would have lied. I could feel that. As he was not, he indicated the shackles on his arms, legs, and torso and said, "These bindings."

"Made from the same metal that you…" I did not finish my question before he confirmed that they were the very same material that he had invented to hold me in my madness. I picked up a set of manacles matching those on his legs and slipped them into a hidden pocket in my skirt.

"Her Majesty's government, perhaps every government, knows of me." He looked toward one corner behind me.

I followed his gaze. A small red light gave away the location of a transmitting camera. Jumping up, I pummeled the camera, destroying it.

Though I had removed my gloved hand from him, I recognized the truth of his next words. "Knows of *us*."

I knew the answer to my next question but I asked it anyway, "Are there any more?"

"No. You and I are the last." I heard the accusation in his voice. He had not wanted to believe what he knew to be true. I had killed them all.

I killed him too. I burned his body. Narrowly escaping the federal agents, I grabbed a red-hot bone fragment and ran. Even if he could heal himself from such destruction, Ed could not do it without every part of himself. It burned my palm so badly that my ability to feel the pain disappeared. When that happened, I slipped it into the pouch at my waist.

∽

Decades before that, in the late 1900s, I neared Pripyat, in the northern Ukraine, on foot. The Incola locater, a compass of sorts, said that the wind had blown me off course yet again. I snapped it in half and discarded it. It was unnecessary now. I didn't know if snow currently fell from the sky because gusts moved the drifts to and fro so quickly and drastically that I was near blind. My night-vision goggles could do me no good here. It was the opposite problem. The white snow reflected light in every direction. I adjusted my course based on my internal locator and set off again.

That same wind that stung my cheeks and any exposed flesh was also a blessing, for it had cleared and hardened my path, giving my snowshoes grip. How far down to solid soil, I did not know. Perhaps there was no land, only snow, ice. The cold was as extreme as any I'd experienced. Yet it did not trouble me much. At my age, any Incola has mastered the ability of repairing one's own body. It was how I survived without sleep. My body remained the same, un-aged, undamaged. I did not know about my mind. Maybe it was like this snow. Maybe it was temporary, unsupported by anything real. No longer did I bother with the lie of what I was. Incola, that which I had always hated, was the nomenclature I accepted.

After that night I would be the only one left in all the world.

I could decide the definition of Incola. The definition I had already decided: final. Finis. Dead.

The frozen pure fat tasted terrible as I walked, but I knew I would need much fuel to keep my metabolism chugging. A train needs coal. The further or faster it must go, the more coal it consumes. After a night spent in the northernmost village, I had loaded up on breakfast and took the seal oil cakes they made and began the walk.

The residents there recognized me for what I was: unnatural. Unlike in many modern places where humans lived removed from the ebb and flow of life, here where death played a key role in life, no one bothered me for my secret. None attempted to buy, bribe, blackmail or beg me for eternal life. They gave me food, shelter, supplies, and directions, happy to see me go.

The fur from the white bear that roamed this longitude graced my shoulders, keeping me safe and warm from the bitter cold. I relished it. Had I been of the current era, worried with the rights of the polar bear and every other such fur-bearing creature, I could not have enjoyed its comfort. Never was my money invested in the fur trade. Call it what you will; I knew fur would become the enemy of modern thinkers. Killing is out of style. Much more will follow in my tale, popular or not.

The rapid wind of the tundra blew the ice sideways across my path but snow did not fall nor accumulate. I marched forward. Though it obscured my vision, my path lay clear. I must end the last enemy.

I issued the same to him as I had to all others. "Invite me to your home, accept the infection, or die resisting." He chose to die. He would have said he chose to fight but I knew there would be no fighting, only ending. Can you battle a tornado? Or combat the tide? No. Such struggles are futile. I wished the last might have been peaceful but it was not mine to choose.

The gaping hole in the ground came into view. It was an unnatural crater untouched by the snow. It was almost as if the snow was as frightened of the dark hole as humans were. I continued on what had been the maintenance road passing in front of reactor four. Climbing over rubble, I stumbled. A hand caught my elbow, steadying me.

Not jerking away was difficult as the hand was dry, flaking, and slick with oozing at the same time. He spoke in Ukrainian, which I understand as well as any of the three dozen languages I am familiar with. Addressing me formally, he said, "Ledi Khvoroby, our Incola hides within the most radioactive area, hoping you will not venture that far. We will bring him to you." He paused and smiled. The genuine smile aged him, spreading cracks along his face as an earthquake does to land. "Though it will cost some of us everything." His second upper incisor fell out. He clapped his palm over his mouth and embarrassment shone in his eyes.

He started stuttering apologies. I stopped him with my hand, gloved of course, on his. The glove, made from the skin of Julian, contained my dead husband's power of touch. The exact opposite of my own. Calm is too small a word to describe it. I'd experienced it hundreds of times during my first husband's life. It was now a tool, instead of a drug. This man's eyes rolled back and around. The smile returned but this time held less pleasure, more peace. This time it made him appear younger.

A change passed over his face and I knew that the Incola now looked out at me from behind his Carrier's eyes. The gift of touch was still strong on his body, no matter who sat in the driver's seat. He was drunk on the touch. It took a few seconds for the cloud of tranquility to clear. A snarl curled his lip but before he could speak the left side of his face exploded.

The man fell to his knees and collapsed in front of my feet. Another man appeared to take his place. He held out his hand and helped me step over his comrade's body. "He knew of the risks; as do we all. Our Incola wants to use us to keep you from infecting him but we will die to end his tyranny." The wind blew his hood from his head long enough to catch a glimpse of his patchy hair. Radiation made it fall out in chunks. "He heals us only enough to keep us alive. Another method of control that keeps us from leaving. If we allow you to him, he says he will let us die." He gazed at me, expectantly. "I told the others that you would not let us die."

I reached up and secured his hood. Taking his offered arm, I neither confirmed nor denied his assumption.

Carriers rose from their hiding places and formed a corridor as I advanced. I walked down that aisle, men flanking me. Here or there a nose was blackened by the prolonged exposure to the extreme cold. I passed many a cheek covered with the blue network of burst capillaries. Bulbous growths graced hand and face. Many reached out to touch my skirts as I passed, as one might do with a living saint. Twice men rose and ran toward me with weapons drawn, only to be shot and drop at my feet. When the man with the rifle who'd been doing the killing was ridden, another rose from the snow and executed him, taking up his weapon and his duty.

They brought their Incola to me bound in chains. He spit at me and cursed the men holding him. When his body went limp and the man to my right stiffened, several guns appeared and pointed at the Carrier. I held up my hand.

"Wait," I commanded in Ukrainian. "Point your weapons at your Incola's body." When they had, I turned to the Carrier who housed the Incola. "Your Carriers are now all infected. There is nowhere for you except your own body."

He smiled through bleeding gums and blood-stained teeth.

There was a time when his defiance would have angered me, made me sad, given rise to any emotion. That time was past and now all I felt was tired. I had won. All by myself, Ramillia, a Victorian peeress twice widowed, defeated an ancient secret bloodthirsty society, hellbent on global domination. I wanted, nay expected, to feel victorious. Alas, only weariness caressed my bones.

I spent a month with those men. That is, those who remained alive that long. Their Incola was able to heal a handful of them before the infection took hold and locked him in his own body. The rest died of radiation poisoning. We burned their bodies and scattered the ashes.

We drank vodka to their memory. We toasted their lives and mourned their passing. Songs were sung, widows tended, orphans cared and prepared for.

The Incola hated me until the last. He saw in the second before I cleaved his head in half that I meant to end not only his reign but his life. I didn't hesitate. Once his skull and brain split, I separated the two hemispheres from his neck. His body was burned in three separate fires. Once the last ember faded, I took a small handful of ash and added it to the pouch on my hip.

2

After Dawn killed Ambrose, I decided the time to die had arrived but Sally and the others overruled me. It seemed I had more personalities living inside my head than just her and me. I gave up. After making arrangements for our daughter Dawn to be well cared for, separate from the Incola world with our friend the Dowager Duchess, I surrendered to the authorities who had a warrant for my arrest. The charges were many and I was guilty of them all. Treason, arson, assault, battery, bribery, murder. I had killed so many. Patricide, matricide, fratricide, filicide. The only crime I hadn't committed was regicide; there is no wonder my queen feared me.

While Sally broke us out of prison, the others kept me in the mental meadow Sally created as the place for our meetings. A beautiful field where we could talk and have tea and roll in the grass. I did not want to be here with *them*. They were not to be trusted and I knew, as I was tied very tightly to a chair, they felt the same about me.

The youngest looking one had actually been with me the longest. Or so she said. I would confirm when Sally returned. Josephine, she said was her name, had been alive when the other two were "born." Jo, she liked to be called, couldn't remember her own birth but she showed me fragmented memories of the West Freeman Asylum for Lunatics where I spent my teenage years. She had been with me then, while Sally anguished in my place, birthing our daughter Dawn while I floated in blissful darkness. Jo, like me, was blissfully unaware of the torture we'd sustained at the hands of the doctor in charge of healing our mental ailments.

Jo seemed locked in a childish age and soon grew bored of my questions, cartwheeling away shouting, "Why don't you ask Friend? She loves serious discussions."

I eyed Friend. She stood confident in the way only a seventeen-year-old could, so convinced and passionate about every issue, even if she'd had no real experiences. She, like Jo and the other, lived her whole life within the walls of my mind. She really was lovely. I had been so lovely at that age.

"Your name is Friend?" I asked.

Friend sat in a chair that hadn't been there before at a table that appeared before us. She served tea, though how I was to drink it tied as I was, I didn't know. "That depends on who you ask. Josephine named herself 'God increases.'"

Friend had only just begun as Jo tumbled by, shouting, "I sure do!"

Friend continued, "She created this meadow. She controls this reality because she survived here on her own without contact for at least a year, maybe longer. Josephine thinks she is a god. The only thing she found impossible to create was another."

Silently, the ground under Jo's feet rose, pushing her high into the air. Spinning until dizzy, she toppled over the newly formed cliff side. I screamed in horror before Jo sank into the ground which had taken on the characteristics of a life net. She bounced twice and ran off.

"When I appeared in her meadow she thought she'd finally succeeded. She screamed, 'Friend!' and grabbed my hand, pulling me away on our first adventure. It is odd to be born as we were. I had only vague memories of before she called me Friend but I knew things."

"What kinds of things?" I urged her to go on.

"I knew humans were born as babies, to mothers who were also born as babies. I understood concepts like gravity and the afterlife. I knew that humans could not fly, so when Josephine said she was god and shot into the air, it seemed reasonable that she was and that I had died, forgetting my previous life when I appeared in heaven."

As if punctuating Friend's statements, Jo leisurely floated by cramming mulberry juice colored comfits into her mouth.

I asked some question and Friend replied using Josephine's name.

"Call me Jo!" Jo shouted.

Friend calmly replied, "I shall, when you refer to me as Effie."

Jo harumphed and flew off.

"So you prefer to be called Effie?"

"It is my name. It is not a choice I've made, simply one of the things I was born knowing."

"Jo, Effie, and…?" I glanced at the third me with us in the field.

"That's Mary Martha. She is new."

"I was born understanding things as well," Mary Martha said with a snarl. "Concepts like freedom and vengeance."

Mary Martha looked most like me, at my current age. A highborn Englishwoman with perfectly coiled and upswept blond hair, she wore the full skirts of a proper lady, not the torn short knee-exposing vulgar skirt I adopted. "What memories do you have?" I questioned my twin.

Mary Martha glared at me through squinted eyes and a hard-lined mouth that reminded me very much of my mother, though my mother had looked more like Jo, frozen in the body of a child. "I know that I was a mother and someone took my children from me." She took a threatening step toward me. "I have the sneaking suspicion that I have you to blame for that loss." She turned on her heel and strode away, pausing here and there to examine a piece of grass or floating dandelion tuft.

"What is she looking for?" I whispered to Effie.

She answered in an even softer tone than mine. "A way out." Her teacup rattled when she returned it to its saucer. She hid her shaking hands below the table edge. The idea of Mary Martha escaping clearly frightened Effie as much as it did me. "She is obsessed with the belief that she can and should get out. Jo's been here the longest and entertains herself by leading Mary Martha on wild goose chases. I just try to show her that this is a wonderful place to be."

"Don't you long to be free?" I asked.

"I am free," Effie answered. "Cold and hunger cannot touch me here. I have no worries, can be or do anything I wish. It isn't safe out there."

"Why do you think that? Because of the asylum? Julian?"

Effie said, "I don't remember the asylum."

"But she remembers Julian!" Jo sang the name in that familiar taunting way of children. She blew by again on a four-foot wave, two fingers of her right-hand sticky from delivering jam from the jar in her left hand to her stained mouth.

Red crept up Effie's neck and cheeks. I remembered how smitten with Julian I was at her age. He could do no wrong. Even when he secretly fed me his blood and rode me as my first Incola, I loved him. She obviously felt the same, as if none of his wrongdoing was clear to her. I feared her reaction to the news that he was dead, at my hand no less. "Do you know where he is now?"

"Julian is with your child."

I nodded. Julian and Ambrose were in the afterlife, if such a place truly existed. I wasn't positive but Effie seemed so. "What memories of him do you have?"

"If you don't mind," she looked at me from below long lashes, "I'd prefer to keep those for myself."

I told her they were hers to share or keep secret as she wished. For a moment I wondered if she and the others were like Sally. Could they take turns at the helm of my body? Had they made decisions and experienced the effects? Did they have memories of their own, as Sally did? I didn't know exactly how to ask, so I said, "Do you all know Sally?"

Effie smiled. "Of course we do. The others don't like her very much, but I do. She talks to me as long as I want."

"Why don't the others like her?" I asked.

"Mary Martha is bitter because Sally won't tell her how to get out." She seemed to consider how to say what she meant. "How to take the reins; how to be in control."

That answered my unspoken question. The others could not control my body. That privilege was reserved by Sally for just she and I. "So why doesn't Jo like her? Surely she doesn't want to get out."

"No, Jo is happy here, but Sally ruined her fun by telling me that I was every bit the god here that Jo is."

A forgotten memory came flooding back. We were inside my mind. They couldn't keep me if I wanted to go. The ropes binding me disappeared.

"You told her!" Jo screamed.

Vines attempted to crawl up my legs but I didn't allow them to attach.

"Grab her!" Mary Martha commanded.

I remembered that this was my mind, my world, and whatever power Sally, Jo, Effie, and Mary Martha possessed didn't hold a candle to mine in this place. Without the usual rumble that would normally coincide with such an event, the ground split and opened. I jumped and fell through, careful to close up the gap before the others could follow.

∽

I would say I woke but it was more like I focused on what I'd been looking at all the while.

A man's knuckles headed right for my face.

I dodged, not wanting to lose control to Sally. Pain was Sally's world. I put my hands up. "I surrender!" I shouted.

Out of the corner of my eye, I saw the man approaching from behind, his nightstick held high, already on its down-sweep. I felt nothing but knew the impact.

I opened my eyes to the three other Ramillias standing over me, whispering. "How long have I been here?" I asked.

Jo shrugged. Effie scolded, "Shrugging is unladylike." Jo pursed her lips and shrugged again.

I should have known better than to ask. Time didn't exist here, not really. Sort of like when you have a dream that feels like it lasts all night but, when you awaken, only a few minutes have passed. Or when you just close your eyes for a little while and wake hours later.

I made a portal and tore the door off that reality. I stepped through.

Right back into the fight. I tried to pull the punch that was midway to a Constable's chin. I must have failed because his jaw spun, followed immediately by the rest of his face, and he crumpled to the ground.

Sally spun us around and headed down the stairs. So rare was the instance when I rode in the background with Sally at the helm that the sensation caught me off guard. I reveled in the details, enjoying the inability to decide our fate. Somewhere we'd lost a shoe. The stone was cold and hard on one foot and knobbly and uneven under the slight heeled boot of the other. Our gait was rough but I could do nothing about it. Our hair came loose of its knots, tickling me as we ran, but I could not lift a finger to smooth it.

I delighted in the sensation of air rushing in and out of our lungs, blood pumping in and out of our heart. As soon as I thought the word heart, I felt it. The damage. I could not look down to see the damage to our exterior so I pulled inward to examine. There was a wound there, just to one side of our heart. Judging by the slight burn around it, I guessed the canal was caused by bullet rather than knife and went to re-knitting my flesh together right away.

Thinking on it now, it seems a strange thing for a woman to do, a woman who had only a few moments prior been awaiting, eagerly I might add, the hangman. "What are you doing?" I asked myself.

Sally must have misconstrued my self reflection for a questioning of her own actions. She answered, "Busting us out of here. What's it look like I'm doing?" She raised her fisted hand but before she could pound the wall into submission, it exploded outward, leaving a gaping but smoky hole.

Andrew and Auley, my second deceased husband's right-hand men, stood blocking the light when the smoke cleared. They helped Sally to our feet but looked as confused as I felt.

"How did you know," Auley began.

Andrew, Auley's father, stopped him. "Later."

I followed the two Hungarian men out of the prison and into the darkness.

The battle, or perhaps healing my own heart's damage, changed something in me. I no longer wished to die. I wanted to live. Immortality wasn't some curse. I could live. I could rule. I was god.

I breathed in that intoxicating thought.

That revelation brought me to the front, pushing the others back.

Sally's presence was faint, from the background, and now that I knew they were there, I could feel the others with her. Their desires pressed against me. Each one was different.

Sally's retreat and my sudden ascension caused me to stumble. My men knew better than to grab me. Andrew and Auley watched as I missed the carriage step and fell.

I heard Sally's voice in my head. *Andrew and Auley met me outside of the prison. They were attempting a rescue break-in when I literally bumped into them on my way out.*

I knew that, had seen it. She had not felt me, looking out from our eyes. *We have much to talk about.* I countered.

I know, Ramillia. I am sorry to have hidden so much from you.

I stood, dusted myself off, and climbed into the armored carriage, with Andrew and Auley following close behind. There on my seat lay the weapon given to me by the Chinaman, Ning Shiru. I slipped it into the inner pocket of my skirts, soothed by its nearness.

It had been such a strange artifact. It looked like no weapon I'd ever seen. Ning Shiru had said it would save the world but I hadn't cared about that. I used it only when I thought it might save Leon and Ambrose. It had not worked. My dead loved ones remained so.

When I thought of Ambrose, my sense of Mary Martha sharpened. It was almost as if her desires became louder. I sat in my leather seat across from Andrew and Auley, who tactfully looked elsewhere, and had an internal conversation with Sally.

Why? I asked her. *Why are they so different than you or me? Why can they never take control?*

She answered, *I have always been with you. We were born on the same day. I didn't just appear the first time your father raped us. I was there the whole time, in the background waiting until you needed me.*

Why? I asked her again. *Why would you voluntarily accept a secondary position? Why would you take only the horrific and leave all the rosy to me?*

I felt her shake her head. When she spoke, her answer shook me. *It isn't because I am good. It just feels natural, right. You are you, and I am you but you are not me. This is your life and I am the helper.*

Are the others my helpers as well? I wondered.

Did they seem interested in helping when you met them?

It was my turn to shake our head.

No, I didn't think so either. I do not know what their purpose is, nor do I fully understand how they were born. The only thing I know is that they are part of you, just as I am. I would never hurt them but I also must never allow them to leave.

Andrew interrupted our internal conversation. "Where to, my lady?"

I blinked at him. I had seen them but until he spoke I hadn't registered that they were real.

Auley looked at me and spoke, "Paetus told us to bring you to the club but we thought you might like to go home. That is where the men await your return."

"The men?" I blurted. "I thought surely you would all have succumbed to the blight with which I infected you. How many recovered from the illness?"

"The survival rate is nearly one hundred percent." I am sure the shock showed on my face. "Yes, you heard correctly. All of your Carriers are healthy and alive."

What good is an illness that does not kill Incola? I wondered. That contagion is hardly a weapon to save the world. What are a few weeks of illness to an immortal? My disappointment and confusion must have been clear; Auley began to speak.

Andrew interrupted his son, "Mr. Hall can best explain it and he's waiting in your parlor."

"Home it is," I decided.

∽

Mr. Edwin Hall, the man who'd torn his own eyes out to avoid a life as a Carrier to evil Incola only to have his actions land him in the West Freeman Asylum, stood in my parlor as promised. His diseased and infected face had terrified me but, when I bought the Asylum and freed him, he became my tinkerer, creating many useful devices.

"Mr. Hall," I said as a greeting. "You made improvements to your goggles," I commented as I settled in my parlor chaise. The room was exactly as I remembered it, complete with the dent in the wall where I threw Leon. The impact broke him and, as he refused to possess another body as his own, killed him. There is something comforting about the familiar, even if horrific.

"Yes, my lady. I was able to shrink them while also hiding their working gears."

"Well, they look very smart and from the way you move with ease, they seem to work as well if not better. What else did you accomplish during my brief trial and incarceration?"

Mr. Hall cleared his throat and straightened his vest. "I took the liberty of extracting some of the liquid from your puzzle box." He had the decency to look abashed. He had tinkered with one of my most prized possessions. Then again, I had given up my freedom and was on the path to giving up my life. I gave the barest of nods and he continued. "I am no chemist but believe it is blood."

"But it was blue," I exclaimed.

"Was? And what color is it now?" he asked.

"Purple," I replied. "When I opened it, some of my own blood mixed with the blue liquid inside."

"Interesting. I did not know. My goggles do not show color." He thought for a moment. Taking a small notebook from his breast pocket, he scribbled down some notes.

I waited. His genius deserved my patience. He must act when inspiration struck.

A man came in and whispered to Andrew, who in turn said, "Paetus is here. Shall we show him in or send him away?" My home was on lockdown, every window and entry shuttered with iron. The only way anyone was getting in or out was with my permission. It might seem overly cautious if I had not only earlier that night broken out of a stone prison while awaiting my execution. There was bound to be someone coming after me.

As soon as I thought of prison, I stood. I hadn't even decided to do it. It just happened. This room was too small for me. I needed open space. I needed fresh air, or as fresh as London of that era could provide. I knew it was too dangerous but said, "Show him around back to the garden. I will walk with him there." The garden was walled and I knew armed guards would be posted. Not one man argued; all hopped to obey.

I waited as they took safety precautions. For my safety, not their own. It is an odd thing to live a life where your well-being is the only thing that matters to every person with whom you interact. The Carriers, at this stage of my story at least, treated me for what I was. Their queen.

By the time I walked outside, Paetus stood there waiting by the sculpture my children and I made of a mother dragon over her nest of eggs. His mask slipped. He wasn't happy to see me, not exactly. It was more akin to relief. Paetus was not really a Victorian gentleman. He was from a much more violent, ancient time. Paetus bowed, as was the custom, but the movement was meant to mock. It dripped with sarcasm when he greeted me for the first time in a manner that would become common.

"Lady Pestis," he said. "How is our precious blight?"

Though night had fallen, the sky was bright. The clouds that blocked the moon from view also glowed with her magnified light.

I didn't answer.

He continued, "Have they told you? Do you know what you've wrought?"

"Are you not well?" I asked, genuinely curious. "I was told almost all the Carriers recovered from the sickness."

"This body recovered." His statement should have sounded positive. Instead disgust was all I heard. He pulled at his clothes to accent his feelings. "This body is well, but I am trapped! I am trapped in this body where I can no longer feel or taste. Trapped! Cut off from even the relief of riding, sensing the world around me for the briefest of moments."

"I don't understand." My admission that I did not orchestrate his current predicament calmed him, as if my innocence of the crime committed confounded Paetus.

"Truly? You did not know that the illness would end our kind?" He stepped close to see the truth of it in my eyes. Several firearms were cocked around us. I held up my hands to stop them from shooting Paetus.

I told him of the weapon. "I only used it in the hopes that it might bring back my Leon and Ambrose. Then everyone fell ill. I assumed the weapon would be genocide on our kind."

"No wonder you sought to end your life." I did not correct his assumption. He continued, "We recovered slowly and then realized that none could ride or be ridden. We are, other than that, unchanged. I can heal this body but cannot break free of it. Those Incola who were taken ill as they rode a Carrier were flung back to their own bodies, if they still existed. My original body was destroyed long ago, therefore I am trapped in this one for all eternity. The illness you brought stole that from us."

You and Dawn were immune. Sally interjected inwardly where only I could hear. *We were never sick. Does that mean we may still ride?*

Mentally shrugging, I knew that Sally did not desire to ride another. She had promised to never leave me again, but now I know that she would. Again and again she would leave me until the last when she would leave permanently. Always for the same reason: to save Dawn.

As if Paetus could hear my thoughts, his went in the same direction. "My only chance at happiness, my only hope to feel anything again, is to have Mistress Dawn in my life." He put his hand on the bare skin showing above my glove but below my sleeve. Paetus' own gift of touch took me over. I suddenly could do none other than tell him the exact truth.

"I need her. Where is my betrothed?" he asked.

"She belongs to no man."

He gripped tighter. "Where is your daughter?" he insisted.

"I have no daughter." I felt the truth of that bizarre statement.

Sally answered my confusion. *Dawn is my daughter.*

Not mine, Sally's. She was the one who suffered our father's advances. He impregnated her, not me. It was Sally who carried Dawn in pregnancy. Sally who birthed our daughter. Her daughter.

Completely missing our revelation, Paetus feared that the illness had weakened his gift. He moved his hand from my arm to the only other bit of skin exposed, my décolletage. Another signal from me saved Paetus from being shot for his impertinence. When my answer did not change, his continued contact with my flesh caught up with him. With no other outlet for his excitement, Paetus shoved a carved stone horse from its pedestal and proceeded to stomp and smash it to tiny bits, his exclamations peppered with foul language.

"Dawn is safe. I sent her away to live with a friend. In secret, she can grow into a woman without the Incola world corrupting her."

"How can you know she is safe?" he demanded. "I've had no contact from her. You've been imprisoned. You cannot know. Tell me where she is so that I may check."

I shook my head. That I could not do. I could check on her though. I decided to send Auley. I located him in the shadows and approached. I whispered my order and instruction. He was to go alone, covertly through back ways and alleys, to check that Dawn was indeed safe with the Dowager.

He left and I returned to the pile of rubble that was recently a statue. Paetus and I stood over it. He whispered, "I miss him."

Knowing he spoke of Julian, Archelaos before he took that name, I nodded. "I know. I do too." It was the truth. Odd, I know. Julian was many things to me. Even the evil deeds changed in memory. I look on his memory now with even more affection than I did on this night. Immortality can do that. The link with any other, be it productive or destructive, is good.

My attempt at camaraderie enraged Paetus. "How can you know? You can't possibly fathom what we had! Your imagination is incapable of envisioning the pain of our separation. You are a child, nay, a babe! He and I walked this earth together for nearly three millennia. Three. Thousand. Years." His anguish was palpable. He pressed his face into his hands. He fisted his hair and pulled. He yelled indistinguishably into the night.

I placed my gloved hand onto his cheek to calm him before I remembered it was Julian's skin they were made from. The touch worked. His rage changed to a deep mourning. The human-leather glove was soon wet with his tears. "Archelaos," he cried, leaning into my touch. He knew what the glove was; Paetus stripped the skin from Julian's body and had them brain tanned. The touch comforted him nonetheless.

"Sophus," I whispered. That was his name before he took the body and persona of Paetus. I still did not know if that was his original identity or just the one before. He used Archelaos so I used Sophus; it seemed appropriate.

"I need my Mistress," he pleaded. He got on his knees. "She can give me the pain to eclipse this loss." He clasped my hands. "You have your Sally. I have no one. I cannot survive alone."

Paetus left only after I promised to allow him to visit the tenebrae where I would see to him. The whole time we spoke I could only think one thing: everyone knew my secret. Since everyone knew, it ceased to be a secret. It was now just a fact.

On that night, I did not question the source of his information. I did not care. It was not outrage that flooded over me. It was relief. We took a moment to mentally hug, Sally and me.

Tonight, my last night, as I remember his anguish, I feel what I should have felt then. Empathy. Sally was with me for thirty years, though I only knew her for seventeen of those. Once she left, I was destroyed. After only seventeen years. Decades passed before I was—I won't say whole for I was never whole again—functional. Paetus was absolutely correct. I could not fathom his loss. I cannot imagine having Sally for twenty-something centuries and *then* losing her, though Paetus would only suffer a few more years before I killed him, while I suffered without Sally for two hundred.

I have not written a journal in so long. The skill escapes me. I should not be tallying score for who suffered worse or longer. I wasn't thinking those things on that night. I should not be writing about them now. Sally excelled at helping me focus. She would say, *We did not know that then* or *Don't forget to mention that happened.* Perhaps she knew I would need my journals. Perhaps she knew she would leave me all alone with my jumbled thoughts.

On that night, Sally and I rejoiced. We could live as we always thought it was intended. We would alternate naturally. Flowing up and down, exchanging places for whichever of us best suited the task at hand. The opportunity for that came more quickly than either of us expected.

Auley burst from the back door with Mr. Hall following close behind. Mr. Hall was pleading with Auley that tests should run before alarming me.

Auley ignored him. "She's gone. They are all gone. The house is empty."

"Perhaps they have gone on holiday," I theorized. After all, I had given the Dowager the fortune of a lifetime, or ten.

"I think not, my lady. Too much blood."

Sally jumped to the front.

3

Blood decorated every surface.

The entrance and front room held the highest concentration, as if men had barged in and killed any who attempted to stop them. I remembered the butler that night that the Dowager agreed to take Dawn. His wig askew, buttons crooked. He lay nearest the entrance. His head askew, body crooked. What horrors had I brought to this house?

I had the luxury of considering such things that night because Sally was in control. Her daughter was missing. I was merely a spectator of her decisions. Detached is the word that I'd use.

Using his collector blunderbuss, Mr. Hall took readings of every spatter and puddle, every chair and bed, every bloodied weapon. Sally remained convinced Dawn was alive. *She must have been taken by force. I would have felt her death. I would have known, wouldn't I? Maybe not. Yes, of course I would.* Sally argued with herself. I did not get involved.

She was right. She would have known. When our family members die, something happens inside us. We didn't learn the details until years after that moment. She was right nonetheless. Later that day, with the sun still low in the morning sky, Mr. Hall would confirm with his readings and his catalog that none of the blood belonged to Dawn. In fact there was very little Carrier blood at all. Mostly that of the Dowager's servants. Humans. But he did find something interesting. Carriers and an Incola had been in that room. It was the same scent that we had repeatedly found while attempting to locate my brother's son, Theodore.

"Whoever has Theodore, has now taken Dawn as well," Sally said aloud. "There will be no end to the pain I will cause them should they hurt her," she exclaimed.

Yes, yes, of course. But they won't hurt her. I attempted to soothe Sally. *Dawn is much too valuable for them to hurt.* Sally knew better than most what could be done to her. Her value, like ours, was in our ability to breed more Carriers.

"We have to find them."

How? I asked her again. We'd been over this before and had no plan. No one had seen anything, not that any of the aristocrats in that neighborhood would speak with us, a convicted murderer escaped and on the run from justice. All the Incola and Carriers had been laid low with illness. I had been locked away and awaiting execution. We did not even know exactly when the kidnapping had occurred.

"We are going to the club. I will need Paetus' help."

∽

Paetus would be very little help to us. That much was apparent as soon as we entered the club. He lay on the back of an oversized, overturned velvet couch. His clothes, the same he'd worn in our garden, were now untidy, untucked, unfastened. Unacceptable. He drank directly from a nearly empty cognac bottle. The label said XO marking it as Extra Old and therefore extremely expensive. The bells on the way there rang noon. Early, even for Paetus, to be inebriated. Very little in the way of furniture or dressings remained in the club.

Paetus greeted us with open arms, gesturing to the room without rising. "They took everything not nailed down. Anything they could sell. And then they left. As soon as they were free to go, they did so."

Sally and I both knew how Paetus treated his Carriers. They had every reason to abandon him. For this I did not, still do not, feel sympathy for him. They may have left him and taken everything they could find but Paetus would remain a very rich man. You couldn't live for as long as he had and not amass quite a fortune. I had thoroughly diversified my assets and I would have bet them all that Paetus had done the same. The expense of the brandy he drank confirmed he wasn't completely destitute.

"We need to use your mews," Sally said without preamble.

Paetus rolled off the couch into a bow. Holding one hand as if to direct us, he gestured to the stairway. "It is the only thing they left me. One last insult, for it is the one thing I will never have need of again."

We started our ascent up the first flight of stairs. The mews was the method by which Paetus transferred his consciousness into a Carrier. That thought halted our steps for a fraction of a second. I did not come to the front but I had enough fear and doubt to give us pause. The only reason Sally would need to use the mews was if she intended to leave me. *What are you doing, Sally?* I asked her but did not bother to wait for a reply. *No, you cannot. You swore you would not.* I had killed my Leon in a blind rage the last time she left me. The last time Dawn had been taken.

Sally spoke to us aloud as we reached the second flight. "Dawn is gone and I will do what I must to find her."

There was a thud behind us and we turned to see Paetus laying awkwardly on the stairs. "Mistress Dawn is missing?"

We nodded. "Taken, most likely. Her hiding place lay in shambles; her guardians dead or dying."

"Why did you not say so immebr…immedri…immedriately?" he asked as he undid his trousers and began to urinate.

Our Victorian sensibilities forced us to turn away. It was not urine that we smelled but alcohol. When he caught up to us on the third flight, completely sober, he helped us step over the dead man sprawled there. He healed himself, cleared his body of inebriation, in a matter of seconds. Would we ever stop underestimating Paetus?

We increased our pace and reached the top quickly. There in Paetus' private chambers sat the mews. I should say lay. There lay the mews. Today we would call it a sensory deprivation tank. The man-sized metal coffin connected to a stationary bicycle was, we knew, filled with salt water.

Sally began to unfasten our bodice and Paetus shooed everyone toward the door. "No, they all stay," she declared.

I panicked. *They can't. I don't want to hurt anyone.*

"That is why we need the mews. It will contain you while I ride Dawn and discover her condition and whereabouts."

Paetus took our gloves and other garments and laid them aside. Then he offered his hand to aid in stepping into the water. "Sally, I presume."

She dipped our chin to him but stopped him when he opened his mouth to ask something. "Another time," she said.

He stared at her face, his eyes flicking around to the various features as if he suddenly saw the differences between us. His breathing increased and he snatched his hand away from ours. Our power of touch lay in the body, no matter who controlled it.

The lid shut and locked. I felt a moment of panic. *What if Paetus refuses to free us? He is quite angry.*

"That is another reason the others had to stay. Andrew and Auley won't let any evil befall you." Just like that she was gone.

Away.

Alone.

Abandoned.

The saying "seeing red" means being blinded by rage. It wasn't figurative with me. It was literal. All I could see, hear, or think about in that dark tube was blood. My own thudding in my head. My dead loved ones. That of those I wished to slaughter. For one of the few times in my life I wasn't conflicted. I had no hang-ups or considerations of others. I wanted to kill.

Death.

Destruction.

Demolition.

I laughed. An insane cackle cleared my throat on its own. I was happy. It was only later when I had time to consider that I realized the truth. I wasn't afraid that I would hurt someone. I was afraid it would feel too good. This state of being without a conscience was addictive. I needed Sally. I wanted her. But if she was going to leave me, I would level the world.

My others—Jo, Effie, and Mary Martha—did not attempt to soothe me. Almost as if they felt how unstable and dangerous I was, they stayed clear of my muddled murderous thoughts. I wondered if I could kill them and began to fantasize about what my methods might be. I would strangle Jo with my bare hands. That way I could watch as the life left her eyes. Effie would be beaten and burned. How dare she remain young and beautiful while I aged! When I got to Mary Martha, that's when my imagination took off. Much like the most famous serial murderer of my time, of all time really, I desired the mutilation of that woman's womanhood. That fantasy took a life of its own.

Details stood out: the futility to her struggle, the first cut depth, the warmth of her organs, the negative space as I removed something of value.

I never saw them. I felt them shy back from me. Their cowering exaggerated my hunger. Their fear fed my fantasy. Just then, Sally's consciousness came into Dawn's mind.

I expected information about her location. I thought I'd see through her eyes. What I saw instead, I didn't understand at first but was every bit as horrifying as my own murder mutilation dream.

As the deprivation tank removed all distraction, I saw as clearly through Sally as I would through my own physical eyes. It wasn't what we expected.

The whip sliced through the air, its sound almost as sharp as its barbed end. Dawn reeled it back in and snapped it again, this time catching Ambrose across the face. It wasn't the baby face he'd had in life, but the visage of his *true* self.

"I'll kill you, you cunt!" the snarled words flew from his mouth accompanied by spittle. Even if his monstrous body hadn't been sliced and whipped to pieces, my son would be revolting as he was completely deformed by bulbous tumors stretching his greenish-gray skin.

Here, Dawn had another tenebrae, one where she was in complete control of not only her victims but of the very fabric of reality. The instrument of pain in her hand changed at her will, becoming a snake. She rubbed its head with her chin, cooing at her new pet as she walked to the wooden box in the corner.

Opening the lid, she became more disgusted by the sight than by that of her brother. "I brought you a gift, Archelaos," she said and dropped the king cobra on top of the old man. His paper-thin skin offered the serpent's teeth no resistance. Three times it struck his face before the lid closed on his screams.

"You can't keep us," the familiar voice argued. "Dawn, they don't deserve this."

Why does Leon insist on defending them? her other asked. *You saved him, allowed him inside our mind after Mama killed him, and this is the thanks he offers!*

Dawn's twin stepped forward. Peace washed over Dawn as her other smoothed her hair. She spoke directly to Leon, *I am the one to speak to should you be dissatisfied with your accommodations.*

"Who are you?" he asked. Leon, seated in a luxurious chair, a fireplace at his back, could drink the brandy in his hand but he could not look away from the torture of the other men. Dawn skipped to him and sat in his lap. She rubbed his eyebrows with her finger and traced the lines of his face, her fingertip gently brushing his Roman nose and full lips. She licked her own.

"My name is Eve' and you should be happy Dawn wants you..." Eve' perused the tenebrae devices, pausing beside the rack. "If it were up to me, I'd see you stretched." A smile spread across her face as she imagined it and I was glad we were hidden in the shadows.

A noise that none of us could hear sounded. Both Dawn and Eve' turned their faces up. A chasm opened in the sky and they fell up into it. Just as Sally and I did in our own field. We were in Dawn's mind.

Sally jumped sideways and flew down and out. She followed Dawn and her other. She attempted stealth. She wanted to use Dawn's eyes to pinpoint her location. Once again, what we saw was not what we wanted nor expected.

Dawn lay on her back in a dark windowless room. Sally used Dawn's peripheral vision to investigate but the task was difficult. Walls were wooden, not bricked nor plastered. Nor were there any decorations of any kind. Looking around was completely out of the question as Dawn only had eyes for the naked boy above her. A silver crucifix hung on his neck, catching what little light came from the candle to one side. Dawn looked and we watched as he trailed his hand over her pubescent chest and then lower. He reached between them. We recognized the angling of his hips and the surge forward of intercourse. Sally screamed and flew back out of Dawn and crashed into home.

Standing in our field, a storm matching our fury in the sky above us, we raged.

Sally yelled, "He is dead!" A lightning bolt ripped through the clouds and struck the ground. Her voice was the clap of thunder; it made no sound of its own.

The rain, heavy and thick, soaked me to the bone. It reflected my feelings just as the lightning had Sally's. "She is so sick. Her mind: completely warped. I should never have introduced her to that world so young. Her mind was not ready for Domination."

"That's what you're most upset about! Her thoughts? No, no. He was raping her. We have to find her, kill him, and save her."

"Of course that is the most upsetting thing. Are you forgetting the tenebrae in her mind? The one where she fantasizes about torturing my deceased son and husbands! The physical can be overcome. Once her mind is broken asunder, it may never come back together."

She pushed me into her memory of Father. The experiences she'd spared me in life. The pain, guilt, and confusion that Father's hands and other parts on our body had caused. "Whatever she's become, she does not deserve that."

I took Sally into my arms and begged forgiveness. So much I owed her. "You are right. We must find her." Sally allowed me to soothe her and the storm clouds rolled away. I reasoned, "You inhabited her thoughts. Did she feel distressed? In pain? Guilty as we did with Father?"

Sally shook her head no. I felt it against my shoulder. "But," she argued, "she is too young to understand. Perhaps it is this experience, and not your instructions in Domination, that fractured her mind. She feels she has no control over the real world and so she created the tenebrae and filled it with figments of her imagination to feel in control."

∽

"Try to remember, were there gaslights in the room?" Edwin Hall questioned us about what we saw. Sally remained shaken for several hours and so I had taken the helm. She was with the others in our meadow, trying not to remember as I fought to recall details.

There had been a light to our left but it was dim, much dimmer than our modern gaslights, and it flickered more. "A candle on a chest or trunk," I replied.

"That is good. You gained more clues than you realize." Mr. Hall went to our parlor door and opened it, calling Andrew and Auley. They came in and he asked them, "If you woke to find yourselves in a small wooden room without adornment or window, the only furniture being a bed and a small chest beside with a single candle upon it, where would you guess you were?"

"A shanty?" Auley guessed.

"I think not," his father contradicted. "In the poorest of homes a single room serves all purposes. It would have been littered with chairs, a table, kitchenwares, other people. No, I would guess quarters on a ship."

"My thoughts exactly Andrew." Mr. Hall snapped his fingers and pointed to him as he spoke.

"I do not see how it would have been possible." Paetus spoke when he paused his pacing. "I have closed down every port; every ship sits idle."

"Perhaps there is one defiant ship, crew, or captain who took them aboard. We should go ask around and see what we can find. Maybe someone will know what ship it was and where it is headed."

"Wonderful idea, Auley." I called them both by their first names from the start. I do not even know their surname. Leon had always called them Andrew and Auley and so too did I. "Go. Now. And take Paetus with you. He might as well put all his nervous energy to use."

Andrew said, "A portrait of Lady Dawn might be of use if we do find someone with information." I directed Mr. Hall to the palm-sized portrait in our desk. "And also a description of the boy could be useful, in case they keep Lady Dawn hidden from view."

Sally and the others froze. They were strangely silent; a deep silence that I could feel. I closed our eyes to help us remember better. I attempted to keep our focus on his face and not what his body did. I did not wish to trigger another breakdown in Sally. "He was close but not yet a man, fifteen maybe. Dark hair with a curl. Cut stylishly and above the chin. Dark eyes and lips and skin." I thought about it. Had the darkness of the room obscured his true features?

"Like this?" Mr. Hall asked.

I opened my eyes to see he held a photograph of my brother, Thaddeus. "No, his features were larger, broader, and his skin darker."

Almost as if Thaddeus had a mulatto child with a Negress. I heard the lawyer's coarse description of my nephew in my memory. "No, no, no, no," I began to chant.

Mr. Hall held up a sketch I'd had made up the previous year. Sally spoke when I could only repeat one word. "Yes, we are looking for Theodore. My brother's son kidnapped my daughter."

4

A ship had indeed set sail while I sat in prison. No one knew where it headed. No one saw Theodore nor Dawn. Nevertheless, it had to be the ship she was on. The sailors were so scared that I knew no other captain would dare ignore Paetus' or, through him, my orders. I released my hold. Post and transportation could resume. I did not wish to further cripple the country I so loved. Paetus ensured that the Incola families understood the fate that would befall them should they share information about me or my precious blight.

For half a fortnight, we could only see the interior of that cabin when we rode our daughter. And, of course, we saw our nephew and the actions they thought were private. The fact that they were cousins did not bother us much. It was not as taboo then as it is today. Aristocratic families often intermarried. At first we thought it rape, which upset Sally to no end. In this modern time, of course, it would be statutory because of her age. At this time, girls of lower station with less options often married and were mothers by Dawn's age. I was a peeress and through my lineage Dawn was as well. She could not marry without the approval of her Sovereign.

Then, through the vignettes we saw, I began to put it together that not only was it consensual but Dawn, in some instances, was the pursuer, instigator. Sally wouldn't believe it, thinking that Dawn did what she could to manage the level of her abuse. For if our daughter didn't resist, there was no reason for their exchanges to become violent. Sally had, on occasion, employed the same tactic for us.

We discussed seeing if Effie could ride Dawn, saving Sally the horror, but in the end we decided against it. That was one door that might not close again once opened. Who knew what beast might escape?

So Sally continued to ride Dawn. We did not know what Dawn's reaction would be if she found us so we hid, sneaking around her mind like a burglar. One ride, Sally stumbled into the tenebrae again. We were shocked to find that even though Dawn and Eve' were elsewhere, the room remained occupied by the figments of Leon, Archelaos, and Ambrose. That shouldn't have been. If they were imagined and tortured for her amusement, they should not have existed in that space without her. Those were my opinions but Sally did not share them as we occupied different minds at the time. I could see through her "eyes" but did not share her thoughts.

Sally stepped into the light, toward Leon, still seated in his chair by the hearth. The vile, monstrous, imaginary Ambrose called to her, to me, from his place on the rack, "Mama!" Every joint below gray skin had been stretched beyond capacity and was out of the socket.

"No," Archelaos called from the crucifix. He had to push up on his nail-pierced feet to get breath to speak. "Do not fall for this trick again," he told the other two.

"Dawn, I will not touch you no matter how much you look like your mother." Leon said this with detachment.

With that statement hanging in the air, Sally stilled. Leon's face changed. He had not seen what he expected to in our face. Struggling against unseen bonds, Leon attempted to stand but failed. He only managed to bring his glass to his lips. Taking two deep breaths, he whispered, "Ramillia?" Sally shook her head and stepped closer, seeing as he could not come closer to us. Then he saw it and asked, "Sally? Is that really you?"

Dawn had not known of my other, not that I knew of. How had she created a figment that had knowledge she did not herself hold? Sally nodded. I knew from our discussions of her previous rides that Sally feared speaking would alert Dawn to our presence. Dawn did not tolerate Incola presence inside her mind. Even when Leon had ridden her with her and my permission, and for her own well-being and protection, she had hurt him.

"If you've come to save us, I do not see how it can be accomplished. Dawn is goddess of her own universe here. She has become fixated with me and relentless in her punishment of these two." Tears streamed down his face.

Sally went to him presumably to get a better look at his bonds. Leon continued talking. "Even when I think I see empathy in her, Eve' steps in and squashes it. Eve' is without mercy. She would see me on the other side of this room."

There were no visible bindings that kept Leon in this position. Not on his legs. Not on his arms. No reason could be seen that his hand must hold the glass of spirits.

"I do not know how you got here but you need to go before Dawn and Eve' return. If they find you here, you will be trapped same as we are." Sally did not move and Leon's whispering became ever more insistent. "Go. Now. Leave this place."

Ambrose cried out, "No, Mama! Do not leave me!" He choked back a childish sob, almost a hiccup, and then broke me by saying, "It hurts so much here. Dawn hurts me so much."

That moment is the most vivid of my life. And it happened in the mind of another. I knew then the terrible truth. These were not figments of Dawn's demented imagination. Somehow, when Leon, Ambrose, and Archelaos died, Dawn had trapped them. I knew she could trap anyone in her mind who attempted to ride her but this was unexpected. She had pulled them from their dying bodies.

I tried to get to them. I didn't know what I could do but I had to try. I thrashed inside the mews, trying to free myself of my own body. I pulled on the cord that connected Sally and me, trying to climb the rope, but it had the opposite result than I wished. I yanked Sally back to me.

This time the storm in the sky above our meadow was my doing and Sally attempted to comfort me. I slapped her hands away. I would not be consoled. "She is a monster!" I shouted.

"She is not," Sally said calmly. "Dawn is a young girl with mental and physical abilities beyond comprehension."

"She murdered my son!"

Sally made sure I looked her in the eye as she argued, "We murdered our father."

"He hurt us!" The lightning began to mirror my speech. "Raped you!"

"Ambrose would have hurt her. He attempted to take her over. She only did to him what we did to Julian when he attempted the same."

"No! We allowed Julian's body to be killed. Then we pushed Archelaos from our mind. We did not imprison him! We did not torture him! And what of Leon? He never did anything to hurt her. He is the one who found her and brought her safely home."

"And he was not hurt," she reasoned.

That stilled me. Sally thought only of her daughter and not at all of the men in our lives. The clouds above us rolled violently but the lightning stopped. "You think what he has endured is less than torture?"

"You are thinking of this in the wrong manner. Yes, what she is doing now is wrong but her evil has given us a second chance. As long as she has them, they are not gone. We will find a way to save them."

She had a point. All three were Incola. Perhaps new bodies could be procured for them. But it was hopeless, for I had destroyed the ability for Incola to ride.

Then an even more horrific realization came to me. "They have no bodies. Her tortures have no end. They cannot die or even pass out from pain. They have no respite. No escape even momentarily from the anguish."

"I know. We will find her." Sally flew to the top and released us from the mews.

But I will kill her for what she's done when we do, I thought, forgetting Sally could hear my thoughts here.

∽

Sally rode Dawn for the briefest of moments only after that. We hoped to catch a glimpse of anything that would tell us where she resided. We steered clear of Dawn's mental tenebrae, not because it was too painful to see, which it was, but because when we approached it the others noticed. If Archelaos/Julian called out, Effie would somehow feel bigger in my own mind. If Ambrose cried, Mary Martha's attention would catch. They were nowhere near able to stand at our helm but they could move further to the front.

We were quite relieved when, at long last, at the end of nearly two weeks, we caught sight of a cityscape that told us their destination. The skyline told us we were headed to New York, in the Americas.

Nothing then moved as swiftly as it now does. Information, governmental decisions, travel plans all moved at snail speed. Though my whereabouts were known, it took two full weeks for the police to organize. Or perhaps the reality that a single unarmed woman had wounded and killed so many of them while escaping prison was too alien to accept and those days were needed to rationalize the events. Maybe they hesitated to make such a scandalous scene in the wealthiest area of all London. In either case, they came calling just as I finished packing for my journey.

Paetus made all travel arrangements. I trusted him to do so, even when my men did not. He was beaten. There was nothing he could do to reclaim his throne; nothing would make him Incola again. We were to travel by ship but, on the day before we were to board, the police came. They demanded that I surrender. When I did not, they shouted my conviction details, hoping shame and embarrassment would bring me forth. When it did not, they began a full assault on my home. They did not know it was impregnable. They could not break through no matter how they battered the exterior.

What they did succeed in doing was forestalling my escape. I could think of nothing but seeing the new world with my own eyes. I could live forever. I wanted to see and experience everything the world had to offer. These police prevented my doing just that.

Sally worried what became of Dawn while we tarried. If she thought that was what upset me about our delay, I allowed her her delusions.

"There is another way," Mr. Hall professed as we stood in my parlor listening to the men outside attempt to pry off the steel window shutters. Sally retreated and I glanced at Mr. Hall. He looked sharp in his driving costume.

"We are to escape by train," I guessed aloud. "But how? The way to the station is just as blocked as the one to the shipyard."

"No, my lady. We will travel in the gondola of your skyship."

"I have a skyship?"

"Not until I built it for you." He offered me his arm and led me to my favorite seat. "I'd been playing with the ideas but once you surrendered to the court, Andrew and Auley came to me asking about methods of escaping the United Kingdom."

I agreed but quickly thought of issues. "Surely this invention of yours is not large enough for all of us." He had only completed his prototype. The scale was much smaller than his plan for a vast skyship that could carry as many people as a medium-sized luxury cruiser. The advantage of that was it was on our roof even now and could be inflated in a few short hours. We would wait until dark. Then Mr. Hall and I would escape in the cover of night. The men would allow police entrance to my home and then follow on the ship as scheduled.

∽

We loaded a few of my trunks, my valuables and my chair in pitch black and then made our escape as silently as possible. The few remaining police stood watch at the exits but none thought to look up to the sky until it was much too late.

To say the view of London at night from the air was breathtaking would be a gross understatement. Quickly we flew too high for details to be made out but with a loss of detail came the gain of perspective. London became a gridwork of roads, littered with flickering gas lights. Individuals could no longer be seen but the whole of the city became one. I was smitten with my city in a way I had never been as a resident. It was too dirty, too crowded, too London. A pang of homesickness struck me as I thought I might be experiencing my last night of peaceful sleep on home soil. Mr. Hall flew in the dark and I fell asleep.

I woke in my favorite chaise. Its feel was quite familiar. When I opened my eyes, the view was anything but. Glass windowpanes surrounded me. The sun had risen recently, and we were over water. I saw the ocean much as I had London, in a completely new way. This trip held many firsts for me. First flight, first time completely surrounded by water. I had ridden in boats before but they were on rivers or lakes. Never before had I seen only water. It was as if I were the center-point of a circle. Water for as far as I could see lay in any and all directions.

Mr. Edwin Hall stood where I assumed he'd been all night, at the ship's helm. "Good morning, my lady," he said, seeming to see me as well as anyone with sight.

"Good morning, Mr. Hall. What an amazing way to wake! What a view." I stood and straightened my skirts. "And please, dispense with 'my lady' as I am certain the title disappeared when I was convicted of murder, arson, treason and then fled the country. Call me Ramillia. You have certainly earned the right."

"If that is what my l…you wish, but only if you will call me Ed."

And so with the formalities over, I followed Ed around the gondola allowing him to explain the mechanics and point out navigation techniques. Passing through clouds, the mist enveloped our vessel. Ed narrated, "We could secrete ourselves by hiding in a large cloud, should we need. That is why I call this a skyship and not an airship. The *Precious Lady* flies higher in the atmosphere than other similar vessels. She also has a special coating which makes her blend more thoroughly."

I leaned against the glass but could not get a good look at the *Precious Lady*'s hull. Gazing down, an oval shadow emerged from the cloud-shaped one. Yet another way a cloud would hide our whereabouts.

When he finished the tour and fell quiet, the silence screamed in my ears. The noise of London had become normalized and now, without sound, I felt a rush. Wind built and pushed me to stay here, hovering above the ground. No one could demand anything of me from here. No pain could touch me. Unless…and just that quickly the world rushed back in. Incola could always reach beyond the grasp of men. The only peace I would ever have would be if all Incola were erased from the face of the earth.

"We are headed to New York, Captain?" I asked.

"No, my l… Ramillia. New York is…dangerous. We do not know what type of reception we might receive there. I have procured a landing site for your exclusive use in a town very near to the island of New York."

By procured, I knew he meant purchased. I had given half of my fortune to the Duchess for care of my Dawn, but even the remaining half was more than a person, even with a household as large as mine, could spend in ten lifetimes. I did not worry even though I might live for ten lifetimes should I so choose.

The revolution of the American British colonies the previous century was still fresh on the collective British mind. If they could overthrow old regimes, what kept other colonies and other segments of society from doing the same? Many had been saying the same for a hundred years: what is to keep the other colonies, the poor, or women from rebelling against the hierarchy? I had the right to vote, through a loophole, my whole life, though that was not the reality of most women at the time. The mere mention of the rebellious colony put an idea in my mind. It didn't matter how long Incola had terrorized, minimized, and negated the Carriers. Overthrow *was* possible. The United States of America has since had a civil war, proving again it was possible to change the imbalance of the world.

Slaves *could* be free.

I had been lost in thought for too long. Ed must have thought I was dissatisfied with his plan because he said, "Sally agreed that your safety was of paramount importance."

Taken aback, I stammered, "Sally? What do...?" Then I remembered, we had exposed our mental instability as I held Ambrose's dying body. Sally and I spoke to each other aloud in full view of all my men on multiple occasions. I sank into the velveteen chaise behind me, defeated. "You must think I'm a lunatic."

Ed hurriedly crossed to sit beside me, though he kept a respectable distance between us. It was only then that my Victorian sensibilities chimed in, reminding me of the inappropriateness of being alone with a man to whom I wasn't married. "I do not use that word and even if I did, I wouldn't apply it to you. Sally explained the situation to us all. She says she is another personality born out of necessity after a great traumatic event that your mind had difficulty handling."

"And you believe her?" I asked incredulously.

"I understand that such a thing exists. The mind is incredible, far surpassing the ability of any invention I might imagine. I, like many of your men, wait for confirmation from you. We reserve our judgment. Is what she said true? Is she another aspect of yourself or is she an Incola riding you?"

I said nothing for a moment. I hadn't, before that moment, really considered the possibility that Sally was an Incola.

Ramillia, we may have had difficulties recently, and for my part in those I am sorry, but in your heart you know. You know me.

Sally was right, of course. "She and I are two parts of the same. Sally has always been with me. She protected me from a reality too horrible to describe. Commands from her should be followed as closely as you follow my own, for that is what they are."

"Are there others, in addition to you and Sally?"

Don't tell him, Sally insisted. *They cannot exchange places as you and I so no one will ever know of them unless we tell him.*

I shook my head no. Ed knew that was directed at him. He started a discussion but I didn't hear him. I agreed to some point he made and pretended to have been paying attention. I changed the subject.

∽

Five days we were alone with Ed. It was unseemly, indecent even, and yet he remained ever the gentleman. No matter how many times I reminded him, he struggled to refer to me as Ramillia, his equal.

There was much manual labor onboard and I found I enjoyed it. My favorite times were when the wind died. If it had not been for the coal, we would have stalled, hanging in the air, dead. This skyship might have belonged to me but it was Ed's in everything but name. He steered and stood at the *Precious Lady*'s helm, calling back to me, the richest and most powerful woman in all the world, when more coal needed to be shoveled onto the fire that drove the fans that pushed us through the empty air.

I saw sea creatures few had seen. Giant whales and intelligent dolphins dotted the water beneath. Fish jumped from the water to glide through the air a few seconds before diving back into the sea. Was their dance for us or were we simply in the correct location at the right time? I wondered. In the deepest darkest parts of the ocean I knew amazing creatures dwelt in places humans would never see. I imagined civilizations below waiting, biding time, waiting for just the right moment to rise and overthrow the prideful, selfish men who walked on dry land.

Most times, when possible, we floated, letting the wind carry us our intended direction. Eventually the ship that carried my men steamed right beneath us. It repeatedly struck me that the air was the only place where none could reach me. Even the men below, at the exact same latitude and longitude, were an eternity away. I was truly free and reveled in it.

Then, the coal ran out. Ed had known it would. The ship below us held reserves for our refueling but that meant landing on its deck. Ed handled the maneuver beautifully. My men were to have been preparing for my arrival, but the looks on their faces told me something hadn't gone to plan. A small group of Spaniard Carriers had joined the passengers before setting sail. They were nothing my men couldn't handle if it came to a fight but the most concerning thing was that they had not fallen ill after coming in contact with those who'd been infected and could no longer carry Incola. They seemed immune. They knew nothing of the illness, thanks to Paetus' quick thinking and his communication ban.

My men took me below deck and stood guard outside while I washed and freshened myself. Some of my belongings had been brought aboard and I put on fresh clothes. As Ed and I had only preserved foods to eat on the *Precious Lady*, we went to the dining hall for a hot meal with more than one course. Paetus joined us, as did one of the Spaniards. His men stood a respectable distance back, giving us privacy but remaining close enough to provide protection.

The man from Spain was an exceptional gentleman. He held my chair, stood when I did, used my title even while introducing himself as Angel. He even poured my wine himself, personally tasting it to test for poison. I watched his lips on my glass. They were very full and lovely. His visage pleased me; every angle was pleasant. He was very handsome indeed. I had never met a Spaniard before and found his accent most exotic.

Angel was an emissary of sorts for his master who never left the comfort of his own country anymore. He'd grown old and was now ready to find another wife. His previous three had died in childbirth along with his children. "I know that your son was killed. Please accept my master's deepest condolences on your loss. As you have no father to negotiate the terms of an acceptable marriage, allow me to suggest the quite favorable match with Master Juan. I know he will find you as lovely as I do. He sent me looking for a woman young enough to bear children but, forgive my bluntness, old enough to have birthed one or two. He hoped to find a wife of stout constitution; he never dreamed of finding a female Incola."

"And what makes you think I am," I paused, feigning thought, "What was it you called me? Incola?"

Angel sat back in his chair, lacing his fingers in his lap. He noticed me looking at his lap but said nothing, in true gentlemanly fashion. "I would like to say that it was purely my powers of deduction, for I have never seen a woman so overly guarded who was not royalty, nor one so rich at such a young age. I cannot, however, for while I did notice those things, it was my man," he gestured to his guards and one bowed to me, "Francisco. He has a gifted sense of smell and can sniff out an Incola easily." He ran his hands along his thighs, as if wiping them on his trousers. "How is it one as incredible as you is not already married?"

"I have been married twice in my life, and widowed twice," I answered him.

"What bad luck to have lost two husbands while you are still so young."

I smiled at him, then took a sip of my wine. "I did not lose them, sir. I killed both."

That women could be violent seemed not to shock this Carrier. He continued, "Even so, I believe the marriage to my master would be found pleasant. He is generous and kind and not unpleasing on the eyes, even for an older man. He does not misuse those beneath him; he only uses us for tasks that we accept." The way he looked at my neck and then décolletage when he said "tasks" told me that this handsome young man served in a bedroom setting more often than a boxing ring.

Having finished the meal and grown tired of the conversation, no matter how attractive the messenger, I told Angel I was not interested in marrying again. He pressed, saying his master would and could give me anything I wanted. Power, influence, land, wealth, whole countries—nay, continents—to worship me. When I told him I had everything I wanted, he argued that once Master Juan knew of my existence, he would not give up, could never accept no as an answer.

This upset Paetus. He stood so quickly that his chair overturned. He was no feminist, though that word did come into use at about that time. Paetus held a knife at Angel's throat. The other Spaniards jumped but my men greatly outnumbered them. Everyone froze. Paetus looked to me to decide this man's fate. At the subtle shake of my head, Paetus sat down and used that very same knife to cut a bite from his plate of food, as if nothing had happened.

I stood to go. "You sir, had better hope Master Juan never finds out about my existence, for if he does, I will have to kill him. No one, Incola or otherwise, can give me what I want, for my only desire is freedom."

~

I spent that night on the ship. While our *Precious Lady* was being restocked, I met each sailor and passenger. They were all very curious about me. Of course it helped that I bought each one a drink of their choice in the onboard tavern. To the ones who could not imbibe at that time, I gave coin to purchase a drink at the time of their choosing.

Games were played, spirits drunk, dances danced, and sensibilities offended. I cared not. While it was fun, I found myself longing for the safety and solitude of flight. Ed and I boarded the *Precious Lady* early the next morning.

The next week was one of the best of my life. I found Ed's company more than tolerable. He had a brilliant mind. We discussed all manner of things in depth. It reminded me most of the time I spent with Julian at the beginning of our marriage. Yes, he betrayed me repeatedly, tried to take over my body, and suppress me completely. Julian was also my confidant, the first man I ever lay with willingly, my benefactor. He encouraged me to develop my skills, my mind.

My life may be completely alien to most but in some ways it is universal. I have come to understand a great many things. Life is not black and white. No person is just good or evil. Neither is it shades of gray. I propose that it is painted with all the vivid colors. True you may not like all of the colors equally but it cannot be argued that removing those less loved would not completely alter the picture. I would not have my picture altered. Sally, whose life encapsulated all of our paint, agreed. She would not give up the pain Father caused because through that pain came Dawn.

Another thing understood from those talks with Ed is that beauty does not always mean good just as ugly does not always equal evil. I found that at times, when Ed and I were so engrossed in conversation that the world melted away, I forgot that he was the same vile, repugnant face I first saw through the door at the insane asylum. I began to think of him as attractive. Not in a sexual manner, mind you. He was a good person and therefore attractive, not the other way around, as most women of my era were taught.

My men had devised a way to communicate with me while I floated in the silence of the air. I ignored them, not wanting to give up my freedom to their worries, but eventually Ed insisted we hear what they had to say. We dropped altitude enough that a letter in a basket could be raised.

The letter was not signed; none claimed it. Information was passed without feeling. The Spaniards had fallen ill after my visit. It was the same illness that rendered my men unable to carry an Incola. Some of the sailors and other passengers had gotten sick as well. They obviously carried the latent Carrier gene.

Ed lamented the loss of his testing equipment. "What I wouldn't give for the ability to test their blood in my laboratory!" he exclaimed.

When he calmed down, he and I together worked out several points:

One: Juan would likely believe we poisoned and killed his men.

Two: The weapon was still active and useful in ending Incola power.

Three: I was now the weapon.

I had but one question. "What are the names of the major Incola families of the new world?"

5

If Sally were still with me, she would say, "Enough exposition!" She is not, but I will take her advice all the same. On with the story.

What I have not portrayed, which I will attempt to do now, is the ever-increasing input of my others. I rarely had a moment alone. Jo, Effie, and Mary Martha became quite vocal during this time. Perhaps it was the lack of exterior stimuli born of flight. Perhaps it was just that I now knew of their existence within my mind. Whatever the reason, their thoughts and opinions came through. Sally did what she could to keep them quiet.

The life, the activity, the vibrant nuance of the new world was supposed to baffle us, delay our rescue of Dawn. It did the opposite.

When we landed, the harbor master informed us that the ship had been quarantined due to an unknown illness and would remain at sea, at a safe distance until all crew and passengers were well. The way he said well also told me that once they died, they might also be cleared to land. After the dead were disposed of, of course.

New England was the common name of this place and it seemed fitting. Perhaps it could be my new home. Ed advised that we should wait for the men to arrive before beginning our mission. The Victorian in me knew he was right but the warrior rebelled. I did not need protection now that I wielded the weapon. No Incola could hold me for long; soon they would fall ill. After discussing with Ed, we realized that now that we were here, there was no option to wait. I needed to infect as many Carriers as possible before word of the illness spread and I became persona non grata. They would soon avoid me like the plague I brought.

I refused to cover my legs. All of my dresses and gowns were altered so that I could run while also maintaining the silhouette of the time. Corseting I kept, as it was all I knew and it bothered me not. But my legs needed to be free to run. In my time in the skyship, running became my daydream of choice and now that we were on land again, I found I could not live without it.

And so I abandoned decency in exchange for freedom. Jo was all for it. Indeed she adopted a similar fashion in our mind's field. Effie thought I should do as I thought best but was less than comfortable with exposed legs. Well, you may be able to guess Mary Martha's reaction. The look was unbecoming for a mother, in her eyes. Quite scandalous was the opinion that continued to penetrate our thoughts.

A modest but suitable home was located and rented near the edge of a massive island of green in the middle of New York City named Central Park. Jo and I found this park to be a lovely place to run. On my first evening in my home, I ignored Ed's misgivings and set off by myself to explore the Sheep Meadow, the largest open area of Central Park.

As usual, Ed was proven correct when a group of young men attempted to detain me in a wooded area just off the meadow. They mistook my exposed, though stocking covered, legs as an advertisement that what lay between them was for sale. When they would not let me pass unmolested, I was gentle in beating them. They were, after all, mere men and nowhere near my level of strength. Careful to leave them unable to follow but not permanently damaged, I turned to go.

One of the men shouted after me using a word I care not to repeat. I sighed, my shoulders slouching a bit. Were men as hopeless as this? Beaten and still defiant? No, I decided. The others had learned a lesson but this one needed tutoring. He did not cower when I turned back and his spittle, laced with blood from the broken nose I'd given him, stained my dress as he hurled insults.

Gripping his jaw in my right hand, I held him still as I taught. I spoke slowly, as his reduced intelligence called for. Then he screamed as I squeezed until I felt his mandible crack. He fell silent, unconscious from the pain, and I continued my run.

Passing a herd of sheep, I decided to take a detour across the actual meadow. It was ever so freeing to run in an open space like that. On exiting the meadow area, I passed the Ladies' Refreshment Salon and considered stopping in for a gin and tonic but decided against it as it was getting late.

Cutting between the people on the sidewalk, I ran right up the stairs, through the door and into the foyer. The butler, who'd been rented along with the house, waited there, looking flushed. I interrupted, "I know and I apologize for being late. Allow me to freshen up and I will be right down for dinner."

He explained, "My lady, this house is yours and I serve dinner when you say it is time. It is only that we have received ever so many unannounced guests since your departure."

As if to punctuate his statement, the doorbell rang. The butler waited to answer it until I'd dismissed him. He brought back an envelope. Inside was a handwritten card where expert golden calligraphy requested my presence for dinner the following night.

"An invitation." I chuckled. One so soon after my arrival in this country meant Incola knew of my location. "Are they all petitions for my attendance?" I asked.

The butler's puffed cheeks and raised eyebrows told me what he thought even before his words. "I am certain I do not know what they contain." He pointed to a small stack of envelopes in the coffer on the entry table. "I would never presume to read an employer's correspondence."

I immediately apologized for any implied insult to his manners or work ethic and warned him that I often spoke without thinking, sometimes aloud but to myself. "Please have dinner ready in one hour. I will be down by then." I grabbed the other letters and started upstairs. "Oh, and please send a gin and tonic up to my room first." Passing Ed on the stairs, I fanned the letters out and showed him, stating, "It has begun!"

∽

I responded to all invitations received in a positive fashion. I was indeed available to meet or dine or dance with them. Playing the ever-pliable widow, I attended every gathering, however large or small. Being sure to cozy up to the highest ranking Incola available, I ensured that every major family became infected with what I came to think of by the name of pestis. Paetus called me Lady Pestis and the name made sense to me. Much like Typhoid Mary, I should be known not for who I was but for what I spread.

Dances and dinners could be described, but what would be the point? All the New York Incola families were neutralized by my tactics.

∽

A series of bank failures made it possible for me to purchase one quarter of the US railroads. All routes in thirteen states were ours mere days after arriving in the new world. That was over ten thousand miles of rail line.

Ed thought we ought to wait for the men to move on to wilder parts of the new nation. I detest waiting and Sally could not bear it. We took the rail to the end of the line. Then I bought the next line. We stopped in each major city along the Eastern coastal states and then the Southern ones. At each we stopped long enough to call upon each of the Incola families we could find. To each I said the same as I had in New York to ensure they all came together, exposing the whole of Carrier society.

After a few weeks we found ourselves in New Orleans, Louisiana. Now that was an interesting city. The influx of boat and train meant that it was truly a melting pot of tradition and yet a birthplace of something entirely American. I found I had much more in common with the freed black man than the poor racist whites.

In the daylight hours, Ed, the others, and I followed leads and attempted to locate my daughter without riding Dawn while we waited on the men. Without the mews, which the men would bring when they came, it just wasn't safe. Not for me and certainly not for anyone nearby when I attempted to control my murderous urges that always seem brought on by the loss of Sally. The men had been cleared to land in New York a fortnight after we left there. I halted all trains save theirs and cleared a path for them to travel directly, or as near a direct route as I could finagle together. Stops would only be made for refueling and restocking.

I have never been much of a music fan but I fell in love with the dancing that accompanied the new music. Our rented home seemed the center of vivacious life. In the evening, I danced on the street corner to a musician who called the location his own. I gained a small following, many calling me indecent as my stockinged legs sauntered, exposed to the world.

Surprisingly, no Incola families had taken hold in this glorious city filled with life. I considered making it my home after finding Dawn. Ed reminded me that as Europe and Asia lay more than the illness's incubation period, I could not settle here until the whole world was infected. I acquiesced and put a pin in the conversation. We all knew I would do exactly as I wished when the time came.

I met Robbie, a Negro who, though he knew nothing of my daughter, gave me a short list of men to speak to, white men that would have paid careful attention to a mixed-race man escorting a white teenage female. Robbie was a quiet yet intense man who supported black emigration back to Africa. He read a lot and collected weapons. I saw myself in him. We spent our nights on the porch drinking iced tea, both of which were new experiences for me. In England tea was served warm in the afternoon with a variety of sweets, biscuits, and pastries. Here, tea steeped early so that it might be chilled prior to serving, sweetened over ice.

Summer descended on New Orleans and I was grateful for the tradition of iced instead of hot tea of the area. The days grew unbearably warm and the nights, though cooler, remained muggy. The cobblestone streets steamed. It didn't seem ominous like the London fog but was filled with life. Everything in that place grew and thrived and I got the sincere feeling that the wild would take over the city if men were to disappear suddenly.

I discovered another favorite drink during this time. Gin was already my preferred spirit so when Robbie suggested I try a New Orleans fizz, I jumped at the chance. The sweetened citrus combined with egg white, cream, and soda was perfect though I missed the gin of my homeland. I doubted any distiller could best the one I'd hired to work at the taproom of my previous butler, Darville.

Robbie and I sat on the porch of my rented house drinking fizz one night discussing, as we were oft wont to do, freedom and equality. Though his people had been free for more than three decades, many still felt the weight of ghost chains. The sting of knowing they would never find and hold their loved ones who were sold and traded again was every bit as sharp as the whip. His narrative concerning freed black men mirrored that of my newly freed Carriers. What was their purpose and place in this world? Should they remain where their slave-owners brought them or should they return to their homeland?

To say I was bad at love was an understatement. Two out of two of my husbands had died by my own hand. I wanted the man before me. Even though I was a, maybe *the*, black widow, it never occurred that Robbie might die as a result of my preference.

I stood to juba, a dance he taught me previously, to a particularly intoxicating tresillo rhythm being played across the street. Then, suddenly I lost control of my left side. Luckily it locked rather than languished and I managed to stay upright. Robbie jumped up and came to me out of concern. All I could do was watch as my ungloved left hand rose and rested itself on his cheek.

His eyes widened. This was our first physical contact. His pupils dilated. My gift of touch.

Palming the back of my neck, his quiet intensity grew and his next bold move shocked me. He kissed me.

A black man kissed a white woman.

In public.

For a few seconds I didn't care of the scandal. I returned his kiss and the further flesh on flesh contact escalated the situation. His aggression increased; I felt the disingenuousness of it as my gift of touch took hold. I wanted Robbie but not because he couldn't resist an otherworldly power I had. I wanted him to want me but in that moment I knew it would never be. I would never know if any other than Leon desired me naturally. Leon's own gift of touch negated mine and I knew the times we were together were genuine.

Attempting to extricate myself from Robbie's embrace, I failed. My left side simply would not comply. I successfully used my right to push his torso away from mine, breaking our kiss. "Don't touch me," I said, hoping he would pull from me. Instead, he gripped my waist. "No," I shouted. "Don't touch me!"

Robbie was torn from my grasp at that. He fell in a jumbled pile with one of the men who gathered there to listen to Robbie's ideas. That man might actually have actually saved Robbie's life by attacking him, if not for what happened next.

Hobbled as I was with one arm completely unresponsive to my wishes, in the time it took me to locate my gloves made from Julian's calming skin, Robbie grew enraged. He rolled on the porch with the other man, knocking over chairs and the small table with our drinks on it. The glasses shattered in a brilliant burst of sound and shards. Getting the upper hand, Robbie pummeled the man below him.

Regulating my inhuman strength as best I could, I pulled Robbie from the now unconscious opponent. He evaded my attempt to soothe him using my deceased husband's gift of touch, ranting about inequality being so great that nothing short of revolution would end it. The crowd that had gathered began to look a bit like a mob.

Police arrived and the situation escalated. They attempted to arrest Robbie and he pulled out his Colt Dragoon revolver. I know its model name because he had shown it and a number of other weapons to me. From where on his body he pulled it, I do not know, as men of color were not permitted to carry weapons. Robbie, not of sound mind, drunk on my touch, stepped forward, straightened his right arm and fired just as the first police stepped up onto the porch. The round hit the lawman in the chest but I only saw that a few seconds later as the massive black powder cloud obscured everything in front of Robbie.

The crowd scattered. Two police fell to the ground. The second had been a step down behind the first. The .44 round traveled through the leader's chest and then through the follower's neck. The first was dead but the second gurgled as blood flowed down his throat.

Robbie stood staring at the men and then at his own hand. He couldn't believe what he'd done. "Run," I told him. "Take your guns and get as far as you can."

One of the men who was always with him, shook him by the shoulders. "She's right. You'll be lynched if you stay," he said as I went down to the drowning man.

I soothed the man's brow using my right gloved hand. I could not prevent his passing but I could ease it. My left arm hung, limp at my side. It had feeling but did not respond to my commands. I caused this. These men's deaths were on me. Looking at Robbie, I knew his life was over as well. He was no longer safe in the city he called home.

I felt a familiar twinge in my heart and then darkness. I fell to the place where I was safe from pain when Sally took over. Only this time, I wasn't alone.

∽

How dare she intrude here! This place was my gift from Sally. We resided in my mind. I shoved at the other.

We fell up through the darkness, past the soil and then grass of the meadow. Only then did I see that my hands gripped the neck of Effie. I do not know who I expected but it was not her. I released the inquisitive blossoming young me immediately, apologizing.

Mary Martha pounced. "How did you do that?" she demanded. "You have to tell me! How did you get out?"

Effie stammered, unable to communicate what happened. Mary Martha raised a hand to hit her.

"No," was all I said but that single word halted Mary Martha mid-strike. A mere thought by me and she found herself unable to speak as well. When Jo floated over, I sat all four of us at a table of my conjuring.

Jo asked, "What was it like, outside?"

"Strange," Effie replied. "I could see but I had no control over anything. I desired the man I saw and I wanted to touch him. Then I watched as my arm reached out and touched his cheek. I felt him. Like nothing I'd felt in this place was solid. Like this life is a dream and his skin woke me."

So it had been Effie moving my arm, whether she knew it or not. Clearly she had no idea what brought her to the surface. The experience of sharing my body was new to me. Yes, I shared it with Sally but never at the same time. She and I switched places, sharing our body as children with a toy taking turns, not playing with it together. We advanced, clearing milestones.

The horizon shifted and Sally came down from the sky and landed in a seat at the table. All four of us fired questions at her. With a wave of her hand, the others flew away in different directions, still bound to their chairs, but well out of earshot.

"How did this happen?" I asked my Sally. "I thought you kept them here."

As soon as I said it, I regretted my words. Sally had controlled and contained these others their whole lives. I had lived in a dream world, free from the knowledge of them and the responsibility of their keeping. Yet another gift Sally provided.

"We were here. And then the mountains opened and hooked Effie, dragging her out. I knew she was up top, at the helm, but then you did not return. You were still with her. I didn't know how it was possible." She stopped a moment to think. "I was only able to displace you both when I felt it. Pain."

I remember what she said to me when first I became aware of her consciousness. *Hurt is where I live.* Sally knew what she was, where she existed, long before I knew of her at all. I am still discovering what I am, still unsure where I belong. The great injustice of her life is that she is most real, most alive, in my pain.

Neither denying nor agreeing with my assessment, Sally said, "That is the only time I can take control."

I shook my head no. That wasn't completely true. Sally took over whenever I felt pain, yes, but she also stepped in whenever I needed her. Had I needed Effie? Had I needed her for some reason and unknowingly brought her to the surface? She said she had desired the man before her but it had been *I* who wanted Robbie. Had I brought her forward to do what I could not? Whatever had happened I knew the blame lay at my feet, not Effie's.

I knew Sally heard my thoughts or at least felt my emotions. I stopped her before she could placate me. I grew exhausted of discovering I was the monster in each horror. Without ascending completely, I sent my senses out. My inner ear told me we were moving. Sally had put us in a carriage, perhaps, considering the curtained darkness, confined space, and clip-clop of shod horse feet.

As always she answered my unspoken questions. “Our Carriers arrived shortly after Robbie escaped. They,” she paused a split second, “took care of the situation.”

I saw in a flash of her memory that more police appeared after the first two died and, as I literally had blood on my hands, they believed I was the killer. Andrew and Auley arrived as uniformed men attempted to arrest me. Sally operated on automatic, preventing the men from doing their duty, struggling to extricate ourself without killing any of the delicate humans. She couldn't allow us to be taken into custody; Dawn had to be found. My Carriers removed me from their hands. I would never be welcome in the great city of New Orleans again after the carnage.

6

As we traveled, Sally and I practiced trading places up top, practiced keeping the others down. As far as we could tell, practice was overkill. At no time did they seem able to control as little as a pinkie toe. Effie hadn't climbed; she'd been pulled. The trigger remained unknown to us, baffling our joint mind.

Alternating between rail and carriage, we saw much of the American landscape. People from all over the world came here searching for better lives. Sadly few of them found what they looked for. Most lived in communities made up of their own kind, keeping separate from others and each treated as second class to the next. The only thing that separated the poor from each other was skin color. They naturally lashed out at each other, attempting to elevate themselves on the backs of those darker or more foreign than themselves.

Each group fascinated me, but none so much as the Chinese. These hard-working people built the railroad, falling off in clumps as the tracks moved west. Every city had a Chinese section. I found them to be the least violent, the most innovative, and serious yet fun loving. I played mahjong at every opportunity, often at tables with men and women three times my age who for some unknown reason treated me with the respect and reverence usually reserved for royalty.

On one such night, the tiles were not being kind to me and yet I was winning and I suspected my opponents let me win. Languages come to me easily. Scarcely had I set foot in some new place but I began to understand those around me. I kept up the ruse of ignorance as it suited me. That night I found it nigh impossible not to react as their conversation went to my nature and the weapon.

Very few of even my own men knew of the weapon given to me by Ning Shiru. The object had baffled me for months and then, when I suspected it might save my child and husband, I opened it and released this illness, this cleansing of the Incola power. Sally kept it on our person at all times just in case it held some ability or further use.

Even with my secrecy these people native to its country of origin knew of it and of me. In their language the man to my left, ironically closest to the secret pocket that held it, said, "I wonder if she carries the weapon right now?"

The woman—at least I believed her a woman though she had hairs on her chin—on my right teased him saying, "You believe it brings her luck, enabling her to beat you?" and then murmured under her breath that no such trinket was necessary to defeat so weak an adversary as he.

He defended himself. "Not at all," he said. "It is only that I wonder how long it will take to cause us illness. You know I only worry about my granddaughter. She may be born here but I fear she will never be safe from…"

The third player cut him off with a sound. The man—I was fairly certain as he not only had hair on his chin but celebrated its existence by braiding its wispy strands—studied me as I lay down my next tiles. He suspected I understood more than I should. I purposefully played the wrong tile to throw him off. The others laughed at my mistake and continued their conversation.

"Perhaps she has yet to open it. Maybe the monks failed to deliver it."

"Impossible. They swore to end Xia's reign."

The third player again cut them off with a sound. He grew agitated when they used the name Xia. I had never heard of that person. The evening went on with no further interesting conversation and the game ended.

I used the mews my men brought with them. Dawn remained with Theodore but now traveled the wilderness with his men in tow. I sketched any landmarks and showed them to locals as we traveled but no one recognized her location. Then I got lucky. I watched as she exited a cone-shaped tent only to see her surrounded by a dozen of its like. She and Theodore resided with American natives.

I knew that this land had once been covered by these people but they were not all one group. Many tribes made up the population and I had no idea how to differentiate between them and so I thought I was no closer to finding them. But some trinket or style of hair, recognized by one of the many men I showed my drawing to, pointed me in the right direction.

No tracks cut the land where we crossed wilderness. Coachmen were hesitant to take so fine a lady as I into wild territory. The caravan impressed our severity to all who witnessed us. My men appeared an army, as heavily armed as any in the known world.

The native people intrigued me. They were unlike any I had ever seen. They lived life naturally and I imagined joining them would be bliss. My exposed legs caused them no pause. I know now that I romanticized their existence, glossing over their trials and hardships. I viewed them not as they were but through my Victorian sensibilities, filtered through my prejudice.

As we neared Dawn, I began to sense her. I had never before been able to sniff out Incola so I attributed the new ability with our familial closeness. I wondered if she could sense me in return. As we did not know her true motives, her reaction to our approach remained a quandary. Would she run to us, fleeing her captors or would she run from us, taking her captives with her?

Her real choice was something I could never have guessed.

∽

When we caught up to the tribe identified by the unique hairstyle recognized by the local, Dawn was no longer with them. She had fled. Alone. Into the wilderness. I could feel it, but I could also feel that she left something, or many somethings to be exact, behind.

We entered the village unmolested. Some of the women even offered us food and drink. The men stood back attempting to appear large, stern, and arresting, but not intimidating. That they all wanted to impress us was my assessment. At the center was a more elaborate tent, which I now know is called a teepee.

All around the dwelling's perimeter, men sat facing out. Some wore shirts but most did not. That would not have been strange if they were native men, but they were European. Each one wore either a light colored leather pouch around his neck or a band of the same color leather around an arm. The dirt under them was darker than natural. The smell told me that the men had not moved in some time, not to wash or rest or relieve themselves. The stain growing beneath them was their own excrement and bodily fluids. I did not know what would enthrall them so. I understood that I was invited to enter even without speaking the native tongue. I did so, leaving the men outside, as I had no indication that any here wished me harm.

It was a mistake.

Light penetrated the dark interior only by the small hole at the peak of the tent, where the poles stuck out into the sky above. A small dark man wearing only trousers and a leather mask crossed that column of light when he lunged toward me. My eyes had not yet adjusted to the dark and so I struggled with him blindly. He had no weapon that I could feel and so I did not even think to call out to my men. We exchanged a few blows but mostly our fight was nearer to wrestling than boxing. His strength was a good match for my own. We could have hurt each other if that had been the intent but as the objective seemed to be subduing me, I did not attempt to harm the man. I refused to be subdued. In the skirmish, I managed to push his mask from his face.

It landed in the beam of light. Even as the struggle continued, my eyes were drawn back to the mask. It haunted me. Something about it reminded me of my own face. Had it been made to represent me? The boy's, for extended contact with his body told me that was what he was, struggle lessened, almost as if his heart was no longer in it. Most fights stop abruptly, when one opponent is bested. This one slowly stopped. He and I stood on either side of the fall of light, breathing deeply.

Assuming the boy was a native, I did not attempt conversation. After all, he had not spoken a word. After I caught my breath, I called out, "Ed! Andrew! Auley!"

The three men entered with Paetus following close behind. No matter who I called, Paetus would not be denied. He'd had too many centuries of being in charge to do anything but exactly what he wanted. I would do well to remember that. Father and son held weapons drawn. Ed moved his head only, looking around with his mechanically enhanced vision, taking in all the details he could. The lack of light seemed no issue to his "eyes." I made a mental note to ask him about inventing a set of goggles for me, to aid my vision at night.

When they moved to apprehend the boy, I stopped them with a word and pointed at the mask. "Who does that look like to you?" I asked them.

Ed shrugged, making me question my internal praise of his vision inventions.

Andrew answered, "You."

Auley commented, "It could be modeled after any fair skinned woman."

The voice from across the light beam startled me. "It is Lady Dawn." The accent was a strange conglomeration from around the globe, but something about the voice made me think of home.

"It could be modeled after Lady Dawn. She is, after all, a fair skinned woman." Andrew reasoned, using his father's logical thinking.

Once again the boy spoke, "Not modeled after. It *is* Lady Dawn's face."

That voice radiated through my memory, and even though I had never heard it before, I felt certain I knew it. "Step into the light," I ordered him. He obeyed without hesitation.

The boy who stood before me could be none other than my brother's son. Theodore looked more like Thaddeus in person than he did through Dawn's eyes. Perhaps that was because she never knew her uncle and saw Theodore as his own man.

Ed leaned down to pick up the mask but Theodore yelled, "No! Don't touch her skin!"

At that, we all froze. I felt the pull of the darkness at the horror of the coming realization but battled the fall. The mask was the skin of Dawn's actual face. Sally fought me for control. She brought up every painful memory she could muster attempting to trigger a switch. She raged inside me, snarling at Theodore through my eyes. She thought he had killed Dawn and stripped her of her face, wearing it, but I knew the truth even before Theodore said it.

"She forces us to wear her skin. There is something strange about it. Touching her makes us do what she wants. Pleasing her is all that matters when you touch her."

My demented daughter had her own gift of touch and she had weaponized it.

∽

Using great caution, I approached the first man sitting in a circle around the outside of the tent. My gloves made from Julian's calming skin helped both the man and me. I couldn't have him get excited as I removed the Dawn-skin band from his arm. Likewise, I could not risk coming in direct contact with her flesh.

"No, you mustn't," he said. "She doesn't want us to take them off."

I laid my gloved hand on his cheek, calming him. "Dawn told me," I lied. "It would please her very much if you would let me remove it. You want to please her, do you not?"

He had been there for many days. His body weakened by the lack of self-care. The calming touch took root quickly. He fell asleep muttering about pleasing Dawn, and I removed the commanding leather. It was a bit more violent than I wished because the leather wasn't dried at all. It had begun to attach to the man's arm. Tearing it loose meant ripping the man's own skin underneath. I tossed it into a waiting basket and moved to the next man. The exchange with him, and every man after, went almost identically to the first. They needed to please Dawn but were weakened and easily convinced of a change in her will. Some did not fall asleep but fell unconscious.

The natives wore similar pieces of my daughter's flesh. They had been allowed to carry out their daily needs and were not weakened. Therefore they took more direct methods. It did not help that we did not speak their language. A few of them had to be removed by force from a couple of men. Once or twice, I thought I saw a flash of anger from inside and wondered if the flesh was not only a way of continued contact and therefore an extension of the gift of touch, but also Dawn's Incola method.

Each Incola had their own means of gaining access and control of his own Carriers. This could very well be Dawn's. The way some of the flesh had taken hold made me worry. Was it just stuck or was it actually healing itself and attaching to the man? Could Dawn not only heal herself, but any piece of herself, even if it was separated from her body? I hoped not.

The lot of them, along with a macabre basket filled with fresh flesh strips meant for me and my men, were burned. The sun set while we waited and listened to Theodore's story. I kept Sally from killing him until we could hear his side. I sat in the only chair to be found. Theodore and Paetus sat together. His hand on the boy's bare shoulder ensured nothing but the truth could be told. My men stood watch around us, their backs to the fire so that Dawn could not sneak up and influence anyone with her touch. They rested inside the circle of warmth in shifts.

I started with an important question. "Do you have a gift of touch?"

"No, not that I am aware of."

I looked to Paetus, who nodded while keeping his eyes on the boy. Paetus thought it the truth. "But what if he has a gift similar to Leon's?" I asked him.

Paetus' face went blank and he turned his attention fully to me. "That weak, worthless excuse for an Incola had no power. He squandered his life and I am glad it was not an immortal one."

With that insult, Effie came to the front. She couldn't take control of my body but they were her words that came from my mouth. Through gritted teeth I said, "Do not speak that way about either of my husbands ever again." I felt that if I had opened my mouth, the screaming might never stop.

"What gift…" he started to ask.

"Ever. Again." I repeated. Sally pulled Effie back down. Paetus and I stared at each other.

"I would never speak ill of Julian. Archelaos was everything to me. You are the one who killed him."

Thankfully, Effie was too distracted by Sally to have heard him.

Andrew, who was very close to Leonus for much longer than I had been alive, turned and answered Paetus' previous unfinished question. There was no doubting the pride in his voice. "His was the ability to negate every other gift." He smiled at Paetus. "Leonus could lie to you. He could remain alert even with Julian's touch." He glanced at me shyly before adding, "He could be in contact with his wife without becoming enraged." Andrew stepped back into his lookout position with a smug look.

"Horse shit!" Paetus exclaimed. "I would have kno… He couldn't have hid… He would have been a very smart man indeed to hide such a thing. If I had known, I would have killed him, slowly, enjoying his pathetic screams." His jealousy must have overridden his sense of self preservation.

I stood. I hadn't decided to; it just happened. Effie wasn't at the helm of my body. She somehow found a way to control my emotions. I could feel it happening but couldn't care. I didn't walk to him because she wanted me to. I didn't pull a knife from my skirt because she wanted me to. I stabbed him in the leg because *I* wanted to. A knife to the meaty thigh would have been too easy on him. Expertly, I slid the blade between the bones of his knee and its cap, slicing tendons and skin so quickly that Paetus didn't react until I withdrew the weapon.

He was the one screaming then. Leon's men chuckled. I had warned him. He cursed and spit, blatantly avoiding any mention of my husbands. He reached down and grabbed his kneecap, which hung down, barely connected to his leg. Holding it in place he growled at me. "Have you any idea how long it will take me to heal this damage!"

"Long enough to hear my nephew's story and confirm the truth of it," I answered what had to be a rhetorical question. I could see defiance in his eyes. Paetus was unaccustomed to being at a disadvantage. He questioned his promise to help me. "You will help me because if you do not, I will strip the skin from your hands and use your brain to tan them, just as you did to Julian."

As soon as the words came from my mouth, I knew I should not have said them. Effie stiffened and grew inside me. Talk of hurting Julian enlivened her.

"Just as you would have done to Leonus, had he any real gift of touch."

I did not readily recognize the one to turn and step toward Paetus at this. He looked to me, the knife glittering with reflected firelight. "Shall I give him a matching pair?" I shook my head no.

I had inadvertently made Paetus a touchable man. Remembering that many of my men had belonged to Paetus or had been abused by him, I made a mental note to speak with them. Paetus had lived for too long, had too many connections, and too much information to be needlessly killed.

"I did not treat Leon's body so, because I love him. I loved Julian as well. You will remember that you were the one to destroy his body and strip him of valuable parts." I gestured toward Theodore, who watched us with wide eyes that made him look much younger than his years. "Your touch, please, Paetus."

Once his hand lay on Theodore once more, I asked, "Did you kidnap Dawn?"

"Yes, but I…" he began but Sally rushed to the front.

She screamed, "Did you rape her?"

Theodore's dark skin paled. He threw his hands up in defense. "No! I swear. I had planned to…mate her as we are the last of our line but I would never hurt Dawn. Even if I had wanted to, I couldn't. When she touched me, pleasing her was all I could think about. Nothing happened that she didn't want."

"Did she want you to rape and kill all of the Dowager's people?" I clawed my way back only because his answer had thrown cold water on Sally's rage. We knew what the skin she put on these men had done. How much more potent was the effect when her skin lay attached to her body?

He shook his head. "My men were as drawn to Lady Dawn as I and we had been trapped on a ship for a short while." He shrugged, but somehow it managed to be apologetic. "Being a good Incola means certain compromises must be made, indulgences allowed. Julian taught me that. He would say, Sometimes," Paetus joined him in unison, "'A man has needs to be met that seem vile to others.'"

Paetus laughed. "The boy isn't lying. He knew Julian. Most of the time, Julian said that about his own needs."

Effie asked, "How well did you know Julian?"

"As well as you can know a person, I suppose," Theodore answered. "Julian was as close to a father as I had. I cannot remember a time when he was not in my life. He was my benefactor, my confidant, my teacher. He gave me my first Carrier, long before I was able to ride."

Paetus snatched his hand away just as I was about to ask Theodore his method of riding. I could have made him tell me but it mattered not. In a few short days he and the men with him would fall ill and find themselves locked in their bodies.

"Then you do ride them," I said, making the question a statement.

He answered all the same. "Of course. How else would I keep order? Without the threat that I could walk them off a cliff on a whim, why would they stay? Surely you ride yours."

Then he had not yet heard tale of the illness I carry. "Certainly not. My men remain with me for a number of reasons: money, duty, loyalty, habit. We have no chattel here; all are equal." As soon as I said it, I knew it was an untruth. I might not have slaves whose body I wore, but there was a hierarchy with myself on top, followed by those closest to me and then those most useful to me and then everyone else. Now, after so long since those days, I was hard pressed to think of more than a handful of the lower men's names.

One of those who will have to remain nameless stepped forward and interrupted. "If you don't mind," he directed at me. "I have something to add." I nodded to him that it would be allowed. "We would do anything for her. Do you not feel it? That overwhelming drive to protect someone so special, she is almost sacred."

Theodore pursed his lips and shook his head. Whatever it was this man spoke of was not an experience or sensation that Theodore shared. He stated, "Nothing could make me surrender my Carriers. No one could make me. The Pope himself came seeking tithe. I told him no but wanted to avoid ill feelings. I am not unreasonable and any Incola that old deserves respect. In the end we came to an arrangement. All he wanted was for me to take communion."

Theodore possessed an almost mesmerizing voice. I could feel myself being pulled into his story. It was entirely unique and yet reminded me so of Thaddeus. We had played together as children. Indeed he was the only child I ever knew. There was no school for a peer and peeress such as he and I. We had only each other among a household of servants and ever absent parents. It wasn't until Thaddeus hit his teen years that Father had any interest in him.

I loved Thaddeus. Sally had spared me of knowing any of his wrongdoings. It was my own gift of touch that caused Thaddeus to act in any manner unbecoming for a brother.

"Julian was not your father. He rode your father and walked him, my brother, straight to the gallows."

"He told me what he'd done. He did it for your release from that terrible place where you would have languished and died, labeled a murderous lunatic. We kill because we must. Does the lion feel remorse for killing the gazelle?"

Another quote from Julian. "But," Mary Martha argued, "should we not feel remorse for the death of our young?" A good question. The lion often kills cubs, usually when they take over another pride. This is often done to stake their claim on females. Maybe Incola have more in common with lions than I'd previously realized. Male lions have been known to kill lionesses who refuse to mate. Julian had attempted to take me over, kill me in the Incola sense of the word, only when I'd been uncooperative.

"Of course we should," Theodore insisted. "Julian loved you. Terrible things are done in the name of far less than love."

I felt Effie sigh and so I held my tongue. When Theodore asked, I allowed him to dress. The night quickly chilled and it seemed an injustice to force him to remain in a state of undress. Clothed, he looked older. Had his skin been lighter, he would have done very well in London society. His bearing, his looks, his voice. When he started talking again, I found myself wondering if we could have categories of gifts other than that of touch.

The night wore on and his story continued. My others had not found their way to the front but they had found their voices. Effie asked only about Julian. Mary Martha and Sally wished to know everything about Dawn and where she might be headed. Even Jo asked questions when Theodore spoke of his worldly travels and epic ocean adventures. This was the first time any of them, save Sally, had spoken. It should have worried me. It would have, if only it hadn't steadied me so. We all had our own thoughts and so each thing he said was quickly analyzed and processed for our purposes.

At some point, the natives packed up and left. They'd had enough of our brand of crazy. I grew tired and my men took turns on watch, sleeping in shifts inside the circle of wagons and carriages around the single remaining tent, in which I slumbered.

In the morning, I climbed into the wagon that carried the mews and got inside. It had been drained of water for ease of travel. I wasn't using it as a deprivation tank anyway. It was a tiny traveling prison; a place that could contain my rage when Sally left to ride Dawn. The chamber had a wheel that, when turned, opened the latch, but for whatever reason, I could not remember how to work it until after Sally would return to us.

This ride was strange. Yes, we saw that she had taken up travel with an older gentleman of some considerable means and they were headed north in some style. Her touch kept the man spending and moving. But before Sally made it to the front to see through Dawn's eyes, she happened upon a new and frightening part of our daughter's mind.

A darkness deep in her recesses repulsed us. Actively. The darkness felt alive. Something within its depths moved. That black inky mass reeked of death and destruction. Having the terrible sensation that making contact would mean the death of us, I screamed at Sally from my mews, "Don't touch it!" I needn't have bothered. She could not hear me. I could see through her eyes when she rode, not the other way around. But Sally was as repulsed, if not more, seeing it in person.

Skirting around the maar put Sally inside a memory. In it Dawn busied herself with Paetus' punishment in her, previously my, tenebrae. Sally went very still. It wasn't like one of Sally's memories, where she had lived so long before I knew of her existence. Neither of these two players were alive. It was a static memory but Dawn's attention could be called to this moment in her life. That is the reason for caution, to prevent any ripples that might signal our presence.

When Sally came back to us, we spoke about what we'd seen. The others joined. Mary Martha and Sally, who had been in agreement more lately than I was comfortable with, thought the darkness might be Eve's domain. For in their eyes, Dawn was all that was light and good and Eve', the opposite. I was not certain. Jo and Effie argued that it could be her quiet place, reminding me of the floating darkness where I went when Sally had taken the pain. That didn't seem right to me either as Dawn's darkness seemed to wish us ill. Effie's argument was smart. The darkness protected Dawn from all sensation and we had seen that the area was surrounded by memories. Those could not be allowed in if the place was to be a sanctuary. Perhaps it only felt unwelcoming and ominous to us. Dawn might find it a pleasant respite from everything.

And so we traveled west, north, and then east, zigzagging in an attempt to find Dawn. Doing so meant that I explored much more of this new world than I would have naturally. Oddly, none of Theodore's men fell ill. I had no hard proof but suspected that he occasionally rode them. I was unsure what that meant.

I loved it. The wild open spaces. The fields where prairie grass grew waist high. The mountains with tops where the snow never melted. The great chasm in the red land that became known as the Grand Canyon. The giant sequoia trees that men sought to profit from but couldn't. The rainforest of the west coast. The big sky country where blue met the horizon in every way I looked.

It was there, in what was called the Montana territory, that a new other was born. We rode north up the Great Plains area when I demanded a stop. The sky was as blue and cloud-free as I had ever seen. I had the men drive the carriages as far away as they would. A handful of guards made a circle around me, paced off forty and ducked down in the tall grasses. It was as alone as I would ever get. For a moment, I felt as though I was the center of the universe. The land stretched out in every direction, only meeting the sky, which was doing the same, at the very extent of my vision. Then, everything changed while staying the same.

I was not the center of the universe. I would only ever be the center of my own life; I could not ride and would never see anything from anywhere but from within my own mind. The universe around me would continue its mechanisms without ever knowing I existed. I was a single ant on a single mound on a single continent on a single world in one of many universes. That was the moment she was born.

"Ramillia," Sally called me from my revelation. "We need you down here."

I called back my men and carriages. Once I was seated safely inside one and I began to feel normal once again, I closed my eyes and went down to our interior mental meadow. Here I was the center of the universe. Or maybe it was Sally.

There, the others waited for me.

Mary Martha demanded, "What did you do?"

Effie took my hand, ever the friend Jo named her. Sally gave it to me straight, "Another other has been born."

Jo could not stop jumping and clapping. "It's the best one I made yet!" She was still operating on the incorrect assumption that she was the one making her friends down in this place. Or at least pretending to believe it.

What was the correct reaction, I wondered. *My mind is getting terribly crowded.*

"Just let her see me," the new one said from behind Sally. Strangely, the voice came from much lower than it should have. It was also an octave higher than my own.

When Sally stepped aside, I saw her. A midget version of myself. Her hair was properly coiled and up-swept; her body, while undersized with dwarfish proportions, was decently attired and corseted. Confidently, she stuck out her tiny hand and introduced herself, "Name's Margaret, but you can call me Marge."

Not quite sure what to do, I took her hand. She shook it. Like a man would greet another man. I had seen midgets before in the freak show as a child, but this one looked like me and I was stunned. Now, I know the term midget has gone out of style and I should call her a little person, but that was not the term at the time and not the terminology I thought. You have had to forgive many things in my tale. This is one of the least of them.

"Heard a lot about ya." She pursed her lips and furrowed her brow. "Naw, that's not right. I haven't heard anything. I…know a lot about you." Her voice was my own, only higher, and the accent was completely different. She was not British. She was…American.

Everything about Marge confused me. Us, confused us. The looks on Sally, Jo, Effie, and Mary Martha's face said they felt the same as I. Marge was an enigma. The others seemed to be me, just at different ages. What was Marge?

"I'm a part of you," Marge answered. I always forgot that my thoughts were not private here. "I may look and sound different than the others but I'm the same."

I could feel that wasn't how she really felt and so I pressed her about it. Her response was, "I'm small and, because of that, most of the world will never know that the sun and stars revolve around me." Funny how I was just thinking in similar terms, out on the Great Plains. She continued, "I'm here to make everything clear. I don't yet know how, but I am the key to everything."

Marge displayed an unbelievable level of confidence. Was it because of or in spite of her size? Or did her stature have nothing at all to do with it?

Then finally, six months later, we came back to the place we landed. New York. There I found my most favorite place of all. Niagara Falls was most impressive. The thought of a simple primitive person long ago approaching the waterfalls overwhelmed me. The noise, the roar, assaulted our ears. Had I not been a woman of science, I could completely understand the superstition surrounding the falls. It certainly did seem a godlike area.

I tried to keep my next thought from the others but failed. "It certainly is like you," Jo said. "It does not matter how often one might hear of it; being in your presence is overwhelming for people."

Marge spoke up. Her American accent still sounded vaguely vulgar to me. Her confidence never dwindled. "I love it too. The water is so powerful. No man could ever stop the flow. The water goes where it will go, just like us."

I allowed Jo and Marge to the front, just enough that they could see the natural wonder more clearly through our eyes. I never let Mary Martha forward. She wanted out too badly and would use it as an opportunity to search for ways to escape me. I knew this made her even more desperate to get out but I feared her release. Effie seemed able to step forward on her own but remained completely unaware of how she did it. Jo liked to see the world but had no interest in leaving our mind, where she had omnipotence over reality. Sally was as always. There to help me, seemingly satisfied with her role as my second.

7

Having discovered my near obsession with mahjong after leaving New York, I was eager to play in New York City's Chinatown. I made sure my men had money to enjoy all the area had to offer and they gave me a wide berth while still ensuring my safety. Most had been with me long enough to know I felt comfortable around unsavory parts of society. I had no problem with the gamblers, amusement caterers, and prostitutes. I found them no more in number in Chinatown than in other parts of the bustling city.

As always the celestials welcomed me readily. I wanted to drink and play the tiles but would not have been able to find a table or open seat without guidance. This area of the city was a labyrinth. People lived on top of each other and businesses filled every alley and nook. My guide finally showed me to my seat where the three other players were much closer to my own age than I was accustomed. They were all men, even the servers and proprietor. I had missed the die throw and took my seat in last place, or North position. I put my money on the table so that they could see that I was serious about playing.

They learned how serious I was when I won all four hands of round one and an extra hand had to be played. After that, it was more evenly matched but I still came out on top. In the fourth round, I won from the wall and doubled my points. The men relaxed after that and began to play in earnest. If I could win that stoutly, I was no outsider. I did not take my winnings for the first game, but rather gave it back to them so that they might all afford to keep playing.

My others contained themselves as long as they could. After the third round a young woman brought the man in the West position beside me a bowl of food. I would never have thought it would make such a commotion, but it certainly did. Every other tried to jump to the front at the same time.

Effie commented about the sweet but yet savory smell of the dish, while Jo wished to know what the strange sticks he used to eat were called. Sally commented that the woman was quite attractive, while Mary Martha determined that the man she served must be the woman's brother and not husband because the familial similarities were so obvious. Marge latched on to the woman's impossibly small feet, commenting that they weren't much longer than her own. Ignoring the fact that Marge's feet weren't real and didn't exist in the real world, I fussed at her callous comment. The woman's feet were clearly bound. I told Marge that binding was a painful process by which the toes were folded under the foot until they and the arch of the foot were broken. This was pain for a male ideal of beauty's sake and I could not support such a thing. I hoped that the tradition would soon fall out of fashion for I would hate to see another generation of girls denied the joys of running and dancing.

I turned my attention back to the game and shuffled the tiles as it was my turn to deal. Soon I realized that the clinking, tinkling sound of my tiles tapping each other was the only sound of the room. Every head in the place was turned my direction. All talk and play had stopped. The only movement was the tufts and waves of smoke from abandoned and forgotten pipes and cigars. In the distance, the end of rain rolled from roofs and splashed into puddles on the cobblestone streets outside.

Going back to shuffling, I tried to figure out just what had happened. Perhaps I took too long with my internal conversation. *Perhaps your conversation was not internal,* Sally told me. I dealt and tried to look less panicked than I felt. This wouldn't be the first time I'd had a conversation with an other out loud but it would definitely be the first time I'd had one with *five* others. I managed to get through the round but didn't manage to win a single hand.

The players finished our game but then left without tallying or collecting their winnings. Everyone else had already made their exits.

As I wove around tables and made my way to the exit, a small girl with dark hair brought me a bowl of the same food the woman had brought the player. I took the bowl and the girl showed me how to use the chopsticks. When I failed, she ran off laughing, her bare feet slapping the floor. The Chinese woman with the bound feet returned and gestured that I should eat the meat and rice with my hands.

Taking a small piece of what looked like duck, I intended to be polite. Once it was in my mouth and the flavors hit my tongue, I was anything but and began to shovel it, all the while making pleasure noises. The meat was tender and moist, rich with fat. Whatever sauce it had been cooked in permeated every part and was unlike anything I'd ever tasted before. Some spices I recognized; some I did not. Some were used in completely new ways. I felt the gentle touch of each of the others and they took turns up front with me so that they could experience the seemingly simple food with exotic flavor.

I complimented her and she nodded her thanks. She understood me but couldn't speak English and I likewise could understand some of what she said. She spoke a different dialect than those I'd played mahjong with along the railways. What I understood was this: Because she was the first daughter, she had her feet bound when she was young to make her marriageable. Her younger sisters had been expected to work in the fields and at other jobs where bound feet would be too much of a hindrance. It had worked and she had made a good match. She was wealthy enough to bring her brother over from China. I was correct; the binding was very painful. But she defended her cultural practice by pointing out that we wore corsets that often kept us from activity and even sometimes broke ribs. All in the name of a male ideal of beauty.

This clarity of thought startled me. I had never considered it that way. Just as I felt comfortable with what I had always known, so was she. I wore my corset and she kept her feet bound. Those things made us feel beautiful and therefore powerful. We did not see them as oppression.

She stood to go and the little girl came running back in to take away the bowl. Smiling after her, she said that her daughters would never have their feet bound. It was no longer necessary. Most Chinese here were men and her daughters would have their pick of the finest husbands, even without lotus feet.

Then I thought of Dawn. How she had wanted to dress more adult for her big birthday party! I had said no. Now I considered why. Mary Martha said I was right to question myself; I had been thinking of impropriety, about how the males in her life would interpret such dress. Jo said she would never wear a corset. Effie silently admired how she looked in hers. Marge and Sally were deep in conversation about if the tiny woman bound her feet inside, would it have any effect on my feet out in the world?

The woman stared at me. Sympathy radiated from her black eyes. "How many death you carry inside?" she asked in heavily accented English. I felt my brow furrow. She asked again in her native tongue but my ability to understand was not much better than hers to speak my language.

"Both of my husbands' deaths weigh heavily on me," I stated.

She shook her head. "No. Not husbands. They not family."

We stood in silence for a moment. Then I decided to try something. "Who is Xia?" I asked her.

The name seemed to resonate around the room. There was a clatter from the direction of the kitchen and then a man barked orders and probably the name of the woman I talked to. Before she left I slipped a bag of coin into her hands. I would say she rushed off but there was nothing quick about the way a woman with bound feet walked. Steps were small and delicate. I could not imagine trying to balance on such tiny things. I hoped I had not gotten the woman in trouble.

Outside my men waited on me with a carriage. I wanted to spend more time exploring the Xia character and why that name seemed to elicit such an extreme response. But night had fallen in earnest and New York was still a strange city to me. Paetus argued that though I had neutralized the Incola, they were still men and might seek revenge for what was taken from them. In the carriage, I studied him from below half-closed lids. Was that how he felt? I felt I had a good understanding of Paetus when Julian lived, and even after, but his behavior had been erratic since his illness.

When we returned to my rented home, a package waited for me. The butler said that a young celestial with a shaved head, save a long-braided tail, brought it and a small note. He was clearly not a fan of the Chinese immigrants.

Understanding a language spoken and being able to read this completely alien pictograph-like alphabet were very different talents. The first, I possessed. The second, I did not. I needed an interpreter. As it turned out the butler knew that a neighbor kept a Chinaman as a servant because he frequently did business with Chinese exporters, importing goods to the United States.

Paetus went to inquire after borrowing the servant's services and returned quickly. The importer had been suspicious at first, clearly worried I was there to interfere with his business in some way but had readily agreed to let us borrow the translator once he heard I had acquired a historic text and had a mere academic interest.

I sent everyone out, save the Chinaman and we sat down at my desk. The letter stated only She Lives To Destroy. "Who lives to destroy?" I asked.

"No, you misunderstand," he replied. It was written, not as a statement, but as a person's title or name. Perhaps that is who the book was about.

The book had started its life as a scroll. Segments had been cut and made into pages. It told the tale of the Yellow Emperor, the first ruler of the Chinese empire, initiator of all Chinese culture, and the ancestor of all Chinese. It spoke of the Emperor's many inventions and conquests. The Emperor, not known for destruction as the note suggested, taught tribesmen basic skills such as how to build shelters, tame wild animals, grow the Five Grains, invented the fundamental blocks of civilization like carts, boats, clothing, and agriculture, and is credited with inventions as advanced as the bow sling, astronomy, the calendar, math, and even the Chinese character writing system. The Yellow Emperor encountered a talking beast, Bai Ze, who taught the knowledge of all supernatural creatures. The Yellow Emperor achieved immortality and, when the time came to pass from this to the next, left only a cap and clothing.

When the Chinaman finished I could tell he was holding back and asked him about it. He said the Yellow Emperor was a well-known story, but this text was much older than any he knew about. His confusion was probably just a difference between ancient writing and modern characters. Chinese writing was not like Western. There were many ways to write any word and the subtle differences held meaning. The way the word Emperor was written in this text was different than he had seen. Had he not been familiar with the tale, he would have read it as the Yellow *Empress*, as the character had the female flourish.

"Makes perfect sense to me," Mary Martha argued. "Of course the ancestor of all Chinese was a woman."

"We are the source of life, not men," Sally agreed.

Marge grumbled under her breath, knowing full well that we could all hear her. "Men! Taking our accomplishments and rewriting history for their own advancement since the beginning of time."

"So the goddess was changed to a god. Who cares?" Jo asked, riding a unicorn in place. We met in our mental meadow to talk. It was easier than allowing them to each use my body. Also, I was becoming concerned that they were so easily coming to the front, sometimes without me even noticing.

"I think our main concern should be *who* sent this to us," Effie said.

"And why?" I added. The book was old, older even than I originally suspected. It must have been of great value, both in monetary and cultural terms. "Why would a person entrust it to us?"

"Because they, whoever they are, know we will do something with it," said Marge.

"Yes, but what?" I asked. We were getting no closer to answering any of our questions than we had been when the Chinaman left. I went back to the top and made a big show of going up to bed in front of the men. I knew their guard rotation and knew it would be easy to slip past them. The one thing we knew was that this book had come from a celestial. I had to go back to Chinatown; I would speak with the woman with lotus feet if I could.

I had no waiting woman to aid me in dressing and undressing so there was no one in my rooms to trick. Instead of dressing in my bedclothes, I put on my least adorned black dress. It was cut to my new specifications so my legs were free to move quickly if need be. It was a matte black and would absorb instead of reflect any light that hit it. Though it had darkened a little with age, my hair was still blond and would shine like a flame atop a black candle. There was nothing to do but cover it with the hood of a dark cloak. My skin was pale but I could not sacrifice my vision by wearing a veil.

I sat and waited.

Jo practically bounced with excitement. She had changed the meadow to a cityscape and turned out the lights so she could practice hoping from shadow to shadow in back alleys. Just in case something happened to me and she needed to take over and get us out of trouble.

"I'm the smallest and could more easily hide in the shadows," Marge stated. "Shouldn't I be the one to take over tonight if needed?"

Now that was an interesting question. Sally and I did have differing physical traits that could be detected by those closest to us. Would Marge be small if she took the helm? Neither she nor Jo had ever taken control. They didn't really know how and we considered letting them try but decided against it.

The hours passed. I knew that the first shift was coming to an end. The guards would be their most distracted and tired. Now was my chance before fresh eyes and ears arrived. I made it outside, after almost being caught twice. I cursed the swish of my skirts, which sounded deafening to my own ears.

I did not wish to walk the whole way, so I took alleyways to a more populated late-night area and hailed a hansom cab. I had him take me to the outskirts of Chinatown. I needed to travel unencumbered and a bit more incognito than the attention a cab like this would get in a place where most were on foot. I had been places seedier than this at night, but never on my own.

I walked with my head down, keeping my face in shadow, all the while trying to look for danger in all directions. I didn't know where we were going nor what we were looking for. Then I saw her. It was hard to tell Chinamen from Chinese women, so alike was their dress, but there was no mistaking the small delicately balanced steps of a woman with bound feet.

She was some distance ahead of me. She turned a corner and I hurried to catch up with her. I caught sight of her back as she turned yet another corner. I sped up my pace. I almost missed her as she turned into an open doorway. I went to follow her and was met by a middle-aged Chinaman. He stopped me and shook his head and hands back and forth saying, "No, no, no. Go back." The door behind him clicked closed and I knew where she'd gone.

I argued as best I could. The strange smoke wafting from the closed door at his back told me this was an opium den, or joint as they called them at the time. Many Victorian ladies such as myself would rail against the immoral behavior in such a place and the owner feared I was there to make trouble by talking reform. I wasn't interested in reform. Opium was used by women in my station quite often, though usually in a tincture to be ingested. As soon as I knew what this place had to offer, I was as interested in experiencing it for what it was intended as I was in finding the woman.

I gestured that I wanted to smoke and jingled my coin purse. His demeanor softened. He attempted to direct me to the door opposite the one she had gone through. "No," I said and pointed.

"Better," he said and went to the other door. When he opened it to show me the lavishness, I could see it was filled by the rich white upper class that probably made up my neighbors in the rented house. I dashed to the other door. I went through. The smoke here was thick. Some was tobacco and the rest was not. A white man stopped me. He was older. I knew instantly that he was the true owner of the establishment. Part of me was outraged. Men like him were getting rich while Chinese suffered under fear of the "Yellow Peril" disguised as an anti-drug campaign.

I punched him in the face.

I don't know why; it just felt right.

I stepped over his unconscious form. This room was smaller, much less populated and less opulently decorated. The items decorating the walls felt more genuinely Chinese. I knew the few people indulging here were enjoying a rare luxury, rather than the addiction of the other, more white, room. I found the woman with lotus feet at the back of the room, lounging on a knee-high bamboo mat. She looked up at me with euphoric eyes and a smile. She tried to offer me her pipe but her arms worked as well as jelly.

"Join her?" asked the attendant.

Taking the pipe from her limp arm, I laid down beside her and handed it to the celestial that followed me. He filled it with new powdered opium and checked the gas lamp in front of us. It burned. He showed me how to hold the pipe above the ornate lamp.

I smoked.

Opium tends to nauseate, so a lot of vomiting was involved. I will skip that part. Euphoria. That is the only word to describe those first few seconds, vomit be damned. I floated, flying. Happiness and joy were all I knew. Calm. I was relaxed and happy. Pain was no more. The others fell asleep. I was alone for the first time in my life. My limbs were weightless.

I dreamed.

Climbing.

Climbing a hill.

Climbing a mountain, hands and feet.

Crawling up, up, up the mountain.

To my left crawled a golden Chinese dragon.

Her mountain matched my own. Each meter I climbed, a new meter appeared above me. The ground rose with every step. I watched her climb. The rocks beneath her feet tumbled down. The thuds were more fleshy than rocky. I continued to climb. Heads rolled. Tiny heads. The mountain was made of babies. The bones and bodies of children, baby humans and baby dragons.

I realized that no matter how fast I climbed, the mountain would grow to meet me. To go further, more babes would perish. I made a decision. I jumped from my own mountain to the dragon's. Looking down I could see her mountain started so far below my own. She'd been climbing for ages. She would climb until the end of time. Reaching up, I grabbed her by the jaw. We fell. I tore off her head; it laughed at me the whole way down.

I smoked more. I had never felt so relaxed. No worries clouded my mind. Cool water flowed down my throat when I thirsted. Warm broth filled my belly when I hungered. I lay with the woman with bound feet. I traveled the world on wings of a dragon.

I woke to a fight around me. Reaching for a pipe and new light, I said, "Do not bicker." I took a puff. Paetus picked me up, chuckling. I was liquid in his arms. People talked around me. I knew them but did not recognize them. I knew there was a carriage ride. I spoke highly of my hosts and left as much money as I could.

∽

Steaming water poured over my head, washing away the soap and hopefully the body odor I had accumulated while chasing the dragon. Paetus and Ed updated me from the other side of the room. A folding screen kept my bath hidden and if the arrangement was shocking to the girl they'd brought in to assist me, she hid it well.

"Finding you was no mean feat," said Ed. "The men all thought an Incola was involved, so we visited every major family in town. We did our best not to give away the fact that you were missing. Paetus used his gift so that we could get through them all in a timely manner."

"We had a chat with the Oriental interpreter then," Paetus interjected. "He knew nothing, just droned on and on about the book you'd had him read."

"The note had no to nor from; only the words She Lives to Destroy. He told us it was a title."

"Sound like anyone we know,? Paetus muttered under his breath.

I could hear the reproach in Ed's voice. "Neither seemed to have any clues as to where you might have been taken." I wondered if Ed's mechanical eyes saw the cloth screen as solid or no encumbrance whatsoever. I sank down deeper into the warm water scented by floating rose petals until nothing below my chin lay above the waterline.

"I wasn't taken," I said.

"We had much more luck after we quit operating under the assumption that an Incola had absconded with you," Paetus said. "We checked all of the gin joints and whore houses. Then we tried the mahjong parlors. Those places are well hidden. Threats did nothing to the Oriental."

"Money talks in any language, but still none of them knew where you were. We watched the neighborhoods and caught a break when we followed a wealthy looking woman into an opium joint."

"It seemed the perfect progression from alcohol and fallen women to gambling and opium. But none of the well-dressed women in that or any other joint we could find had seen you."

"The problem was that at each establishment we asked where a wealthy peeress would partake. Each time they took us in the opposite direction as we needed. It wasn't until we watched a celestial woman go in another entrance, that we realized there are two sides to every joint. We went back and searched the other side and found you."

"It took us four days."

Sally sat up at that statement. "Where is Dawn?" she asked them.

There was a pause, a moment of silence, as if neither wanted to answer. It must be bad news. In the end it was Paetus who spoke. "We've lost her."

∽

After dismissing the girl, Ed, and Paetus, I sat at the mirror in my bathing gown, allowing it to absorb the bath water while I combed out my long blond hair. It had always been a vanity of mine. Short hair was the sign of insanity, as no woman would ever voluntarily give up her locks.

As soon as the thought crossed my mind, Jo ran with it. She altered her appearance by severing hers right below the ear. She laughed, running to and fro in our meadow, enjoying the light and loose feeling. Jo had always despised brushing our hair. She complained every time of the feel of tearing knots and the sound of ripping strands.

We, the others and I, spoke about our opium experience. We had all come out with a revelation of sorts. We had only one body and mind so a drug of that type would affect us all. I hadn't expected that they would each have a different experience.

Jo dreamed of power like she had in our mind, but more godlike. The power over others. She still never wished to be out in the world. The opium fog let a secret longing out. She wanted what Dawn had. Jo longed to rule over people here in our mind. She hoped to pull people in. Even as I had been repulsed by Dawn's mental tenebrae, Jo had been drawn.

Effie dreamed of love, in general and specifically. Hers was one of being reunited with Julian, Leon, Robbie, even Theodore. My nephew was near her age; it did not seem strange that she would have an attraction to him. The feeling of seeing them again for the first time left her intoxicated. What exchange of lovely words would set her heart to flutter? How would her body react to the embrace of each? How would each feel pressed against her? She cut off her descriptions then, like any respectable Victorian lady.

Mary Martha dreamed of laughing children, protecting her family, savoring their innocence. She wished for something that she'd never had. She was homesick for a time and place that never existed. We had never been a happy, normal family. My children's laughter was not a thing to seek but to fear.

Marge dreamed of space. She floated, weightless, watching the stars flicker and flash. She watched clusters and constellations float past. Galaxies collided and fought in the darkness and she just swam by, enjoying the light shows. They never knew that they danced for her, the center of everything.

And Sally. She thought only of being whole, of pulling us all and somehow corseting us together. It was more complicated than just us being one again. She wanted us all to have our own place, our own control as an individual but as part of a greater whole. What she had seen in her mind made no sense to me. She longed not for something that had not only never existed but that never could exist. How wrong I was. She had dreamed of their final fate, in an almost prophetic manner.

Now that the haze had lifted, I knew my dream had been one of Xia. She was the yellow dragon, the Yellow Empress. If I stayed on my path, desperately trying to keep up with her, people on both sides would be stepped on, crushed, and destroyed. I had to find her path and join it to gain access to her, in order to stop it all. It was too philosophical to be helpful in the physical world. I didn't know who she was or where to find her or how to join her path and destroy her destiny.

Brushing my hair had become automatic while we met. Now that it was thoroughly untangled, I braided it for night to keep it from re-knotting itself during sleep. I knew I would not be able to sleep. Since hearing that Dawn was once again missing, I had been excited, wound up. Sally worried, but not I.

"Of course you're excited, Ramillia," Marge said. "It means more adventure."

Mary Martha praised our daughter. "Dawn has given you what you always wanted."

It was true that this had been a great adventure. I'd never been more free. So much of the world had been too dangerous for me before. The Incola were no danger to me, the living weapon, Lady Pestis. Dawn being kidnapped and now disappearing had given me the excuse I needed to travel the world. I could see every place, have every experience.

A knock at my door interrupted my thoughts. "A letter has come for you," came a familiar voice from the other side.

"Bring it in, Auley. I am decent."

While I was covered, I was far from what would be considered decent at the time. The door opened and he came through, careful to only open it wide enough for his entrance and not enough that any other might see inside. Even so, I stayed facing away and watched in the mirror as he deposited the letter on a bureau.

"Thank you," I said as he made his exit.

The letter looked official and the letterhead told me it was from my family's solicitor. The lawyer, whom I did not recognize, wrote to inform me that my father's older sister, his only sibling, had passed away two weeks prior. She had no children of her own and had been preceded in death by her husband some years ago. I had never known her but may have met her on an occasion or two as a child. She had left everything to me. The law meant that fortunes passed from father to son so my father had gotten everything long ago. My aunt had little to leave. She had married for love but married well enough. Her husband used her dowry to buy them a small estate. An estate that would now be mine if only the state had not confiscated it. The lawyer had managed to keep a small chest of family memorabilia and would store it for me until such a time when I could retrieve it, if I should so desire to take the risk of reentering Britain.

"When did she die?" asked Marge.

I told them the date. Sally and Marge firmed in my mind. A thought had occurred to them both. "Why?" I asked as I met them in our meadow.

Effie and Mary Martha scrambled, trying to understand. "What date were you born, Marge?"

It had been the same as my aunt's death. "Coincidence?" Marge asked.

I asked each of them when they had been born and discovered they all coincided with the death of a family member of mine. My mother had died in childbirth, my own. Sally had been here with me since birth. Jo had been born when father died. Effie, around the time Julian had walked my brother, Thaddeus, to the gallows. Mary Martha's appearance could have been the result of my son's death. And now my aunt led to Marge.

These were my closest genetic relatives. Not just someone close to me, for no one had been born at the death of my father's wife, whom I thought was my mother but was not. I remembered the woman with bound feet's words, *How many death you carry inside? No. Not husbands. They not family.* Could she have known? Could she have been asking how many *others* I carried?

Everything clicked into place. Not only were my others' births linked to the time of those deaths, but they each had a connection to the emotion I felt most strongly at the time. Jo was strong and free and in control. Effie was love, lust, and devotion to my husbands. Mary Martha was motherly rage and protection. Marge was small and insignificant but also the center of her universe.

Sally, born at my own birth, had told me when first we met that the pain was hers. She lived in the pain. There was nothing more jarring and painful than birth. This all might mean something else. I rushed to the top, away from the meadow where they could all hear my thoughts. Sally could always hear me and it was in her I confided.

I now knew how the others came to the front. I knew how they could escape. It was a secret I needed to keep from them as long as possible. Only Sally could help me do that.

8

The familiar squeak of the mews door closing above filled me with dread. Not the normal level of anxiety that normally accompanied the impending loss of Sally. This was something more. I worried about Dawn. True, I did not feel about her as I once had, but I had promised to protect her and I was failing. Sally shushed me, assuring me that everything would be all right. Then she was gone.

Normally the others kept quiet when Sally left. A healthy sense of self-preservation in action. *This* time they started screaming at me. All of them. Talking at once. This was not smart on their part. In my rage at having lost Sally, I turned on them. I knew in that moment that I could just kill them all. I would. Kill. Them. All.

In our mental meadow, they jumped and yelled at me. I couldn't make sense of anything they said. I didn't want to. I had a single focus: murder. In an instant I had them bound and gagged. Jo, Effie, and Marge stared at me, panic in their eyes, their words mumbled behind the gags but they never stopped trying to tell me something.

"Mary Martha!" I roared. "Where are you?" I reached out and tried to grip her as I had the others. I had all the power here. They never should have spoken to me without Sally to protect them. But I could not find her, could not grab her. I spun on the three I did have. "How is she evading me?" I demanded of them. "You think to ambush me in my own mind!"

I removed Effie's gag so that she might answer. "That's what we were trying to tell you. Mary Martha is gone. She followed Sally. Mary Martha escaped!"

Their bonds fell away. I flew to the front, leaving them to lick their wounds. Seeing through Sally's eyes as she rode came simply. She was looking through Dawn's eyes. Dawn seemed to be looking down into a pail with an inch of soup at the bottom. I moved on. Sally could explain when she got back.

I tried. The mechanics of seeing through an other's eyes were unknown to me. Once I made it to Mary Martha, I still had no idea how. At first I didn't think I'd done it because I couldn't see anything. Then I realized that there was nothing to see. Mary Martha was floating in warm darkness. The relaxing effects were soon interrupted by a violent jostling. Then quiet. Then convulsions again. Had Dawn found Mary Martha? Was this some new kind of torture?

When Sally came back to us, I pounced. "You have to go get her! Mary Martha followed you into Dawn."

Sally soothed me and we talked where the others could not hear. She could tell them later. "I cannot get Mary Martha. She is trapped. Dawn is traveling by ship again. I couldn't find any information about her heading because she kept vomiting."

I nodded. "Choppy seas can make even the most experienced sailor lose his lunch. Why would that ensnare Mary Martha?"

"It is more than that. Our daughter is with child and that child's undeveloped mind is where Mary Martha is trapped."

∽

We needed to go after them but I was in no condition for travel. My mind raced. I hadn't needed Mary Martha until she'd been born. Now that she was part of me, living without her was chaotic. The meadow ripped itself apart and reformed in the strangest of ways. Mary Martha wasn't just born of my motherly rage and need to protect. She contained the sum of those feelings. Without her I had none.

Sally worried about Dawn, wanted to help ease her suffering and protect her.

I cared not.

What I did care about was that the others didn't figure out how Mary Martha had escaped. I could not do without my emotions of love, lust, freedom, power, hubris, and humility. I kept them so busy with the tasks of righting the meadow's wrongs that they had no time to consider the how of what she'd done.

Then Sally decided that she must ride Dawn again. She did not ask nor allow me to prepare. She took over while I was distracted, walked me to the mews, and put us inside. She left before I realized what was happening.

The others, showing high intelligence, kept quiet. I might not have motherly rage but murderous rage was still mine to call when needed. All I was feeling at the time was betrayal. Sally chose Dawn's well-being over my own.

I watched through Sally's eyes as she cautiously approached the tenebrae. It was relatively quiet, meaning Dawn and Eve' were otherwise disposed and not actively torturing. When Sally entered, the scene was shocking. Ambrose, Leon, and Archelaos sat around a table eating a feast as quietly as possible. Dawn, looking lovely and more mature than I had ever seen her, fluttered around them, tending their wounds.

Leon sensed Sally's presence first. With a finger to his lips, he gestured that she should join them. I hoped Sally knew better than to eat anything. The food could be a way of trapping her, like that used by the Fae of myth. He spoke in a hushed tone, little more than a whisper. "This is Ilene. She is Dawn's…" He paused, clearly searching for the right word.

Ilene was Dawn's other. It made sense. I got Marge when my aunt died. Dawn got Ilene. I wondered what Dawn had been feeling at the time of Ilene's birth. What emotion was she?

Ilene answered without Sally speaking, finishing Leon's sentence. "Happiness. I am Dawn's happiness." She came around the table, arms spread to hug. Once clear of the men, we could see her fully. Her belly was swollen in a way that meant one thing. Ilene was with child, or at least appeared pregnant. Sally shied away and Ilene dropped her arms but not her smile. "Ilene means bright shining light or pleasant light."

Leon assured Sally, "It is safe. Not a trick, not unless the setup has been an elaborate one."

Ambrose, who still looked every bit the giant gray monster, sounded small. "Ilene brings me sweets." He said something after that too but it was muffled behind the fistful of tart he shoved in his face.

Archelaos added, "She is kind and would never betray us to Dawn. She can't or Dawn would know about her."

Sally took a breath. "Where are they?"

The men did not know. Ilene spoke and her voice portrayed everything good and beautiful in Dawn. If Dawn could harness this other, she could rule the world. Even I was drawn to her, felt the need to be kind to her. Combined with Dawn's gift of touch, she could become unstoppable. "Our pregnancy is advancing." She rubbed her tummy. "Since boarding the ship, those two have been busy, distracted. Dawn is sick most of the time."

"Too sick to come hurt us very often," Ambrose said between bites.

"Morning sickness will pass," said Sally.

The men and Ilene froze. Only Ambrose kept eating. What were we missing, I wondered. "It is more than that," Ilene said, her smile didn't disappear but did seem dimmed somehow. "Come, I can show you."

Traveling through the mind of another is difficult to describe. Sally and Ilene passed through different parts in different ways. Sometimes they passed through memories, posing as characters in the back of the scene. Other times Ilene stepped into Dawn's role as they passed. At one point they were but sparks of electricity traveling on a path from one fire to the next. It looked very much like Marge's opium dream.

Sally must have felt what they were approaching; she attempted to stop them but they only stopped when Ilene decided. The darkness loomed before them, larger now than it had been when Sally first discovered it.

"What is it?"

Ilene answered, "A tumor."

One of Dawn's memories from the time she lived in the house of ill repute with women of the night, quite fuzzy and generalized as it was from a time when Dawn was very young indeed, stretched. The timing elongated. The very edge of the memory curled around itself and hooked the darkness. The tumor slurped it up like soup. It disappeared in the darkness.

"We lose some every day, more each day as it grows. It eats more the bigger it gets and the bigger it gets the more it eats."

Sally pulled Ilene. They traveled back to the tenebrae. "Why does she not heal herself?" she asked.

"Quite simply, she does not know how," answered Archelaos.

"How can that be? She has been healing herself her whole life."

Sally had to be right. She'd healed her skin, surely. We would have heard of a walking nightmare vision of a girl without skin crossing the country.

The three men continued to eat. Ambrose shrugged his giant shoulders in a very childish gesture. Archelaos placed his utensils beside his plate. He laid his hands in his lap and spoke in a firm but knowledgeable manner. I recognized it as his teaching voice. "Our bodies are born with a certain amount of natural healing ability. It is almost impossible to kill us. But to become truly immortal, we must stop or even reverse aging. We must actively heal, not just passively. That is what she would need to learn."

"Why doesn't her body heal the tumor?"

"Every surgeon knows that children do not get cancer. Tumors are part of aging."

"But Dawn is a child!"

"No, she is an Incola who has trapped another three Incolas in her mind, two of which are ancient."

"You have to teach her how to heal herself," she said to Archelaos. When he rode and lived as Julian, Archelaos had been the one to teach me. I remembered the moment. Such power. I could be hurt but there was little I could not recover from. I would never have to age if I did not wish to.

"Absolutely not," was his answer.

"She is dying," Sally argued. Ilene had gone back to applying unguent to my son's back.

"We know. Ilene told us when she arrived." Archelaos stood and opened his shirt. The damage to his chest spoke volumes. The flesh was gone. Heartbeat was apparent behind exposed ribs. "She will never stop. We cannot die if she does not. I thought I wanted to live forever in any circumstance. This is too horrific for me to ever have imagined."

Ilene ran her hands over his chest, millimeters from touching it. An ultra-thin layer of flesh appeared. He visibly relaxed, sat, and began to eat again. The food, I realized then, was not physical. It was mental, magical. It comforted them, eased their suffering.

I knew that Sally was thinking that she—we—could help Dawn. We could teach her, mentor her, ease her suffering. I wasn't so sure. I had my own need for violence, my own desire to maim and kill. I pushed the thought away before that seed became a full-grown tree.

Archelaos didn't look at Sally again. As far as he was concerned the conversation was over. I remember that face from my years of marriage to him.

"She'll die!" Sally pleaded. No reaction from my first husband. My second was not as sure. Sally saw the softness in his expression and switched her focus. "Please. Our daughter needs us. She cannot be unredeemable. Not so young."

Leon had stopped eating. He stared at Sally's face. "You look so like Ramillia."

"Please," was all she said.

His chest expanded with a deep breath. He whispered, "I never could say no to her."

"Don't. Please teach Dawn to heal herself. We will figure out a way to free you."

"No." I said it at the same time as Ambrose and Archelaos.

"Teach Ilene." Sally hit on the solution. Dawn did not know of Ilene. She did not have access to the other's memories and knowledge. I did not want Dawn to have the secret to immortality. Sally did not want her to die so young. This was the compromise. I wondered why Sally did not teach her herself. Surely she had access to that, my memory. I had an epiphany. I had access to my others' memories and knowledge. They did not know everything I did. I could have secrets. I vowed to teach Sally. It might be necessary for survival. I could be unconscious; she would be our only salvation.

In the end Leon was convinced to try. I will not relay the method. Perhaps there are some of you who will ferret out the steps from within these pages but I will not hand them over to you freely.

Ilene learned and immediately went to the tumor. Sally followed. I had never been without Sally for this long. I began to feel…good. Before, I felt the loss of Sally would allow me to kill without feeling. Now I knew life without Sally meant life without pain. She took my ability to feel pain with her when she went. I breathed that in. It was a freedom I had not dreamed of. I pushed it away. It was a dangerous train of thought.

The tumor pulsed at their approach. It responded to Sally and Ilene in the same measure but in vastly different manners. It hated Sally. I felt certain, if given the chance, it would lash out at and destroy her. Ilene, it loved. She reached out to work the Incola magic. Magic is the wrong word. Medicine, maybe. We were not supernatural beings. We were completely natural, just an unknown nature.

Time moved strangely here on the edge of that darkness. Now I know it behaved much as time does on the horizon of a black hole. Then, we could only observe and try not to be lost. A memory came from behind them. It stretched. I recognized the moment, though it took on a rosier hue here than it had in my own memory. We were in my parlor. Leon had said something kind and Dawn sat perched on his lap. Something inside me had snapped and Sally had screamed at him to get his hands off of her. Here in this memory, the moment before we freaked out expanded.

Dawn stared into Leon's eyes. She was happy.

Ilene was Dawn's happiness.

Even as it happened, we could do nothing. The memory swept over them and past them. The darkness swallowed the memory and because it was a happy one, Ilene was sucked away and swallowed with it. One second she was there and the next she was not.

In the memory, Sally and I were on the outskirts. It had been Dawn's memory so she was the center. We were still on the outside but for a second, Sally got stuck in the version of us in that memory. I began to scream. Sally elongated and I thought that was the end. Just a fraction of a millimeter before she hit the darkness, Sally snapped back to us.

My relief was so overwhelming that I almost did not feel that of the others. I needed my pain. What painting would be as beautiful, as impactful, as realistic, without its shadow? The others needed Sally, for without her, they would have no protection from my baser instincts. I was not myself without Sally. I could not believe I had entertained such a thought for even a moment during her absence.

A loud banging filled my ears. I was pounding the mews from inside. When I stopped it went silent. The deprivation tank did its job well even after my abuse. The method of releasing the latch and opening the lid came back to me when Sally returned. As I opened it I wondered, if the tumor had devoured Sally, would I have been trapped inside until someone on the outside opened it?

It took a moment for my eyes to adjust to the sudden light. When they did, I could see that Paetus and Ed waited patiently. Ed handed me the Julian skin gloves, which I put on before Paetus offered me both his hand and help out of the mews. I normally struggled in quite an unladylike fashion and got out of the mews alone without aid. The men had been instructed to steer clear of the mews while in use. It sat in one of the underused front rooms of my rented home. "What's wrong?" I asked, straightening my skirts. The mews gets warm when all closed, even if the weather is cold. Here inside the windless heated space of a fine New York house, it got downright hot. Ed handed me a small hand towel to wipe my dripping sweat.

"The Pope is here," was Paetus' reply.

A moment of panic arose that I hid behind cleaning up my face and neck. The most powerful and well-connected Incola in the known world was here. How? Why? The first I learned of his existence was when he had sent his cardinals to collect what he called tithe. He wanted ten percent of my Carriers, as he took from all Incola. We fought hard to keep knowledge of Dawn from him. He wanted a relative of mine. Any would do.

It seems he got what he wanted. The only person seated in my parlor was Theodore. He lounged in his seat, somehow making it look like a throne and he, a bored prince. He played with the crucifix at his neck.

He did not stand at my entrance. Paetus made a move to go around me, presumably to teach the man some manners. I held my arm out, blocking him. I must be seen as strong in my own right. I dismissed my men and crossed to the Pope riding Theodore.

He held out his hand, presumably for me to kiss the proverbial ring.

I slapped his hand away.

He laughed.

"You are in my seat," I said. It was not my favorite chair but I attempted a power move to assert my dominance.

"Of course," he said. "My apologies." His voice was Theodore's but his accent was something else. I would call it an Italian accent but it was older, thicker. Perhaps this was how a Latin accent sounded. He stood and moved to a footstool near the chair. It seemed a submissive move but was just the opposite. He intended to stay very close to me and now I had to sit in the seat I forced him to vacate.

I sat, acting as if it was what I wanted. I did not offer him my hand but asked abruptly, "What do you want?"

He took my rudeness in stride. He smoothed his hands down my nephew's chest. "He is very fine indeed. Usually I prefer my tithe younger. I will require a female offspring eventually but he will do for now. I know you killed my cardinals and hope you know there is no animosity on my part because of it. I would never harm him, just as I do not want to harm you. You are far too precious as the only living female Incola." Again he idly fingered his crucifix.

Then he did not know about Dawn nor Xia. Not knowing about the existence of my daughter was understandable as she was a young person yet to make her mark on the world. How could the Pope be ignorant of one as old as Xia? Either she was very good at hiding or he was not as all-knowing as he thought.

Without warning I yanked the crucifix from his neck, breaking the delicate chain, and tossed it into the fire. Again he laughed. I had hoped that was his method of riding and removing it would sever his connection. I should have known it would not be that easy.

"Value aside, simply put, my lady, I will have my tithe. You will pay me. Or…"

"Or what? *Or else!*"

"No. I do not resort to threats. There is no need. I was merely going to offer you a simple alternative to war you cannot win that might cost you everything. All you would have to do is take communion and I would relinquish my claim on your tithe. Of course I would insist on watching."

Pervert! Marge declared.

It could be worse, said Effie.

Men are gross, Jo added.

Then, in that moment, Sally and I saw the whole picture. Communion was the Pope's method of riding. It was how he'd acquired Theodore. I could not accept his request because it would be a surrender. Theodore had accepted, and now was the Pope's Carrier. Family now was the ultimate danger and through my family Incola could always get to me.

Perhaps I was stronger than before. Theodore's head seemed more easily removed from his shoulders than with my other kills. His body tilted and fell to one side, legs up in the air at an odd angle as they were still resting on the footstool. The position meant that the last few pumps of his heart pushed the majority of his blood out of his stump of a neck, instantly ruining the lovely rug of this room. I would add a generous amount to the owner in the payment of my bill.

"Why did you do that?" Effie screamed at me out loud.

In her rage, I remembered her attraction to our nephew. Or was that my attraction? I explained, "Anyone related to us is immune to the illness. Theodore would be an Incola for as long as he lived. And, as you can see," I gestured to the corpse, "He was susceptible to more powerful Incola."

"No, Ramillia," said Marge. "She means why did you do *that*?"

I looked inside myself at what Marge pointed to. There inside our meadow sat, or should I say huddled, a new other. Her knees tucked under her chin, arms wrapped around her shins, she made herself as small as possible. Wide panicked eyes looked to each of our faces in rapid succession. Sally attempted to soothe her, but any touch set her to screaming. Sally backed away and a cave appeared behind the new other, who quickly backed into it, disappearing into darkness.

"Thank you, Jo," said Sally. She looked at me and I knew what she thought because I was thinking the same thing. What on earth had I been feeling or thinking at the time of this other's birth to produce such a damaged reflection? Then I remembered. Paranoia. Fear of my family. How incredibly unfortunate timing for her birth.

They all heard my thoughts and spoke at once.

"Unfortunate!"

"You alone decided the timing."

"How could you be so careless!"

I had done this; I made an other by killing my nephew and I had not even considered the consequences. The method of making others I had suspected but when the time came I did not hesitate. All of my others suffered under the cloak of whatever emotion I felt at their birth but this one would live in fear and paranoia our whole life.

In that moment of guilt, the situation worsened. Mary Martha slammed back into our mind and she did not come alone. The meadow shrank. The eight of us stood in a small cube, pressed together, on top of each other. The vistas of our meadow had become hanging painted backdrops on four sides of a tiny stage. I could feel a tightness on every part of me, even those parts which did not touch the others. The paranoid other started screaming. This was too much to bear. Jo began to struggle for freedom. Effie cried. Mary Martha hyperventilated. I picked up Marge and put her on my shoulder to keep her from being trampled. The newest other apologized with her last breath. I looked right at the screaming one, whose name came to me, and said, "Stop it, Dierdre. We are not family. We are you. We won't hurt you. There is no danger here."

She stopped. Effie and Marge looked at each other. I could feel them thinking of Mary Martha's exit and my murderous rage. I told them to stop. They did.

Sally had the idea that saved us. "Imagine yourselves as very small. There is still plenty of room for us all but we must make use of that space. We are tiny. Minuscule ants on the savanna."

It took some time to achieve but slowly the backdrop of painted meadow backed away. The space we had to stand increased. Our breathing became less labored. I set Marge down on the ground. They stood in a circle around me. Sally, Jo, Effie, Mary Martha, Marge, Deirdre, and the newest other, who continued to apologize. "I did this. It is all my fault. I am so sorry. I would take it back if I could but I can't."

"You can stop apologizing," Sally told her.

This newest addition to my emotional menagerie was my guilt.

"What is your name?" asked Effie.

"I think it is Ruth."

"You *think*?" Jo asked rudely. Effie nudged Jo, who defended herself. "What? Who doesn't know her own name?"

Ruth answered, "I've never thought about it. I guess I've never thought about anything. How can that be? I am so sorry. I'm not making any sense. I feel like my name is Ruth but I also feel like everything I know is wrong. My apologies."

Then Marge asked a question that shattered the moment. "If Dierdre was born when Ramillia killed Theodore, who died to make you?"

Sally spouted a string of expletives and flew off.

Except, she did not fly off. The sky opened up just as it always does when one of us wants to go to the front. She fell up but it was so incredibly slow that in the time it normally took for her to disappear, she'd barely moved a meter. "Dawn!" she screamed.

If Dawn was dying, Sally would never make it at this speed but then again, we knew that time passed differently in this place. Perhaps we had plenty of time. I did not want Sally to ride Dawn again. I feared what our daughter's mind might do to her.

Dierdre rose to follow Sally. She felt my fear and paranoia and was going to do something about it. Whatever she did was my fault; the blood would be on my hands. With that feeling of guilt, Ruth began to rise as well. I turned to Mary Martha. The look on her face told me everything. She hadn't known how she escaped before, just as Effie was not quite sure how she had done it. Now, watching it happen in slow motion, feeling me cycle through the emotions that triggered a switch, she knew. Mary Martha was a prisoner here no longer.

Mary Martha pushed her core emotion right into me. Dierdre feared Dawn. Scared people were dangerous. Deirdre might hurt or kill our daughter preemptively.

Mary Martha succeeded. She rose to follow them and I to follow her. Marge grabbed Effie and Jo by the hands and pulled them. "They're not leaving us here. Come on!" I felt a quick sequence of emotions and all eight of us were on the chase.

Quickly I changed the gravity in this place. We all shot off to the west while Sally was affected the least as she was further ahead than the rest of us. Then I opened up a new hole, a new path, one that was much closer to Sally. I might not agree with her all the time but I trusted her above all the others.

A flash through the emotions and again, the race positions changed. The others were getting better at manipulating me for their own advantage. We had accidentally set up the perfect practice laboratory for them. I did not know how to stop this outcome so I continued to try to give Sally the advantage.

This battle dance continued until Sally reached the front. She immediately left for Dawn's mind. I got to the helm shortly after and felt Dierdre slip by me and follow Sally's path. The others were locked back in the meadow. I puffed myself up so that there was only room for me at the front. With two gone, the balance returned and the meadow worked as it always had. I was careful to remain emotionally blank.

Not using my own eyes to observe where our body lay, I looked through Sally's eyes. Dierdre and Sally continued to struggle along the path to Dawn. The paranoid other tore and tried to destroy the path. Sally screamed at her, "No, fool! You'll trap us there!" When they popped into Dawn's mind, they could not act covertly. They burst onto the scene in a tumble of petticoats and nails. But what they saw froze them.

Dawn's "Sorrow" sat in a field of memories, growing on an electric vine. We did not know her name but we knew she was Dawn's sadness. She had been born at the death of our granddaughter. All around her were our daughter's memories. Even the ones I recognized as happy times were blanketed by sorrow that stained them blue and cold.

I could feel the motivations of no other that left our mind. I could not hear Sally's thoughts. She grabbed Sorrow's hand and pulled her away. Dierdre stayed behind while my vision went with Sally. She took Sorrow to the tumor. As soon as I saw the location, I knew what she intended to do.

Sorrow seemed mesmerized by the darkness. It was a home that called to her. She went to it, reaching out, tears streaming down her lovely face the whole time. Sally had the opposite reaction. That darkness repulsed us, pushed us away. She stayed as far as possible. Sorrow reached the barrier of the tumor and looked back. Sally nodded to her that it would be fine.

Sorrow stepped into the tumor.

Something was changing. Sally tried to get back to Dierdre but the mind of our daughter had become scrambled. A maze. Like the work of M.C. Escher that would become popular much later. Pathways circled around and ended where they began, led up and down at the same time.

Just as true panic began to set in at the idea that Sally might be trapped, she tumbled into the memory garden where Dierdre stood. "What did you do?" Sally whispered.

Dierdre pointed toward herself. "What did, what did I do? What did *you* do?" Her hand moved from her own chest and gestured out to the memories. When Sally looked at them, I could observe their evolution.

The blue had been stripped away. What was left were pale versions of the original memories. The events of Dawn's life thus far were mainly black and white and shades of gray. Here and there in the distance shades in the yellow range flashed along with a color that had no name, no equivalent in the real world.

We had been wrong in our first interpretation. The memories hadn't been blanketed by sadness, masked by sorrow. The rosiness had drained from all of them, leaving everything a bluish tone. Ilene was gone, devoured by the darkness. She was Dawn's happiness and without her even Dawn's memories had had their happy hue removed. Now, with Sorrow gone as well, the layers of sadness and blue had leached away.

Dierdre said, "So you killed Dawn's melancholy after watching her elation die? What have you left her with?" She pointed angrily at the yellow. "Anger and confusion is all!" Her voice rose in both volume and pitch. "Whatever danger she was to us before is increased tenfold! She has nothing to temper her. She is made of rage! It is all she has left! What do you think will happen when the next other is born? Then she will have nothing but insanity!"

Dierdre's tantrum caught Eve's attention. "How did you get here?" Dawn's other shouted.

Sally grabbed Dierdre and pushed her back to us. I waited for the shrinking of the meadow but it never came. The all over tightness returned. It was uncomfortable, like an unreachable itch, but Victorian ladies are taught to present a certain facade no matter our discomfort. I felt it was something I could live with.

I turned my attention back to Sally. Through her eyes I could see that she and Eve' fought. A better description would be to say that Eve' attempted to hold Sally but could not. Sally did not attempt her own blows, and merely evaded Eve's attempts. Eve' continued to scream about the place where Sally belonged. They had a special place for intruders like her. Eve' yelled for Dawn to no avail. When Sally easily escaped every hold Eve' tried and Dawn never came, Eve' broke down. She said she hoped a threat like this would snap Dawn out of it but she wouldn't even save herself.

Sally assured her, "I am no threat to Dawn."

"You are. You have to be," said Eve'. "It feels wrong to have you here."

"That is only because you are fighting me," Sally pressed her luck. "Accept me." Before Eve' could argue, Sally continued, "Dawn never could accept a rider but you are her strength. If you can do this, I will bring Dawn to you."

"Swear on whatever you find holy that you won't hurt Dawn."

"I swear, as a mother, from one other to an other, I will never knowingly hurt Dawn. I will always protect her. I will give my life to save her if needed."

Even I could sense the truth of those words. Eve' tried to relax. Sally wasted no time. She marched straight to the front and brought tiny Dawn back in her arms to Eve'. As she handed her daughter over, she said, "You tend to her here. I will go and tend to your body."

Then she was at the front and we could see through Dawn's eyes. In fact we had possession of all of her senses. The room aboard the ship reeked of old blood and other bodily fluids. Rats had unabashedly taken up residence in her room, feasting on a clump of placenta at the foot of Dawn's bed. The fetus, for it could not be called a baby yet, was wrapped in a cloth which was clutched by Dawn. She had protected it from the rats. Wrapped as it was, we saw only its face. So underdeveloped was it, that its eyes were on the sides of its head, ears closer to the neck than the sides of the head. The skin was mottled and almost completely transparent. It weighed next to nothing and fit in the palm of her hand. We wrapped it tightly, covering its face, and set it aside.

It was clear that she had been wallowing in her own miscarriage filth, her sorrow gone but her happiness not returned. She lived in the gray.

Sally washed as best she could in the water in the bowl and basin on a stand in the corner. When it became unusable, she stuck her head out the door, shocking some sailors resting there in the corridor, and demanded clean water and a doctor. "Tell the Captain we will need a burial at sea for my stillborn."

The doctor came and went, doing what little he could. Sally finished cleaning Dawn and had servants clean the room and change the bed linens. Then donning a dress fastened loosely without restrictive undergarments, and two shawls, she took the fetus up to the deck where the Captain waited. The burial at sea service took only a few minutes. It was night. The starry sky twinkled beautifully and the tiny white bundle disappeared within seconds.

Sally went back to her room, ordering food along the way. When the broth, bread, and cheese arrived, Sally ate every bite. Then she took the dose of laudanum the doctor left and laid down in bed. Dashing away from the front before the strong drug could take hold, she headed straight down the path to us. We noted that there were color sparks in some of the memories now and hoped the opium-based tincture we drank for Dawn would work its healing magic. Eve' watched us go.

Eve' knew where the path lay.

Dierdre began to panic.

Sally slammed into us. We breathed a collective sigh of relief.

Each of the others pressed at me. Their emotions struggled to get at me. They had learned how to gain control and get to the top but I too had learned. I kept myself emotionless, cutting my feelings off and barricading them in my memories. I did my best to build a labyrinth, a memory castle, where they would get lost in those memories that reflected their particular emotion back at them.

Except Sally. I would never trap her in the emotions where she had lived for so long in the pain. She and I met in the meadow and I held her as she wept for her daughter and lost grandchild. I did not feel the same way but I kept my thoughts to myself as best I could. I had seen Dawn's growing insanity. Her immense strength and power should not be housed by one so unstable.

Sally was consoled and sleeping.

Slowly, back up top, I opened my eyes.

9

Opening my eyes took more effort than it should have. The lights were bright and stung my vision. My throat felt dry and painfully stuck to itself when I attempted to swallow. I made little pained sounds when I tried to speak. *Water, I need water*, I tried to say. My noises and minor movements brought about a commotion around me. I could hear voices and feet running to and fro. The air smelled of chemicals but under that was the smell of sickness and death.

One arm seemed to be nonfunctional so I used the other to shield my eyes. More footsteps. Then all around me shutters closed and the dimness soothed my eyes. Someone held my head and pressed a cup of cold water to my lips. I choked and spit and it was taken away to be replaced by a cup of warm broth. This went down much more easily. I was suddenly aware that I was ravenous. I would have gulped down the whole bowl but someone removed it from my lips. An unfamiliar female voice said, "There, there. Slowly."

Looking up, her features came into focus. She spoke again, "We thought we'd lost you. The doctor will be pleased you're back." With the mention of the doctor, I saw her uniform for what it was: that of a nurse. I tried to sit up but couldn't. Looking down I could see that my arm was strapped to the gurney. Strapped. Trapped.

I was trapped in a hospital.

"No. No," I began muttering. Not again. I wouldn't live in an asylum! I struggled but strong arms held me down. Lots of arms. Men. Touching me. Nothing good would come of this. "No. No. No! No!" My objections became increasingly loud. I'd rather die. I was so weak; they must have drugged me.

Shouting filled the air around me. Someone close said my name repeatedly. I couldn't see. I couldn't move. I had to get out. I was strong and I would be free. Jo joined me up front; she took the helm. Gasps all around. Jo said, "Get your damn hands off us."

They did. Jo's arms were smaller, like they were when I was a young girl. She easily wriggled out of the straps holding our arm. A tearing feeling burned in the hollow of the inside of my arm opposite my elbow. Sitting up brought pain and Sally replaced Jo. Again the room filled with gasps.

A man's voice, somewhat familiar, said, "Get it out of her now."

That set a new panic. They were taking my baby from my womb without consent. "No! No! Do not touch her!" said Mary Martha as she roared to the front, replacing Sally. Murmuring rather than gasps followed but the effect was the same.

"Ramillia, Ramillia, it is us." Mary Martha's eyes shot to the face of the man speaking. His eyes were obstructed with some sort of goggles covered in gears. I recognized Ed. He continued talking. "Please let the nurse remove the needle from your arm. You are hurting yourself."

We looked down at my arm and saw blood. We also could see that the gown had become tousled in my struggles and more skin showed than was proper. Effie shot to the front and Mary Martha went back to the meadow. We were young and thin again and the gown could be adjusted to cover more. Now I knew what the gasping was about.

Each time an other came to the front, I physically changed. It must have been incredibly shocking. I was thankful Marge hadn't come to the rescue. I would have ended up in a circus sideshow. "Thanks a lot," she said sarcastically through my mouth. Her American accent came through.

"That is not what she meant and you know it," Effie chastised.

I pushed them back. Perhaps nudged them was a better fitting word. I gestured the nurse forward. She hesitated for a second and then came and removed the needle connected to a tube and hanging container of water. When she left I told Ed, "I cannot have hospital gossip."

He replied, "Your nurse and doctor are very rich people now. They would not do anything to jeopardize that."

Auley jumped in. "We also used more traditional threats. They know what would happen to them should the new hospital owner's secrets get around."

They had purchased the entire hospital in my name, bought my attendants' silence, and threatened their lives. "What were they doing to me?" I asked suspiciously.

Ed's face lit up. "It is a new technique. They put fluids directly into a person's veins. When you would not wake up, I offered a small fortune to any doctor who suggested a treatment to keep you alive. It worked."

"Barely," I muttered. Or maybe it was one of the others. "Wait, how long have I been…" I could not think of a more appropriate word than, "under?"

"Nearing a month now," answered Auley.

Andrew confirmed, "Since the day the Pope came to see you."

Theodore! "What about the…?" I could not bring myself to say body but they knew what I asked.

"Taken care of," was the answer.

The discussion in the meadow grew intense and required my attention. Each other had an opinion about how long we'd been unconscious, Theodore's death, owning a hospital, needles delivering liquids, and doctors taking liberties with our unconscious body. They all talked at once. "Quiet!" I yelled.

Ed pulled a chair close to my bed. "It is not just you and Sally in there anymore, is it?" He nodded to my head.

I said nothing but he looked as if I had.

"Some of us suspected as much. Is there anything we need to know?"

I liked the way he'd phrased it. He wasn't intruding. This wasn't about gossip. He asked if there was anything they *needed* to know. My men were still my men; concerned for my well-being and safety. I shook my head no.

"Do you need our help…dealing with any of them?"

I blinked at him for a moment. Every other had fallen eerily silent, as if awaiting my answer. "I often may want to kill them but no. The others hold parts of me without which I would cease to be myself."

Some of the men took me at my word. Others looked at each other and I knew they thought I was insane. It mattered not. None of them could do any harm to my others, not from out here. And I wasn't completely certain that I was fully sane either. Was that the reason for so few female Incola? I had tried to commit suicide via the legal system and my others had stopped me.

I looked around and noticed the room. It was massive, one that might be used to house hundreds of people during an epidemic, but I was the only patient. There were just as many beds as normal but they were occupied by my men. They had moved in with me, surrounding me with protection. Not all of the beds were occupied. I started to ask, "Where is everyone?" but I did not make it to the last word.

Andrew scrunched up his face in disgust. "Paetus fled. He abandoned you as soon as you fell."

At first I was angry too. Then I remembered that without me, Paetus had little protection from the men he had used so harshly as Carriers. "He had little choice. Are the rest of the men lodging elsewhere? What of Theodore's men?"

Auley spoke then, keeping his face neutral. "Theodore's men fell sick with the illness as soon as he was dead. It was more severe and many of them died."

Ed elaborated, "We believe it was because he was unaffected by it and the contagion built up in their systems. As soon as his hold on them released, the illness exploded."

"The few who survived were allowed to leave with any of our men who felt the same way."

I sat up straight at that. My arm hurt and so I favored the other. Andrew assisted me and added a pillow behind my back for support. Sally spoke to me internally but when I did not echo her thoughts, she jumped to the top. She said, "They could have families and birth new Incola. They could undo all we are trying to do."

No gasps this time. Most of the men did not notice the small differences between Sally and I. The scant centimeters difference in height was negated by our seated position. Our eye color too was a fluctuation of shade, nothing noticeable with the shutters closed as they were. The ones that did notice knew Sally and made no sign.

Ed, the most versed in medicine, explained. "We gave each man a choice. Any could leave if they so desired but would have to submit to a medical procedure that assures they never become fathers. At first only a handful chose to undergo the surgery but then the longer you were in the coma, the more men got the surgery. It helped that they could see the success stories of the men before them. They accept that they will never have families."

I shied away from thinking about what such a procedure would entail. That solution satisfied Sally. I was not so sure.

∽

Spain would be our next location and then we would go straight to Rome.

Dawn had sailed to India but these other places had ancient Incola, both of which knew of me. We needed to visit and infect before they knew the extent of my methods of freeing Carriers. Spain was closer to New York than Rome and so we went there first. Same as before, I traveled with Ed in the skyship, *Precious Lady*, and the rest of the men traveled by boat below.

We dropped down for supplies but mainly enjoyed the solitude. Ed showed me his notebooks where he jotted down ideas and sketches for inventions he'd been thinking of. We discussed them and he made little changes and I made suggestions about things I might need for our travels. It was great fun. I felt as close to Ed as I had ever felt with anyone in my life.

We had no trouble at port this time for there was no reason to quarantine the ship. We were greeted by Incola Juan's men and taken to him straight away. We dined and I pretended to entertain his marriage proposal. He showered me with gifts, even giving me a beautiful Spanish castle. He was a perfectly gracious host and had he and I been normal, well as normal as ultra-rich nobles can be, it would have been a reasonable match.

We left and headed across water for Rome before he and his men fell ill. It must seem odd to a modern person that I was able to travel faster than the news about me. This was a time before modern advancements. The world now is so much smaller than the one I was born into. Additionally, people had a tendency not to spread word of me. I killed almost as often as I left Incola alive. I believe they feared my retribution should they gossip and hinder the spread of my blight. They were right, for in the end, I have returned and killed every one, even those I loved.

Rome was as beautiful as you might imagine. Opulent, grandiose, gilded; these are the words that come to mind when remembering that place. It all paled in comparison to St. Peter's Square, St. Peter's Basilica, and the Apostolic Palace. Here there was a display of wealth at a disgusting level. To think of all the good that could have been done with the money all of this had cost. A charitable organization, if that truly was at its core, would have put the wealth to better use.

The piazza and colonnade, four columns deep, in front of St. Peter's were a great waste of precious space. There were and are fountains and statues, all honoring past Popes and apostles and saints. The Basilica is the largest church in the world and a complete flaunting of wealth. It took one hundred and twenty years to construct and the dome dominates the skyline of Rome, even to this day. As we watched people approach, they appeared to shrink, being dwarfed by the scale of this building.

Inside was even more impressive and worrisome. I always lived in fine houses, but I never built myself a palace nor set my home up to be revered as sacred. Inside were a number of sculptures in niches depicting popes and founders of religious orders, all hailing them as great and holy men, and a variety of elaborately decorated chapels. Every surface was covered with sculptures, paintings, or was gilded with gold. The baldachin, a giant sculpted bronze canopy over the high altar meant to intimidate, did its job.

No one would listen to me and indeed many tried to show me the exit. I made a scene. Not enough of one to cause us to be arrested, but enough that a group of bishops took note. As they approached me I noticed that my antics amused a cardinal standing in one of the alcoves with his acolytes. His smirk was momentary and only when the men around him looked away did he smile at me. He was lovely, so unlike the other high ranking church officials. Young, having just reached his prime, to be so advanced in career. His hair was dark, shiny, and full. His eyes, clear and sparkling brown. His teeth were straight and stain-free, and his long, lean body was kept fit with exercise.

I felt my budding wrinkles smooth themselves. I was growing younger by the second as Effie floated to the top. I looked away from the man who attracted me. As my lust faded so did Effie. When I looked, the cardinal and his group had left me at the mercy of a group of bishops and lower priests.

The Pope was too busy to see me, I was told. I assured them that, if they would only pass word to him that Lady Ramillia had come, he would see me. The bishops refused; most had a look as if I were less than an insect. I could practically hear them thinking about the audacity of a foreign, non-Catholic woman demanding audience with His High Holiness. With uncovered legs no less!

It wasn't until an inquisitive younger bishop's attention caught on Ed's mysterious goggles that we got anyone to pay attention. He was an inventor as well and spoke with Ed, through me as an interpreter in Italian, at great length about the goggles that could allow the eyeless man to see. We told him about our blunderbuss and catalog and how it worked, though Ed said it was for the detection of men "possessed by evil and in need of exorcism." It was a stroke of genius. We convinced him this was the reason for our visit. He too was interested in the marriage of scientific technology and religion.

He managed to do what the others had not. He had me exit the church. The Pope did not reside in the basilica, after all. He certainly would not hold audience there. We went to this young bishop's workshop. He spoke mostly of science and technological advances. He and Ed fed off each other's energy and intellect. I knew he was one of these religious men who chose this life, not for zealous belief, but for the time and access to education it afforded. He was likely from a lower-class family. Without the church the world would have lost this genius. I planned to use my power to make sure the church did what good it could by elevating this tinkerer.

He did not have the ear of the Pope, though he would speak to his superior. This new man—his higher station and ranking of cardinal shown in the ridiculousness of garb, hat, and adornment—agreed to mention me to His Holiness if he got the chance. I knew at first glance that this man also did not join the church for belief. He was greedy. Glutenous. Gross. He joined for the food. The power. This was the type of man I wanted to see laid low.

I told him that the Pope would recognize my name and asked him to say that Lady Ramillia and her tinkerer were here and would like to discuss a spiritual discovery. He warned me that I would never be granted an audience dressed as I was. I would be required to cover up and dress more appropriately. I smiled. He did not know but I had all the power. If someone would just tell the Pope I was here, I felt certain I could dictate *his* dress in order to meet *me* in person. I did not say such a thing, as it would be too shocking and might hurt my chances rather than improve them.

We sat in the bishop's workshop, having left the rest of my men in the public area, and had refreshments and some of the best wine I had ever smelled. Sally knocked the goblet out of my hand before I could take a drink. I couldn't believe I'd been so foolish. Julian had laced wine with his own blood and fed it to me as a means of riding. I already suspected the Pope used communion in much the same way. Communion consisted of two parts and could be every bit as much about the wine as the wafer. The scientific pontiff scurried about, cleaning my spill, and apologizing.

The pompous cardinal returned in a huff. His face was red and glistening with sweat. He was not alone but had returned with an impressive escort of holy men and brightly colored guards. I leaned back in my chair, enjoying the pontiff's discomfort at my exposed stockinged legs. He bumbled along not making any sense and then blurted out, "You cannot keep His Holiness waiting."

"I thought he was too busy to see me."

"No. No. His schedule opened up and he can receive you now."

The torture had gone on almost long enough. "But what of my inappropriate attire? Surely I should go away and come again another day, when I am properly covered."

This buffoon was clearly unaccustomed to apologizing but I would settle for no less. We stood as he stuttered. Sally commented that I might give the man a heart attack and so I ended his suffering. "Please lead the way." I insisted that the young bishop accompany us as well. The cardinal did not like that but knew he was to do whatever I wanted.

We went directly to the Pope's quarters. He could have played power games with me, leading me all over the palace, showing who was really in control. He did not because he did not have to. Not toying with me was a power move all its own.

The quarters were large. An office, parlor, and sitting room all in one. There were both more and fewer social rules for this Incola. He did not meet with women and could be more informal, but he had a religious facade to retain. The Pope sat on a throne of sorts. Three young boys, dressed in white robes with gold embroidery, sat on footstools around it. Their pose should have read as relaxed but I could see its forced nature. The rest of the room narrowed until I could see only them.

"Please pour our guest some wine," he said in that odd accent. His ring-laden, sausage-fingered hand reached toward the boy on his left, whose cringe at the touch was minuscule but noticeable. The Pope saw me notice and anger welled inside. I knew him, his nature. He was like my father. A lover of children. I knew he would punish the boy. He liked pain when the hurting belonged to someone else.

Mary Martha threatened an appearance. Then for a second, when I thought of how it was my fault, Ruth did as well. Sally did her best to keep them placated in our meadow. This was too important a meeting to shift as I almost had in the cathedral.

"None for me," I said a bit more crassly than necessary. The swift intake of breath by the cardinal at my side said I had breached some rule of etiquette. I knew how I should act but just did not want to. I might be small when compared to this Incola's religious world but maybe he did not know I was the most important person he would ever encounter. I threw that thought away abruptly when I felt Marge move. That shift simply wouldn't do, not when it meant that drastic of a physical change.

The Pope had the boy fill his ornate golden goblet, which he quickly drained. I watched him. He was fat, grotesque even, under his beautiful robes. Wispy white hair, yellowed against his mottled, liver-spotted skin. Just under the edge of the gold and jewel encrusted hem of his gown peeked a foot, or at least I guessed it was a foot. The wrapping showed both old, dried pus and fresh seepage. The size and shape spoke to a swollen, misshapen appendage, probably due to gout or maybe leprosy.

He must have seen me looking because he said, "I care not for this mortal flesh. For I will live forever in God's holy embrace." His smile was another study in disgust.

He meant that he would ruin this body just as he had all the ones before it. Then he would jump to a new body, probably the young attractive cardinal who had smiled at me earlier, and do it all over again. As old as he was, pain was likely even less of an issue for him than it was for Paetus. Who knew how old he was?

"How many Popes have there been?" I asked him.

He knew that I was really asking how many times he had stolen a Carrier body. "That depends on how it is counted and who is included. I am the two hundred fifty-sixth Bishop of Rome."

I wondered if they all had been him, in a different body. Had he invented Christianity? Did it even matter? To those that followed the teachings of Christ, the Pope was a symbol. The man mattered little. They did not know that he was truly evil. I felt certain that my escorts had no idea what sat at the head of their religious governing body.

"May we speak in private?" I asked.

"You may certainly not!" declared the torpid cardinal. He huffed, "His High Holiness has given you too much freedom and too much of his precious time." He turned to the Pope. "Surely she should be censored."

"Leave us," was all the Pope said. Everyone except the altar boys turned to go. They knew their place.

"Wait," I commanded. "I think you should offer me a gift."

"What did you have in mind, my child?"

"This bishop has a strong mind and, if given the proper support, could invent world-changing things. I would see the cardinal's living quarters, holdings, and possessions given to the bishop to fund his research."

The cardinal grew red faced but said nothing, sure the Pope would refuse such an indignity.

"Done," the Pope agreed. "Anything else?"

"Yes," I added. "I would like very much that the church stops taking young children into service. They should be old enough to choose for themselves if a life of service is what they want."

The Pope frowned. I had found his weakness. "That I cannot do. You see, Christ himself said, 'Let the little children come unto me, and hinder them not, for the Kingdom of Heaven belongs to such as these.' Having them near me is Heaven. And even if it were not, I could not cast them out. These had nothing, nowhere to go, and would have died on the street."

"Then, please promise me that they will be educated. The next great mind could be among them and I would have them learn of the whole world, not just the Kingdom of Heaven."

The Pope did not know where I was headed and that scared him. He nodded and I continued. "I request that the bishop be given control over their education."

He could not see my goal and so he granted my second request. My others worried what the Pope would ask in return.

The bishop took a moment to thank me during the mass exodus. I did not know if proximity infected, so I leaned in close and breathed on his face as I instructed him to never give up his inquisitive nature and open-mindedness. I would not have the Incola Pope take this man over and ruin the genius. Whispering, I told him to give the children a safe place and make an excuse that they must all spend the nights together and in his careful watch. I did not tell him that his pontiff was evil. He'd had enough change and revelations for a day. His head spun and he was too useful to confuse further.

When they were all gone, Ed included, the boys went to a lounge and lay together. The movements were so in unison that I knew this was not a spur of the moment choice but a common nightly practice. I tried to remember that their protection approached and ignored them.

The Pope did the same. When I addressed him formally he said, "Please, call me Peter."

I froze. Was he saying that he had jumped from Pope to Pope since the Peter of Christ's time? He mistook my pause.

"Or John, if you prefer. I will take any familiarity you choose." He laughed nervously and for whatever reason it reminded me of Paetus. I missed that man and wished he was here to help me navigate this new world I'd woken up to. He was not one of my great loves but he had a place in my heart. I wondered how many new people would be able to say that. My capacity for making space in my life dimmed with every other born. I could only protect myself. He spoke and broke my concentration, "It has been many years since I took audience with a woman. It is an unintentional effect of my religion. There were no female Incola so I created a religion that focused on men. Now I do not know how to relate to you. I cannot take a wife."

The last statement was almost an apology. I tasted bile in my throat. This monster thought I wished to wed, and worse *bed,* him. "It seems you have less need of me than most Incola, having established your kingdom so fully encompassing the world."

He chuckled at my compliment. "Even though I need it not, taking tithe is necessary. I hope you understand. I liked your nephew and was saddened by his passing."

I moved closer, slowly, as not to alert him. I wanted to kill him, but to do so now, before he was trapped in this body by the precious blight, was to give him a new body to start with. I wanted him to suffer the consequences of mistreating a Carrier so completely. "I liked him as well as I could for knowing him as little as I did. I killed him for you."

"I have not required a death in some time."

"You needed to see how little I value my Carriers. I am different than any you have known for I can easily replace an army of Carriers. My body is the miracle you portray your god as. I can live forever in the body of my own making. I can do that which other Incola can only dream of."

My approach became too intense. He believed what I was pushing. He turned to pour himself another drink. The altar boys tried to stop me when I sat in his lap. The throne was big and I pulled my feet beside us, getting as comfortable as possible in the Pope's symbol of power. Careful not to allow him contact with my exposed skin, I leaned back into him. "I will make a child with all of the major Incola. I will belong to no one man."

"I thought your only son was killed by a rival Incola."

I breathed all over him, even though his stench gagged me. *Do not tell him about Dawn. She would never be safe again,* Sally warned. I hadn't planned on telling him. I said, "I have no rival Incola, only subordinates and suitors." I wiggled my backside ever so slightly. I had a plan, if only I could keep from vomiting while I executed it.

"My apologies. This body no longer responds to the feminine wiles."

I jumped down off his lap. Hand on my hips, I turned to face him, as stern a look as I could manage without giving away my disgust at his implication. His body only responded sexually to young boys.

He rushed to explain, "They all respond to women at first but gradually over the first year my own preferences push theirs out." So they were his own evil preferences. "No need to fret, my child. This body is old. The Pope can die and I can ride a new one of your choice."

I clapped my hands and bounced. *Laying it on a bit thick, aren't you?* Sally mocked. This Pope was so unaccustomed to interacting with women that he did not notice my erratic behavior, or if he did notice, he assumed it was normal female behavior. "How many do I have to choose from?"

"Theoretically, any baptized male Catholic can be Pope, but tradition says it will be one of my cardinals. There are a little over one hundred and fifty."

"I want to see them all today to choose." I needed to infect as many as possible so they would all fall ill at the same time.

"I can arrange something. I will have to lie about your identity; my cardinals do not know of my true nature." They probably did not know about the child rape either. At least they better not. The idea that a group like this would know of such abuses and overlook them was unconscionable. He continued, completely unaware of my growing anger. "Of course, depending on which you choose, it may take some time to maneuver that man into a position where the others will vote for him to be Pope."

"That is acceptable. I am on a grand tour of the world. Meeting all of the great Incola families has been fruitful thus far and I haven't ventured into the East at all."

"Do be careful. There are places in this world much less civilized than mine."

I waited with Ed, after having seen and assured my men I was whole and safe, for the Pope to arrange an up-close viewing of all of his cardinals. He told them I had graciously donated to the church, having recently converted. I was to be royalty from some far away country choosing an emissary from among their ranks. I had spoken in a variety of languages already, and though the cover story was thin at best, it seemed a passing excuse. I spoke to each one, getting close enough and spreading my disease throughout the Pope's highest ranking Carriers.

Again, we left town before the illness took hold. The Pope believed my exit was his idea, to give him time to position my choice for his replacement. He told me that he would feign illness. Nothing too abrupt that might be mistaken for poison; just a man getting old. The various bishops and other clergymen spread around the world would gather around him. That worked for me. I knew he wouldn't be feigning at all and when they all came back to Rome, he would still be contagious. The fall would take care of itself.

10

For months we played the same roles, traveling through Eastern Europe as the only female Incola searching for the right Incola family with which to align. I infected as much of the world as possible all the while searching for Dawn.

Our daughter was quite insane. Each ride Sally went on, it grew more and more difficult for her to find her way back. It was as if, though Dawn had lost her grip on reality, her grip on the thought world had tightened. On the last ride I allowed, Sally saw something that shook us to the core. For the first time I was truly frightened of our daughter. Not just for her but of her.

Sally, after hours of wandering in the memories that managed to grip tight to the peripherals around the tumor, found herself in the tenebrae. The devices of torture were gone. My son and two husbands remained. They were empty, unable to speak more than a few words in a row. Dawn was cannibalizing them, harvesting and consuming parts of them, their emotions, their memories, hoping to replace what she lost.

Ambrose had it the worst. Perhaps she thought being siblings might make the connection closer and more likely that his memories might heal her. She had allowed him to return to his childlike form and away from the monstrous one she saw him as. The left side of his body was gone; the right side pecked at, mangled but bloodlessly. His head suffered the same fate. It looked as if a massive melon baller had scooped it and the skin had grown over the wound. His single remaining eye did not look at me but straight through me without recognition.

Archelaos/Julian and Leon were in the same state but more whole. Their bodies looked like Swiss cheese. Some places showed light from the other side. Again, there was no gore, no blood, as if they had been born this way.

His spine missing, Archelaos lay on the ground, completely paralyzed. I hoped he could feel nothing but knew that was too much to hope for when Sally looked. His mouth was gone. No lips, no opening, just a smooth expanse of loose skin, because his jaw and teeth had been taken too. The nostrils of his nose were closed and smooth as well but he breathed through the bridge. The hole there showed us the cartilage and bone, where we could hear the passage of air. Tears streamed down his face and fell into a deep depression in his cheek. He felt everything.

Leon sat in his chair but the closer Sally moved the worse he looked. His right ankle was crossed over his left knee and his arms crossed over his chest. Except they weren't. His right foot grew out of his left knee and his arms through his chest. He looked as if he'd been posed and then melted into himself. He could not move much and when Sally went to him, he spoke two words.

"Kill her."

∽

Sally came back to us nearly as insane as Dawn. She refused to accept the truth. Dawn was unredeemable. The end of the suffering of those three men could only be achieved by Dawn's death. My others had varying opinions. I cared not. I knew what had to be done. Leon spoke true. Dawn must be stopped.

My ability to hold the front on my own improved with determination and focus. Sally was not allowed to leave anymore. We relied on more traditional means to find and follow Dawn. It took longer but I would not risk Sally again. I could not.

Here in Europe, contrary to the Americas, the population was consolidated, too dense to escape the illness. It was not necessary to visit every single location. Carriers would take the blight from town to town, household to household. In a small city, in a cold country before we reached Eastern Europe, I went to the theater so that we might expose an isolated Incola family that only came out to see actors. On that stage I saw a familiar face behind a mask.

Satisfied that the exposure had been enough, I dashed backstage and tore the tragedy mask from Paetus. Careful not to touch my skin, he led me into a dressing area. I stood next to a clothing rack filled with hanging costumes which stank of stale sweat and greasepaint makeup. He shrugged and said, "There is nothing quite like a Roman play."

Confused, I asked, "But isn't this a Greek tragedy?"

He smiled and for a moment I could see how handsome he probably was in his youth. "It is. As I said, there is nothing quite like a Roman play." He looked as he always had and I remembered that this Roman body was not his and had been stolen.

"Did you think we wouldn't find you?"

"On the contrary, it is why I took up with this troop." He untied a small sack, more like a large coin purse, hanging from his belt and placed it in my hands. He said, "Once my mission in the Americas was completed, I targeted the most secretive Incola family by joining their favorite entertainment. Then, when I heard you approached, I pressured the troop to move in the same direction." He untied and unbuttoned his coat, vest, and shirt and removed them all as one piece. He hung his costume with the others on the rack.

"What was your mission in the Americas?" I asked. He gestured to the bag in my hands. I pulled the drawstring closure and opened the bag to find it empty save fine gray ash at the bottom. I looked at him questioningly.

Bare chested, he sat at a vanity to remove his stage makeup with a rag and a jar of petroleum jelly. His back was a mass of scar tissue but, as I had placed many of those scars there, this was not shocking. Looking at me in the mirror, he explained, "That purse you hold carries an ounce of ash from every Carrier who abandoned you." He smiled at me, clearly proud of himself. "I hunted, killed, and burned every last one of them." Resuming his face wiping, he continued talking. The energy increased as he ranted, "Worthless traitors, the lot of them. Carriers without loyalty should not, nay, shall not be allowed to live. They either live to serve or they die. How could they think they would be allowed to live forever, completely free of service to Incola! Incola should never have taught them to heal themselves! If I cannot jump bodies, cannot ride, then living forever is all that sets me apart from the common riffraff! No Carrier will ever be allowed to live forever! No Carrier will ever be allowed to live without an Incola master!"

I took the sack and put it in a pocket of my gown. At that moment I was angry at Paetus. He had killed and would continue to kill innocent Carriers. Later, I would completely change my mind. There is no such thing as an innocent immortal.

My men went ahead, scouting both Dawn's location and Incola that must be infected. In Russia, everyone learned what the state of her three prisoners told us. She had been taken by madness and must be stopped by whatever means. At this time, the Tsar and his family were still alive, as was the extreme segregation of wealth from the masses. Over eighty percent of the population were peasants. These people lived in small communes and few were literate or traveled much beyond their own village. This isolation meant that there was significant diversity of ethnicity, language, and culture. It was intensely patriarchal.

These factors led to more difficulty for me. Each group was different and I did not know all the languages or dialects. Even if I did, many men would not speak with me, as a woman, and many forbade any woman from visiting with me. I became frustrated quickly that I had to leave the detective work to my men while I waited silently. I did enjoy quite a bit of vodka.

In the more isolated areas of Siberia, the most inhospitable place for human habitation, and especially down into Mongolia, I found much more warmth and welcome. I drank vodka and fermented milk with wizened women and mustachioed men. We laughed at the same silly drunken behavior even without a fully understood language between us. At one of these late evenings, we heard of a rumor of a young woman who had taken over a nearby village with violence and madness.

As soon as I heard them speak of it, I could sense Dawn's touch. I could smell her proximity. I also could sense that as soon as I knew she was close, she knew my location. She got further from me with every second but I could not give chase. To say it was cold out would be a vast understatement of the devastating weather. Locals seemed unconcerned but did not advise leaving at the moment.

We left at first light and were all glad we'd skipped breakfast. The three round dwellings stood on a plain surrounded by mountains. It was a small area and we did not see it until we were almost on top of it. Here the cold was dry. Hardly any snow fell, in direct contradiction to snowfall in Russia. The thin layer of snow surrounding the village was no longer white but stained red.

I saw the children first. A child, fully dressed in traditional garb, lay perpendicular to each side of the door, their bodies forming a border for the path to the entrance. Each one had been laid carefully and purposefully. Every one had their throats cut. Other than that aspect, they appeared peaceful compared to what we found inside each home.

The first we entered appeared to be a slaughterhouse of sorts. Headless bodies piled to one side. A short table had been converted to a chopping block, I assumed because of the gouges in the red-stained wood. Some of the bodies had a limb missing.

The second yurt had been used as a cooking tent. The stove fire was out but still had a cast iron frying pan atop it. "How did they get scrambled eggs? I've seen no sign of chickens."

Paetus held up a blanket corner. "I've found the heads but they're all missing their brains."

I spun my head back around to look into the pan more closely.

Brains.

Human brains.

Your daughter is eating folks' brains, said Marge.

She spoke internally. Sally shook our head, saying, "*No, no,*" repeatedly.

Emotions overwhelmed me. I would say the world started spinning but it was I who was spinning. I feared for Dawn; Mary Martha rose. I feared her, feared what she had become; Dierdre flew. I feared what I would now be forced to do but also felt freed that the decision was already made for me; Jo and Marge soared. Effie remembered what Dawn had done to our husbands and Ruth reminded me that if I had done something about it then, these people would be alive. Sally reflected them all back to me, amplifying them.

What did she hope to accomplish?

You mean, why did she do this?

The real question is how could she do this?

We are not innocent. What would we not try if we were as broken as she?

Who says we aren't?

This feels the same as in her tenebrae. She was hoping to regain what she's lost by consuming some part of another.

She is broken, completely insane.

No one is beyond redemption. We must try.

Taking time to try and save her gives Dawn more time to commit these kinds of atrocities again.

She won't do this again. Whatever she attempted either worked and she won't need to or it did not work and there would be no point in trying it again.

The others discussed the situation. I did not know who said what because they were all me. They all reflected some part of my own feelings. My thoughts were reeling and so my others argued.

Then a thought occurred to me that I could not remember ever having before. I should have let Father take Dawn before she was developed. That abortion would have saved so many people, myself included. I dismissed the thought. It was but one step away from saying that everyone would be better off if I'd never been born and that just wasn't a path I was prepared to travel. Dawn had her role to play, just as I did.

I watched as Paetus walked around examining the bodies. His face reflected not horror but pride in Dawn's actions. He turned and I saw evidence that he felt excited and aroused. It was disgusting. Then I remembered how long he had lived. That body was increasingly numb. The longer he lived the more pain and gore he required to stimulate him. If there was no limit to how long he could live, there would be no limit to the heights his depravity would grow.

Feeling unstable but anxious to push forward, I went to the third yurt. I thought it could not get any worse. I was mistaken.

At first my mind had difficulty making sense of what my eyes saw. This room had been set up more along the lines of an operating room. Every horizontal surface of significant size held a body. A few of them showed a level of decay but most had frozen before decomposition began. The bodies here were not missing their heads or limbs. In fact, most of them had extra parts attached.

We moved through the room silently. If it had not been for that fact, I might not have heard it, heard her labored breath. The poor thing lay on a soiled bed with another corpse. At least, that is what I thought at first glance.

Upon further study, I realized that the dead head lying on the pillow next to hers was attached to her neck. A second rattling breath told me that infection had taken hold.

"Ed," I called. My whisper sounded like a shout in this silent place.

When Ed moved the blanket down to better view the situation, he exposed the junction between the decaying dead head and her infected, clammy dying body. There between the two lay a perfectly rosy-pink strip of flesh. I kept Ed from touching Dawn's skin. The woman, on which my daughter experimented, woke. Her cloudy and yet bloodshot eyes shot open.

The arm closest to me reached out. Though it was attached where her arm would normally be, it could not have been hers. She was a young woman and the arm was thick. A man's arm had been attached where hers had been removed. And yet it responded to her command just as hers would have, with a thought. The same type of healthy pink flesh connected the two.

This monstrosity with our daughter's skin attaching both dead and living parts from other people looked at me. I expected her to plead with us to kill her or to kill Dawn for what she'd done. I expected tears of anger or groans of pain. What I got was more horrifying.

Contentment.

She was doing what Dawn wanted. She pleased the owner of the flesh that kept her together and so this real-life Frankenstein's monster was satisfied to lay there and rot until she died.

Something happened then that had not happened that completely since my stint in West Freeman's Asylum. The darkness came. I fell into the darkness that protected me from pain throughout my childhood. I floated in ignorant bliss while the world went on without me.

∽

I floated to the top. The others were mercifully silent. Attempting to stretch my limbs revealed that I was bound. Since I had never met a binding I could not break, I pulled. When the metal shackles and chain did not break, I applied real pressure. Two loud cracks sounded as I broke my own bones. Pain meant that Sally came to my rescue and I again sank into the darkness.

∽

I floated to the top. Again, the others were mercifully silent. Sally kept control of our limbs to prevent a repeat of the last time I awakened. I was still bound. My eyes were mine to control. I opened them and found myself aboard the *Precious Lady*.

Ed stood at the helm. I cleared my throat and he rushed over to unbind me. He explained that Sally had asked him to devise a means of binding an Incola and the metal of these manacles and chains were the result of his work. He apologized but also excused his own actions by reminding me that I had said Sally was to be treated the same as I. She was me and her instructions were my instructions.

I wondered if I ought to change that. We might butt heads in the near future over what to do about Dawn and I needed to know my men were my men and not hers. Ed took my train of thought off of those particular rails as he showed me the new kind of metal strong enough to hold even Incola.

My right arm, stronger than my left, had broken itself in two places during my struggles. I set to healing that damage as Ed talked about chemical composition and metallurgy. When he finished, I asked about the monstrous woman who had caused me such distress that Sally felt the need to take us over.

"We killed her," he answered quickly. It was a mercy killing. "We burned the entire village and reduced every body to ash." They had done just what I would have. We had to ensure that any remnant of Dawn's power of touch was eradicated.

"How long was..." I searched for the right question and settled on, "Sally's visit?"

Ed backed away from me and feigned interest in some reading on his instrument panel. "Ed, I need to know."

He wrung his hands. "Sally said not to discuss her time with us."

"Let me see if I understand this. I tell you that Sally is me and that you are to treat us equally, then Sally tells you not to treat me equal to her and you just jump to her command."

"No, my lady. She just did not wish to upset you."

I was happy to decide what I wanted to know for myself, so I asked him again, "How long was Sally's visit?" He hesitated and so I pushed until he answered.

"It depends on if you count the time that Sally was gone."

Sally had ignored my order not to and had ridden Dawn. If I was in the darkness and Sally rode, then "Who was in control while she was gone?"

"All of them. None of them. Sally left Mary Martha in charge but she could not hold control exclusively, thus the shackles."

That concerned me. Mary Martha and Sally had become too close. It was the mother bond. Mary Martha was our fear for our children, our desire to protect them at all costs. That would not do, for when it came time to deal with Dawn, those two could not be strong enough to overwhelm my will.

Effie would be my choice, or maybe even Jo. Dierdre was too paranoid and anxiety ridden. Marge was unpredictable and Ruth a useless ball of guilt.

"Why not put me in my mews?" I asked.

"The *Precious Lady* will not fly with that great weight. Here aboard is the best place for you so the shackles were fashioned and used while Sally was away."

"Anything useful about Dawn uncovered while I was out?"

"Quite a lot, actually." He retrieved a leather-bound notebook from his workstation. He held it against his chest, protectively. "Sally worried that it might bring on another episode. Are you sure you wish to know?"

I felt much better now that some distance had been placed between me and the monstrosity that was created by the monster I had created. I felt safe hearing the details when not facing the real-life result of those details. I nodded.

Ed came to sit beside me and opened the book. It was a journal of some type, medical by the look of it. It was filled with sketches and descriptions of procedures. Ed told me that he had found this in the last yurt where I had passed out. Dawn had a doctor traveling with her now. He did what she wanted because he, like everyone her skin touched, was under her spell, but he did not know her motivations, did not know her goal. Dawn did not speak aloud.

The doctor did not know why she needed to consume brains. He did not know what the point of his experiments were or why the skin she donated to his operations adhered and healed the tissue below so thoroughly. For whatever reason, his new ward needed to know if body parts could be grafted on and eventually if a person's head could live on another person. After the first success with an arm transplant, Dawn had him put her arm on another person. It worked. The arm functioned but for whatever reason, this was not enough. There was some outcome unknown to him that she desired. He wondered if the head had worked; was that her goal? Did she want to transplant her head onto the body of another? The way her own arm had reattached itself to her body, after his surgery to transplant it back was completed, was nothing short of a miracle.

"How is Dawn? Is she well?" I asked. "Do we know where she is?"

"We do. Physically, she is recovered."

I was aware that mentally she was equivalent to a vase dropped on the cobblestone. Broken was too tame a word. Dawn was shattered. For all my experience within my own mind, I knew nothing of how to heal one.

"Where is she? Are we headed there now?"

"We are. This is another thing Sally asked us to keep from you." He paused to allow me to decide for myself if I wanted to hear or if I wanted to trust Sally.

I said, "It will be fine. Please go ahead and tell me."

"Lady Dawn is with Chinese royalty—a woman or organization, it is difficult to tell for certain—by the name of Xia."

I went inside to the meadow to confront Sally. I do not know if Ed continued talking or if he knew I was preoccupied. *I understand why you would keep riding Dawn, against my wishes, from me. I would have been angry. I am angry. But why must Xia be kept a secret from me?* I asked her. *I know of the Yellow Empress, mother of all China.*

There is something strange between you. Like a moth to a flame, you are attracted to what I fear will kill us. Sally answered me internally but I and the others could hear her all the same.

As always, Sally knew me better than I knew myself. I needed to meet Xia. How had she lasted so long completely undetected by the most powerful Incola in the world?

11

China is the most amazing place on this planet. Its landscapes are so magnificent that the millions of songs, poems, paintings, and sculptures cannot even scratch the surface of that depth of beauty. Simply describing the varied landscapes could fill a library, so I will only say that I fell in love with that land and understood why Xia would choose it as her eternal living place.

We flew over the most beautiful place in the world and I knew I was the first to see it from this height. Now such a view is commonplace in photographs but then it was a magical first experience for all of humankind. The Yangtze River was, and is, gorgeous. Approaching Xia's home like this served for more than a pretty view. It meant that I did not spread my illness during the approach, hopefully avoiding alerting Xia to my intentions to infect her whole household.

I had not been awake when Sally rode Dawn and looked through her eyes to find her with Xia. No one seemed worried that our daughter was within the clutches of the oldest, most secretive Incola in the whole world. The others were not anxious and so I felt only a sort of excitement. I wanted to meet Xia. She must have answers to the many questions I had about Incola.

Xia's home was a compound on the edge of the coast of China made up of a dozen buildings arranged symmetrically around a series of courtyards that led to a large main palace. A wall surrounded the entire complex with a wide strip of land between. The wall itself seemed to be a building made up of two walls with space between and a flat roof on which soldiers patrolled. It was breached by an elaborately decorated gate to the north and south. On the east and west sides, small stages or large altars, stood covered in little bundles and burning incense. Many Chinese participated in ancestor worship and since Xia might be the Yellow Empress, the ancestor of all Chinese, it made sense that her altars would be overflowing with offerings. As I watched, a woman laid one more carefully on the top of the pile and then went back to her husband.

Our approach and landing was met by rows of soldiers in formation and servants who stood lining the walkway. We were greeted by a man about my own age, who spoke English and was dressed very finely in elaborately woven silk robes decorated with none other than the Yellow Dragon. He had an entourage of men with him, all high ranking in this court judging by their robes and how the Yellow Dragon was displayed. I noticed two peculiarities. One: every man there, including soldiers and servants, bore the Yellow Dragon on some article of clothing, whereas I had believed that only an Emperor could wear its likeness. And two: every person there was male.

My own men were shown great respect and treated without suspicion when they came in the main gate. Our belongings were carried inside. My men received rooms in the two buildings closest to the main one, in which I was given a room. We were invited to rest and freshen up as there was to be a great feast in our honor that night.

The feast was elaborate and flavored with exotic spices. We were all served individual bowls of rice and then the large dishes were placed on the center of the table for all to take from. Whole fish, cooked with head and tail on; a whole goose with golden braised skin; meats and vegetables cooked in unfamiliar styles; noodles; deliciously sweet fruits that were completely unrecognizable; and dumplings filled with a variety of fillings made up the meal.

All members of the household ate with us so I feared no poison. At first my others did not want to eat for fear that was Xia's method of riding but I convinced them that even if it was, she would soon be too sick to ride anyone. I ate and drank and listened to beautifully strange music played on some plucked string instruments and some flutes. The musical scale used was different than in Western music and seemed alien but calming, if not a little sad, to me.

"Here we eat unfamiliar food as not to insult our hostess but she cannot even appear in person. How can I not take that as a personal affront? I have traveled around the world to meet Xia and she cannot be bothered to come from her chambers to greet me?"

The man who had been spokesperson at our arrival looked puzzled. Then he gazed at me and said calmly, "I am here."

"You! I do not even know who you are. I am here to see Xia, Yellow Empress, ancestor of all Chinese, ancient female Incola, friend of the talking beast, Bai Ze, keeper of the knowledge of all supernatural creatures."

Comprehension dawned on the man's face. He turned to me and I met his gaze. He said, "I am Xia." Before I could question that statement, every member of that household stood and in unison repeated, "I am Xia." My dinner partner continued, "There is no one here who is not Xia. She looks through all of our eyes, uses us to speak her words."

How could she ride so many at once? I wondered. Then I thought of the time when Sally rode Dawn and Mary Martha rode the unborn child. I had been able to see through both of their eyes. Maybe she had others just as I did, but she gave her others their own bodies. How could I ask her without sharing the details of my own mind? "But where is she? Physically. Where is her body?"

Sally could stand it no longer and shouted, "And where is our daughter?"

He stood. "Come. Xia will see you with her own eyes but it will take some time."

Why? Why would it take time? I did not understand but I followed him, leaving my men feasting. We went down a hall, passing closed and open doors on either side. The man stopped at one of the open doors and gestured that I should look. Dawn sat eating while a tattoo was applied to her arm. Her hands were bound in a sort of mitten so a man sat next to her feeding her. When she saw me, she neither ran from us nor to us. She simply raised her skirts, showing off her tattoo covered legs.

Sally showed me a memory from when she last rode Dawn. Her hands were covered now because when she arrived at Xia's palace, she would not stop picking strips of her flesh and putting them on the men. Strangely, the Xia men did not seem affected by Dawn's gift of touch. They threw the bits of skin into the fire. She had put her hands on them, attempted to seduce them into giving her more children, but they had no difficulty resisting. Her will could not overwhelm Xia's.

"Doesn't Xia wish to use her to birth an army of Carriers?" I exclaimed out loud.

"Goodness, no. Why would anyone wish that? No, I do all I can to keep down the number of us. What do you call them?"

"Incola is the word I was told meant leader, owner, rider. That one person has Carriers, human cattle to be ridden when the Incola wishes to jump bodies, leaving his own for a while," I explained to the man who, as he was ridden by Xia, could be centuries older than I.

We descended a staircase, then another, and then another. I would have thought that a basement would be less ornate, less fancy than the residence above but here quite the opposite was true. Once we were well below ground, light filled every corner. The man who was Xia saw me examining one of the fixtures on the wall and explained that it was electricity that so well-lit Xia's personal chamber. I did not think having all of that power, basically lightning, flowing through a home was safe. I knew of the inventions but preferred the safety and comfort of gaslights.

The stairway opened into a small entry room, dominated by two giant doors painted bright red, which symbolized happiness here, and decorated by a yellow dragon each that culminated in large metal door knockers forged to look like the dragons' heads. Every surface of that room was lacquered and polished so that it seemed to have a mirrored finish.

The man who was Xia asked me to avert my eyes. The door was locked in a hidden fashion similar to Julian's secret room at our home in London. I heard a series of clicks, slides, and groans. The doors opened toward us and I looked into a gargantuan empty room. Empty is not the correct word. Columns carved with minuscule Chinese characters filled the space. I walked in and immediately a painting to my left caught my attention. In it, an octopus' tentacles caressed and trapped a nude woman. The *petite mort* on her face said she enjoyed the sea creature's touch. The painting next to it was similar in subject matter. Every painting was similar. Some were more or less graphic. Some had men. Most featured a woman and an octopus or squid.

"Are you a fan of shunga?" he asked me.

At the time I did not know that word but did not wish to offer offense before meeting Xia so I asked a question instead. "Aren't these Japanese works?"

He complimented me on my eye for detail, stating that most outsiders would not recognize the differences.

"Why would the ancestor of all Chinese collect Japanese art?" I pressed.

"Come," he dodged the question. "You can ask Xia. She wakes."

"I thought you were Xia," I mumbled mockingly.

He pretended not to hear or perhaps he did not care. He led me to a bed at the back of the room. The word bed is a bit of a misnomer. This pillowed platform was wide enough for eight people to lay side by side, maybe more. It held but one at the moment. A woman, so elderly, dried and wrinkled that at first I thought her a mummy, lay on her back on the right of the bed.

Her white hair, spread out around her head, began to change first. It went gray, then salt and pepper. As the pepper began to outweigh the salt, the age spots on her face disappeared. The number of her wrinkles halved and then halved again. She opened her eyes. Her cataracts faded and her dark sparkling eyes looked deep inside me. I knew her and she knew me. There would be no secrets between us.

Xia sat up, the sheet sliding down, exposing her above the waist. I should have looked away but I could not, so great was the transformation. Her breasts tightened and lifted, her skin as well. Dark hair fell straight down her back past her waist, the last of the gray having vanished. She pushed down the covers, making me aware of her complete nudity, and slid out of bed.

Her waist, thin without the aid of corseting, and her strong but small body disappeared in the robes that the man who had led me there held for her. The first layer was thin but several more were added and cinched, pinned and tied. She had her own cultural rules to follow just as I did, but I knew she was nude beneath the layers. The knowledge that she wore no undergarments sent tingles down my spine.

Xia stood before me a gorgeous woman no older than I, when I had thought her a desiccated ancient mummy only moments before. She held her hand out to me. Her tiny, delicate, dainty hand entreated me from the loose folds of her large sleeves. I reached my hand out but Sally remembered our gift of touch and snatched it back just in time. I shook my head no, even though I wanted to touch her more than anything.

Her lips plumped and smoothed, turning the most pleasant shade of pink. I longed to kiss her but then she spoke. “There is no need to worry. Your power will not work on me or mine.” I scarcely understood the words she said, so caught up was I in the timbre of her voice. Again she held out her hand. This time I took it in my own. “It seems counterintuitive but touching me helps fight the…” She paused, searching for the phrase to express it best. “Fight the hold my glamor has over you.”

She was every bit as lovely as she had been before we clasped hands but her beauty was less intoxicating. I did not feel obsession rearing its ugly head. Xia pulled me to a painting. Xia was a small woman, her head barely reaching my earlobe level. We stood and admired the skill of the artist, for it appeared that the octopus moved through the water. All I could think of was how Xia's naked body would look as water lapped over it.

She spoke, breaking my fantasy. “The octopus is a most interesting and alien creature. Did you know that they have a brain in each of their eight arms in addition to their central brain? The arms have literal minds of their own and can act completely independent of the head.” We moved to the next painting. They were wood carved imprints. This one did not feature an octopus, just two women engaged in sex. “The suction cups on the octopus' arms can taste what they touch.” The next piece was of big waves breaking apart a small boat while an octopus dragged a man down into the depths.

“You asked me why the mother of China would collect Japanese art. In your travels, have you noticed a similarity in appearance, language, and culture with Han Chinese, Japanese, and Korean?” I had never been to Japan or Korea but it felt like a hypothetical or leading question so I just nodded. “The people I come from originated near the mouth of Yangtze River area and moved over the Korean peninsula and into Japan. We have a common ancestor but our genetics are now so distinct that I cannot count people from Korea or Japan as family. I cannot use them as vessels. The Japanese and I are connected. They are not mine; I cannot own them but I can own their art. I lived there for many years, hiding from what I was. I became obsessed with shunga, Japanese erotic art. But the longer I denied who I was and what I needed, the more split I became. With no vessels for my splinter selves, I went insane.”

“Dawn is insane.”

"Is that her name? Dawn?" She pulled me to another painting. It was more erotic than the last and I tried to concentrate on what she said, rather than allow my imagination to run wild again. "Yes, she is. But it is different. Her mind feels empty, as if she made room for her splinters but they never arrived. You are the opposite, almost full." Before I could question her statement, she continued. "I have gone my entire life without ever having encountered another woman with my abilities and now within such a short span, I have met two. I have not allowed her to see me as I fear it would complicate matters."

"She cannot ride you."

"Of course not." When it became clear that I did not understand why she assumed she was safe from Dawn's possession, Xia said, "She cannot become one of us until she kills her mother. Killing the body that birthed us is the only way a female Incola can be born. You should have ended her in infancy. She will always be a threat to you."

Deirdre threatened to make an appearance because Dawn was a threat. Mary Martha grew when Xia said we should have aborted our daughter. Ruth felt guilty about killing our mother at birth. But Sally was too close to the surface, too intrigued by what Xia said. There simply was not room at the front for us all.

"Even if she did kill you, she would never be able to ride me."

"Because you're too powerful of an Incola." I said it as a statement, so convinced was I that I understood.

"No," she said, furrowing her brow. "Do you really not know? How can you be so powerful, have consolidated so much power, destroyed or taken over so much of the Incola world and know so little about yourself?"

I released her hand. "The Incola I've met are not as forthcoming as you." She was what we would call a church-bell back in London. A talkative woman, this Xia.

"They would be secretive. They did not want you to know all you are capable of and most of them weren't aware that our abilities differ from theirs." She turned so that we might look directly at each other. "Dawn can never ride me because we, female…Incola, can only ride our direct descendants. You share the same wretched blood as your daughter. She is your vessel. You and I are at the top of our family tree. No one can ride us."

"But my first husband was able to ride me."

An eyebrow lift was the only hint that she recognized the unintentional double entendre. That beautiful, perfectly arched eyebrow lowered. "You were young. Since you are still you, I assume that ride did not end as he wished. I have been able to kill anyone who tried to ride."

I nodded. The movement set my eyes on Xia's toes peeking from beneath her robe hems. I was glad she did not have to suffer the pain of lotus feet. But then I thought of how her feet would be comely no matter. "I can push Incola out. Dawn can trap them in her mind."

"You can ride her without becoming trapped though."

Again I nodded. My words failed me. How did she know so much when we'd only just met? So breathtakingly gorgeous. So intoxicatingly wise. That isn't a real word but her dazzling self muddied my mind. Xia waited for me to catch up. "Not me. I cannot seem to ride at all. I am stuck in this body. One of my splinters, I call them my others, rides and I see through her eyes."

"That *is* how we ride. We are not like our male counterparts. They can only have one body at a time, killing off their previous form. We must stay in our original body but our splinters, our others, can be sent to ride our descendants. We can see through their eyes, live many lives through them concurrently. Controlling so many minds at the same time is easier when I put this body in stasis. I find the most deaths I can carry is eight. Any more after that inside my mind leads to insanity. I can feel yours pressing to get out. You must be close to that."

Her voice made speaking coherently difficult. I managed four words. "I carry seven others."

"You need vessels. Dawn is your only living descendant?"

Ask her! Effie pleaded.

Ask her what? I asked silently.

About Dawn and if our men can be saved.

No, not yet. I replied to Effie and then answered Xia's question. "Yes. I had a son as well, but he died."

"He died, bringing about the birth of one of your others." She spoke it as a statement. She did not need me to confirm. In fact, she confirmed for me our suspicion of how the others were born. "Then Dawn is your only vessel. One splinter could permanently take residence but you need room for all." We walked to another painting. I didn't even look at it. I only had eyes for Xia. My eyes would not drag themselves away from her glorious face. No detail was too minute to memorize. I counted her eyelashes and wondered what I wouldn't do for Xia. Her almond shaped eyes looked at mine and she smiled knowingly at me. She reached out and took my hand. The world around Xia came back into focus.

She spoke, further strengthening my grip on reality. "I apologize. The effects of my glamor seem to have increased manyfold while I slept in stasis. It is why I lock myself away, allowing my body to grow old. This body cannot go into the world anymore. Being in public is too dangerous. Even my own splinters cannot resist."

"Will that happen to us?" Sally asked aloud.

"I don't want to live in a cave!" added Jo.

I reprimanded them aloud. "Xia was sharing a personal pain and you made it about us. For shame, for shame. You think we will ever be as Xia is!"

"It is possible. My touch, at first, just made people attracted to me, made them desire my company. Then, around the time I turned one thousand, mere proximity began to trigger the effect. After two thousand years, the area around my home became congested with people just hoping for a Xia sighting. That is when I started putting myself into stasis. Only a few months at first and then years."

"How long was this stasis?" I asked.

"For the past two centuries or so, I have lived only through my splinters."

No wonder no other Incola knew about her. She was old enough to be a myth. I wondered how old she was but did not ask. If she really was the Yellow Empress of lore, she could be over four thousand years old. "That is why they bring their offerings to your altars outside the gates, because you are a deity."

She flinched as if my words stung and I wished instantly to take them back. How could I be so callous? I hurt Xia. I began to stutter apologies.

"No, no. It is I who is sorry. I wish you had not seen that. It must be impossible for an outsider to understand the need for such a loss of life."

I thought back to the woman I had watched lay a tiny bundle on the altar. Tears glistened on her cheeks. Her hand lingered on the bundle. The moving bundle. A baby. Peasants were leaving their babies on the altar to die of exposure. I yanked my hand from Xia's. I tried to run, check on the baby, see if it still lived. Sally stopped me. She knew only pain awaited me outside those walls.

Even with my back to her, being in the same room as Xia meant her glamor hit me hard. I tried to keep my outrage and yelled before it vanished completely. "I'm glad I brought my precious blight to your home!" I pulled the weapon from my pocket and brandished it at her.

She retrieved something from under her pillow. Bringing it back to me, she held out a cylinder similar to mine. "I used mine long ago, when I was relatively young. I thought we were evil and sought to end it all. Did the monks give that to you? I tried to develop a weapon and was able to make these two. I used one and the other disappeared."

"Why didn't you use yours as I am trying to do?"

"I did. I traveled as far as I could, travel being what it was back then. I was arrogant and thought only the Han had this power. There were very few large populations living together. Most people lived isolated and I never found them. You have a chance. Then there will only be you and I." Her glamor mesmerized completely. When she said that last sentence, I could no longer feel the earth beneath my feet. I soared with the thought of it being just she and I.

She came and took my hand once again allowing me to manage my wayward thoughts. She spoke again, and I knew she kept no secrets from me. I only had to ask and she would tell me everything. "The villagers bring their baby girls to the altar if they are my direct descendants. I commanded them to do this long ago for two reasons. The first is that if they were my descendants then their death would bring a splinter and that splinter could be used to possess a male descendant. I did not want a male Incola, immune from my weapon, to rise in power. My splinters ride them all.

"Now that so long has passed, so many generations between me and those babies, the connection between us is so minuscule that their deaths no longer make a splinter. The second reason is that I did not want a country filled with insane women. Very few would have killed their own mothers so they would continue to splinter as their family died. Those splinters would build inside their minds with nowhere to go and make the women go mad."

Xia paused for a few minutes. Whether it was to allow me time to process or herself time to recover from sharing such a dark part of herself, I do not know. We looked at more art, all the while holding hands. When she spoke again, it was soft and gentle. "Do you know how many deaths Dawn carries?"

That was difficult to answer. If others were made when our family died, she should have more than she did. "Dawn has a tumor and some of her splinters were absorbed by it. She only has one other that I know of and then there are my son and two husbands."

"Dawn imprisoned them, those who attempted to ride her?"

"Any who have ever entered her mind, even if they escape for a time, whenever they do die, they are trapped. When she tires of their screams, Dawn cannibalizes them."

Ask her! Effie begged me.

Before I could ask, Xia volunteered the information. "I have never heard of such a thing. What a horrific end to any creature."

Ask her! Effie insisted.

If she'd never heard of it then she has no solution, I reasoned. I asked anyway. "Is there any way to save them?"

Xia shook her head. "Even if you killed Dawn, and your son and husbands did have bodies to return to, if they are as consumed as you say, they would never be themselves again."

12

I wanted to stay the night with Xia but she did not know what prolonged exposure to her glamor might do to me while I slept. I did not care but Xia said no, for my own safety. I went up the stairs with the man who had led me there following closely behind. Xia spoke to me through him, the whole way. She assured me that she was still with me but it mattered not. I grew more melancholy with every step, my head lowering until my chin touched my chest. So distracted was I by the intensity of my feelings that I did not notice that the door to my room was not only unlocked but also ajar.

The room was dark, especially when compared to the bright electric lighting of Xia's chamber. My chin resting on my chest as it was, I saw nothing but the polished wooden floor. I did not see the antique jian falling toward my neck. The once beautiful double-edged Chinese sword had succumbed to the ravages of time. It made contact with the back of my neck and the force alone allowed it to split my skin but when it hit the bones of my spine, the ill choice of my assailant became clear.

The jian blade was not only dull but brittle. I fell to the ground, stunned and temporarily paralyzed. I went to work healing myself right away as the battle began beside me. The man who was Xia had not been far behind me and he met the second swing of the sword with his dagger-ax. It was a long weapon, designed for use in much more open spaces than this. The sword lost length with every blow. When my healing neared completion and I started to rise, the man who was Xia shouted that I should stay down. It was said in her own native tongue so that I, but not my assailant, would understand.

I watched as the man who was Xia thrust the spearhead near our enemy's head as a feint. Then the scythe-like cutting blade, angled optimally, beheaded my assailant, who still had not spoken a word. For a second I thought that it might be Dawn, since she no longer spoke, but the thought was dismissed just as quickly. This was clearly a man. His body collapsed with his stub neck near my face. I can still feel the hot, thick, blood gushing to the rhythm of the assailant's last few heartbeats. It sprayed and covered my face, neck, and chest. I would have screamed but I did not want that fluid in my mouth.

Light filled my room as guards with lanterns, both mine and Xia's, rushed in. The man who was Xia knelt between the bloody stump and myself. He offered me help standing, which I accepted. I followed the trail of bloody spatters to where the head had rolled under my platform bed. I sat. The man who was Xia reached under and pulled out the severed head of Paetus.

A nightcap drink sat on a small table near my bed. Needing it to calm my nerves, I went to grab it only to have Ed knock it from my grasp. He explained quickly, "It smells of poison. Before Paetus was Paetus he was a Greek. Ancient Greeks often executed by use of hemlock."

"He was going to behead me and poison me?" I questioned. "Isn't that rather butter upon bacon?"

Ed replied, "Perhaps he planned for just this type of situation where you bested him."

My others began to speak over each other and I shouted, "Quiet!" My others and the men in the room went silent. I did not know if the next thought to cross my mind was my own or one of the others. *Perhaps he intended to drink it himself after he killed you.* "Strip him," I ordered.

They did. There it was, just as I suspected. A strip of tattooed flesh against his. Dawn sent him to kill me.

No, argued Sally. *Not possible.*

She wants us dead. He had no choice but to do what she wants.

You heard Xia. Dawn cannot be whole again until she kills her mother and can become Incola.

Even if she did, she has no descendants to ride. She would still be stuck with her splinters.

I noticed that she used Xia's name for them rather than mine. That was a little too close to home. I was stuck with my others.

Ed began to disrobe. I averted my eyes and asked him, "What are you doing?"

He answered without stopping his disrobing. "You need to know that Lady Dawn did not get to anyone else." Soon all my men followed his example. I examined them and they each other.

The men who were Xia stood and watched. "Strip," I told them.

The one who had saved me said, "I have already told you that we are not susceptible to gifts of touch. We are simply too old."

My men drew their weapons. Some of them were still nude but pointed weapons at Xia's men nonetheless threateningly. "Either you take off your clothes and prove my daughter has no influence over you or my men will kill you."

"No, you can't," he exclaimed. "These bodies are my descendants. Killing them would create more splinters and since Xia has not had a descendant vessel born in many centuries, we and the new splinters would have nowhere to go except back to her mind. She would be insane instantly. The world would not survive."

All around us, guns cocked. Calmly, I said, "Then I would advise you to disrobe quickly."

They did, no trace of Dawn's flesh anywhere except on Paetus. He had always been her creature, her submissive. I was only ever a placeholder. I looked at his head, face muscles now slack in death, and wondered how long his consciousness lingered. Had he ever ridden Dawn? Was he now trapped in her mind, a new captive for torture?

After they had dressed and began to drag Paetus out, I called, "Wait!" There was more Paetus could do for me.

∽

When gloves had been made from the hands and forearms of Julian, Paetus had been the one to do the dirty work. Since his was the body from which gloves needed to be created, I was left to do it myself. When I was done, I allowed the men to take his body out to be burned. I would collect a sample of ash later. The man who was Xia took the arms and brain of Paetus to a local tanner.

Xia's men took Dawn to another part of the complex, where my men, the only ones susceptible to her touch, were not allowed. She seemed content with the arrangement, as long as her tattooist was allowed to accompany her.

He was happy to have such a canvas on which to practice. If he did something wrong, or when her whole body was covered, she simply made a clean spot for him to apply another tattoo. He burned all the discarded pieces.

I washed all traces of Paetus from my face and changed dresses. I could not go back into Xia's presence wearing anything shy of my best. That was the only place I was interested in being. I descended the stairs unaccompanied and found the large, lacquered doors standing open. "Xia," I called. When there was no response I entered. No Xia. Crossing to the bed, I saw bright lights shining from the crack in the wall behind it. I pushed ever so gently and it sprang back toward me.

I opened the door only enough to look inside. A room just as large as her bed chamber, just as well-lit, lay behind that door. Xia was there but she, shockingly, was not what caught my attention.

Aquariums were the televisions of the Victorian era and I had seen many in the parlors of our same social strata of my youth. They were called Ocean at Home at first when they held salt water but those were difficult to keep in balance and alive. Then they were supplanted by the Lake in a Glass because freshwater creatures were easier. So the sight of an aquarium in this beautiful luxurious foreign home would not have shocked me, had it not been for the enormity of size.

A round well, how deep impossible to tell, dominated the center of the room. Its glass walls stretched above my head. Xia walked around it, dragging her hand along the panes. Before she made a full circle, the beast appeared from the depths.

This beast looked like the octopuses in Xia's art except it was colossal. Guessing, I would have to say it was over forty stone, the size of three big men, with tentacle arms each at least four meters long. The length of the arms were easy to estimate because several of them, white in color, came out from the lowest visible point on the monster, over the glass and reached for Xia.

"Xia!" I called, this time making myself heard.

She spun toward me and stepped out of reach of the beast. The tentacles, quickly turning red, sank back into the water. Xia held her hand out to me and I walked forward and took it. The octopus once again changed color from an angry red to a calm bluish green. "This magnificent creature is older than I, maybe older than humankind. She taught me to heal myself. She returns to me every time I wake from stasis." The giant octopus turned so that its eye, the size of a dinner plate but with a horizontal slit like a goat, very nearly pressed against the glass.

She continued, pulling me toward the aquarium. "Its blood is the main ingredient." Water sloshed as the beast hovered at the top. "We have its blood inside us." The gargantuan octopus flashed a rainbow of colors in rapid succession and Xia laughed. "She is so excited to finally meet you. We wondered if you would ever come."

Xia pulled us closer and a gigantic eye pressed close to the glass. "She can read your mind and communicate if you allow them to touch you." Tentacles reached for me but I yanked away. Xia said, "There is nothing to fear. The suction cups can leave marks but it is not unpleasant." She went to the tank and when the arms reached for her, she did not flinch. One wrapped around her torso, one around her leg, and another slipped in her sleeve to encircle her wrist to elbow. It lifted her off the ground.

A tentative touch on my wrist; I did not pull away. It began to explore my clothes. Xia called out from above me, "She is a very inquisitive creature. She has never seen clothes like yours." An arm wrapped around my wrist. Suction cups attached.

The octopus could sense my fear and sent me waves of comfort. It did not communicate with words but rather through images, colors, and sensations. While I was distracted by attempting to decipher the octopus' communication, two of its other tentacle arms continued to explore my clothes. I saw a flash of pain and then the octopus pulled all of its arms from me. Octopi do not make sound, but I could hear it howl in my mind just before it disconnected. I looked down to see that one tentacle held my weapon and another was covered in ash from the pouch Paetus gave me.

The weapon's needles had activated, just as it had with me, piercing the octopus' flesh. There had been two indications of pain. Could it be that the ash had hurt it as well? The tendrils under the octopus skin told me that the mixed blood in the cylinder traveled up its arm. When it was finally allowed to release the weapon, the octopus did. It clattered to the floor and shattered. A small amount of purple fluid was mixed among the shards of glass and wood. It must have nearly emptied itself into the octopus.

I had come to be with Xia, not this beast. I wanted to leave but my others stopped me. They were not interested in Xia but they were quite taken with the sea creature. We stood there while once again tentacles came out to touch our skin. I had been overruled. My others communicated with the octopus all at once.

Its name was Bai Ze. She had been waiting for us for so long. We spent hours there in her embrace while Bai Ze showed us her story. Each other got to hear the part that most interested or benefited them.

I am a woman of science, or at least I strive to fly above the superstition so common in my time but there is no other word but magic that describes it. Bai Ze is magic. Communing with her like this was healing, rejuvenating areas I had not known were deteriorated.

When it was over, I was exhausted. For the first time that I knew of, the others slept. I went back to my room so that I might join them in slumber.

∽

I woke to find that Sally had taken the front. While the others and I slept, Sally had retrieved Dawn and brought her to Bai Ze. Xia had allowed it; there was no bloodshed in getting her out. Sally had hoped Bai Ze could heal Dawn, help her, make her whole again.

Then everything happened so fast. I will tell every action but know they all occurred in the shortest of time spans. As soon as she read Dawn's most central core desire and knew her insanity to be incurable, Bai Ze released me but not before I saw the truth. Bai Ze tricked Sally. She wanted us to believe that she would never let Dawn kill us, but the reality was that she did not care about Dawn. She only wanted to kill any connection we had to the world. Bai Ze wanted to be the most important thing to us, the only thing that mattered. She knew that killing Dawn would kill Ambrose, Leon, and Julian. They were the last of the people I loved.

Bai Ze dragged Dawn into the water. Bubbles rose to the surface as Bai Ze squeezed the air from Dawn's lungs. Each burst brought the sounds of Dawn's screams. The struggle sloshed water over the top and then it splashed on the floor, soaking my feet, and filling the air with the smell of salty sea water.

I could have stopped it. I did not want to.

Dawn pulled at the tentacles holding her to no avail. Her nails were not sharp enough to hurt Bai Ze. Everywhere she grasped, grasped back. Suckers latched on to every available surface. Dawn's face went slack and her struggling ceased. At first I thought she was dead but then realized that Bai Ze had flooded her mind with calming colors.

This whole time my others screamed at me. They all had varying opinions of the whys and hows but there could only be two sides. Either they thought Dawn should die or that she should not. It was no surprise that Sally, Mary Martha, and Ruth wanted to save Dawn just as Dierdre, Effie, and Marge wanted her dead. The only one that I wasn't certain which side she'd choose was Jo. In the end she sided with those who wanted Dawn dead, not for the same reasons as they. Jo wanted freedom and we would not be free until Dawn was dead. I did not care how any of them felt. Dawn needed to die. There had never been any other way for this to end.

Sally jumped from our mind toward Dawn's, to help her escape Bai Ze's clutches. I felt the familiar rage that always accompanied Sally's departure. Then there was an audible crack as Bai Ze broke Dawn's neck. A fight started in my mind meadow. Dierdre blocked the path back because she feared Dawn and Eve' would use it to invade. The struggle did not cease even when my eighth other crashed into our meadow like a meteor. Debris from the crater obstructed the path and I felt Sally slipping away.

"No!" I screamed and I dropped down from the front to the meadow with all my others. Earthquakes rocked the whole place. It was breaking apart. Tornadoes whipped rocks and plants around, stinging and cutting my skin. I smelled smoke and tasted ash. I tried to gain control as I had managed to do before. Everything went silent, but when I unclenched my eyes I found nothing had changed. It was only muted.

Then I felt a voice. Bai Ze spoke to me. She said, *Release them. Be whole.*

One by one, my others were pulled from the turbulent meadow that had always been their home. With them, parts of it disappeared until nothing was left. I found myself back at the front, standing before the aquarium. I tried to go back down, to find them, but there was nowhere to go, no one to find. I should have felt hollow, fragmented, lacking, but I didn't. This new feeling could only mean that I was alone in my mind for the first time in my life.

"Ramillia," I heard someone saying repeatedly.

Looking up, I found Xia staring at me from in front of the aquarium. "Ramillia, are you all right?" Xia continued, "I felt it happen." She was shaking her head. "I did not know it was possible. Your splinters are with Bai Ze."

"You lie!" I screamed. The rage at being alone grew. "You have them. Give them back to me!"

Xia had obviously never felt anything for her splinters. They were just parts of her. She did not understand why being without them upset me so. She never guessed that my blinding bloodlust would overpower her glamor.

Another said my name but it was not aloud. *Ramillia, it's me, Sally. I'm here. We're all here. The weapon held your blood. Now that mixed blood flows through Bai Ze and she holds us.* Sally spoke to me through the tentacle wrapped around my wrist, but not with words. Images and feelings flashed through me and I translated them.

My others, now each occupying her own individual arm, lifted Dawn, now limp, out of the water and laid her at my feet. Sally spoke one more time. *Finish what we started and come back here. When the last is neutralized, we will come and you can join us with Bai Ze.* Then she pushed feelings of confidence and peace before pulling the suckers off of my wrist.

Bai Ze and my others sank to the bottom of the well and swam out to sea. I could no longer see through my others. They no longer had eyes, except Bai Ze's. They were hers now. They had no thought for me. I was alone. Bai Ze had everything.

This hit me hard. All that loss compounded and I snapped. Xia reached to console me and I killed her. I would like to say that it was justified or that I did it in a humane manner but the truth is I just killed her. I blinked and when I opened my eyes, everything within a two-meter sphere was covered in her blood, including me. A sound emanated from my throat that was somewhere between a scream and a moan. It was more wounded animal than human.

A few of my men rushed in to help. By then I was flinging myself around in uncontrolled anguish and loss. In my thrashing, I hit Andrew. It felt so good that I hit him again. Each strike was a momentary void of the pain. Sally was not there to take the pain. I was blinded by it. I preferred rage.

Andrew did not fight back but tried to soothe me. A few others tried to help. I broke the arm that tried to hold me. I tore off the hand that attempted to take Dawn's body. It is easy to destroy a dozen men when they are holding back in concern of hurting you but you have none of the same concern for them. I kicked knees so they bent the wrong way. I caved in chests that got too close.

More of my men got to the entrance. I paced back to Andrew and yanked him up by his blond hair. "Tell them to run. Save your son. Everyone here is going to die."

He must have heard the truth of my words because he yelled, "Run!" Then I broke his neck. Those who could run, did. I killed the ones who couldn't. They closed the doors, locked me in. I could have broken the doors, followed my men but I did not. The rage subsided.

13

Something had to be done with these corpses or I would have the living dead with which to deal. Even I was not up to that so I burst through the door and began the laborious task of dragging Dawn and the handful of other bodies up the stairs and out to the courtyard. There I planned a massive funeral pyre.

At the top of the stairs lay the man who had been Xia. I had not thought of what would happen to her others and Carriers. He was dead. No, not dead. He moved, made a gurgling sound, and blew bubbles in his spittle. He was not injured and did not speak when I spoke to him, only wailed when I yelled at him.

Every one of Xia's Carriers was in a similar state. Some lay on their backs, some on their stomachs. One was on his hands and knees, rocking back and forth. Though it had only been a few hours, the smell of human excrement and urine choked me. They cried, laughed, and cooed, helpless as babies.

Babies.

Xia's glamor had dissipated when she died, but I hope that even if it hadn't I would have been able to see how monstrous her actions were. She had ridden these men, sent her splinters into them, when they were mere babies. Now that those splinters were gone, the men, frozen in development at the age when the splinter had taken them over, reverted back. They had never learned to speak, walk, crawl, or feed themselves.

Xia was no better than any other Incola. How could I have been so blind? She used Carriers just as completely. She stole the lives of these men and now they would die without ever having known life. There were hundreds of them. I could not care for them even if I had been so inclined. I ignored them as I dragged body after body by them. There was nothing to be done.

The funeral pyre burned bright long into the afternoon. When it died down, and I had added their ash to that of my bag, I flew my airship down to the tanner's house to retrieve my gloves of truth. Ed had always flown before but he'd explained it so thoroughly that watching him had been lesson enough.

On the return, I noticed a woman making the walk toward the altar. My flying ship startled her but that was to be expected. I landed it and exited. I told her the news. Xia was dead and tribute was no longer required. She should take her baby home and tell everyone she knew to do the same. I exposed her and eventually all of Xia's descendants to the blight. With her gone, they were no longer immune to my strain.

As soon as she left, I turned to the altar and gave in to my anger. Xia could have stopped this tribute tradition with minimal effort. I was glad she was dead and even proud I had been the one to do it. I carefully moved all of the little bundles and laid them in a pile under a nearby tree. Then I smashed the altar with my fists, pummeling it into rubble. I took those stones and piled them on the bundles, making one large funeral mound.

Bai Ze did not return to the well that night. The next day I took the *Precious Lady* in a new direction and exposed another ethnicity of Carriers to the blight. When I returned, Bai Ze and my others were still at sea. The next day I did the same but I went further and stayed away longer before returning. Each time I tried not to hope but found myself disappointed that the well was empty and Bai Ze had not returned for me.

Years continued like this. I gave up the hoax I had used for so long. No longer was I looking for a husband or ally. I demanded an invitation into Incola houses. If they refused, I met them with force and aggression. Victory was mine, not because I was superior in strength or determination but because this was a time when women were considered so lesser that I was underestimated constantly. It did not matter that I was the biggest threat to their lifestyle and lives; no man wanted to be the one to hurt or kill the only female Incola.

I allowed myself to grow old. I was alone for the first time in my life. There were no voices, no battling of wills, no one to talk to. I did not use stasis as Xia had done because I was not certain I could rouse myself. I experienced every moment. Then one day, on a walk to the gates to check for the food left there as offerings sometimes by the peasants, I found a letter addressed to me. From the look of it, the letter had been there for some time. The writing was faded and I had to heal my aged eyes a bit before I could read it.

My lady,

I leave this here so that you may consider the situation and decide your action, or inaction, according to your own conscience without pressure. Immortals now rule the human world, in the open. In some ways it is worse than the secret power wielded by Incola.

Your Servant

There were instructions on the ways to access my fortune. Also in the envelope were several articles clipped from newspapers from around the world. The Pope had not managed to jump to a new body before the illness took hold. After recovering, he set himself up as the Eternal Pope. He appeared younger now than he had seventy-five years earlier. The Church followed him. No matter what he was accused of. It made sense because why would God grant him eternal life on earth if he was evil? I thought of the boys in the Pope's chamber and how many had suffered at his hands in the last seven decades. The young, smart, and scientific bishop was most likely dead and could not save anyone.

Juan was now the Emperor of Spain, having led a revolution. He promised anyone who helped him would live forever just as he would. Emperor Juan had hundreds of wives and a thousand children. The article did not say but I knew he was attempting to resurrect the Incola gene, ever hopeful to regain the power and abilities of the pre-blight era.

Similar revolts and power grabs happened all over the world. I had ended, at least temporarily, the terror of the Incola but had unleashed a new threat. It was not being an Incola that was evil. It was immortality that was the real enemy. What lengths are too far to go to for immortality? There are none too far, nothing too horrific, for any who have tasted eternity.

I healed my old body and brought it to my prime age. The *Precious Lady* had fallen into disrepair and though I knew how to fly it, repairing its mechanics were beyond me. I would have to go on my final great adventure on foot.

It is odd that I spent so long describing in detail the first thirty years of my life but would find that I have very little to say about the last hundred and twenty. I had no idea who I was, and I had spent my time working out the details of my existence, finding myself. Now without the others, I am completely myself, unfiltered, unabashed, certain. Yet, I have nothing to say. I did not discover any major truth, just accepted the simple ones.

Incola were almost extinct. I've already told you about finding the last one. With that finished, I moved on to locating and killing any who knew the secret of immortality. I killed more than I can remember. Some I will never forget. Ed, the Eternal Pope, Emperor Juan; these are just the big names. They aren't any more special than the fisherman who bedded every girl around in hopes of producing a Carrier. They all died by my hand. Auley killed himself to spare me. He shouldn't have bothered. These deaths were not dark spots on my soul. They are what I existed to do. I brought death to the immortals and reminded them of what they had forgotten. Death abides.

Yes, I am the monster in my own life. I am the evil. I accept that sometimes good cannot do what is needed. The world needed a bloodthirsty immortal murderer. I was that. I was good at it.

I returned to Xia's palace to find Bai Ze and my others waiting for me. At last I had done what she willed and could join them. I took the time to write this all down on my last night as a human. Until it was down on paper, I thought I would join, live as one with Bai Ze, but now I know that cannot be. As long as Bai Ze lives, immortality threatens the world. In a few minutes I will take my last breath, feel my last heartbeat, and I will kill the last immortal.

ABOUT THE AUTHOR

Natalie Gibson writes novels filled with otherworldly violence, sexuality, and the supernatural, and she enjoys mixing horror, magic, fantasy, and romance into her writing. Her stories always have powerful females who change the world, magical creatures that battle their baser natures, and seriously evil bad guys who don't. She resides in central New York with her family.